HANDY DISCOVERY

"I'm not getting in that van," Vonn said, shaking and pale.

"What's your problem?" May asked.

"He's scared of misterbob," Winters said.

May shook his head. "In case you missed it, they *got* misterbob."

"Not all of him," Vonn said, trembling.

Grumbling, May slipped up to the van and pulled at the door. It opened with a metallic grunt, and something drifted out from inside that choked him and caused his eyes to water. He swallowed and peered in. His breath stopped.

It was lying on the middle of the deck. It was long and brick red, and yellow fluid still seeped from one end. On the other end, stilled and peaceful, were two sets of opposable, chitinous fingers.

By Joe Clifford Faust
Published by Ballantine Books:

A DEATH OF HONOR

THE COMPANY MAN

Angel's Luck
   Book One: DESPERATE MEASURES
   Book Two: PRECIOUS CARGO
   Book Three: THE ESSENCE OF EVIL

THE ESSENCE OF EVIL

Book Three of
Angel's Luck

Joe Clifford Faust

A Del Rey Book
BALLANTINE BOOKS • NEW YORK

A Del Rey Book
Published by Ballantine Books

Library of Congress Catalog Card Number: 89-91539

ISBN 0-345-36089-3

Printed in Canada

First Edition: April 1990

Cover Art by David B. Mattingly

For David B. Mattingly; artist extraordinaire, nice guy, and a handy person to know in The City

ONE

"It was a dream, Captain May, a brilliant, mad dream, and there are people out there who desperately want it to come true."

James May was busy learning how difficult it was to reason with an Arcolian.

He was walking beside the short, hulking creature at a slow pace so it could keep up with him. Its legs were hidden by the flowing purple robe it wore, but May could hear them scrabbling and clattering on the metal deck of the *Angel's Luck*.

"You don't understand," the merchant said. "You're no longer in an area where people are used to the idea of seeing Arcolians. We can't screen everyone who'll be boarding this ship for xenophobic tendencies like they did on the *Hergest Ridge*. I don't want anything to happen to you should someone go Psych 13."

The Arcolian's head bobbed up and down. A rattle rose in its throat, and its mouth parts flexed to form the noise into words. "Indeed. Have I not demonstrated that I am capable of self-protection? Although it is not considered proper, adjustments of scent could sufficiently alter the Sapient fearscent reaction."

May shuddered. Having been through the Arcolian's barrage of pheromonal influence once before, he was anxious to avoid the experience again and determined to prevent it from happening to anyone else.

"misterbob," he said calmly, "it's not just that. You have to remember that the people who will be coming here are going to charge me for repairing this ship—"

"Yes," the Arcolian croaked. "bigguy indicated that mer-

1

chant vessel *angelsluck* was damaged during a procedure called kickass. I must experience that sometime.''

You're going to experience it now, May thought, if you don't get out of my way. "These people will think that I have money and influence because you are here, misterbob. They will ask for more money to do the repairs. Considering that I have no money right now . . .''

"I can assist," misterbob purred.

"No," May said quickly. "No, thank you. I'll have more money than I know what to do with as soon as Duke finds the nearest branch of the Essence Company. I just don't want anybody to know you're here.''

The Arcolian stopped its shuffling gait. "jamesohjames, you must understand that I have departed from the others—''

May rolled his eyes. "I know. I know. 'To study the Sapient A-forms and their natural interactions to promote better understanding between the races.' ''

misterbob gurgled. "I do not understand this. Your words scent of understanding of purpose, yet your pheromones indicate agitation.''

May sighed and folded his arms. "What's the best way to explain this?''

misterbob's head cocked. "A most curious trait in the A-forms. The object of certain questions has no knowledge of correct response.''

"Let me try it this way." May sighed. "You wish to observe the way I interact with those who are coming to repair my ship. Correct?''

"Correct.''

"But if you are present, I will not be able to carry on a normal interaction with the others. Those who come here have not been exposed to Arcolian E-forms before, and their fascination with you will hinder the normal communication process. Therefore you will not observe a normal interaction between Sapient A-forms, but rather one which you have directly influenced.''

misterbob shook its head. "You do not understand, jamesohjames. I wish to observe, not interfere.''

"But I *do* understand," May explained. "You must understand, Ambassador, that I do not fear that you will pheromonally interfere. You have given me your word that you would not—''

The Arcolian's eye narrowed, and May's voice cut out. It was unnerving how the aliens mimicked human body language.

"What," the ambassador asked, "have I given you, james-ohjames, other than my presence on your ship *angelsluck*?"

Do you really want to know? May thought, giving an exasperated shrug. "Never mind," he said. "It's an idiomatic phrase commonly used between Sapient A-forms to indicate an intangible value which has passed between them."

"Then I must strive to understand your ways. The way you put value on that which has none: The Word, The Life. The ritual bondings between your genders. I must study all of this in detail." The creature shifted and began to walk again.

"Fine," May said, watching it get ahead. "But you're not going to stay."

The Arcolian stopped. "But, jamesohjames, I have not scented sufficient reason. I have given you The Word that I will not interfere—"

May drew breath and studied the creature. At last, an idea came to him on how he could convey understanding.

"Even if you make no scent," he said, "even if you make scentkill, the other A-forms who come will still scent you."

"Indeed?"

"Indeed," May said firmly. "They will scent you with their eyes. And when they do, your eyescent will interfere with our conversation."

Again the Arcolian's double-pupiled eye narrowed. "But how can this be, jamesohjames? I fail to scent the Sapient A-form fixation on the false senses."

The merchant shrugged. "That's what we do," he told the creature. "Sad but true."

"The dependence on the false senses is beyond my immediate comprehension," the ambassador said. "Yet I am able to scent your concern over my presence to observe. It is a most confusing phenomenon."

The corners of May's lips turned up. "Nobody is asking you to understand us. We don't often understand ourselves."

"Interesting," misterbob said.

"All we're asking is what we ask of one another, which is friendship."

On each hand, the Arcolian's opposing fingertips closed. "This obsession with intangibles—"

"I know," May said. "I know." He gently put his hand on the ambassador's back to hurry it down the hall. "You can't scent it, and it's something you must study more. No problem. Listen, misterbob, I think I have a compromise worked out so you can observe our initial . . . interaction . . . without influencing the other A-forms with eyescent. Are you interested?''

It went without saying that the Arcolian was. The plan, as May described it, was for misterbob to conceal itself in a small storage compartment that was part of the *Angel's Luck* library. Not only would the Arcolian be able to hear and smell the goings-on, but May would set up a video monitor that would allow the ambassador to watch the negotiations.

And so it came about that when Roz arrived to announce the first appointment, the merchant captain was busy making sure the Arcolian was comfortable. Pleased with himself, May looked around the library, which had been hastily rearranged into a conference room.

Roz hesitated on seeing misterbob, but she quickly recovered. "May? The representative from CompuFarm is here to see you.''

"Fine," May said, closing the door on the Arcolian. "Send him in.''

The merchant kept his hand on the closet door as if to make sure that misterbob would not unexpectedly emerge. He fixed his gaze at the door and waited for the door to budge. It didn't.

"Captain May?''

The person May turned to see was short and rumpled and had a smile that conveyed both good humor and enthusiasm for his line of work.

May extended his hand. "You're the agent from Compu-Farm?''

"Actually," the man said with a grin, shaking hands with May, "I *am* CompuFarm. I'm Del Hickman.''

May laughed. "Well. Nice to meet you. I've heard a lot of good things about your work—''

"Although you were expecting someone taller, right?''

"Well . . .''

"Never mind." Hickman strolled to the center of the library and tossed a handful of slates onto the table. "Shall we begin, Captain?''

Sniffing the air cautiously, May waited for Hickman to take a seat, then placed himself to one side of the storage compartment so misterbob's view wouldn't be obstructed. For a brief moment he thought of how ludicrous the situation was. Certainly Hickman did not know about the Arcolian's presence, but May himself did, and that was enough to taint the conversation. He decided that this was as good as it was going to get. He had made a promise, some-

thing else that misterbob had not understood, and he figured that
the best way to teach the Arcolian the value of something it considered intangible was to live the example.

Well, he thought, here goes nothing.

"Absolutely," he said, taking a seat at the table. "But you
can drop the 'Captain' business. It's one aspect of the merchant
business I've never gotten used to."

"Right." Hickman grinned. "Then you should call me Dirk.
Everyone else does, although I'm at a loss to explain why."

"All right." May took a moment to look the man over. Duke
and Dirk, he mused, thinking of his copilot. Where is this all
going to end? "I trust you've had a chance to look over the ship's
electronics systems. What do you have for me?"

As it turned out, Hickman's quote was substantially less than
May thought it would be. Hickman himself showed amazement,
as well, saying that the circumstances that took out many of the
simpler circuits should have played total havoc with the more
complex ones. The fact of the matter was that most of what May
thought had been destroyed was merely damaged or program-
wiped. Complete replacement of the merchant ship's electronics
would not be necessary. A work crew could replace the dead
chips in a matter of days, and then the systems could be repro-
grammed.

"You're looking at three weeks of work," Hickman told him.
"Plus another ten days after the ship has been completely refitted. The total cost—" He paused for a moment at May's sharply
drawn breath. "Are you all right?"

"Fine," May said, waving his hands. "It's a reaction I seem
to have developed over the last few months. I get this pain in
my collarbone whenever someone mentions money." He rubbed
his hand across his upper chest.

"I hope this doesn't hurt too much." Hickman laughed.
"Your total bill for this is going to come to twelve million credits, and that's going to include a new Vasac controller. Looks
like you had a little piece of tin stuck in—"

"I'm well aware of the inadequacies of my former controller," May said.

"As long as you—"

"Tell you what," May continued, "I'll give you fifteen, and
you put in the best Vasac controller you can find. A Galactrix
9000 or better."

"Captain, that's really more than you—"

"I insist," May said, "Call it a stupid childhood dream. I want a Vasac that's not going to go bad on me at a bad moment."

"That's the 9000 all right. Although with normal use—"

"The way my career has gone," May told Hickman, "there's no such thing as 'normal use.' "

"Very well." Hickman keyed notes into one of his slates. "It'll be a few days before I can get my repair crews in, but I'm going to send a master programmer up and start on the equipment in the bridge to make sure I haven't missed anything."

May straightened in his seat. "I thought you were a master programmer."

"I am." Hickman shut off the slate he was working and folded his hands. "But do you have any idea how tough it is to run your own business?" He shrugged. "Of course you do. You're a merchant. What I'm getting at is, I've got to spend all of my time with administrative matters and authorizing paychits and coming to do estimate inspections—no offense, of course. It leaves me very little time to do the stuff I like to do, which is why I went into business for myself to begin with."

"But you've done very well."

"It's been an embarrassment of success, really. Well, I don't want to tell you my problems. Rest assured, though, that Cheech is a fantastic master programmer, quite possibly better than I was at my youthful peak."

"Cheech?" May asked. "Your master programmer is named Cheech?"

"By choice," Hickman explained. "As I understand it, a bunch of them have formed some sort of goofy coalition where they get together and discuss recent development in microparticle bits and subatomic engraving—"

"I get the idea," May said.

"A quick study you are. In any event, I'll have Cheech come by to start looking things over in the next day or two, and we'll get started from there on the hard stuff."

The meeting ended on another handshake, and May folded his arms as Hickman left, feeling good about what he had just accomplished. If the meeting with the ship refitter went as well, he could be back in business by the beginning of the next fiscal year.

There came a low croak from the closet. "jamesohjames?"

May opened the door. misterbob was patiently sitting on the other side, nodding its head. "Are you all right?"

"I am quite well. You were correct, jamesohjames. This concealment of the eyescent from the Sapient A-forms is a most effective means of observation. The olfactory communication between the two of you was most interesting.''

"Olfactory," May said. "The smell? What about what we were saying?''

The Arcolian nodded. "That was worth observing, as well, although I have noted that aural communication is inefficient and makes for a high ratio of misunderstanding between the Sapients.''

May glared. "I thought we did pretty damned good.''

"Still inefficient. Perhaps you do not realize how much of your conversation was wasted in the discussion of the extraneous and intangible.''

"That's called small talk." May sniffed. "It's an important part of our culture. If you keep bugging me about it, I'm going to get pissed off.''

"Indeed," misterbob said. "We must both avoid the state called pissoff. It impedes the efficient—''

"Enough already," May said. "I think Roz is coming." He thumbed the door shut, walked to his seat at the conference table, and waited to greet his next guest.

2

It was a star.

It was a star, but for a handful of coins you could rent time on a stereoptic telescope and single it out with crosshairs, lock on to the image, and zoom in until you could tell exactly what it was.

Duke already knew what it was, but he pumped coins into the machine for a closer look in spite of that. He stood at the Danforth Observatory on a mountaintop on Council 5 and focused the optical device until an image fixed before his eyes.

"That's not a star!" a nearby child exclaimed to his father. "That's an old piece of junk.''

"Let me try it," the father said. "Maybe I can find Jubilo for you.''

"I want to see a commsat," the child insisted.

"You'll see a commsat," the father said grudgingly. "But it's my money and we're going to see Jubilo first.''

Duke laughed and his breath rolled out as vapor in the cold night air. He put his eyes to the device and twisted the handlebar controls with his hands. The star grew, blurred, then pulled into focus to reveal the battered hull of a ship, scarred with plasma burns and smeared with dark blisters from Vacc Fighter weaponry and fastened to the dark hull of an orbital platform. The name of the ship had once been prominently displayed across a major piece of plating, but all that could be seen were a few random letters and numerals.

Duke knew what they added up to. *Angel's Luck*. Three seven four nine one. Registered to James Theodore May, a certified merchant captain who was certainly on board, waiting for the arrival of businessmen who would begin restoring the *Angel's Luck* to its former glory.

On further examination, he could see a tug attached to the merchant, a ship so small that the name could not be read, even with the observatory's sophisticated optics. But Duke knew the name of that ship, as well. It was the *Jamming Jenny*, and it was registered to a new business, ChibaCo Speculative Salvage Unlimited. The company's owner, Peter Chiba, and his untrained but willing-to-learn assistant, Roz Cain, would also be on board the *Angel's Luck*. The gig of hauling the burned-out hulk of a merchant ship had been their first job. The money from it would give a good start to the fledgling business.

The telescope beeped, and words scrolled across the field of view, informing Duke that to continue his perusal of the heavens, he needed to add more coins. He straightened and looked straight up, regarding the flickering star that was the *Angel's Luck*. Next to him, the father and son were engrossed in looking at a communications satellite. The rest of the tourists, who had not numbered all that many because of the cold of the night, were beginning to disperse, leaving sparse numbers behind.

Duke took a deep breath. He held the cool air in his lungs, then let it out slowly, watching the vapor billowing from his lips and dissipating in the night air. Like the crowd, he thought. With a sigh, he started away from the telescope, checking his watch. His observations had gone ten minutes over. Had he found the star he was looking for, perhaps he would not have lingered so, but atmospheric conditions had effectively blocked his attempts to find Tetros. He told himself he would have another chance. There would be many other chances before he went back, but he could not help wanting to look. It was almost as if the sight of the star in his lens would bring him news from back home.

It might have. It might have even made him feel better, but it would not be happening that night. Duke walked off of the observation deck and started down a long flight of stairs. At the end, he walked across a large plaza crowded with people milling in the cool of the midseason night.

Crossing to the far side, he made his way to a line of stone benches in an isolated corner. Two men were sitting with their backs to him, looking out at the lights of the city below. One was big-boned and had a head that was almost too large for his body. The other was lean and wiry. His right hand was swathed in bandages, and he was balancing a gravity knife on the back of his left hand, point aiming out between his fingers. With a jerk, the blade was flipped up in the air, and the wiry man tried to catch it by the handle. The weapon made a slit across the palm of his hand and clattered to the ground.

"Dammit," he said, sucking blood from the wound. Even under the artificial light, Duke could see hash marks left by previous attempts at the trick. "I'm never going to be able to get it."

"Why don't you wait until your right hand gets better, Mr. Vonn?" the big man asked.

Vonn plucked the knife from between his feet. "Because it may be out of action for a while. I don't want to be unarmed."

Duke shoved his hands into the pockets of his neowarm jacket. "You get caught with that toy around here," he advised, "and all of you is going to be incapacitated."

"Duke." With a flick of his wrist, Vonn slipped the blade back into the handle and pocketed the weapon. "It's about time. We've been waiting for you."

"You've been waiting for me," Duke scoffed. "I waited for you half an hour before I decided to go stargazing. Where the hell were you?"

"Let's say I had some business to take care of," Vonn said. They skirted the plaza, making for a second set of steps.

"Did you find your star?" Winters asked.

Duke shook his head. "Too bright out," he said.

"Maybe tomorrow."

"Maybe."

"I don't see what your big obsession is, Duke," Vonn said, shaking his head. "I mean, if it was me, there's no way I'd want to go back to some class C world and marry a couple of—"

"That's enough." Duke's voice was cold.

"Maybe you should explain it," Vonn continued. "I'm getting tired of meeting you here and having you show up all down and moping like some damned Psych 13—"

Duke grabbed Vonn by the shoulder and jerked him to a stop. "I told you to watch your fucking mouth."

The air around them froze to crystal. For a moment, nobody moved. The breath stayed in their lungs, waiting and warming.

Duke looked from Vonn to Winters and back. "What's wrong with you two? You're looking at me like I'm some common criminal."

Slowly Vonn's head shook. "No. Not that at all. I'm sorry, Duke."

"We're worried about you, Mr. Duke," Winters said.

"Worried." Duke dropped his grip on Vonn and brushed invisible dust off of his hands.

"We hear you talk like that," Winters went on, "and we think maybe you're getting sick again."

"I'm not sick," Duke said. "I never was sick. Yeah, I've got a passenger, but things are under control. It's been three weeks since the last episode."

"The blockade run," Vonn said.

Duke cocked his head and gave a wry shrug. "Stress brings out the best in me."

"That's not all," Vonn muttered under his breath.

The trio passed through the observatory's ornate gates and stopped to board a metrobus that would take them down the mountain to the city. They went halfway back, and Winters took one bench seat to himself, while Duke and Vonn shared the one across from him.

"So," Vonn said, trying to change the subject, "did you find out anything for us?"

Duke nodded. "I have. It seems we've had another serendipitous turn of good fortune."

"Angel's Luck," Winters whispered reverently.

"I'll be the judge of that," Vonn said. "What have you got?"

"The reason why Li had us running to the Jubilo system. He was using an indirect path to shake the *Yueh-sheng*, and Jubilo was handy because it's a short hop from here. And the nearest Essence branch to here, my friends, happens to be right here. Not just any branch, mind you, but one run by the son of Maximillian Burris."

"Who?" Vonn asked.

"Maximillian Burris. He was the one who finally got the Essence Phial program off of the ground. He made the contracts with people and was responsible for filling the phials we rescued."

"I'm still withholding judgment," Vonn said. "How did his son get stuck in charge of a branch that's out in the middle of nowhere?"

"How did a planet that's out in the middle of nowhere get to be the diplomatic center of the galaxy?" Duke countered.

"Nothing's real," Vonn said. "Me, I'm not going to believe it until I'm counting my share in my hand."

"Fair enough," Duke said. "In the meantime, what's on the agenda for tonight?"

"There's a place I want to check out," Vonn told him. "It's called the Black Orchid."

"Sounds like another one of your mercenary bars," Duke complained.

"It is," Winters volunteered.

"Dammit," Vonn said. "Didn't I tell you not to say anything?"

Winters shrugged. "But he guessed, Mr. Vonn."

Duke folded his arms and sank back into his seat. "You know how I feel about those," he said.

"But this is different," Vonn protested. He waved the bandaged hand for emphasis. "You don't think I'd be going out into the field with this, do you?"

"I don't see why this can't wait until we've collected from the Essence Company. I don't like the idea of your running off and finding another job before this is all over with."

"Relax. I learned my lesson on the *Hergest Ridge*." Vonn cradled his wounded arm. "It's not that at all. It's the camaraderie. I don't expect you to understand it, although at one time I thought you were getting close. Even the hard cases, the ones who have to get brought in on grav chairs, they keep it up because it's something you get in your blood."

"Well," Duke said sniffing. "We all have our cross to bear."

"Didn't you have something similar on Tetros? What did you do after hours at your father's abattoir? You and the other meat cutters get together to compare wounds?"

Duke looked down at his hands, his little fingers. He thought for a moment that he had lost one of them, but he saw that it was not so. "No," he said calmly. "I never did anything like that."

"What's wrong? You afraid to mix with that type?"

"My uncle always said that he had good people working for him, but that didn't mean I had to hang around them. Their lives were different from mine."

"I see." Vonn nodded. "So instead you spent your time impregnating the local girls."

"Something like that," Duke answered, "although I'm not proud of it. I'm not proud of leaving them, either, but I intend to make that up."

"Yeah," Vonn said. "Well, we've all got our plans. And mine are to get somewhere and plan out my future, and friend, my future begins at the Black Orchid."

"Then it's understood," Duke said coldly, "that our paths are going to diverge once the Essence Company makes their payoff. Therefore, you won't be too upset with me if I pass on the opportunity to visit this place."

Vonn gave him a hard look.

"For tonight at least," Duke added. "I'm not up to handling it."

"You've changed, Duke," Vonn said.

"We've all changed. I've lived enough stress for a lifetime, Vonn, and now it's twice as important that I avoid it. I don't want to be a hero, and to tell you the truth, I'm not sure that I want my share of the reward money other than what it would take to repay my uncle for a misappropriated shipment of meat. All I want to do is go back to my green little world and settle down with my women."

"That's your choice."

"I know." Duke thumbed a switch on his armrest, and the bus began to slow. He rose from his seat and smiled at Winters. "Don't let Vonn get into too much trouble."

Winters smiled. "I won't."

Duke looked straight at Vonn. "See you later, brother."

"Yeah," Vonn said. "Brother."

Duke pointed at Winters. "Don't let him stay out too late, big guy. We've got medical appointments in the morning."

The metrobus stopped, and Duke got off on a well-lit street near a complex of stores. In spite of the late hour, there were still good-sized crowds in that part of the city, many more than had been up on the mountaintop earlier. He made his way through them, happy to be ignored, unhappy at the prospect of being on his own at the hotel.

Being by himself and knowing—knowing that he was not alone.

3

Roz led the next guest in, and instantly May was intimidated. The man was pear-shaped and had drooping eyelids, and his suit was the best thing short of K'Perian Silk. May noted that he had a good, strong handshake, and that there was a constant squeaking sound as the man breathed through his nose.

"Captain May," Roz said, "this is Wieland Emeht, owner of the Starforth Orbital Shipyards."

"I feel important," May said, extending his hand, "meeting the owner of such a renowned—"

"It's company policy," Emeht growled. His right hand twisted a large bauble that hung on his left ring finger. "I personally inspect and quote on ships over a certain size." He glared at May's waiting hand and took a seat.

"Uh," May said, "Well, Roz, I guess that'll be all. If you'll excuse us."

She nodded and closed the door behind her.

"Nice woman," Emeht said.

"I'm sorry?"

"That's a nice woman you've got there."

"She's a salvor," May said, hoping to dampen the possibility of Emeht asking for any physical favors. "I'm letting her use space on the ship until her business gets going."

The man grunted.

"So, Mr. Emeht, I trust you've had a chance to observe the damage that's been done to this ship."

Emeht nodded and stroked his thick mustache. The man's eyebrows were as dense as the hair on his upper lip, and they effectively shadowed his eyes from view, making him look distant and unapproachable.

"And your conclusion?" May asked, thinking *this is going to take forever if I have to draw everything out of him with a question.*

Emeht locked his hands together and rotated them, raising a chorus of crackling from his knuckles. "You have one hell of a mess on your hands."

A shocked laugh slipped from May's lips as he sat. "Tell me something I don't know. That's why I called you."

The broad-shouldered man pulled a slate from inside his vest, laid it on the table, and turned it on. He sucked his lower lip as he studied it. "You have a major plasma blister on a section of your lower armor plating that accounts for two percent of your total coverage. That's going to have to be replaced. You've got minor plasma burns—that's pinhole to fist-sized—over another twelve percent of the ship's outer hull."

"That's not so bad," May told him.

"No, but it takes time." Emeht punched a button on the slate. "Every one of your major external antennae needs to be replaced. Some were ripped out, some were melted, and what's left have so damn many of those pinhole burns that they're useless."

"I expected as much."

"Of course I can install new ones, but they're going to be current technology, and you're going to have to recalibrate your Vasac and other appropriate computer systems. I don't do that. I rebuild ships, and rebuilding ships is all I do."

May stared blankly at Emeht and worked his tongue in his mouth. I wonder what this guy smells like to misterbob? he thought. It must be a real learning experience. "Go on."

Emeht laughed. "Then there's your engines. You don't have any."

"I was aware of that," the merchant said dryly.

"But before we can put them in, we've got to rehabilitate the entire engine compartment structure. The backflash from the jettison blackened the entire compartment. At the least, we're going to have to go in with solvent and strip the walls and recoat them with all the different magic mixtures. At the worst, we're going to have to reinforce some of the bulkheads because the jettison charges may have overstressed them to the point where they won't hold up under a fully functioning drive system."

"What's your opinion for this particular ship?" May asked.

Emeht snorted. "I think we're going to have to reinforce at least one of the bulkheads. Maybe two."

May started to nod, but he stopped to sniff the air. No, there was nothing there. Perhaps it was Emeht himself. He blinked, and the feeling passed. He had spent too much time in the company of an Arcolian.

"Interior repair," Emeht continued. "You've been handling most of the painting and cleaning, so you've saved some credits there. As far as the doors, a full half of them had their servo systems fried so we're going to have to replace them. But someone's got to wire them into the main logic controller, and someone's going to have to program them. I don't do that."

May tugged at the collar of his jumpsuit. The library was becoming uncomfortably warm. He hoped that the ambassador was all right.

"Now on top of that, we've got to buy and install the engines. You said you wanted the B3-Es. Those you've got to get on your own. I can act as a purchasing agent, but you'll have to pay me for them up front. It's two standard months' delivery on those, minimum, plus you pay the shipping from Fontanalis 13. The exterior paint job after the patch job will have to be done inside one of our atmospheric hangars; you're looking at a week's time at a by-the-hour rate. With replacement of the transgear system, you're looking at nine months' work with a total of—"

"*Transgear.*" May coughed and shivered from the stifling air in the room. "What's wrong with the transgear system?"

"Lube congealment," Emeht said. "Structural integrity's been severely compromised by extended burn and pressure fractures."

"How in hell could that have happened?" May shouted.

"You don't take care of your equipment, you pay the price."

The merchant choked. His throat was getting dry, and he found himself constantly swallowing. "That's impossible. I had the transgear system serviced—"

"I write these the way I see them," Emeht said coldly. "And I see this job as running nine months, seventy-eight million credits less the engines, twenty-five percent up front or a lien on the ship proper."

"That's outrageous."

Emeht punched a key on the slate, and it went dead. "You want the job done cheaper, you go somewhere else, Captain. You want the job done by the best, you pay for the best."

May took a moment to calm himself. "All right," he said. "As for this transgear, will you accept salvaged materials in lieu of part of the payment?"

"No scrap metal," Emeht said. "I don't deal in that."

"This is an intact transgear, rated for a dreadnought."

"Never fit," he scoffed.

"I'm talking about credit," May said. "You take this thing and install it somewhere else where you can cut a really nice profit. Meantime, you give me a break on the repair bill."

Emeht sucked his teeth and ran some figures through the slate. "I can cut it to seventy-five million."

May drew breath. The air seemed thick and humid, making him sleepy. "That's only five percent. A transgear of that class is worth—"

"I know what they're worth," Emeht snapped. "And I also know that it's going to be salvaged material. It's going to need minor repairs, and chances are it's going to have to sit in a safe bay long enough for the radioactivity to decay down to a safe level. I'll take the transgear off your hands, but the truth, Mr. May, is that taking it on will be almost more trouble for me than it'll be worth. My final offer is seventy-five millon on the terms I've previously set down, take it or leave it.''

May's throat became tight, and he felt as if the room were closing in on him. What was wrong, other than the fact that Emeht's estimates were going wildly beyond his own expectations? He tried to shake the effects of the miasma with no effect. ''Well . . .'' he started.

Then something pricked his nostrils. It was a sharp, sweet scent that reminded him of burning pipe tobacco. May quickly turned to look at the door to the storage compartment. What am I doing? he thought. Why am I doing this?

His eyes burned, and he blinked to rid them of the irritation as he turned back to his guest. ''I'm sorry,'' he said. ''I seem to have gotten distracted.''

''Understandable.'' Emeht grunted.

May sighed. The air in the room seemed crisp and clear. ''Where were we?''

Emeht stared blankly at his slate. ''Well,'' he drawled, ''we were discussing the price for refitting this ship.''

Things drew into focus for May. ''Oh, yes,'' he said. ''I appreciate your coming out here to do the inspection, Mr. Emeht, because I did want the work done by the best people available, but your estimate is way out of line. My experience at refitting may have been a quarter century ago at Merchant Academy rates, but I still know that your figures—''

The corners of Emeht's lips turned up, not into the hard, cruel grin he had displayed earlier, but a kind, benevolent smile. ''Are grossly inflated,'' he said.

May's mouth dropped open. *''What?''*

Emeht nodded. ''That's the trouble with being the best,'' he confessed. ''Sometimes your ego gets in the way and you lose sight of your original goal. You start making people pay for your name, not your work.'' He started to run figures through his slate. ''You mentioned a dreadnought-class transgear that you could provide?''

''Yes,'' May said.

''With a little expansion into the unused space in your engine compartment, I think it could be installed. It'd make your drive system more efficient, and even with the extra installation work, you'd save twelve million on your bill."

"What about the half-life of—"

"We can give the transgear a special coating that'll keep it from being a hazard while it's decaying. Once the radiation is below safe levels, it'll start to flake off. You'll have to sweep up the bay every couple of days, but the savings will be worth it.

"You're also going to save money on rehabilitating the engine compartment. I've already tested the walls and found them structurally sound. You're going to get away with that for a couple of coats of primer and paint. The repainting of the exterior can be done in three days, and the drying bay charge will stand only as long as I have men inside working on your ship. That's how every other refitting yard does it, and I should be no different.

"With the savings from all of that plus the credit for your old transgear, which there's nothing wrong with, by the way, the total amount comes to fifty-one million credits."

"Fifty-one—" May stared at Emeht in disbelief. He felt there was something about the exchange that should have been bothering him, but he could not quite tell what it was.

"Which is still high, I know, because I tend to inflate my prices because of my reputation. So I'm going to knock off fifteen percent of that and give you a final quote of forty-three million flat for the job. If it runs over that, I'll eat the cost. Unfortunately, the nine-month delivery has to stand." Emeht pushed back in his chair and stood, holding his hand out to the merchant captain. "Is it a deal?"

"I wish you'd let me think about this," May said. "There's something—"

Emeht grabbed May's hand and pumped it. "Nonsense. I insist. I want you to be able to tell all of your friends that you got the best refitting job in the universe from my yard, and that I cut you a fair, honest deal." He shut off his slate and slid it into his pocket.

"Listen, about these terms, don't you think—"

"Too late." Emeht's eyes twinkled. "We already shook on it." He stepped to the door and it slid open to accommodate him. Giving May the civilian courtesy salute, he said, "Thanks for making it so I can sleep at night," then slipped off down the hall.

Astonished, May watched the door close. "What the hell. What the hell. What the—"

Something in his head snapped, so strongly that he recoiled. *"misterbob!"*

"Yesssss." The voice came from behind the storage-compartment door.

May bolted to the door and opened it. "You did that, didn't you? I thought you weren't going to interfere!"

The Arcolian clicked its chitinous fingers together. "I did make such a statement, jamesohjames, but the circumstances of my intervention were most necessary. My observation of your conversation scented many interesting things. You yourself scented most interestingly. It was a fearscent of entrapment."

"Let's just say I was having a bad day," May said. "But still . . ."

"More interesting was what I scented in misteremeht. Quite interesting indeed. I have not scented such malevolence before, although I have scented that it was expressed often in the early days of the Accord."

"Malevolence?"

"Perhaps not a direct malevolence," misterbob explained, "but most certainly a combination of scents the sum of which would indicate such. What you have described as avarice, something misteremeht said was called ego, and dangerous levels of apathy. He meant no direct harm for you, but what he was doing certainly would have harmed you. Since I have previously scented your concern for my welfare, it was not a viable option for me to let you be put into such a position."

May erupted in gooseflesh. "Thank you," he said, trying to smile. "That means a lot to me, misterbob, but what happens when Mr. Emeht gets back to his office? What if your phero-monal influence wears off?"

The Arcolian nodded. "Indulge me for a moment. Think back on margarethearn."

A lump formed in May's throat. "All right," he croaked.

misterbob watched him for a moment and purred. "I can tell even from my vision that when you think about margarethearn, you remember your ritual bonding."

Unable to speak for the moment, May nodded.

"A fascinating aspect of the Sapient A-forms. They have strong bonds which can be so easily forgotten."

"Get to the point," May choked.

"As with you and margarethearn, I did not use influence, which has been found to be fleeting. Instead, I find scent of long-forgotten bonds and restore them. It is most satisfying to see the reaction of A-forms when they find something which has been lost to them.''

"And that's what you did to Emeht?''

"Yes.''

May shivered and sighed. "All right. But please watch it—'' He saw right away that the Arcolian hadn't understood the idiom. "Please . . . exercise caution when restoring these bonds, misterbob. We Sapient A-forms are just getting used to the idea of dealing with Arcolians, and I'd hate to go back to the days when there had to be a dog in the room—'' He stopped short, and his eyes fell to the floor. "I'm sorry, misterbob. I shouldn't have said that.''

The Arcolian lifted its hand and laid it on James May's shoulder. "As you might say, 'nonsense.' That is the reason I am so intent upon studying your ways. Full effort must be made between our two races to ensure that there is not a return to those days.''

"Well,'' May said with a weary smile. "Our work is certainly cut out for us.''

4

Duke was lying on a table. He wore no shirt, and his right arm was fastened down with loose straps at the shoulder, elbow, and wrist. Tiny electrodes were poked into the tips of his fingers and thumbs, and sensors were glued to the skin over each of the arm's major muscles. From the base of the table, blue light filtered up to monitor what was happening.

"Now, Mr. Arbor,'' one of the doctors said, "we're going to be testing the nerve connections and the quality of muscular response in your arm. It won't hurt, but you might find the process a little . . . alarming.''

"All right,'' Duke said. He looked over at his hand.

"Here's a sample of what we'll be doing so you know what to expect.''

His fingers jumped. The rest of his body tensed.

"Relax, please, Mr. Arbor. As I said, the test is harmless, but we can't do it unless you totally relax that arm.''

Duke took a deep breath and closed his eyes. "Okay. Sorry.''

"No need to be.''

Duke could feel his arm moving. Curiosity overcame him, and he looked again. The hand was making a fist, and then it flexed out, fingers spread wide. Then, in sequence, each finger stretched over and touched the pad of the thumb. The sensation was amazing. Duke knew that his hand was doing the work, but he was putting forth no effort. It was like watching as someone else went through the motions. He looked back at the ceiling and closed his eyes. A moment later, he heard a familiar sound. When he looked, he was snapping his fingers.

"This is really strange," he said.

"It's the same principle as a Comealong," he was told, "only a Comealong projects a line of control and centers it in the spine. The victim of one has no choice but to follow given orders."

Duke watched as his hand flexed and unflexed. "I'm told that the best thing to do is not resist a Comealong."

Another of the doctors spoke. "Signal's a lot stronger. Could hurt you if you're not careful."

The test went on for another ten minutes, and then the doctors ran the accumulated data through their systems. While that was being compiled, Duke's arm was freed from the restraints, and he was told he could dress. He went to sit up, but his right arm did not want to cooperate. It hung limply at his side.

"Side effect," the attending doctor said. "It'll wear off after a while."

With a shrug, Duke picked up his shirt and put the sleeve around the dead limb. It seemed to take just short of forever to get it around his shoulders and left arm, and as much again as he fastened it up. By that time, the doctor had returned with the results of the test.

"Good news," he said. "Your arm's almost good as new."

"Almost?"

"You're going to have to take it easy for a while," the doctor advised. "Don't try anything overly strenuous or attempt any zero-gee bravado. The wrist will be sore for a while, and your grip will be weak, so make sure that you exercise it on a daily basis. Whenever you think of it, flex it, make a fist, snap your fingers, squeeze in and out on something soft. In a couple of standard months, you'll be as good as new."

"All right. Thanks." Duke's shoulder budged, but his right arm stayed at his side. He grabbed it with his left and held it out to the doctor, who laughed and shook with him.

From there, Duke made his way to the cashier's desk, where he paid for the testing, and then joined Winters in the waiting area.

"How's the arm, Mr. Duke?"

Duke flopped the lifeless limb into Winters's lap. The big man's eyes went round with fear.

"Oh, no. They made it *worse*!"

Duke picked the arm up and laid it in his own lap. "No, they didn't. That's from the testing. The doctor said I'm all healed."

Winters clapped him on the back so hard that it almost sent him sprawling out of the chair. "Great! When Mr. Vonn gets some new fingers we'll all have to celebrate."

Duke started to say something about celebration, but his words were cut off by a bitter obscenity that was shouted from the other side of one of the clinic doors. The waiting room fell silent, and after a moment, the door slowly opened. Vonn shuffled out, right arm in a sling, eyes glaring hatefully at the floor.

Winters's mouth dropped open. Duke stood and went to the mercenary's side. "What's wrong?"

Vonn cradled his slung arm. "Let's just get the hell out of this—"

"Winters," Duke said quickly. It took another shout to bring the big man to his side. Duke put his hand on Vonn's shoulder and inched him toward Winters. "Take him down to the street," he said. "Don't get on the bus. Flag down a taxi and make him wait for me. I'll be down in a minute."

Winters nodded and ushered Vonn out.

Duke hurried back to the cashier, paid for Vonn's examination, then caught the elevator down to the street. A taxi was waiting with open door when he stepped out of the building, and he climbed into the back with the two mercenaries.

"Where to?" the driver asked.

"Just drive," Duke said.

The car lurched out into traffic, snapping them back in their seats.

"Give us a privacy screen. I'll ring when I figure out where we're headed."

A wall of static formed between their compartment and the driver.

"Now," Duke said calmly, "you want to talk about it?"

Vonn stared at the fresh bandages on his hand.

"Come on, Vonn. It can't be as bad as all of that, can it?"

"They want to give me a hand," he whispered.

"I thought that was the idea."

"A ServoHand," Vonn said, voice rising.

"So?"

"They're slow," Vonn snapped. "They're damned ugly. And they're unreliable. I wanted the fingers. The Neuroflange fingers." He was trembling.

"All right," Duke said. "Why don't you start at the beginning?"

Vonn squirmed in his seat. "Well, they hooked up these wires to my fingers, and where my thumb and index finger were—"

"They did the same to me."

"And they ran all these tests, trying to get my hand to move, seeing how much damage was done, all of that. When they got done, they said that half of my middle finger was going to have to come off, which I figured, because it hadn't been right since I got hurt. But I wasn't too worried about it, because I thought I could get a Neuroflange for it, too. In fact, that's what I told them, and that's when things went to hell.

"They told me that they noticed something wrong with the remaining two fingers, even though they weren't hurt. What the hell did they call it? 'Decreased tactical ability'?"

"Tactile ability?"

"Something like that. Well, I told them about my injuries, and they decided that when that piece of metal went through my hand, it damaged the nerves and muscles and all of that connecting stuff in there. That's when they first pitched the idea of the hand." He paused. "I told them that I couldn't really use the hand, not in my line of work. I really wanted those damned fingers." He pulled his right arm close to his chest and held it there with his left.

"What did they say to that?" Duke asked.

"They said they were sorry. Can you believe it? Like they could do something about it to begin with? They said that I wasn't a good candidate for the Neuroflanges because, while the partial middle finger would be okay, there was irreparable damage to the remaining nerve endings where the thumb and index fingers had been. I told them they could damn well scrape down to a usable nerve ending, and they said—" His voice caught. He leaned forward and rocked in his seat. "They said," he continued quietly, "that in order to get a usable nerve ending, they'd have to go all the way down to the wrist, which would leave me with a ServoHand."

"I didn't think your hand was that bad," Winters said.

"It wasn't," Vonn said distantly. "The problem is that I've got something called global neural hardcasing. My whole nervous system was shocked from drug abuse and started to form this dense outer coating that they likened to wood. They said that while my nerves were working fine for me, it would make the application of fine prosthetics a real bitch. The smaller nerve bundles tend to separate and fragment during the attachment process.''

"Why did they say that about drugs?" Winters asked. "I thought you didn't like drugs, Mr. Vonn."

"Outside of alcohol, I don't," he answered.

"Alcohol wouldn't do that," Duke said. "Would it?"

Vonn shook his head. "This damage is recent," he said, raising his bandaged hand. "After I was hurt, I stole drugs from the hospital on the *Hergest Ridge*. I knew what most of them did and had heard about the rest, and I shot myself full of them. I had to keep going. I had to keep Bachman from taking the Arcolians.''

Duke found that he had regained some motor control over his arm. He propped it around Vonn's shoulders.

"A ServoHand," Vonn said. "A damned ServoHand. Nobody's going to hire me with one of those."

"You could learn to shoot with your left hand," Winters suggested.

Vonn spat. "I could be a sharpshooter with my left hand and still starve to death. You know how easily spooked sponsors can be. They see me walk in with one of those plastic mothers, and they'll turn me around and show me the door."

"Maybe you're lucky," Duke said. "Getting out of the mercenary trade before your number gets called."

"I'd rather be dead. I'd rather be in hell."

"Look at what the mercenary life has cost you, Vonn. You've lost your best friend, you've lost a woman that you really cared about, you've lost your physical well-being. And now that you're hurting, what does the brotherhood do? It turns its back on you."

"You watch what the hell you say about my brothers," Vonn barked. "I'm not like you. I can't just make planetfall on a place like this and get a job. I'm not going to take some damned institutional vocational rehabilitation program and learn how to vacuum-mold plastic into parts for sensu-droids. I'm not made of that kind of stuff."

"You're going to give up, then, is that it? Just because you got dealt a lousy hand of cards, you're going to fold and leave?" Duke shook his head. "What a coward you are, Vonn."

The back of the cab went silent. The two mercenaries stared at the commodities broker.

Duke shrugged. "I'm sorry. That was bad of me to say. I guess when things go right for me, I expect them to go right for everyone. Galaxy's not built that way, is it?"

"No." Winters sighed in relief.

"Let me make it up to you since I'm the one with all of the money right now. How's that?"

"It's not necessary," Vonn said quickly.

"Nonsense. I insist. Your spirits need a lift, and I know just the way to do it." He punched a button and the static screen dropped.

"You rang?" the cabbie asked.

"You ever heard of a place called the Black Orchid?" Duke asked.

"Are Zytean women horny?" the driver replied.

"All right," the broker said with a laugh. "Take us there." He sank into his seat and closed his eyes.

Winters and Vonn exchanged uncomfortable glances.

"Actually," Vonn said suddenly, "I'd rather wait."

"Wait?" Duke gave him a look of disbelief.

"Until we've taken the stuff back to the Essence people. If I'm going to be drinking on your tab at the Black Orchid, then I want to be in a mood to really enjoy it. As it stands now, I'm too miserable to appreciate the place. I should reconsider getting a ServoHand, and I think I should be sober when I do it. Might not be such a bad idea after all." He looked at Winters for support. As usual, Winters missed the point and stared at the two of them blankly.

"I don't believe this," Duke said in disgust. "After all this time I've been hanging around you and trying to avoid the places you liked to go, and when I'm finally ready to be friendly you turn on me."

Vonn shrugged. "Sorry. That's the way I feel."

"All right." Duke sank back in his seat. "Cabbie, scrub that last order. Stand by for new directions."

"They're your credits," the cabbie shot back.

"Honestly, Vonn," Duke said, shaking his head. "I don't know what to make of you. It's like I hardly know you anymore."

Vonn just stared back at Duke. It's the same with me, brother, he thought. It's the same with me.

5

They watched as a long, silver ship circled the field, losing altitude with each consecutive spiral, until it was close enough to be identified as a pleasure craft. When it was near enough to tell the model by its silhouette, jets kicked in on the vehicle's underbelly and it began to slowly descend toward a square of blue lights in one corner of the field. By the time they could read the name that had been painted on the pleasure craft's side— *Reconnez Cherie*—it had landed, and the dust it had raised began to settle.

Duke fired the van's engine. "Are we clear?"

Vonn, who was sullenly staring out the passenger window, nodded.

Winters opened the back door of the van and scanned across the landing field. "Clear, Mr. Duke," he said.

Duke put the van into gear and drove it straight up to the nose of the pleasure craft, then waited while Vonn climbed out and rapped a distinctive rhythm on the hull. After a moment, the nose of the craft split and a set of stairs descended. At the top of the stairs was May, who was lugging a large crate.

"Go help him, Winters," Duke ordered.

The big man jumped out the back of the van and met May at the foot of the stairs. He took the crate from him and, in a moment, was tossing it into the back of the van.

"Open it up," May said.

"You're pushing your luck," Vonn complained.

May gestured as Winters opened the chest and squealed in delight. He pulled out a machine pistol and began to fondle it affectionately.

Vonn grabbed May's lapel with his good hand. "Have you lost it? If the Council Port Authority catches us with this stuff—"

"They won't do a thing." May removed a shotgun from the chest and pressed the trigger action into Vonn's left hand. "I've got a temporary permit to use these in a high-security convoy. As long as we go straight to the Essence Company and straight back to the ship, we'll be fine." He pulled out a shoulder holster weighed down with a pistol and handed it to Duke. Duke took off his jacket and started to put the holster on.

"Straight back to the ship? What about the reward? What about the transactions it'll take to credit our accounts?"

"Quit whining, Vonn," May growled. "It's going to take

time for all of that to come together. I'm assuming that the Essence Company will want to spread the word about their fabled product being returned safely, and we need to keep a low profile until the excitement dies down. Anyway, we're going to be stranded until the *Angel's Luck* is refitted.''

"Speak for yourself," Vonn said. "I want to get out of here."

May put his arm through the sling of a machine pistol and went back to the *Reconnez Cherie*. "Cover me," he said. "I'm going to bring out the merchandise. And I'm going to shoot the first man who says anything about 'the stuff of dreams.' All right?"

The two mercenaries nodded and took their positions on each side of the stairs. Duke pulled the van around and backed up until the rear doors were no more than a meter from them. After a moment, May came down, lugging a stained box that had once carried bottles of transgear lube. He slid the box across the bed of the van and motioned for the mercenaries to climb in with it.

"Anybody tries to open the door, you guys blow them away, no questions asked. All right?"

They saluted.

May slammed the doors, then climbed into the passenger seat as Duke put his jacket back on.

"Drive straight to the Essence Company field office. Follow all of the signs and the speed codes. If someone unauthorized tries to stop us, you know what to do."

Duke patted the bulge under his coat.

"No," May said. "You won't have time. Run over them."

"Got it."

Duke drove them from the airfield to the Essence Corporation at the opposite end of the city. The transport went off without a hitch, with only some minor traffic snarls to cause the van's occupants any anxieties.

They were all amazed at the size of the company's complex. A two-story building sprawled in front of them, and vehicles of various makes and models cluttered a parking area of equal size. Separating them were large expanses of lawn, and around them were thick groves of trees. The expanse was surrounded by a tall chain-link fence, which broke only for the occasional guard shack.

May reached into his breast pocket and pulled out a handful of plastic cards. He handed one to each man in the van. "Clip this to your clothes somewhere on the right side. It's a permit to carry our weapons in the open."

Duke looked at his before attaching it. It carried the hologram of the Council system branch of Port Authority, the words CON-DITIONAL WEAPONS PERMIT (SECURITY ESCORT), Duke's full name, and a period of validity that came to thirty-two hours.

"Did you get us a permit to fire these things?" Vonn asked bitterly. He fumbled with his card, trying to get it onto his right side. With a sympathetic smile, Winters reached over and clipped it for him. "You're treating me like a cripple."

"You always treat me okay, Mr. Vonn."

Vonn shrugged. "Okay, Winters. I understand. Sorry."

They stopped at a guard shack long enough for Duke to show his weapons badge and announce his appointment with a man named Burris. The guard checked her slate, asked for their names, and then waved them through when satisfied with their identities.

Following the guard's directions, Duke took the van across the vast parking lot up to the Essence building and around it until they reached the main entrance. He started to take the van down one of the parking aisles, but May ordered him to park right along the curb.

"But the sign—" Duke started to protest.

"Ignore it," May said. "I don't want to waste any more time, and I certainly don't want to have to walk an entire kilometer out in the open with this stuff. Park us there."

Duke obediently stopped the van directly in front of the doors to the building, then leaned against the steering wheel and stared out the window.

"Gentlemen, we are here," May announced. "The time is finally at hand for our big payoff. Winters, shoulder your weapon and carry the box with the phials. Vonn and I will go in on each side of you, and Duke will take up the rear."

There was a bark of affirmation from the mercenaries, and they all began to ready themselves. May checked the clip in his weapon and chambered the first round, noticing that Duke was still staring out the window.

"This is it," May said, thumping him on the shoulder. "Kill the ignition, get your weapon out, and cover Winters's flank."

"Sorry." Duke shut the engine down and reached down to unfasten his driving harness. "You know there are times when I thought I'd never see this place."

"Well, you made it, farm boy," May said. He opened the door and stepped out. "Are we ready?"

There was a double "yes" from Winters and Vonn. Duke,

he saw, was still staring out the windshield of the van. May slapped the side of the vehicle with the palm of his hand. "Wake up. It's payday."

Duke slowly turned to face the merchant. "Have you thought about what it's taken us to get this far? Have you thought about the cost?"

"I've thought long and hard about my share of this," Vonn growled.

"Is it going to replace Anders? Is it going to bring back Bear or Li? What about Sullivan? What about the crew of the *Roko Marie* or that *Ebitsuka* craft that was destroyed?"

"Stop that, Duke," May complained. "The next thing you know, you're going to tell me that you miss Hiro."

"It's crossed my mind," Duke said. "And what about the way we dragged Roz away from—"

"Duke," May said sternly, "the way I see it, you have two choices. You can sit here and get lachrymose over absent friends and the ultimate cost in human suffering, which no amount of money is going to even touch, or you can come in with us, let them cross your palm with more money than you'd make in your whole frigging career as a commodities broker, and get on with the rest of your life."

Duke considered that. "You're right. I need to get back to Tetros." He opened the door and stepped out onto the sidewalk.

"His idea of getting on with life and mine differ greatly," Vonn muttered.

"He's paid more for these than any of us have," May replied.

Winters slid the box out of the van and lifted it into his arms. Vonn laid the barrel of the shotgun in the crook of his right arm and wrapped his left hand around the trigger mechanism. May raised the machine pistol with one hand and waved for Winters to start toward the door. The three of them started toward the building, and Duke followed, hands in his jacket pockets.

They made a brisk walk across the plaza and pushed through the doors into the Essence Corporation building. To a man they began to slow as they saw the wide-open space that made up the reception area. Before they could decide where to go, an older woman was up from behind a desk and heading their way, eyeing their weapons nervously.

"Guns down," May said, thumbing his safety and dropping his barrel toward the floor. Vonn straightened his right arm and let the business end of his shotgun fall.

"You must be the high-security party we're expecting," the woman said, relaxing.

May tapped his badge with a thumb and nodded. "We're here to see Mr. Burris. We have an appointment."

"Very well. If you'd please let me check your weapons, I'll notify him that you're here." She held out her arms expectantly.

May surrendered the machine pistol and nodded at Vonn, who relinquished the shotgun.

"The box?" she asked.

"Stays with us," May said.

The woman thanked them and told them to have a seat while she contacted Burris. In spite of the luxurious-looking furniture, the four stood huddled together, their backs toward Winters, who remained in the middle, box crushed against his chest.

"Nice digs," Vonn said.

"Real nice," May returned.

"I thought this was supposed to be a small operation."

"Me, too. Not doing too bad for missing their main product, are they?"

"Shoulda become a biochemist. Then I could grow my hand back."

"If you had been a biochemist," Duke said, "you wouldn't have hurt your hand to begin with."

"I hear you on that, brother."

The woman returned and gave them a strange smile. "I'm to show you right in. If you'll follow me . . ."

They did, falling into the same formation they had used to enter the building. The woman led them straight down the hall and to a section that had been labeled ESSENCE CORPORATION MANAGEMENT—COUNCIL 5 BRANCH.

"You'll have to forgive us," she said, turning to face them, "but Mr. Burris can only accommodate two of you in his office at a time." She waved her hand to indicate a row of soft-backed chairs in the hall. "Two of you will have to wait out here."

"Take Duke," Winters said quickly. "I'll wait out here with Mr. Vonn."

"This is your big chance," May said. "You sure you don't want it?"

Winters shook his head. "I'm too nervous around big shots. Bear always got my share for me. I don't like doing it myself."

"Duke?"

The younger man shrugged. "Have it your way."

"Keep the box here until we call for it," May blurted. The others stared at him. "It'll make things less complicated."

The woman led May and Duke a little farther down the hall to a door that was marked BRANCH MANAGEMENT. "You may ring whenever you're ready. He's expecting you."

May nodded. "All right. Thank you."

The woman returned the nod and walked away.

"Well," Duke said. "What are you waiting for?"

May smiled and thumbed the button. The door raised and they stepped into a plushly furnished office with a flatscreen hanging on one wall. Behind a smoked-glass desk, a man with folded hands studied their entrance.

"One of you," he said, moving his fingertips away from his mouth, "must be Captain May."

"I am," May said. He stepped toward the desk and extended his hand. "You must be Mr. Burris."

"I am." Burris motioned to a pair of chairs, one at each corner of the desk. "Please sit."

May nodded in approval as he took a seat. "Pretty nice place for a little biotechnics firm."

"Diversification," Burris said. "That's the key." He waited for Duke to be seated before speaking again. "I understand you wanted to speak with someone about our biochemical Knowledge Storage Program."

"We do," May said. He pushed his hand down his legs in an attempt to wipe the sweat from the palms. What's wrong with me? he thought. Is it this guy or what? I wish to hell that misterbob was here . . .

"So . . . speak," Burris said.

May cleared his throat. "Well, sir, you have doubtlessly heard that the Essence Phials have been rescued. Uh, by them, I mean of course the two hundred phials of stored information taken from the great scientists and thinkers of the last—"

"I know what you're talking about," Burris said. "The Essence Corporation Series One Legacy Distillations."

May said, "Right. Those."

"I have heard. In fact I've heard it a number of times—"

"Big news," May said. "Really big news."

"It's been really big news for a while." Burris pulled a small terminal from a drawer and began to tap the keys. An image flickered on the flatscreen over his shoulder. "I've been keeping track of them for some years now."

Years? May boggled at the word. It was strange—Myron Li

had made no mention of years when recruiting them to rescue the phials.

Yet, as May looked at the words materializing on the flat-screen, he saw that it was so. The headline he was staring at read ESSENCE PHIALS TURN UP IN MORANGA SYSTEM? and was dated a dozen years in the past. Burris stabbed another key and NO TRUTH TO RUMOR OF PHIAL RESCUE ON ELPHEX 6, SAYS T'GAL AFFAIRS appeared. The date of that story was only a few months after the first one. Another keystroke and a third appeared.

"The stories come in at the rate of about three a year," Burris was saying. "We subscribe to a systems service, and they make sure that we get transcriptions of them and any related material."

ESSENCE PHIALS TRACED TO SOL 3.

"You'll notice that these are reputable news services, too. None of those sleazy slates. We don't even take those into account."

ESSENCE KNOWLEDGE PHIALS DESTROYED IN COLONIAL RAID.

"What is your background, Captain May? I take it that you have a merchant's background?"

"I *am* a merchant."

BIOPRODUCT NOT ESSENCE, TESTS REVEAL.

Burris folded his arms and relaxed into his seat. "Let me tell you a story, then. A long time ago, there was this group of pirates who had managed to eke out a living in a colonial area that has long since become civilized. They decided to specialize in biological merchandise, because in that particular sector, bio-product had to be imported at great cost. They developed a burgeoning trade with black-market goodies, and were quickly becoming rich beyond their wildest dreams.

"One day they jumped a little courier owned by an outfit called Universal BioConcepts. To their surprise, this courier put up a hell of a fight, even though it was easily outgunned by the pirate vessel. Needless to say, the pirates crippled the ship and were able to magnet it in and board it with no problem.

"Only there was a problem, Captain May. During the battle a stray shot from the pirate cruiser led to an explosion in the storage compartment of the courier. The crew didn't know it at the time, but they were walking through a ship that had been contaminated by an engineered organism.

"The organism was a bioreplicant, a critter that was intended to be administered to victims of cryonic freezing. It was sup-posed to go through and repair damaged vessels and organs as it went. The pirates were very disappointed to find out that the cargo was damaged, and aside from the courier ship itself, they had come away empty-handed. Only they hadn't come away totally empty-handed, if you know what I mean.

"Before long, the crew of the ship was noticing that the wages of their decadent life-styles were beginning to disappear. They were actually recovering from damage done by substance abuse, alcoholism, and sexually transmitted diseases of all manner. and injuries among them healed at a rapid rate. They were, of course, too stupid to realize what was the cause of it all.

"The next state was that of perfect health, and after that came something that none of them expected. The crew of this ship thought they were *evolving*. They began to swell, to grow monstrous, limp appendages from their abdomens; they grew so corpulent that many of them couldn't move. Of course, what was happening was that the bioproduct they had absorbed from the courier had run out of things to do, so it had taken the initiative to start making things on its own.

"It was just a matter of time until the entire crew had been transformed into a handful of monstrous, ulcerous masses—and the hellish thing was, they had a drastically extended life span. If an injury occured or a disease developed, the organisms took care of it in a matter of hours. The only thing that could do one of them in was a sudden, instantaneous death.

"Of course, in their line of work, that's going to happen on occasion. So these pirates still prowl the galaxy, looking for people to replenish the crew. Their favorite tactic is to lie in wait like a derelict along a trade route and snatch up salvors when they happen along. And it isn't long before the salvors become one of them . . ."

"You're talking about the *Rough Trade*," May said.

Burris nodded.

"It's a folk tale. I've heard versions of that in every bar and port from here to Sigma Alphaeus, although I must admit that yours was among the most detailed."

"A folk tale. A story passed off as gospel from person to person although the events seem vague and unverifiable. Very good." Burris tagged another key on his terminal, and the headlines began to change, appearing on the screen just long enough to be read before going on to the next. May stared as the data flashed.

"It's our own nature to take something out of real life on

which to base these tales," Burris continued. "They hold so much more validity than, say, the one about Argos."

"The planet of gold," Duke said. "I've heard that one."

"I collect them," Burris said. "My favorite involves three Terrans named Disney, Presley, and Apostle John, who have been traveling around the galaxy together for thousands—"

"Get to the point," May said. "Surely you have one."

"My point," Burris said, "is that the Essence Corporation Series One Legacy Distillations have fallen into that category. It was a dream, Captain May, a brilliant, mad dream, and there are people out there who desperately want it to come true. Imagine being able to take the accumulated knowledge of a human being and pass it on to the next generation. What a gift, Captain. What a gift."

"You're talking as if—"

"Let me finish. Add to this dream, Captain, the one thing that appeals to seventy-five percent of the galaxy. Add instant riches and notoriety. Heroism, Captain. The supposition that anyone crazy enough to go in and take the phials from the gangsters hoarding them would surely give their name immortal status. It's what everyone wants."

"Not everyone," Duke said.

"It comes with the territory," Burris replied.

"But it doesn't have to."

Burris shrugged. "Have it your way. But there's still the prospect of more money than someone like you could imagine spending in a lifetime."

"Try us," Duke said.

"Suffice it to say that the Series One Legacy Distillations have captured the imagination of the galaxy. So a couple of times a year I receive someone in my office, someone of your background and caliber, who seems to think that they have discovered the shift route to Argos."

"The phials," May said blankly.

"The phials," Burris said. "Can I tell you something with complete candor? You and I have lives that are worlds apart, Captain, yet I appreciate what you have done on behalf of the Essence Corporation. It is the feelings of people like you that have kept us in the forefront of the public's attentions, and you have made us what we are today. We could not have become what we are without you.

"Yet for all of my appreciation, my respect for your capabilities and plans, I can in all truth say that I can't condone—nor show any enthusiasm for—your desire to liberate the phials from what you have determined to be their place of concealment. The *Yueh-sheng*, after all, is notoriously vindictive, and the Essence Corporation cannot be liable for your well-being should you cross them. We will not sanction or underwrite your project, nor will we give any form of tacit approval. If word was to get out—"

"Now you know why some people wouldn't want the publicity," Duke said. "There's too much to lose, such as the lives of the surviving team."

Burris narrowed his eyes. "What?"

"And even if the *Yueh-sheng* decided not to tangle with a handful of people who were galactic heroes, there are still the sycophants and hangers-on, the ones who would be out for their piece of an enormous reward. They alone could make the lives of the heroes miserable."

"Which is why," May said, rising, "we want to receive the reward in *cash*."

Burris laughed in spite of himself. "Of course, of course. This is not unusual. Once every few years we get someone in who claims to have—"

"We claim nothing," May said, stepping to the door. "We have them." The door slid open, and he stuck his head out into the hall. "Winters," he shouted, "would you please bring in the merchandise?"

Burris placed the tips of his fingers together and nodded. "Absolutely," he said. "Please bring them in. Of course, I'll have to have their authenticity verified by our laboratory."

May smiled. "We wouldn't have it any other way."

Winters appeared in the doorway with the tattered box and looked nervously around the office. Burris gave the box a reproving look, then smiled knowingly.

"Right here," Duke said, pointing to the floor beneath his feet.

Winters gently laid the box down, then backed toward the door. "Can I go sit with Mr. Vonn now?"

May nodded, and the big man disappeared.

"This is most amusing," Burris said. "I must admit, you two are doing this with more panache than I'm used to."

Duke pulled the flaps of the box open and reached down inside. "Catch," he said, and flipped a thin bottle into the air.

"Duke, you son of a bitch—"

Burris grabbed it out of the air and cradled it in his hands.

"You careless—" He looked down at the phial. May and Duke watched as he grew pale. "Mother of the Fifth Region," he said.

"Surprised?" May asked.

Burris caught his breath, exhaled, and made a feeble attempt to casually roll the bottle onto the tabletop. "I thought your associate was going to spill something all over my—"

"Something valuable, perhaps? You haven't even looked at the label."

"I don't need to—"

"Then here's another," Duke said, and another phial arced toward Burris, who swore once, loudly and very vulgarly, and clapped the container into his palm.

"It's someone named Acker," Duke continued. "Of course, that name means nothing to someone of my caliber."

"Acker. Ack—" Burris glanced at the type on the cap of the phial and gasped. He looked up as Duke was reaching for another. "No," he said. "That's quite unnecessary."

"You're convinced, then?"

"Of—" Burris paused to take another breath of air. "Of course not. I mean, those phials look *very* authentic, and you've certainly done your homework on some of the donors involved with the original program. However, it has been a number of years since they turned up missing, so I'm going to want to have them tested in the biolab to confirm their authenticity."

"You've said that twice now," May said. "Are you going to do it or not?"

"Of course," Burris said nervously. "Of course." He rose from behind his desk and skirted around it toward the door. "If you'll excuse me for a moment, I'll have one of my techs pick them up."

"Fine." May smiled as Burris walked out. Once he was out of sight, May spun on his partner and grabbed him up out of his seat by the lapels. "You bastard. If you ever pull a stunt like that again—you realize what you could've cost us?"

"May," Duke croaked. "Something's wrong—"

"I know," May said. "It's got to do with Eric Dickson running through your veins. I'm going to have Mr. Burris take care of that just as soon as he figures out that we've got his hot little product in our hands."

"May, I've got this feeling—"

"Is it your Tetran sense of observation?"

"Not exactly—"

"Then I don't want to hear about it. You've got knowledge or intuition or something from that war hero inside of you, and it's been doing more harm than good of late. I'm sorry, but I can't trust you, not now, not when—"

"Then why did you let me come along, May? Want to explain that? If I'm such a high risk—"

"Is that Burris?" May asked suddenly. He stepped into the doorway and peered down the hall. "Where the hell are Vonn and Winters?"

With a shiver, the hair on the back of Duke's neck stood. He suddenly felt as if there were wide bands around his chest constricting his breathing, and the office began to close in on him.

Oh, no, he thought. Not again. I'll never be able to convince him, and we'll never be able to convince them that—

His eyes fell on Burris's desk where the two phials sat, waiting for confirmation.

That's it—

He grabbed the phials as May stepped back into the room.

"Mercenaries," the merchant spat. "You haven't been able to get a good one since the war."

Duke eased into his seat and casually placed one of the phials back in the box. "Since when were you an expert in hiring mercenaries?"

May leaned back and tried to prop his feet up on Burris's desk. It was too high and too far away from the chair to be comfortable. He abandoned the idea and sat straight. "Ever since this damned thing started," he said, "I feel like I've become some kind of expert."

The second phial was cool as it rolled against the palm of Duke's hand. He wrapped his fingers around it, then stuck both hands into the pockets of his jacket.

"I'll tell you one thing, Duke. I'm tired of it. I want nothing more than to get the ship fixed and get on with the rest of my life . . ."

Duke uncurled his fingers. He could feel the extra weight drop into his pocket.

". . . not sure what your plans are, I know you're thinking about going back to Tetros, but I've been giving this pleasure craft racket of yours some thought—"

The broker smiled. "May," he said. "It's all right."

May blinked and came out of his reverie. "What? What's all right?"

"Never mind. You were saying?"

"Well," May said, as if broaching a sensitive subject, "If you're not in *too* big a hurry to get back to Tetros, I could sure use your talents as a broker. And you'll certainly be cut in for a substantial portion of the profits. And when I get a new copilot, he'll be on a regular *salary*, because I don't ever want to treat anyone the way I treated poor old Dexter. I wonder whatever happened to that son of a bitch." He laughed wistfully. "If he's not rotting in a jail somewhere, he probably owns his own brothel by now. He always was kind of twisted." He turned to Duke as if he was about to deliver a longer speech when Burris appeared in the doorway, a green-coated technician at his heels.

"Captain," Burris said, "this is Dr. Melrose from our research department. He's going to take what you have and test it for authenticity."

"No, he's not," May said.

"Captain—"

"Perhaps he doesn't understand," Melrose said, stepping in. "No harm will come to what you've brought us. The Series One Distillations were packaged in a very special way, and a very simple analysis will determine their authenticity."

May nodded. "All right. Duke—"

Duke rose and lifted the box. Melrose took another step and held out his arms.

"Duke will carry them."

"Please let Dr. Melrose," Burris said, a bitter twinge in his voice. "Surely you're worn out after carrying them halfway across the galaxy."

May glared, and Duke handed the box over. Melrose turned and started out, and the merchant waved for Duke to follow. They were blocked at the door by Burris.

"I'm sorry. You're not permitted in the lab. Insurance company rules."

"Where they go," May said, "I go." He started to walk past, but Burris checked him with his shoulder.

"Sergeant," he said.

"That's Captain," May growled.

"No," Burris answered as a shadow grew behind him. "I meant sergeant."

The sergeant was no taller than Burris but carried a fully charged Comealong.

"Sergeant Emerson is going to show you the way out of the building. Aren't you, Sergeant?"

The sergeant smiled.

"Dammit," May said. "We're not just another bunch of crooks trying to pull one over on you, and we're not trying to hit your laboratory with a bomb. *Those are the real phials!*"

"May," Duke said. "He knows. Beyond a shadow of a doubt."

"Sergeant, if you would—"

"Mr. Burris," Duke said quickly. "Aren't you going to tell us about the settlement you got from the insurance company? Aren't you going to explain to us how you parlayed that money to make Essence a galaxy-wide business and how you don't give a righteous damn about the status of the phials?"

Burris blinked at Duke and then turned to the guard. "Sergeant Emerson, if you'd excuse us, please."

The sergeant gave Burris a civilian salute and stepped away.

"Duke," May said, "what the hell are you talking about?"

"I think I should let Mr. Burris explain it."

Burris thumbed a button and the door slid shut. He paced to his seat at the desk. "Your young friend is only half correct, Captain. I do care about what happens to the phials. I care very much about them."

May put his hands on his hips and stared hard at Burris. "So you're admitting the possibility that what we gave you were the real thing."

"I have no doubt in my mind," Burris said. "It's been a dozen years since I held one of the bottles in my hand, but I haven't forgotten what they looked like."

"Then where's our reward money?"

Burris turned to one corner of the desk as a computer terminal appeared from beneath its surface. He sat down and punched orders into it, stopping to ask for May's full name. After another bout of typing, the terminal rattled and spit out a long slab of plastic. "Right here," Burris said, taking it out with a flick of his wrist. "A certified credit voucher which can be instantly converted to cash at any reputable bank on this planet."

May took the voucher and scowled at it. "Wait a minute." he said. "This is only five million credits."

"That's the entire amount of our authorized reward account."

The merchant's hands closed around the voucher and snapped it in half. This is *nothing*," he growled. "This would buy you three of the phials at most. Where's the rest of the money?"

"What makes you think that there's any more?"

"The man who hired us," May said, "promised us a cut of

seventy-five million credits. If you base that on the conservative and entirely reasonable assumption that we were receiving a quarter of the promised reward for bringing in the shipment, the rest is easy to figure.''

''All right. You've made your point, so I suppose it's best to level with you. You want to know where the rest of the money is?'' Burris spread his hands. ''You're looking at it, Captain. You're looking at it.''

May stared around the office.

''The building, May,'' Duke said. ''This whole complex. It seems Essence isn't Essence anymore.''

''How right you are,'' Burris said, entreating them to sit. ''Captain, you've been in space for far too long.''

May turned to Duke. ''Then maybe you'd like to share your insights with me, because I'm not getting a thing out of this.''

''It's only because I've recently made the transition into space,'' Duke said, ''and because of my background as a broker. Money works differently in space. The numbers are grossly inflated, yet everything rises to compensate. You make runs from planet to planet, but—and correct me if I'm wrong—the real money comes in when you take something into deep space, like the beef you wanted to sell on the *Saint Vrain*.''

May tossed the halves of the voucher onto the desk. ''Are you trying to tell me that this is the entire worth of those phials on this planet? Well, that's bullshit because—''

''That's not the reason,'' Duke said calmly. ''Try it this way. You probably move more money in a year than my uncle's company does in a decade. Remember the abattoir, May, that big, fine abattoir? The price you had committed to pay for the *Angel's Luck* would buy that complex, brand-new, twice over.''

May drew breath. ''Or it could buy a complex like this.''

''Exactly,'' Burris said.

''So if you had the phials insured at a rate to justify the proper amount of reward money, you could have used the proceeds to finance—''

''A business, Captain May. We deposited the insurance settlement into a rather complex account which allotted us a rather high rate of interest. Working with the yearly interest from that, we were able to build the company. A whole new Essence Corporation that is quickly expanding into the field of biotechnology. Maybe you've seen people with the Cateye implants. Those are ours, our first real success since the debacle with losing the distillations.''

"You're *lying!*" Duke snapped.

"I beg your pardon—"

"You couldn't have expanded that fast, not using accumulated interest. Not to develop something like the optical implants. A fledgling company like Essence couldn't have floated the loan, not after losing their main asset. And you couldn't have banked against the reward as collateral. You spent it, you bastard!"

May was up from his seat. "What are you saying?"

"The terms of the settlement would have to allow for some kind of reward account to be set up, and the amount would be determined by the likelihood that the phials would be recovered. The rest could be used to rebuild the business."

"Then," May said, "you had to be pretty damned sure that those phials weren't coming back in order to get away with spending all but five million of the settlement. This means . . ." He looked at Duke—and Duke looked at Burris.

"That you knew they weren't coming back," Duke finished. "You set up with the *Yeuh-sheng* in order to have the phials stolen."

Burris slowly nodded. "Very good—Duke, is it? What gave it away for you?"

Duke rose and crossed over to Burris's desk. He reached down and pushed a key, and the screen came to life, replaying the headlines about the theft of the Series One Distillations.

"You were so proud of this file," Duke said. "You so enjoyed rubbing our noses in all of this rumor. It's free advertising for the Essence Corporation. What you've done isn't necessarily right, but it's damned good business."

"Very good," Burris said, smiling. "Very, very good." He gestured at May. "You hang on to this one, Captain. He's good, observant—"

"Burris," May said, too loudly, "the way I see it, you owe us an explanation—"

"No," Burris snapped. "I owe you *nothing*, Captain. But since you were so valorous as to bring the phials out from the grip of the *Yeuh-sheng*, I can see fit to appease you. This whole thing has to do with responsibility."

"Responsibility." May said it with a sneer.

"Exactly. My colleagues and I, you see, had contracted with the various donors and had gone ahead with the first series of distillations. The original group numbered two hundred seventy-five, but several of the less courageous reneged, and several potential donors met with rather violent accidents which, unfortunately, left their brains useless to us. Another handful were deemed unfit before their demise, and we revoked their contracts; and a handful of others were pared out to bring the number to two hundred.

"Once we had the distillations in hand, we were faced with the prospect of marketing them. And that, Captain, is where the responsibility reared its ugly head. Immediately several surviving families of the deceased filed injunctions to prevent us from selling the legacy we had legally contracted for. Keep in mind that we weren't complete ogres—we had every intent of paying a rather healthy royalty to the beneficiaries designated by the donor.

"These injunctions only served to raise more questions within our ranks, and we began to have defections from within. Several of our top people left, claiming disgust with—"

"Forgive me if my heart's not breaking," May said, "but I've heard this story before. It didn't do anything for me the first time, either."

Burris folded his hands and carefully studied the merchant's face. "Very well," he said. "The upshot, Captain, is that we had the perfect product at the perfect time, and it blew up in our faces. Those it was intended for didn't want it. Those who sought it didn't deserve it. The lawsuits were beginning to bury us. The assets on which the Essence Corporation had been founded had become a huge liability and were threatening to put us out in the vacuum. We had to do something quickly before the worth of the distillations was completely devalued."

"So," Duke said, "it was a simple matter for you to give the phials to the *Yueh-sheng.*"

"Yes."

"*Yes*—" May pitched forward in his seat, but Duke held him back with his arm and a curt "Let him finish."

"Conceptual Protection Insurance had downgraded the value of the phials twice by then," Burris continued. "Their current standing was a fraction of their original worth. Those of us who remained decided that it was time to cut our losses and run. It was a simple matter to lose the phials under the proper circumstances. With great fanfare we announced that we were moving them to the high-security facility we were building here at CPI's insistence—"

"Via Malaysia Prime."

"Precisely. Of course, the *Yueh-sheng* just couldn't resist something so ripe for the picking. Especially not when we made it known that several experts in the law-enforcement field were among the distillees. My own theory is that the phials were never even loaded onto that Freight Bus. They just put the torch to it to make things look dramatic.

"Of course, when they made the ransom demand, it was much too exorbitant. They had undercut the last announced market price by half, but CPI wouldn't pay. There were other offers, but they were for individual donors—not the entire series. They were stuck.

"In the meantime, it worked out rather well for us. With the profits from our little enterprise, we added on to our high-security facility, diversified, and are doing quite well for ourselves. Our Series One Distillations became legendary, and we've got the toughest bunch in the galaxy guarding them. After all, *nobody* is fool enough to go up against the *Yueh-sheng*." Burris cleared his throat and shifted uncomfortably in his seat. "Well, until now, that is."

May calmly stood and smiled down at Burris. "I appreciate your candor," he said. "Now we can get down to business. Since you're doing so well, you're certainly not going to mind rewarding us for our efforts. I can understand that you don't have access to the reward fund anymore, but I'm sure that you have other assets that you can liquidate."

"Liquidate . . ."

"Of course." May smiled. "If the reward is based on the last depreciated price of the phials, then you owe us for the return of one hundred eighty-seven phials."

"One hundred eighty-six," Duke corrected.

With a shrug, May continued, "Whatever. Let's call the base amount owed two hundred eighty million and leave it at that. We will negotiate down to a point, but understand that we don't want credit, we don't want payments, we want cash. And we prefer to remain anonymous."

"After all of this," Burris said, "I thought that you would understand. There will be no negotiation. There will be no financial remuneration other than what you so deftly destroyed. The Essence Corporation cannot possibly raise the kind of cash you want—"

"Liquidate," May sang.

"—even if we wanted to, and I can assure you, Captain, that we most certainly do *not*."

"What's that?" May said sarcastically. "I thought I heard a negative."

"Captain, as your friend explained, the disappearance of the Series One Distillations has made the Essence Corporation a household word. You can go from Sol to the Inner Fringe, and everyone you meet will know our name. In every bar and pub in the galaxy you can hear whispered rumors. They've turned up somewhere. Some brave souls from such-and-such risked life and limb and made the ultimate sacrifice. They've turned up on this planet or that. A handful of people have made a career of searching them out over the last decade."

"Then imagine the publicity value when you can announce that an anonymous band of mercenaries actually *has*—"

"*No*, Captain. That would mean a windfall of publicity for us, true, but it would be terribly short-lived. People would forget, and we certainly can't have people forgetting the name of the Essence Corporation, can we?"

May folded his arms with firm finality. "All right," he said. "That's it. We're out of here. We're taking the phials—excuse me, the *distillations*—and—"

"What distillations?" Burris spoke with a deadpan expression on his face. "Do you see anything that resembles our missing product?"

May looked around quickly and then the memory returned: Melrose. And the little bastard had smiled as he had carried the phials off. A string of obscenities erupted from the merchant's mouth, and he lunged at Burris's desk. Duke came out of his seat and wrapped his arms around May, pulling him back as his fingers were centimeters from Burris's throat.

"May!" Duke shouted. "Stop it! It's all right!"

Burris shook his head. "Just as I thought." He smiled. "Another couple of crackpots trying to besmirch the good name of our company." He fingered a button, and the door roared open to reveal the sergeant, weapon at the ready. "Would you remove these two . . . *beings*."

Sergeant Emerson brandished his weapon.

"You haven't heard the last of me, you bastard!" May shouted.

Duke grabbed him by the shoulder and tried to urge him out the door. "It's all right, May. We'll handle it."

The merchant leaned toward Burris and shook his index finger. "We cart your stuff halfway across the universe, put our lives on the line—"

"Let's go, May," Duke urged.

"—and this is the way you—"

The sergeant's finger bit down on the trigger, and the air was filled with a sharp crackle. Ozone pricked Duke's nostrils, and May came out of his hunched stance into one that was stiff and upright.

"Ahhhhhhhhhh *shit*!" he bellowed.

"Follow me," the sergeant said calmly.

May began to plod out of the office, one stiff leg at a time, like Frankenstein's creature relearning how to walk.

"You . . ." May grunted, fighting the effect of the neural override, *". . . are . . . dead . . ."* The last word was a choked strangle, and saliva began to foam on the merchant's lips.

Duke looked at Burris and gave an apologetic shrug as May staggered out into the hall. "It was a nice try, wasn't it?"

Burris said nothing.

Duke looked to check May's progress and then turned back to Burris. "Let me tell you a secret. My partner's right." He narrowed his eyes and whispered conspiratorially, "You're *dead*."

Burris began to laugh as if that was the funniest thing he had ever heard in his life. "Oh, you mercenaries!" he said, wiping a tear of glee from his eye. "You're all the same!"

6

The scream echoed across the plaza and sounded like a shot in the ears of Winters and Vonn. They pushed open the rear doors of the van and jumped out in time to see the source of the commotion. One of the Essence Corporation guards was leading May out under the control of a Comealong, and the merchant was making the mistake of fighting it every step of the way. As they cleared the first set of stairs, the sergeant ordered May to bend over, put the flat of his shoe against May's buttocks, and shoved as he clicked off the weapon. May literally flew half a dozen meters and then hit the concrete hard.

"You're going to *pay* for that!" he rasped. "I'm going to remember your name, pal, and I'm coming back to slice off a big chunk of your—"

"May!" Duke said, kneeling to check on the fallen man. "You're not supposed to fight those things."

"He's dead," May whispered through clenched teeth. "So's his family. If he's got pets, they're—"

"Nice to see they were happy to get the phials back," Vonn said bitterly. He squatted and lifted one of May's arms. When he let go it fell lifelessly. "You're going to feel like hell for the next couple of hours," he pronounced.

"What are you doing out here?" Duke asked. "I was looking for you in the lobby—we needed help."

"They kicked us out," Winters said sulkily.

"Vonn?" Duke asked.

"True." The mercenary sighed. "We were sitting there when I noticed this little shit of a guy in a lab coat carrying the phials off. I got up to investigate and was met by a few uniformed individuals who escorted us out here."

"We've been screwed," Winters said.

"It's not as bad as all that," Duke said. "Listen up—"

"—and then I'm going to hardwire his car," May continued. "And then I'm going to burn his house to ash. There isn't going to be enough left for him to make—"

"Hang on," Vonn said. He took one of May's arms around his shoulder and stood, pulling the merchant up with him. "Can you walk?"

"—but it's got to be a *lingering* death," May said. "A thousand tiny razor cuts—"

Duke took May's other arm, and they started to walk him toward the van. "Is he going to be all right?"

"I think," Vonn said. "the more you fight one of those things, the worse a hangover you get from them." He paused for a moment to listen to May's ravings. "He's actually delirious. This is one of the worst cases I've seen. He must have been madder than hell."

"That's a quiet understatement," Duke said.

They walked May to the back of the van and waited as Winters climbed in the back ahead of them. The big man grabbed May under the arms and unceremoniously hauled him into the vehicle and plopped him down, oblivious to the torrent of profane disparagements that salted the air.

"I never heard anyone talk like that in my whole life," Winters said, brushing his hands off against one another.

"Do you suppose he learned that at the Merchant's Academy?" Vonn asked.

"You're asking me?" Duke said.

Vonn climbed into the back to tend to May while Winters made his way into the driver's seat. Duke opened the door and, on seeing him, stopped for a moment.

"May said I could drive back to the shuttleport," Winters said.

Duke bit his lip. "I know," he said. "But that was if we'd gotten the money. Better let me drive."

Winters's face began to droop.

"It's because I've got something important to talk to you about, big guy. Private stuff."

The thought intrigued Winters, so he worked his way into the passenger seat while Duke climbed in and fired the engine. After a few moments they were out of the Essence Corporation's gates and on the main boulevard. Duke casually leaned forward and turned on the cockpit radio, tuning through the stations until he found one playing Funtime. He turned it up loud, then looked at Winters.

"Vonn," he said quietly. "How long do Comealong hangovers usually last?"

No reply came. Winters looked back into the bed of the van. "He didn't hear you, Mr. Duke. Mr. May is being too loud."

Duke put his finger to his lips. "I know he didn't hear," he said, maintaining the soft tone. "I don't want him to."

Winters wriggled in his seat. "Secret stuff, huh?"

"Yeah. You know how May can be. Something goes wrong with his plans and it's the burning end of the universe. He's too sick right now to appreciate what I'm about to tell you, and I'd rather that Vonn not know about it yet, either, not until we get some good plans made."

"Okay." Winters was rubbing his hands together.

"I want you to keep something for me, Winters, and I don't want you to tell anybody about it until I tell you it's okay. Have you got that?"

Winters gave him a solemn look and bit his lower lip. "I promise," he said, pounding his chest with an elaborate series of hand signs. "I swear as your hired gun that—"

Duke wagged his hand at the big man to quiet him.

"—I, Irvin Winters," the ritual continued, "will so execute the duties given to me until the point of death, for there is no greater honor and no greater loyalty than that of the lone gun—"

"Winters—"

"—and there is no greater, uh, prize —no, reward—than that of the lone gun—wait."

"That's okay," Duke whispered urgently.

"Good." Winters blushed. "Because I forgot the rest."

"That's fine, Winters, just fine." Duke dug into his pocket and fished out the phial. Cradling it from view, he reached over and let it roll into Winters's lap. "Do you know what that is?"

Winters nodded, eyes wide with disbelief.

"Keep it safe."

Winters looked at the tiny bottle as if it were contaminated. "I don't know if I can do that, Mr. Duke," he said. "I mean, I think maybe you should keep it. Really. I might break it or something."

"I can't keep it," Duke said. "I can't explain why right now. It has to be you, Winters. Keep it where it won't be broken. You can find a really good hiding place, I know you can."

Winters gave an uncertain "all right." He was getting used to the idea.

"And don't tell anybody."

"I won't."

"Not even Vonn. Not even May, not until I tell you that it's okay."

"I won't. I won't, Mr. Duke. You'll see." Winters gingerly picked up the phial and slipped it into his right breast pocket. "Because I swear as your hired gun that I—"

Duke watched as Winters struggled to remember the oath, and was amazed at the smile that grew on the big man's face as he realized that he was an integral part of something important.

7

Appropriately enough, Duke thought, it started to rain on the way to the port. Large drops fell from the sky and hammered the windshield and roof of the vehicle, and the steady roar it produced seemed to calm May to the point where his planned atrocities trailed off into silence.

At the landing field, Duke pulled the van up to the *Reconnez Cherie* and leaned on the horn. After a moment the pleasure craft's maw opened and Roz came running down the steps, hand on the rail to steady herself. She walked right out into the downpour, circled around to the back of the van, and threw the bed doors open.

"How much did we get?" she asked brightly. On seeing Vonn with May, who was haphazardly sprawled across the floor, her face fell. "What happened?"

"He's all right," Vonn told her. "He's just not feeling very well.'' He looked at her. ''We got took. The Essence Company wouldn't pay us.''

''Well, then,'' she said indignantly, ''we'll just take them somewhere else.''

''Easier said than done, dearest. They took the phials from us.''

She stood with her arms crossed, letting the downpour soak her. Duke and Winters appeared next to her.

''Let's get him into the ship. He needs to be on the *Angel's Luck* to show the master programmer around. He's supposed to arrive sometime tomorrow morning.''

They slid May out and carried him toward the pleasure craft like a limp log. Rain splattered his face, making him blink and sputter.

''Is he going to recover in time?'' Roz asked. ''I mean, I could show this guy around, but I don't know what May wants done.''

''He should,'' Vonn said. ''He won't be in a very good mood, though.''

Once up the stairs of the ramp, the procession went to the nearest suite and strapped May in to one of the berths. Shaking the rain off of themselves, they stepped out into the hall to make plans.

''Vonn,'' Duke said, ''take us up.''

''No,'' Vonn said flatly. ''I'm staying here.''

''Give it a rest, Vonn. We need you here.''

The mercenary looked at Roz. ''Is your friend on board?''

''Yes,'' she answered.

''Then you don't need me.'' He turned and started for the stairs.

''Dammit,'' Duke said. ''Can Peter fly this thing?''

Roz shrugged. ''He assisted May on the way down.''

He sighed. ''All right. Have him take it back up. Park back in the cargo hold of the *Angel's Luck*. I'll be up in a few hours.''

Roz put her hand on his shoulder.

''It's all right,'' he said. ''We've just suffered a setback and our morale is low. We need to regroup and figure out what we're going to do next. I need Vonn's help for that.''

''Be careful,'' Roz said as Duke started down the stairs. He hurried across the tarmac to the van, where Vonn was sitting in the driver's seat, battering the steering yoke and cursing.

''The drive must have gotten wet,'' he said. ''Doesn't want to start.''

Duke blinked water out of his eyes. "Good. I'm coming with you." He circled around and climbed in on the passenger side.

"I don't want you around," Vonn said in low tones. "My life has officially come to an end."

"You've been around May too long, you know that? This is a setback, Vonn. There's a way out of this."

"I don't want to hear about it," Vonn snapped. He leaned forward and tried to get the van to start.

"Where are you going?"

"Me? Hell, I don't know. I thought I'd go somewhere and drown my sorrows, see if anybody is stupid enough to hire a one-armed mercenary and a frigging retard." He fiddled the controls again and the engine fired.

"The Black Orchid?" Duke asked.

Vonn glared back. "Probably. I don't know. What difference is it to you?"

"A big one. I'm going with you. I want to be around when you snap out of this streak of self-pity because *I* want to hire you for something that needs to be done. You've pulled us through some close scrapes, Vonn, and I want you on my fire team. I won't let you get away."

"You'd have to match me drink for drink, farm boy," Vonn said.

"So be it."

Vonn knocked the vehicle into gear and it lurched. "This is going to be a pleasure," he said with a smirk. "I've had this urge to kick your ass ever since we met." He lifted his foot off the brake and started to steer around the resting pleasure craft. Once out of the way he started to accelerate, and as he did, a hulking figure appeared in front of them. Vonn yelped and mashed the brake, and the van stopped short of running the figure down.

Hissing through his teeth, the mercenary popped the window open. The figure slid that way, and a wet, smiling face appeared.

"Hey, guys," Winters said.

"What now?" Duke asked.

"Roz thought I should come along and watch over you two guys. She said she and Mr. Chiba could get the ship back okay."

"It isn't a good time for this," Vonn said.

"But I got to stick by Mr. Duke because—"

"Oh, let him come," Duke blurted.

Vonn turned to him and mouthed, *Are you crazy*?

Duke shrugged. "What's the harm?"

"Hell." Vonn turned back to Winters and gave him the okay. Winters shouted with glee and clamored in through the rear doors of the van.

"Might as well," Vonn said in mocking tones. "Might as well make a bloody party of it."

8

There was nothing exceptional about the woman, save for the fact that she was green. Her looks were plain, her dark hair a common cut that hung about her face and shoulders. A dark Duraflesh one-piece molded her figure to the galactic standard, shiny leatheroid boots ran up her legs to midthigh, and matching gloves covered her arms to the shoulder. She was on her hands and knees, head swaying in time to the pulsating music that filled the bar, mouth opening to smile and moan.

What made the scene unusual was the green man standing over her. He had close-cropped hair and wore nothing but Duraflesh briefs. He had a barrel chest and was solid muscle from head to toe. High in his right hand he held a vicious-looking whip, which he swung in time to the music to lash the woman's back. The woman reciprocated with another lustful smile.

Winters stared at the couple with an open mouth. He squirmed uncomfortably in his chair and all but ignored his drink when it came. The scene on the tabletop had him transfixed.

"What's wrong, big guy?" Vonn asked. Two rounds of drinks had come and gone, and his emotions were beginning to subside. "See something you like?"

Winters shook his head. "He shouldn't be doing that to her," he said, wiping beads of sweat from his face.

"Hot in here?" Vonn laughed. "Come on, big guy, what's the problem?"

"Lighten up," Duke said. "It's not real, Winters. See those lines going through them?"

Winters squinted and studied the cruel dance on the table before him—but not too closely. If he squinted, he could see what Duke was talking about: tiny, uniformly spaced lines where the color did not seem as vivid, as if the performance were taking place behind a strange set of clear glass bars.

"Those are rezzlines," Duke explained. "This is just a hologram. In fact, if you watch it long enough, you'll notice they do the same thing over and over again."

Winters shook his head. "I don't want to watch it that long."

Duke stuck his hand into the scene. Green light splayed across his palm, and the figures disappeared where it blocked the light. He wiggled his fingers for effect. The image bent and skewed. "See? They've got one of these in a bar back home, Doctor Bombay's. That's where I met May."

Winters nodded and picked up his drink, trying to get interested in Duke's story. "He still shouldn't be doing that to her."

"I agree."

Vonn laughed. "You guys lose your spines in the war? Why don't you just relax? Enjoy this place. It's the pride of Council 5." He grinned and raised his glass in a silent toast.

"Of that, I'm sure," Duke answered sourly. "What's the attraction of a place like this?"

"I'm sure," Vonn said between sips of his drink, "that you've noticed Council 5's planetary government to be rather . . . repressive."

"It's understandable," Duke said. "The planet is full of the type of people you don't want to see gunned down in the middle of the street. Face it, Vonn, if the wrong person is even struck by a cab, it could result in a planetary war."

Vonn shrugged. "This is the only mercenary bar in the Council system. The planetary government tried to discourage having one at all, but one place or another always ended up catering to the crowd. So the government just decided to look the other way."

Winters squirmed in his seat. "I don't blame them." He tried to find a place where he could look that did not have an upsetting scene, but the green couple was on every table. "I wish I could look the other way."

"What are we looking for?" Duke asked.

"Nothing," Vonn said. "We wait."

"Great. Just great." Duke looked down into the bottom of his glass and slumped in his seat. Vonn chuckled at the holo between sips of his drink and mentioned something about his favorite part. His comments were ignored.

"Some friends you are," Vonn complained. "You're supposed to be cheering me up, but you won't even share in my fun."

"This isn't fun," Winters said in a low tone.

"What the hell." Vonn held up his empty glass for a passing waiter to see. "Another round on the outsider's tab," he said, pointing at Duke.

The trio sat through another round of drinks and nothing

happened. After a while, Duke began to form a dim understanding of the mercenary mind-set. Perhaps it was because of those interspersed periods of intense danger that the soldier of fortune enjoyed nothing more than sitting in a dark place that he or she knew to be safe, knocking back a few drinks, and enjoying the sensation of nothing. As he looked around to study the others in the Black Orchid, he observed that a great many had adopted the same posture as Vonn: generally ignoring the goings-on, slouched into the chair, slowly drinking, and not letting the waiter take the old glasses away. It was as if the accumulation of glasses was some kind of talisman, or perhaps a mark of one's courage and tolerance. It was all so foreign to him. The only one besides himself who looked out of place was Winters, who was busy looking about the bar, trying to avoid the endless scene on the tabletop.

The waiter returned again. Vonn asked for another. Duke shook his head. Winters seemed unavailable for comment, so Duke told the waiter to bring the check. As he vanished in the direction of the bar, Winters turned around and brought his fist down hard on the surface of the table. The accumulated glasses bumped and clanked against one another.

"I'm sorry," Duke said. "I didn't think you'd want another."

Winters thumped the table again.

"Lighten up. I'll catch the waiter when he comes back."

Winters smiled. "It's not that, Mr. Duke. I'm trying to make that picture go away." He thumped the table a third time. The image of the man and woman scrambled momentarily, then reassembled. He raised his hand for a fourth blow, but Duke stopped him.

"You're going to break it," he said. "Whatever gave you that idea?"

Winters turned in his seat and pointed. Duke grabbed his hand and slowly pulled it to the table.

"Not in here. Just tell me."

"Way over there in the corner. The man there knows how to make the scene go away."

Duke searched until he saw what Winters was talking about. A man was seated at a table littered with glasses, in the traditional position of downcast stare, slump, and drink in hand. As Winters had said, the hologram was not visible. It suddenly reappeared. The man's eyes came up, and then his face, and with a blow from his fist, the image flickered out.

"See?" Winters said, "I said you could do it."

Duke stared in astonishment.

"Don't look so shocked," Vonn said without looking up. "Sometimes the holo gets a short in it."

"I know that man." It came out in a whisper.

"Then buy him a frigging drink," Vonn said. "You're here to make contacts."

"Not that kind of contact." Eyes burning, Duke squinted hard and tried to conjure up the name that went with the image. *Deakes!*

No, it's not Derrald Deakes, but it's someone just as bad.

Vonn looked up from his drink, disturbed. "What did you say?"

Duke startled and turned back to the mercenary, heart hammering wildly. "I didn't say anything."

"Who is this Deakes character?"

Duke shook his head. "That's not Deakes. That's someone who stole something from us."

Vonn put his drink down and looked over at the man, who again pounded the holo out of existence. "Is he that Dexter character that May keeps bitching about?"

"No. He owes money." He closed his eyes and a figure popped into his head. "Fifty-five million credits."

"Then how can you give that kind of price on a two-year-old pleasure craft? You could get seventy for this, easy."

"Fifty-five? That's a hell of a pile of money."

"It can be explained," Duke said.

"It had better be good or I'll have Business Affairs on your case so fast that you won't have time to draw breath."

"It's a personal favor," Duke said quickly. Vonn looked at him, puzzled. "We might as well level with him. He's got a right to know."

Vonn studied Duke's face. "Are you all right?"

"Hartung," Duke said. "That son of a bitch is named Hartung."

"You're sure? I mean, you're absolutely—"

"It's him, Vonn." Duke brought his hand up to show how it was trembling. "I can't help myself."

"We should confirm this, though." Vonn took a deep breath and then shouted out the man's name.

Hartung slowly looked up from the table.

"Remember those diamonds I got from your sister?" Vonn shouted. "I gave them to your wife."

Hartung shook his head and began to look the party over.

Vonn smiled at him. Winters waved. Duke did nothing, but when Hartung saw him their gazes locked, just for a moment. There was a flare of recognition, and then he quickly turned away.

"Well," Vonn said, sounding pleased with himself. "It appears that you haven't lost your Tetran powers of observation." He stood, the sudden action causing him to weave for a moment. He steadied himself, then said, "I think we should go have a little chat with him."

"Yeah!" Winters shouted, bolting up from his seat. "I'll kick his ass for you, Mr. Duke!"

"Winters, no." Vonn stepped in to block, but a gentle shove from Winters sent him sprawling back into his seat. *"Winters—"*

In slow motion, Duke pushed back and started to rise from the table. It was not fast enough. Winters's strides were long, his air confident, and he had closed half the distance in the seconds it had taken Duke to get to his feet.

That's not gonna get it, boy, that's not gonna cut it—

Duke was stepping back, trying to get around the table, muscles tensing for a mad sprint. Winters was almost there, his big hand stretching out toward the man hunched at the table. The voice that followed was loud and booming.

"Hey, Mr. Hartung!"

Look at him, boy, look at the way he's moving, you know what he's doing, you know what's going to happen to your pal—

"My friends want to talk to you—"

Are you going to stand there and let it happen, or are you going to do it, you're going to have to do it, do it, son, do it—

Winters's hand fell on Hartung's shoulder and clasped on it. Hartung started to rise, one hand dragging a glass, the other sunk under his coat.

"—but first I think I'm going to kick—"

"Winters!" Duke's hand grabbed at the inside of his jacket as Winters looked his way. Hartung was coming out of his crouch, and in his hand was something long and dark. Duke could hear it warning—*beep beep beep*—as he sidestepped and forced his newly healed right arm out in the direction of the scuffle. Hartung brought the weapon in the air—its noise was getting faster and faster—and struck Winters full in the face, making the big man loose his grip. He took one step toward Duke and started to aim.

There was a concussion, and fire erupted from the end of

Duke's arm. Hartung snapped back and hit the wall. Duke screamed.

"No no n—"

Then he smiled. Hartung was recoiling off the wall, the weapon held limply in his hand.

"Duke, whatthehell do you—"

Keeping the aim, Duke fired again, and Hartung bounced back into the wall, a look of astonishment on his face.

"The other guy did it," someone was shouting. "The other guy pulled first—"

The comment was cut short by another shot, and then another, and more in quick succession until the total reached ten. Then silence returned to the bar, leaving the patrons to deal with a mad ringing in their ears.

"Coulda burned a hole clean through that big guy."

"Duke!" Vonn was shouting. "You stupid bastard! Do you realize what you've just done?"

Duke said nothing but tossed his pistol onto the table. It skittered across to the hologram, partially obstructing it and causing it to look as if a swarthy green man were whipping a smoking gun.

"You don't do it like that." Vonn shook his head. "You just don't do it like that."

Duke smiled. He was enjoying the smell of the cordite.

9

The air smelled of spring. The snows were gone, plants were beginning to green and burst from the ground, and everything felt fresh and new. The scent was fresh and reassuring.

It was making James May sick.

"If you don't stop that," he growled at misterbob, "I'm going to throw up. We'll see what you can scent off of *that*."

The Arcolian, which was shuffling down the hall behind the captain, knitted its hands together. "But, jamesohjames, I detect that you are not altogether well and am merely trying to—"

May stopped and turned. "I—" He winced at the volume he was using and toned it down. "I know I'm not well, but when I reach this point, anything I do makes me sicker. While I appreciate what you're trying to do—" He stopped again to check his volume. "I appreciate it, but you have to understand something. This is one hangover I want to cherish." The Arcolian's head cocked. May held up a finger to keep misterbob from speaking. "I know what you're thinking, misterbob. 'Indeed, why should the Sapient A-forms put so much value on their suffering?' I can't speak for the people who make a habit of getting blind drunk and then laughing off their hangovers, but in my case, I want to remember what it feels like to crawl up from the bottom and get kicked down further than I was before. It's going to make my moment of triumph that much sweeter."

"You are euphemistically speaking, of course," misterbob said.

"Of course," May agreed, resuming his walk. "There's something else you should know. Most Sapient A-forms don't enjoy their suffering like I do. Keep in mind that I'm a frigging lunatic."

May could hear rustling as the Arcolian's head nodded. "This is understood, jamesohjames. This frigginglunatic is a coalition of spiritual comrades much like The High Order of Jehovah or The Church of the Fifth Region."

May shook his head slowly.

"This is not correct?"

The merchant answered with a sigh.

"This rasp of breath is to mean something? If my interpretations are not correct, then I must learn what is correct."

May turned and—almost—put his hands on the Arcolian's shoulders. They stopped inches from their target and froze. "Look, misterbob, I'll be happy to explain it later. As for right now, I've got to meet with the guy who is supposed to repair my computer systems and tell him that I can't afford his work right now. It's time for you to take your hiding place so you can observe."

misterbob's mouth opened, and for a moment, May thought the creature was smiling. "Indeed. Yes. This observation is most rewarding."

"And no interfering," May said, opening the door to the library. "If this guy tries to mess with me, I'll take him apart with my bare hands."

"Yes," the Arcolian rattled. "I would recommend that, as well. I have been anxious to witness this spine-removal procedure since you first spoke of it to mistervonn."

May's mouth dropped open as he ushered misterbob into its hiding place. "I don't know what you're talking about," he said. Before the creature could make another of its interjections, May slapped the switch and the door closed. "Calm," he whispered as he took his seat at the table. "Calm."

He closed his eyes and tried to picture himself afloat on the tranquil sea of the main planet in the Linus Mahoning system. The water was crystal clear and warm, the sands on the beach a pure white. A cool breeze was blowing, and light filtered down from the high gray clouds, and his back was being rubbed with lotion by Maggie—

May's eyes jumped open, and he swore again. After a moment, he remembered his resolve. "Calm . . ."

The main door opened and Roz peeked in. "The representative from CompuFarm is here," she said, raising her eyebrows.

May rose. "Send him in, by all means!"

With a shrug, Roz disappeared. In a moment, a small figure appeared in the door. The first thing May noticed was the hair, which had been done in a triple mohawk. The center band of hair was combed straight back, and the ones that flanked it went straight down over each ear. May's first thought was, Oh. One of those.

His eyes fell from there, taking in a plain, smiling face, a Laotex shirt that swirled with changing shades of blue, the fading black denims all bent into shapes by—

The merchant smiled. "Well," he said. "I'm glad Mr. Hickman sent you, but I think there's been a misunderstanding. Well, at least you can run the initial diagnostics on the system."

"What are you talking about?" the woman asked. "You're James May, aren't you?"

"Yes, but—"

The woman extended a hand in fingerless gloves and let her thumb point up in the air. "I'm Cheech."

May's eyes grew wide. "You're a—"

"Say it," she said, circling the table and wagging her index finger as she came. "Go ahead and say it. *Techette*. Because if you do, I swear I'm going to tear off your—"

"Don't say it," May moaned, "or I'll have to explain it to misterbob."

Cheech stopped as if she had caught herself about to commit a mortal sin. With a loud sigh, she dusted her hands off against her shirt. The colors melted under her touch. "Whoa there. I'm sorry, Mr. May. Or should I call you Captain?"

"Call me James," he said uncertainly.

"You won't tell Dirk—I mean, Mr. Hickman—will you? I get flat, rolling pissed sometimes, you know? No, I'm afraid you don't know. It's just that people don't take us—techettes—

seriously. They think we're some kind of technological groupies who get off on hanging around the people that do the work. They don't know we take this stuff seriously, that we can pull a board apart and rewire it, besides being able to program. So we get typed as secondary users like programmers, pilots, and paramilitaries. It really gets my hackles up when my clients type me like that.''

May studied Cheech and the shape that her clothes molded her into. Somewhere underneath that tangle of syncloth lurked an attractive figure. "I'll, ah, bet that happens a lot," he said.

"An awful lot," Cheech admitted. "Most of the time, in fact. Just because my taste in dress is a little *unusual* . . ." She looked at him nervously. "Not that there's anything *wrong* with being a techette, I guess. Don't misunderstand me, Admiral—"

"Captain."

"Captain—"

"James."

Cheech nodded. "Right. I'm not one of those militant types you hear about, the bushwhackers with the big, sharp knives—"

"And what does Mr. Hickman say when he hears what happened?" May asked, trying to change the subject.

One corner of Cheech's mouth turned up. "Usually, he laughs. See, by the time I get back to tell him what happened, he's heard from the client already because they felt bad about doubting me and when they see the job I did they're *really* happy."

"Well," May continued, "Mr. Hickman did say you were his best, ah, master programmer."

"He did?" Cheech beamed. "Bless his heart. Well." With a nervous smile, Cheech retreated back around the table and took a seat. After a polite shrug, she said, "I'm told that you're looking at a complete reprogramming and revamping of this system, complete with restorative programming and a possible upgrade of ship intelligence to a KEVIN model. I'd like to suggest that you start with a simple reintegration of the existing systems so you—"

"Ah," May interrupted. "I'm afraid that we're not going to get into reintegration."

"You've decided to opt for complete replacement, then? I can give you—"

"No," May said. "I'm afraid, Cheech, that there's not going to be anything done to the *Angel's Luck* right now."

Cheech pointed her nose at the table and raised her eyes in a glare. "What do you mean?"

May shifted uncomfortably. "It's that CompuFarm won't be doing any work for me in the near future."

"It's not because I'm a—"

"Techette?" May said quickly. "No. Heavens, no. The problem, ah, Cheech, is strictly financial. The money I had coming to me when I spoke to your boss is no longer coming, and I've got to have some time to consolidate—"

"You're lying," Cheech snapped. "You're just saying that—"

"No," May said, anxious to keep the argument suppressed. "I honestly and truly have bottomed out. You've got to understand that. The most important sale of my career has gone haywire, and I don't know how I'm going to make docking costs on this ship, let alone—"

"Council 5 is one of the charter members of the Interplanetary Trade Association," Cheech said. "They subscribe to the standards and practices of all ITA concepts, including that of strict interplanetary price regulation to prevent profiteering. There's no way your cargo could have—"

"I know all about it," May said. "What I was carrying would have fallen under the precious cargo exception. That's why I've avoided runs to this place. There's no way to make any real money off of any ITA members." He caught himself and gave Cheech a long stare. "Wait a minute. Why am I even arguing with you? This is my ship and I can damn well do what I want with it, including not having it repaired." He walked to the main door and opened it. "You, my dear friend, may be excused."

Cheech was motionless.

"I mean it," May said. "And believe it or not, I think I'm going to miss having the chance to work with you. You're sure a feisty little—"

"Then let me work on something," Cheech said quickly.

May sighed and leaned against the bulkhead wall. "I can't," he said. "Really. A big business deal has fallen through."

"I believe you," Cheech said. "I do. Honest. I'm afraid, though, that Dirk is going to think that my temper flared—"

"It did," May said.

"I can't have that happen. See, even if you're on the level, Dirk's going to think that the reason I'm not doing the work here is because I opened my mouth, which I did, and which I'm *terribly* sorry for, Captain . . ."

May sniffed the air suspiciously, then cast a glance at the compartment in which misterbob was hiding.

"Is something wrong, Captain?"

He did not smell anything unusual. Of course, with the Arcolian, that was usually the point. "Uh . . . no," he said.

"Then will you think about it? You'll have to pay the consulting fee anyway."

May slowly walked toward the ambassador's compartment, then stopped cold. "What?"

"It's a standard thing that Dirk—Mr. Hickman—does. See, he's got this reputation for doing the job right—"

"I know that part."

"So what some people were doing was having one of his techs come in and explain what needed to be done, then they'd contract out with someone else to do the job. It's a significant fee, but all of it is completely deductible from your final bill."

"I don't believe this—" May started.

"Tell you what," Cheech said. "I'll give you some work on a cut rate. How about if I fix your CHARLES unit for you? That usually runs more than the consulting fee, but I can fudge the figures a little and—"

May quickly walked to the chair, took Cheech's arm, and began to escort her to the door.

"But, Captain May," she protested. "I really need this job!"

"Look, Cheech. Would you mind stepping out for a moment?" he said grimly. He gently shoved her out into the hall, then with a single finger gesture told her to wait, and closed the door. After a deep sigh, he turned and, taking short sniffs of the air, walked to misterbob's observation room and opened the door.

"jamesohjames," the Arcolian purred. "I am scenting—"

"Cynicism, perhaps? Outrage? What the hell are you doing to me, misterbob?"

"Doing?" misterbob pondered that. "I was merely observing interactions of daily business between the Sapient A-forms."

"You know what I mean. I can't smell anything. Did you scentkill me again so I couldn't tell that you were bringing back Cheech's childhood horrors?"

The Arcolian sat straight up in its seat, as if taken aback by what the merchant had said. "Indeed no. Did I not assure you—"

"Then what did you do to get her to change her mind, make

me smell like one of her old lovers? misterbob, this has got
to—"

"jamesohjames," misterbob said. "Any alteration of emotional state was done by lookcheech herself. I did scent that her
menstrual cycle is to begin in three point two biological days,
but that does not account for or influence the dramatic drop in
confidence that registered. There were distinct levels of fear and
panic, followed by—"

"You're serious," May said. "That was really her, then? You
weren't doing any more of your restoration of spiritual bonds?"

"I assure you with the solemnity of the Fifth Region," misterbob said.

May bit his lip and stared up at the ceiling. "Why is it that I
get every hard-luck case in the galaxy?"

"There are pheromonal considerations—"

"Forget it," May said. "It was a rhetorical question." The
Arcolian raised its arm as if to punctuate a comment, but May
cut it short. "Yes, I know, most fascinating, you'll have to study
it. But please, don't make me explain it now."

"Then, jamesohjames, are you going to hire lookcheech?"

"Looks like I don't have much of a choice now, do I?" May
sealed the compartment and went back to the door. "I thought
it over," he said as the door opened. "You're hired. I don't
know how I'm going to pay your boss, but—"

The words cut off in his throat. Cheech had turned into Vonn.

"Hey," the mercenary shouted down the hall. "The captain
says you're hired!"

There was a whoop, and then quick footfalls.

"Vonn, what are you doing ba—"

May was cut off as Cheech hit his chest and threw her arms
around him. "Thank you, Captain," she said. "You won't re-
gret this. I'll get started right away."

"So much for flagging levels of confidence," May said as
the technician vanished down the hall in search of her equipment. He brushed off his jumpsuit and eyed Vonn suspiciously.
"Now what's your problem?"

"Duke," Vonn said, "is in jail."

May narrowed his eyes.

"I'm not kidding, May. Bring in the dogs if—oh, shit, I'm
not supposed to say that anymore, am I?"

"What happened?" The merchant's voice was low and calm.

"Well, me and Duke and Winters went to this place for a couple of drinks—"

"What place?"

"I doubt you've heard of it, May—it's just a little hole in the wall."

"Was it one of Duke's places, or one of yours?"

Vonn took a step back and cleared his throat. "Well . . ."

May grabbed him by the lapels and began to shake him. "You son of a bitch," he shouted. "You were supposed to watch him and take care of him. Can't you even do your frigging job, Vonn?"

"Will you let me explain? We saw this guy in the bar, and Duke said it was someone that stole something from you, a pleasure craft."

May dropped his grip. "What happened?"

"Well, you know how Winters is. When he heard that this guy had wronged Duke, he went over to take care of him. This guy started to draw on Winters, which would have landed him in jail right there—"

"Get to the point, Vonn."

"Only Duke killed him, smoked his ass right dead. He was still wearing his gun, May, the one you gave him on limited permit for escorting the phials. That and the fact that this other guy drew a weapon first would have been enough to keep Duke out of trouble on the weapons charge . . ."

"What happened?" May asked.

Vonn shivered. "Duke, he, uh—he emptied the clip into this guy. All ten shots."

May slumped and bent at the back. "Oh, hell," he said, shuffling back into the library. "Oh hell oh hell oh hell."

"It turns out that this other guy didn't have a permit for the weapon, and he had a history as long as your arm, but the law said that what Duke did was violent and malicious and they took him away."

"The whole clip?" May asked.

"Yeah."

"What do you think? Eric Dickson?"

"Maybe. Could be. Entirely possible. There was one thing, May. This smile he had on his face as he put the gun down. It wasn't him, May, not the Duke I know."

"Dammit!" May leaned against the table and called for misterbob. The compartment opened, and the Arcolian ambled out. Vonn shifted back against one wall.

"Yes, jamesohjames."

"You understand the concept behind the transferred knowledge that Duke is carrying?"

"Yes, although I fail to scent the novelty—"

"Do you think it is possible that you could scent if there is another Sapient A-form inhabiting Duke's . . ." He looked up and down at the Arcolian. "Shell?"

The Arcolian purred. "This would be a most interesting experiment. It might explain some of the anomalies I had noted about misterduke's behavior."

"All right," May said. "Our first order of business is to get him out of jail and have you see what you can find, misterbob. Then we take him to the Essence Company and we make them fix whatever is wrong."

"Providing it can be done," Vonn said.

"All we have to do is get him out, then. Was a bail set, Vonn?"

The mercenary gave a sad shrug. "There was, in the millions. But I don't have enough fingers left to show you how much."

"Would it help," misterbob asked, "if I exerted nonpheromonal influence in his behalf?"

"Political influence?" Vonn said. "Not a bad idea. He *is* an ambassador, May."

May shook his head. "I don't want to take the risk."

"There would be no risk," misterbob said. "The others are here, laceylane and killerjoe, redbutler and leighbrand, and they are visiting other places, studying what you would call the high order of things. I am no great loss. Any accumulated knowledge I have would—"

"We value The Life in ourselves," May said, "and we value yours as well, misterbob. But that's not what worries me. It's the publicity that it would bring. I want to keep this as quiet as possible until we can prove our right to the reward." He slammed the tabletop with his fist and swore. "If only I hadn't handed over all of the phials. I'd have had all of the evidence I needed right there."

"I probably don't have to tell you this," Vonn said, "but our speed in dealing with this is of utmost importance."

"I know," May said, and he struck the tabletop again. "Dammit. All I need is for one more thing to go wrong. One more thing—"

"Captain," came a voice. "Could you tell me where the CHARLES—"

May and Vonn and misterbob all looked up as the voice cut off. They all saw Cheech as she screamed at the sight of the brick-red Arcolian, dropped her tool kit, and fainted dead away.

10

The memory was there. It was showing little of itself, just enough to be a recognizable irritation that kept him from sleep.

Wake up.

It was the sensation of suddenly finding one's muscles rock-hard and bulging, of surveying a bad situation and knowing without a moment's hesitation that one could turn it around, alter the inevitable outcome. The feeling of it made a friendly burn in his belly and made the corners of his lips turn up. It was the feeling of heroism.

Wake up.

But the image he had was fogged by sharp-smelling clouds. He pushed against them, and they began to clear, leaving behind only a sharp, familiar scent. There was a weight in his right hand, and the tip of the weight was still smoking, still putting that smiling scent into the air. His hand lowered and he looked across the room to a figure that was momentarily pinned against the far wall, leaking fluid from a series of punctures on his chest. The figure's eyes were glazed over in shock, and a bleating instrument fell from his hands, which someone immediately picked up and turned off. A tall, broad man looked at him and muttered his thanks in a simpleton's voice. Others who were frozen slowly began to thaw and move about and the figure pasted to the wall slowly peeled from it and hit the floor. *Yessir, we perforated that bastard good.*

"Oh, no," he said. "Oh no, oh no—"

Wake up, dammit!

Duke bolted upright, shivering and looking around the room. He was sitting on a thin insulating pad that kept cold from the concrete bed from leaking into his bones. The furnishings were Spartan and all-too familiar. It was all coming back to him, and it did not seem to be as much of a mystery as it had before.

"I got to hand it to you, farm boy. You got one hell of a knack for landing yourself in The Small Room."

Duke looked around to find the source of the voice. There was nothing. Distressed, he started to lay back down and was overwhelmed by a tingling sensation, the feeling that someone was there looking over his shoulder. "Jail," he said.

"You are correct." The other laughed. "Have a cigar. You've got problems, son. Big ones. On the other hand, you won't have to worry about that acquaintance of yours burning a hole through any more of your brothers. Or stealing from your business associates, for that matter."

"Go away," Duke said, turning his back to the door.

There was more laughter. "You do something right, you've got to live with it."

"You killed him," Duke shouted.

"No," the other said patiently. "You killed him, Duke. Better get used to the idea."

"I have no memory of that."

"No, of course you wouldn't. I wouldn't, either, but for a much different reason than you. I have no memory because it was just another damn thing I had to do to preserve my life and the lives of the shrinking number of the people I love. You were in the same situation and you acted admirably, but you've got no memory of it because you can't deal with it. You're a loser, Duke."

Duke closed his eyes against the feeling and curled into a ball. "Leave me alone."

"I won't. Not until I've shown you something."

"I don't want to see it, Eric. I've seen enough of your life."

"Have you, now?"

Duke turned to where the other would be, only to find it was not there. No matter where he turned, it always seemed to be lurking behind him. "I have. And you might have been a hero and done a lot of great things, but you were a miserable human being."

"You don't know me very well, then."

"I can see what you've done to me. Look where you've put me, Eric. Just *look*." He closed his eyes.

"And now it's time for you to look, Duke."

Duke clenched his eyes shut in defiance, but the bed seemed to shift and revolve beneath him. A sharp shiver ran up his spine, and he rolled onto his back. His left arm flopped straight out, and something warm pinned it down at the shoulder. The fingers of his right hand were running across something cold and jagged, and he was aware of thick, humid air.

Equatorial Tetros? he thought, and opened his eyes. He was looking up at a water-stained ceiling, the plaster cracking and flaking. A single bulb hung from the center, and shifting colors of light filtered in from a cracked window. His fingers were playing with a rip in the wallpaper, which had a small, nondescript design.

Something warm blew across his chest, and the weight against his shoulder shifted. Duke looked over and saw a woman's face, framed by hair in a short pilot's cut, blond with roots showing black. He shifted to get a better look at her, and she flopped her arm across his chest.

This was the room, Duke thought. This was the room or something like it that Dickson kept putting me in, the one where Leigh Brand keeps trying to seduce me. The one—

His breath caught short in his lungs. Something was wrong. The layout of the room was not quite right, and there was something about the woman, the unnatural blonde, at his side . . .

Suddenly Duke caught the something that burned bright as a phosphor.

. . . not her but it looks like her not much but enough like Leigh oh Leigh why did those bastards and now you're gone let me take you to bed just one more time not really her but it looks like her not much but enough like Leigh . . .

He tried to sit up but could not.

It's not time for that yet.

Eric, he thought, what are you doing?

But the phosphor had gone back to its litany: *. . . those bastards and now you're gone let me take you . . .*

Duke closed his eyes and pushed against the resistance. He sat straight up, shaking the woman off his chest and getting a good look at her face. It was not Leigh Brand and did not even resemble her, except for the pilot's cut, *unless you've got half a bottle of Aiaagan gin in you, in which case she looks a lot like prettydamngood.*

"You're not Leigh Brand," he told the woman.

The woman pulled the sheets up to cover herself. "No," she said bluntly. "Bering's Gate was fifteen standard months ago. Eric's been in here, on and off, for the last twelve." She lifted a lock of her hair up and let it fall lifelessly down over her forehead. "It was his idea to do the cut and dye. I wish he'd let me be me, because I think I could help him."

"I've got to leave," Duke said urgently. "Something's about to happen."

The woman put both hands on his chest and pushed him down. "I know," she said. "Wait here. Thomas Fortunado will be here soon, and if you want I can show you what I showed Eric, something Leigh didn't even know.''

Duke rolled so his back was to the woman and stared hard at the pattern of dots on the disintegrating wallpaper.

"What's the matter, darling?"

Don't call me darling, please don't call me that.

She put her hands on Duke's shoulders and kissed his back. "Whatever you say."

Duke closed his eyes and pushed against the resistance, harder this time. When his eyes opened he was back in his cell. The feeling was still dogging him.

"What are you trying to prove?"

The thing seemed to shrug. "Just a simple explanation, Duke. I'd appreciate your permitting me to continue."

"Then get to the point of it. I don't need to be indulged in your reveries over some whore—"

"She wasn't a whore," the feeling said too loudly. "She wasn't. I never paid for it, never."

"Get out of here," Duke ordered. "I mean it, Eric. I don't need you around."

The other shrugged. "And miss the last mortal appearance of poor old Thomas Fortunado, the man who set a record for cratering his flyers, the man who defied death until—"

"Good-bye." Duke closed his eyes again and settled into a relaxed state.

"A shame," the voice said wistfully. "You should've seen him that night. It was the happiest I'd ever seen him. We'd been through it all together, were the only ones left out of that entire group of us on Narofeld. And they'd just announced the cease-fire so they could lay groundwork for the Accord.

"Old Thomas, he had such a smile on his face when he kicked open the door to tell Rhea and me the news. He had a bottle in each hand, a woman under his arm, and that red beer-foam all in his mustache. Those squinty eyes of his, they were shining like lights, and his grin was so wide you could count every one of his big white teeth.

"And he said, 'It's over, Eric. They've made the cease-fire official. We held the xenos back.' I remember that." The feeling sighed. "It's your loss. I just wanted to show you what you were fighting for."

"It wasn't my war," Duke muttered.

"Oh, yes, it was."

Apprehension spiked Duke's stomach, and he quickly sat up.

The shadow was gone. He settled down in the darkness to wait for the advent of sleep. When it came, his mind blanked, and he was out before his eyelids came down.

We held the xenos back. Why don't you and Rhea come and join Madeline and me for a little physical celebration of unusual proportions?

He waved his comrade off. "Get out of here. You're drunk."

"And I'm going to get drunker," Fortunado said. "I want to remember the fact that I couldn't remember this evening."

He closed the door to the room and wandered off down the hall with Madeline, singing an obscene training song in sour bass notes. "Bunga," he sang. "Death by bunga."

Of course it would all come down to this. Bering's Gate was it—the climax, the final act of disgrace. The human response to it had been murderous, and they proceeded to exact a terrible price from the misshapen Arcolians.

And then, some nine months before, something strange had occurred. A lone Arcolian transport ship that was skirting the frontier near the Darness system was jumped by a sortie of light cruisers. The transport surrendered without firing a shot and allowed itself to be boarded without incident. The boarding crew, which had been dispatched to make sure the vessel had not been booby-trapped, was shocked to find a creature that had never been seen before. It stood on a vertical axis, had two arms with two sets of mutually opposable fingers on each hand, and its head was mounted on the front of a barrel chest, giving it the appearance of a small hunchback. Just below the head in the center of the chest was the olfactory communications organ common to the other four creature-types they had been fighting, and after a time, this new discovery was dubbed the E-form Arcolian.

The creatures were taken away for study. To the wonderment of those who were studying them, this new Arcolian form made no attempt to use its scent against its captors, and for a while it was thought that they lacked the ability.

This was soon found to be an incorrect assumption, but not until after another startling discovery had been made. As a public-relations ploy, Admiral Eugene Studebaker decided to visit the laboratory where the Arcolians were being studied. The commander of the entire Arcolian theater of operations brought with him a corps of media representatives with the intent of showing that "all human capability, military and civilian, artistic and scientific, was working hard to bring an end to this miserable conflict.'' And during the climax of his speech, a slit opened on the head of one of the Arcolians and it proceeded to make a noise that could only be interpreted as speech.

It said, "studebaker, our races must have peace."

When the initial shock wore off, it was determined that the captive Arcolian E-forms had been studying humans as intently as humans had been studying them. Of course, the hard-line interpretation of the statement made by the Arcolian who had taken the name stalwartwhite was that the xenos were indeed suing for peace. What wasn't such common knowledge was the fact that the Arcolians were shrewd in their negotiations, and to insure that they were not being manipulated by undetected pheromonal influence, the human side of it revived a nearly extinct canine breed, the bloodhound, and taught them to react in certain ways to various Arcolian manipulative scents. The dogs were a constant fixture throughout the negotiations, so much so that interest in the breed was revived and the expression "if you don't believe me, bring in the dogs" became part of the vocabulary. Now, just like that, the war was over, and humankind was going to be friends with the savage xeno bastards.

He sniffed angrily. If that was the sentiment, then to hell with them all. He knew better. He knew what it would really be like, that at least two generations would pass—the one that fought the war, and their offspring—before Arcolians would be accepted on human worlds. Too much hate had been generated by the jingoistic furor, too many sacrifices had been made . . .

He turned and looked at the woman next to him, her hair shorn into a mockery of the pilot's cut.

Too many dear lives had been lost.

Biting his lip, he closed his eyes, trying to ignore the shouting and pounding that was coming from down the hall. That blasted fool Fortunado, can't he let a guy suffer in peace?

At that point a shock wave rattled the door in its frame and shook the thin walls of the room. The counterfeit Leigh Brand came awake with a screech and rolled out of bed, taking the covers with her. He was up in an instant, pulling a jumpsuit off of the cheap dresser and yanking a pistol from one of the drawers. Draping the suit across his frame, he crept to the door on the tips of his fingers and toes and cracked it open.

Out in the hall, the sounds of abandon had changed to a high-pitched wail that choked off into a series of sobs. A short, swarthy man had Madeline by the neck and was dragging her away *from Fortunado's room. Her eyes fell on the crack in the door and her arms reached out.*

"Please, Mist' Dickson," she said, tears flooding down her cheeks. *"I don't want to go."*

He let the door swing open and chambered a round in his pistol, letting it clamor in the hall for effect. The swarthy man stopped and raised an autoshot. A wisp of smoke curled out of the twin barrels.

"Don't get in the middle of something you got no business being in," he advised.

"Pimp?"

"Husband. Although, I don't know, maybe I oughta been. I seem to attract the ones like Madeline. I'm determined I'm keeping this one, though."

He let the pistol roll back in his hand, the barrel pointing down at the floor. "I won't stand in your way."

He watched as Madeline and her husband went to the end of the hall and started down the stairs, then turned and ran to Fortunado's room.

The door was standing wide open when he arrived, and a crowd had gathered around it, keeping their distance and murmuring. He pushed through the people and his nose caught something—

Cordite

—mingled with something heavier, something that had not filled him with dread since Bering's Gate. He paused for a moment to search, but the reference memory would not come to him. He stepped inside the room.

Thomas Fortunado was sprawled naked across the bed with a large hole punched in the center of his chest. Still clenched in his right hand was his cutlass, the one he kept under the bed, its blade creased and dented from pellets of shot. The walls of the room were streaked and splattered with drying blood, and carnival sounds came from the hallway.

"Bastards!" he roared, turning on the crowd. "Stop it! Stop it! Why doesn't one of you call the law?" Tears stung his eyes and burned his cheeks as he slammed the door on them, then slowly turned back to Fortunado's body.

"Amazing," he said to it. "You got through the war, the entire war, with nothing more serious than a skull fracture." He shook his head. "And now the ink's not even dry on the Accord, and this happens. Dammit . . ." He sank to his knees beside the bed.

*The door opened and Rhea slipped into the room, battered
work clothes hiding her frame. "I'm sorry," she said.*

"It's not your fault."

"I knew about Madeline—"

*"Hell, he knew about Madeline. But do you suppose he'd
listen?" He turned back to look at Fortunado. Rhea's hands fell
on his shoulders and tightened.*

*"You'd better get out of here," he said. "The law's going to
be here soon, and you aren't going to want your name dragged
through this."*

The hands tightened and started to shake him.

"Rhea—"

*Now they were snapping against him, trying to crack his neck
with a series of sharp thrusts.*

"Dammit, Rhea!"

"Rhea? Who the hell's Rhea?" A bearded face looked down
at him. "Wake up, Duke. I've got to talk to you!"

Duke blinked his eyes and looked around the cell. "May?"

The merchant gave him a wistful look. "I've got to get some
help for your condition, but first I'm going to get you out of
here."

Shaking his head to clear the cobwebs of sleep, Duke looked
about the cell, confused. "May," he said. "I can leave?" He
started to rise.

May took him by the shoulders. "Not quite. It'll be a little
while yet."

"But you've paid the bail . . ."

"No, I haven't. It's high, Duke, and I don't have the resources
to put up the money, but—"

"Then what are you doing here?" Duke puffed air out of his
lungs and fought the haze behind his eyes. "Wait a minute.
Winters—"

"Winters is fine," May said. "He was scared to death after
Hartung drew on him, but I think he's learned his lesson."

"Hartung." Duke puffed out his cheeks again. "May, the
Star of Bolivia."

"Gone," May said with a twinge of sadness. "Law enforcement couldn't find a trace of it. He probably ditched it somewhere for cheap and spent the money in a manner only the Fifth
Region could tell you." Duke started to bring up the subject of
Winters again, but May cut him off. "You're not to worry about
it, though. Vonn and I have thought of an angle." The corners
of his lips turned up a trace.

"I've seen that look before," Duke said. "I'm not sure I like what I see."

"It's not as bad as all that," May said. "We've decided to let Mr. Burris intercede on your behalf. Once we tell him that you're carrying the Eric Dickson distillation inside of you, he's going to want to get next to you in order to find out how the stuff performs—under actual field conditions, you might say. He knows that we had the real phials, so he won't be able to resist the prospect. At the same time, we'll try and get your condition straightened out. Simple as that."

Duke looked around the cell. His head felt thick, and what he was seeing seemed to swim slowly around him. A troubled look crossed his features and he fought for a memory fragment that had been more than substantial only hours before. "Winters," he said.

"Winters is fine," May said.

"No. There's another way, May—another way we can do it." Duke started to rise, but May gently took him by the shoulders and eased him down onto the bunk.

"I know," May said. "And you did it. You kicked the *Yueh-sheng*'s ass and saved all of our lives."

"May . . ."

"Duke, let me tell you something. Heaven help me, but I've come to almost look at you as the son that Maggie and I could have had if things had gone a bit differently. I know some things that wouldn't have been—you never would have grown up on Tetros, for one—but for the most part, you've got the courage and the integrity and the intelligence that Maggie and I admire. So calm down and let me do something for you for a change." He patted Duke on the back. "I expect to have you out of here in forty-eight hours."

Duke searched but could not find the memory he had been trying to grasp. It had become lost in a swirling vortex of thoughts about the *Yueh-sheng* and May and Maggie and Hartung and the *Star of Bolivia*. Then out of the dark thickness, something emerged.

"May. About Burris."

"Yes?"

"How do you know that he'll give you another audience?"

"He won't. We've already tried that."

"Then how are you going to get him to listen to you?"

That smug look returned to May's face. "You leave that to us."

11

May sighed and finished loading bullets into a long clip. He slid the clip into a weapon and handed it up to Winters, who sat behind the wheel of the van. "Ready to go."

Winters took his hands from the steering wheel and picked the weapon up. "Almost ready." He wrapped two big fingers around the bolt and snapped it back. "There."

"Remember," May said, "and this goes for you, too, Vonn— try to avoid firing if at all possible. Do it only if there's serious trouble."

Vonn smacked his lips. "Heh."

"I mean it," May said loudly. "Everything we've done up to this point will be worthless if we mess this up, and we'll mess up if we show these weapons, because our permits have expired. Even if this goes right, I don't want to have a weapons charge hanging over us."

"Yeah? Well, what if—"

"Stow it, Vonn! You need to clean up this attitude you've gotten or else—"

"Guys," Winters said loudly. "It's about time."

He pointed out the window. Through the trees they could see a high-gloss red Minisport headed in their direction.

"Are you sure?" May asked.

"It's the right time." Winters wriggled in his seat with excitement.

"You know what to do?"

"Yeah," Winters replied. "I got to make the timing good." He squinted at the approaching vehicle, and when it passed an outcropping of rock, he began to count. "One, two, three." He held up one finger. "One, two, three." He held up another. "One, two, three." He held up a third finger, stared at them for an impossibly long moment, then mumbled to himself. His foot slammed down on the gas, and May was pitched from between the seats to the van bed. A series of klaxons dopplered past, and one came screaming closer amid the squealing of tires and a grinding of metal. It stopped for a brief instant, and then the van shuddered with impact and skewed sideways. May rolled across the floor and looked up to see that the rear quarter panel had been crushed his way.

"The rental service is going to scream," he said.

"How the hell else do we stop the man?" Vonn complained, reeling from being thrown against his safety harness.

Winters slid the window down and a torrent of obscenities rolled in from the outside.

"He's getting out of his car, Mr. May. He don't look happy."

"No," May said, crawling to the rear doors and throwing them open. "He wouldn't."

The merchant jumped out of the van and ran around to the red car. The driver had gone into a skid when they had pulled out in front of him and had slammed broadside into the bigger vehicle. Some of the red paint had transferred from the car, looking like streaks of blood against the van.

The car door was standing open, and Burris was at the window, loudly haranguing Winters and making vulgar insinuations about his lineage. The big mercenary took it all in stride, smiling politely and nodding until May had closed the distance.

"Excuse me," he said to Burris, "Could I have a word with you?"

"It's about time, Officer." Burris turned away from Winters. "This microcephalic refuse pulled out—" His words cut short and his jaw went slack at the sight of the merchant. *"You!"* he said, outraged. *"You're* responsible for this. Well, you're not going to get any money out of me this way, not one damn credit. And you're going to jail, my good man, as soon as the law gets here."

"We won't be here that long," May said.

"Well, that suits me fine, although somebody is going to pay for the damage to my vehicle, and it might as well be you, Captain." Burris started to walk away, but May grabbed him by the arm.

"I've got some news for you," the merchant said. "You remember my partner, Duke? He's gotten himself in a little trouble with the law."

Burris jerked his arm from May's grasp. "That doesn't surprise me. You're going to join him if you don't watch it."

"He got in trouble because of your product, your *distillations*, Burris. Now you can stand there and pretend that we didn't really have them, and I might pretend that you were right in declaring them bogus, but deep down we both know the truth, don't we? And pretty soon a lot of other people are going to know the truth."

"You don't frighten me, Captain." Burris walked to the driver's-side door of the car.

"Eric Dickson," May said. "The name sound familiar? It

should. He was one of the people you contracted for a distillation.''

''Purely a public-relations move,'' Burris said. ''He had nothing real to offer us except for his name, which he was ruining with his drinking. He was no big loss.''

May smiled. ''Then I know you know what I'm talking about. You should know by now that his phial was missing from those we returned, so it'll give some credibility to what I'm about to tell you.'' He closed the distance between himself and Burris. ''It's my associate, Duke. He's *got* Eric Dickson. He swallowed the whole damn bottle.''

Burris shook his head. ''Ingestion would ruin—''

''It was injected,'' May said. ''And now he's having all sorts of strange experiences: nightmares, memories of things that weren't in his past. Under the right conditions he can even fly a stellar vehicle. There's just one catch. He's also learned to kill. That's why he's in jail.''

May grabbed the car door and held it open while Burris climbed in, trying to look away. ''Maybe you heard about the shooting at the Black Orchid a couple of nights ago? That was Duke, and he shot a pattern into some poor son of a bitch that Eric Dickson would have been proud of.''

Burris tried to slam the car door, but May held it fast.

''Don't you hear what I'm trying to tell you? Your product— the distillations—works. Granted, there seem to be some rather unpleasant side effects, but for the most part it does what you said it would do.''

''You're not getting any money out of me, Captain, no matter how outlandish the story.''

''I'm not asking for money, Burris. I'm asking you to save my friend's life. You're the only one who can do it. All you have to do is explain to the authorities that Duke is under the influence of another person's memories and instincts.''

Burris shook his head. ''This is a trick,'' he said. ''Once you get me to confess to the authorities, then you've got your precedent for a claim to the reward money.''

''In return, you'll have a chance to study the way a distillation would work under actual field conditions, not in some laboratory. And maybe you'll be able to find a way to reverse the process in my friend.''

Burris laughed. ''Captain, even if what you said happens to be true, there's no way to reverse the process. In order to purge someone's mind of the absorbed knowledge, you'd have to go in and physically excise the affected memory centers of the brain.

"I must give you credit, though, for a most intriguing attempt to con us out of the money. You should be aware, though, that others more clever than yourself have tried and failed." He gave May a polite smile. "You can forget it, Captain. The money is gone, tied up in an industry that'll soon be worth its second billion. Against that kind of money, one life is a pittance."

"I'll take this to the law myself, then."

"Go right ahead, Captain. Give it a try. It's your word against mine." Burris mockingly gave the merchant a child's salute and slammed the car door. The engine fired and he pulled out, the car scraping and leaving a scar down the van's length.

"What happened?" Winters called. "Is he gonna do it?"

May's shoulders slumped. He turned and started toward the back of the van

"Mr. May," Winters called. "Vonn wants to know what happened."

May stopped and watched the scarred car as it vanished down the length of highway. "Tell Vonn . . ." He sighed. "Tell Vonn that his attitude is contagious."

12

And there was poor old Thomas Fortunado, dead on the bed in a cheap hotel, not even the one who had called herself his woman at his side.

And while Duke stared at the scene, he found Eric Dickson standing next to him.

And Eric Dickson was saying, "Don't you see, Duke? Don't you see?"

13

James May stared sullenly out the window. Below him, the purple-blue terminator appeared to crawl across the gray surface of Council 5. He stared hard, not daring to blink, fearing that if he did it all would come to an end.

And why not? he thought. Everything else in my life is headed that way.

A brief tone sounded through the small *Sky Subway* shuttle, and he unbuckled and rose from his seat, flowing with the others out into the halls of the orbital docking platform.

The platform was, by galactic standards, spacious and immaculately clean. One never saw pullers or suiters in grubby clothing loitering and filling the air with their colorful euphemisms, and the walls were bone-white and free of graffiti, residual dust, and smudges and smears of the various fluids of galactic travel.

Innocuous music filled the hall as May walked, piped in from hidden speakers in the ceiling. The people around him ignored it and chatted with one another until reaching their destinations or parting ways at one of many intersections. To May, the music grated and irritated. It was so damned cheerful, like the stuff piped into his room in that hospital on Tetros.

May sighed and rubbed his collarbone. The knot that had formed during the healing process had shrunk until it was no longer a worry for him, but there was still enough of it there to make him remember how it had all started. There was Dexter and his dreams of glory, a sultry woman on a street corner, and a cop named Albert who had been lightning fast with his baton.

The merchant turned a corner. It all seemed so long ago, the memories dim like some poorly remembered course in Ancient Terran History. There was a parade of barely remembered faces: Hiro, Li, Anders, Bear, Sullivan, Dawn, and others. The feeling was that of matching faces to memories, an X over the face of those killed and a question mark beside those presumed still living.

The biggest question mark of all surrounded the name of Eric Dickson. It frustrated May that he did not know how to approach the matter of the long-dead pilot. When Duke seemed lucid enough to talk about what he was going through—which seemed to be whenever there was no pressure bearing down on him—he was reluctant to talk of the events that had led to his saving the *Angel's Luck* from the *Yueh-sheng* and, beyond that, his escape from the brig on the *Hergest Ridge*. Were it in his power, he would give any amount of money to know what was going on inside the young commodities broker's head.

May thrust his hands into his pockets, probing with his fingers. They felt nothing but string and lint. His lips turned up in a cynical smile. It was easy for him to talk about giving up money for knowledge because he was lacking in both. Had he the money, would he really give it up to help young Duke? Or was Burris right in his assessment of Duke's situation, that even a human life had its price? The thought depressed him more than he could bear.

"Cheer up," he told himself, deliberately slowing his pace. "I don't want misterbob to get scent of this."

Indeed, how would he ever explain it to the Arcolian, who was stricken with awe over the reverence that human beings gave to the life within themselves? He could almost hear himself trying to rationalize that yes, life was precious and sacred, but there were those who were able to coldly put a price on it. And caught in the middle of it all was poor Duke, whose present value was wildly oscillating between the two billion minus of Burris's multiplanetary corporation and the nine million asked to free him from the detention center.

May stopped at the pod where the *Angel's Luck* was docked and stuffed his access card into the lock. Explaining it all to misterbob was going to take some doing.

May blinked as the door opened. There was a distinct scent drifting out from the ship, an animal heaviness that reminded him of the outskirts of Tetros. Impossible, he thought. Impossible . . .

The door finished its ascent to reveal misterbob, patiently waiting in the hallway. After a momentary wave of panic, during which May checked the platform's halls to make sure that nobody had seen the Arcolian, he put a smile on his face and walked onto his ship, sealing the door behind him.

"Hello, misterbob," he said in his most cheerful voice. "How are your studies of the Sapient A-forms coming?"

The Arcolian's head cocked at him in a frighteningly human gesture. "Fascinating that you should speak in such a festive tone, jamesohjames, when all of the indicators read that your mood is quite contrary."

"Dammit," May said, face falling. "That was my best face, too. Even Maggie used to fall for that one."

A trilling sound came from deep in misterbob's throat. "Indeed, if you feel at a disadvantage to me, you might wish to purchase one of the negotiating species of canine in order to balance things."

"No," May said emphatically. "I'll make no such affront to you, Ambassador."

The Arcolian raised its hand.

"I know," May said. "I know. *misterbob.*"

"Am I correct in interpreting that this the Essence Corporation did not, as you say, listen to reason in the case of misterduke's incarceration?"

"The only reason they understand is—" May stopped short,

remembering his earlier thoughts on money and life. "Is their own brand of twisted logic."

"Indeed, perhaps you would allow me to persuade them."

"No," May said quickly. "I can't allow that. I've just gotten used to the idea of your accompanying us. I won't have it said that I used you to my advantage. I'm not ready to ruin my life over a few lousy credits."

The Arcolian knitted its fingers together. "Is this an indication, jamesohjames, that you would be willing to engage in such ruin for a set amount of recompense?"

May winced and his hands balled into fists. Dammit, he thought, I've got to watch what I say! "No, misterbob," he said slowly. "I wouldn't. It's a figure of speech—an idiomatic expression used to indicate ill humor among the A-form Sapients."

"Most curious. Such expressions usually originate from a basic truism expressed by various cultural groups among Sapients. Is this to say that there are those among you who would indeed engage in such ruin for monetary gain?"

May closed his eyes and took a deep breath in an attempt to look into the next sixty seconds of his future. The Pandora's Box had been thrown wide open, so his only chance was to minimize the damage.

"misterbob," he said, "I apologize, but I'm going to have to explain this later—if that's all right. I have some matters which require my immediate attention."

misterbob put the eight fingers of its left hand to its chin and looked up. The sight made May shiver.

"Yessss," the Arcolian said. "I understand, jamesohjames. We will discuss this further, along with the other things you have promised to discuss. I am most anxious to corroborate this monetary concept with what mistervonn does for a living. Also the use of liquid depressants as entertainment, and why some consider regurgitation in an intoxicated state to be humorous. And I still cannot conceptualize why you and margarethearn parted ways in spite of the clear bonding between you, nor why you deny that there was a marked exchange of discreet pheromonal information between yourself and lookcheech during what you termed the initial consultation."

May put his hand to his eyes.

"I scent you are tiring, jamesohjames. I must leave you to your work."

"Thank you," May said, not looking at the Arcolian. He waited until the scrabbling of the creature's legs on the metal floor of the ship had dimmed into silence, then turned and said, "And I haven't laid a hand on Cheech, either!" He tugged at the lines of his jumpsuit. "Or anything else for that matter," he finished under his breath.

May went through the ship to the bridge and found the door closed. He looked at it with a certain curiosity, then knelt down to crank it open. To his surprise, the crank access plate had been bolted back into place. The merchant straightened, then put out a tentative finger and stabbed the access button.

The door hissed open. He smiled in delight and walked into the bridge, where he found Cheech sitting cross-legged on the floor, parts from the CHARLES unit scattered in a wide arc around her.

"You fixed the door?" May asked.

Cheech looked up at him. She was wearing a pair of magna-lenses to work on some of the smaller circuit boards, and her eyes looked as big as saucers. Her head feinted back; she blinked, then reached up and took the lenses off. "Oh," she said, almost embarrassed. "Yes. I did."

May turned back to the door and closed it. He stood there for a moment with misterbob's words about discreet pheromonal exchanges ringing in his ears, then he punched the button and let the door open again. "Works good," he said sheepishly, walking to the pilot's console and leaving the door open.

Cheech shrugged. "Well, I like to work in privacy. No, actually, I don't, but I thought the door should work—now don't get me wrong—because of the *Arcolian* being around here."

"I understand." May nodded. "misterbob's curiosity gets to me, too. I'm hard-pressed to explain some of the—" He looked at Cheech, who had put her lenses back on and was intently studying the circuit board. Now that he thought about it, she did have a rather appealing figure. He cleared his throat. "Some of the things he's asked me about."

"I don't mind that so much," Cheech answered. "Don't get me wrong, Captain, but I'm just not used to the critter yet."

"I understand," May said. "And call me James."

She turned and looked up at him with exploding eyes. "Pardon me?"

"Uh, nothing," he said quickly. "I was empathizing. Some of misterbob's questions can get pretty personal."

"I don't mind that either," she grunted. She picked up a test probe and touched several of the board's components. "It's that he looks like the guest of honor at a rekkfich boil."

"Well," May said, trying to change the subject. "How's the work going?"

"It's going." Cheech nodded. She took the lenses back off and reached over to pick up the CHARLES's head. "I feel like I'm getting somewhere." Reaching inside the bottom of the android neck, she clicked a switch. The CHARLES's eyes jumped open.

"Hello," he said.

"Hello." May smiled.

"Hello," the CHARLES replied. "Hello hello hello. *Hello*. He*llo*. Hello? *Hello hell*o hell*ow*!" The unit's eyes rolled and its mouth flapped, reminding May of a ventriloquist's dummy.

Cheech shrugged, cutting the power. "Still some bugs in the linguistics circuit."

"I understand," May said. "I want you to pay special attention to the personality board when you get there. I think it was in need of recalibration."

Cheech mumbled to herself, then went back to her work. "So," she said slowly. "Were you able to raise the money to help your friend?"

"No," May said. "The Essence Company wouldn't listen to reason and nobody is lending money to bail people out of jail except for some bail bond places that look like *Yueh-sheng* fronts. I guess I'm going to have to sell the *Reconnez Cherie*."

"Would that be so bad?"

"It could be worse. I won't get that good of a price on it here, and I wanted to get as much out of it as I could to get my business going again. I hate to liquidate it just to get my hands on nine million credits."

"Well, then," Cheech said. She put the board, tools, and lenses down and rose in one fluid motion. "I *might* be able to help you." Crossing over to one of the consoles she had gutted, Cheech picked up a small slate and handed it over to May. "What you need to have is a scrap component auction."

May looked down at Cheech's hand-stylused notes. She had headed the slate with the word SCRAP and had made a listing of thirteen components she had pulled from various sections of the *Angel's Luck* computer system.

"This is a partial listing. There might be seven or eight more—I'll know for certain when I've finished my assessment. I could put these on the Auctionnet and have your money for you in a matter of hours."

May smiled at her and shifted the slate in his hand. "This is nice of you to do this, Cheech, but I'm not going to be replacing these components until I get my monetary situation straightened out. That means it's illegal as all hell for me to sell off these components as long as they're a functioning part of the ship.''

"First of all," Cheech said, taking the stylus back, "these *aren't* functioning. They're dead. That's why I listed them as scrap. Second, as I understand it, you can do any damn thing you want with this ship, including selling it down to the last rivet if you wanted."

"I appreciate your concern, but you'd better leave the merchant's law to the merchants and stick to what you do best.''

"But this ship doesn't fall under merchant's law, Captain—that's what I'm trying to tell you. I'll be the first to admit that I don't have a knowledge of the kinds of law that a spacer would, but I've picked up enough from our clients to be of some use.

"Now you told me this funny story about how your ex-friend seized this ship from you at a bad moment and then sold it back to you for a token fee?''

"Ex-wife," May corrected. "Go on."

"By doing that, she claimed it in the name of whoever she worked for. By doing that—and subsequently selling it to you—she took your ship out from under the auspices of merchant law and placed it under salvage law. The difference is, under salvage law you can do any damn thing you want with this ship. If there's a mortgage on it or a lien against it, you can kiss it good-bye. If you want to turn it into an orbiting bar and grill, you can. You could reregister it with a new name and number, or you could sell off whatever parts strike your fancy, right on down to the aforementioned last rivet.

"Now I know a lot of these parts are trashed, Captain, but I think we've got enough to get a fairly good price on the Auctionnet.''

"What would it take?" May asked. "How long?"

"The system runs constantly. All we'd have to do is go in through a sharesys, wait in queue for our turn, and sell the stuff off when our turn came. I'd have to have a main terminal to do it, which means either going planetside to use mine or renting one and doing it here. The cost of rental would be about the same as the trip down, so take your pick.''

"Are you at a stopping point?" May asked, looking across the floor at the stacks of CHARLES parts.

"I think so," she said.

"Great. What do you want to do first—pull and inventory the parts or go coreward to rent a terminal?"

14

Thirty hours later, May gave Cheech a platonic peck on the cheek and walked off the *Angel's Luck*, weaving between members of a crew that had been hired to crate and deliver the scrapped equipment to the proper buyers. In his hands was a certified plate worth seven point six million credits. There had been more than that, but Auctionnet had deducted its percentage, planetary tariffs had been paid, and the crew had been hired to ship the equipment. Cheech tried to apologize for actually netting less than the target amount, but May told her that was nonsense. He had enough funds to cover the difference, and in any event, he would not have had the money at all if Cheech had not shown him the way. With that, he gave her credits worth ten percent of the gross for coming up with the idea and left for the planetside shuttle.

At the shuttle station, May sent a lase to the hotel where Vonn and Winters had camped out to await word of their next move. May had felt reservations about leaving the two mercenaries planetside on their own, but Duke's jailing had given Vonn a focal point for his anger. He no longer seemed restless and mad at the universe, and he no longer felt the need to haunt the Black Orchid. May could see hints of the old mercenary cool returning. While Vonn was still far from being the same mercenary he had met on Aiaaga 12, he was becoming increasingly easier to reason with—something that had been close to impossible since he had lost most of his right hand.

On the way down to Council 5, May leaned his head back and closed his eyes, trying to plan the next few days of his future. Obviously, the first order of business would be to get Duke out of jail. Naturally Duke would be obliged to stay planetside until a hearing could be held to determine his legal status. That might take months, which they would have if the *Angel's Luck* was to be refitted. The problem was financing the work since Essence had defaulted on the reward for the phials.

In the meantime, he had to find a way for them to live. Padding out his auction profits from the remaining operational expenses that Li had given them would put him dangerously short of money. He still had to pay Cheech for the initial consultation, and there were still docking costs to account for. As much as he hated the thought of it, it looked as if he would have to sell off the *Reconnez Cherie* in order to stay afloat.

Unless, of course, he could get the Essence Corporation to fork over the money.

That was the problem, May thought. If only he'd had foresight enough to take only a handful of the phials in, enough to draw Burris's interest. Even if he had retained the presence of mind to keep one phial back, he would have had something to use as leverage. He could have threatened to take the matter to Transgalactic Affairs or even the media. If only . . .

Well, that battle was not over yet. Having fought and scraped to keep his precarious grip on the *Angel's Luck* for better than a dozen years, he was not about to lose it all now because of some greedy bastard with a love of folk tales. If there was a way to get his money out of Burris, then James May would find it. After all, he had faced off the *Yueh-sheng* and run the Arcolian Blockade and come out shining. He had faced the worst the galaxy had to offer and had lived to tell about it. A corrupt businessman like Burris should be no trouble at all. If worst came to worst, he supposed, he could always take misterbob up on its offer to use its ambassadorial clout to negotiate. He hated to do it, but perhaps that or a little pheromonal stimulation would be all it would take to get Burris to behave more reasonably.

May was brought out of his thoughts when the shuttle lurched. They were touching down on Council. His hand went to his breast pocket and patted it, making sure that his money was still there.

He walked off the shuttle and through the general reception area, looking for Vonn and Winters. They were nowhere to be seen. The merchant nodded to himself, changed course, and headed for the nearest lounge. He was not at all surprised to find them there, Winters rattling the ice around in an empty glass and Vonn nursing a dark, oily looking drink.

"What," May said to them, "no tumultuous reception?"

Vonn smacked his lips. "We knew what the reception area would be like. All these hotshot government types and ambassadors in fancy clothes, high-tech businessmen who wouldn't take the time to look down their nose at us. Happy-ass rich people greeting their loved ones who were coming back from the rejuv tanks and saying shit like, 'Oh, Delancey, you look *sooo* good.' "

"Mr. Vonn figured you'd find us here," Winters said.

"He would," May said.

Vonn picked up his drink and let it ooze into his open mouth. "You're becoming like one of us," he said, wiping his lips on his sleeve.

I hope not, May thought. I really hope not.

"Come on," Vonn announced to the bar in general and May and Winters in particular. "Let's go and get our brother out of jail." He tapped the chromed surface of the bar, and Winters obediently laid down a stack of credit chips.

May took the big man by the shoulder as Vonn sauntered out the door. "Look, Winters," he said. "You don't have to step and fetch for him. You don't have to buy his drinks for him."

"It's okay," Winters said patiently. "It's his money. He just asked me to hold it for him."

"All right," May said, patting him on the back. "You're a good man, Winters. A good man."

"People trust me." Winters beamed. "They're always havin' me hold stuff for them that's too important for themselves to carry."

"That's because you do such good work."

"Yup," Winters continued. "When I get asked to keep a secret, I keep it real good and I don't tell anybody. Bear used to have me carry stuff for him like that, and so did Mr. Duke. And Mr. Vonn has me keep his money all the time because he's afraid he'll drink too much and I can tell the transport drivers how to get us to the hotel."

"Hmmm," May said absently, hurrying Winters along to catch up with Vonn. "Do you mind if we go with you, pal?"

"Forgive me all to hell," Vonn said. "I got a lot on my mind."

"Yeah," May said bitterly. "Like I don't."

"Let's not fight," Winters said. "Okay?"

"I've been thinking about this son of a bitch Burris," Vonn said. "I mean, really thinking about it. There are several options that we could pursue, but I think our best option is decisive military action."

May groaned. "Do you realize what you're saying? There's no way we'd even get past the front gate."

"Like hell there isn't. Look, May, we've got the *Reconnez Cherie*, and we could drop that sucker right down into the main parking lot and go in with guns blazing—"

"Vonn," May said, shaking his head, "would you listen to reason?"

Winters dropped a massive hand on the merchant's shoulder. "He's been drinking Qzelthian Sludges. Those make him mean."

"We go straight to where the phials are and straight out, no problem."

"What, Vonn, the three of us? Sure. And we just leave the *Cherie* running with the keys in it, right, like we're going into the market for a bottle of Leuten's?"

They stepped out of the shuttleport and onto a bright plain of concrete. Vonn waved his bandaged hand to flag a taxi.

"I've thought this all out, I'm telling you. We hire your Ori friend Chiba to fly the *Cherie* for us. Your ex could use her influence to run interference so we can drop down and take off without any hassles, and there are some brothers that I met on the *Ridge* who owe me in a big way. They'll be more than happy to beef up our manpower."

"There will be no more killing," May said emphatically. "I've had quite enough of that. We're going to do this in a civilized manner. I can get in touch with Maggie and—"

"What?" Vonn said, turning on him. His breath smelled of something heavy and metallic. "You want to get Ambassador Bugface to go plead Duke's case before the courts or something? They'd have so damned many dogs packed into the courtroom that it wouldn't be funny, and only half of them would be to keep their noses on the xeno."

"Vonn," May said quietly.

"The others would be to sniff out the crowds. There's still a lot of anti-Arcolian sentiment around, May, and if you don't believe it, you're living on Fool's World. Taking those frigging phials back is the only way, you mark my words."

"You're the one on Fool's World," May said as a taxi pulled up. "We wouldn't know where to look, and if we did, we'd have to go in with an explosives team because they've probably got that stuff in a vault."

"Taxi's here," Winters said, opening the front door.

Vonn waved him on. "In a minute." He looked back at May. "Like I said, May. I got this figured. We get the Tiger Lady to help us."

May looked up to the sky as if beseeching help. "Tiger Lady? Is this one of your acquaintances from the Black Orchid?"

"I'm getting in," Winters said.

Vonn smiled. "No. It's that spooky bitch you hired to do the computer work, the one that has the hots for you."

May opened the taxi door and tried to herd the mercenary in. "Stop that," he ordered. "You're as bad as misterbob."

"She could do it," Vonn said, resisting May's muscle. "All she'd have to do is tap in and find out through the Essence Dataplex where they've got the stuff. Hell, she could have the vault standing open when we got there. All we'd have to do is slag a few guards."

May grabbed Vonn by the collar, spun him around, and slammed him into the rear of the taxi. "All right," he snarled, closing nose-to-nose with the drunken mercenary. "I know you're mad at the whole universe, and I know that things haven't been going well for you, but that's no excuse to take it out on the two sentient races."

Vonn started to crack a smile, but May growled it down.

"Those phials aren't worth it, Vonn, not anymore. People have been dying over those things since the day they were taken, and it's all got to come to a crashing halt. They're not worth it. Nothing's worth it, not even what's in those bottles. They don't feel, Vonn, and I know in my heart that they've got no soul. You lost your best friend, Winters lost his, we've all been down and hurt and deprived. Don't you see it? They aren't worth it anymore."

Vonn's eyes rolled and he sniffed. "Anders."

"Nobody wants a piece off of Burris's ass more than I do, Vonn, but we're going to do it without anybody being killed. Have you got it? We're going to do it straight and legal. We're going to bring him down with our brains, not our balls. *Have you got that?*"

"But I've got it figured—"

The mercenary was cut off by an angry bleat from the taxi's horn.

"Coming," May shouted.

"I do," Vonn insisted.

"Then you're going to have to figure it another way," May told him. "I suggest you get to work on it." He turned Vonn around and herded him toward the rear door.

"Where to?" the driver asked as May climbed in. "Or do you wish to discuss it?"

"He's running the meter," Winters told them.

"The Planetary Detention Center," May said.

The taxi lurched out into the traffic, snapping them back in their seats. The driver eyed Winters nervously, but before he could say anything, Vonn gave a noncommittal shrug and turned his blank stare out the window.

"So," he said, "some weather you've been having."

The driver cast a sideways glance into his mirror, trying to catch sight of the mercenary. "It's, ah, average," he said. "Just, ah, average."

"That's us," Vonn said in a menacing tone. "Average guys. Isn't that right, Winters?"

"That's right." The big man smiled benignly at the driver, who shrugged into his seat and locked his eyes onto the road.

May glared at the mercenary and shook his head. He would have to find some way to vent Vonn's anger in a more efficient way once Duke had been taken care of. Certainly, the one real solution to the problem was to restore the man's flesh-and-blood hand. True, he had sustained the injury in a most heroic capacity, but the reward had been too slow in coming and bitterness was quick to set in.

"What are you going to do," May said, trying to sound low-key, "when we finally get paid?"

Vonn looked up at the driver and rolled his eyes. "You mean after I spend a week blind drunk?"

May pursed his lips. He should have known better.

"I thought I'd spread a little joy around," Vonn continued. "I've got some brothers who have been rather impoverished of late. I've been thinking of hiring them on for some work I'd like to have done."

"I see. And what type of job did you have in mind?"

"Depends," Vonn said, "on how long it takes for this next money to come in, and how much it is."

So that's it, May thought. He's going to go after the Essence Company's throat. He's going to make one last stupid gesture of disgust and then fade into oblivion.

The vehicle rolled to a stop at the Detention Center. Winters bounced out, dragging Vonn, while May lagged behind to pay the driver and then joined them on the street.

"Well," Vonn said, letting a puff of air out of his lungs. "I suppose this is it."

"Let's go get our brother," Winters said.

"Let's," May agreed.

They pushed through the door and walked across a crowded, smoke-filled lobby to a central desk where a pear-shaped woman in a uniform was harriedly juggling the attentions of a handful of tattered-looking people.

"No," she was telling one. "Your husband is not here, I'm sorry to say. If he's been missing that long, I suggest you start checking the Bioparts clinics while there's still enough of him left to recognize."

With a wail, the woman turned and ran out of the building.

"Hell of a touch with the public," Vonn said.

The woman at the desk summarily dispersed the others in the crowd, telling two different people that their friends weren't going to get out until the boiling sun of Velthos froze over, another that his wife had already been extradited off-world, and still another that the person he had come for had been executed that morning.

"Maybe," Winters suggested, "we're at the wrong desk."

"Nonsense," May said. He slid his hand into a pocket and nervously cradled the credits he had accumulated. "Duke's here."

The desk officer looked at the merchant with dark, beady eyes. "What can I do for you?" she asked coldly.

May cleared his throat. "I'm here for William Arbor."

"What," she growled, "you come to take his place or something?"

May pulled the credits from his pocket and laid them on the counter. "No," he said. "I'm here to pay his bail."

"Is this the right desk?" Winters asked.

The officer looked up at Winters and knit her eyebrows. "Who wants to know?"

"His bail," May said quickly, "has been put at nine point three million credits. It's all there."

The officer ruffled through the plastic chits. "Oh, sure, yeah. I'll just take it and buy myself a Nimrev Company coat, right."

Face filling with color, Vonn started to bolt toward the counter. May reached back and laid his hand across the mercenary's chest to stop the advance.

"You know," she continued, "with this kind of money, you could have helped the last three or four people I've sent away. Why waste this on just one—"

"Spare us the acerbic insights," May said, voice rising in pitch. "We're here on legitimate business."

"*Nobody* is worth this much," the woman continued. "Take my advice and run with this money."

May slapped both hands down on the counter. The sound echoed like a shot through the hall, which fell strangely silent. "You know, I've got a lot to be proud of in my life. I've never hit a cop, even when one beat the hell out of me, and I've never *ever* hit a woman. But there's a first time for everything, and I sincerely wouldn't mind ruining my reputation on the likes of you."

The officer tossed the credits down on the desk and waved her hands. "Ease up on your thrusters there, spacer. What was your friend's name?"

"Duke. Uh, William Arbor."

She repeated the name into a small microphone and looked down at a screen. "Nope," she said. "No Duke William Arbor here."

"Would you try William Arbor, please? Duke is—"

The woman gave May a knowing glare. "I know."

"It's what we call him."

She repeated the new variation of the name into the mike, eyes on her terminal. After a brief pause, she shook her head. "Not here," she said.

"Not here?"

"Gone." The officer shrugged.

"That's impossible," May said. "Flat-out impossible. He was here not forty-eight hours ago."

The woman studied her terminal. "He's been bonded out already. Good thing for you, you can hang on to your—"

"Who?" May snapped. "Who bailed him out? Tell me."

She shook her head. "I don't have access to that information. All I'm showing is that a William Wesley Arbor—is that his real name? I'd kill myself it I had that name—was released from this facility late last night."

"We've got to get up to the ship," Vonn said. "He'll be coming up to find us."

"No, he won't," the woman said, shaking her head. "He can't leave the surface of the planet."

"How do you know?" Vonn asked.

The officer tapped the terminal. Her fingernail made a clicking on the glass surface. "Terms of release state that he's indentured to whoever released him. He's going to have to stay here until he works off his bail."

"Slavers!" Winters exclaimed. "Let's go—"

May held out a hand to calm the big man. "No," he said. "It's not slavers. Not this time. But just as bad."

"You don't think—"Vonn started.

"No," May said. "I know." He turned to the officer and

gave her a polite nod. "Thank you, ma'am. You've been more than helpful, in spite of yourself." He started toward the door.

"May," Vonn shouted, following him out. "May, what are we going to do? We're not going to be able to find Duke. We're not going to even get *near* the Essence Company now."

May looked up and down the city streets, at the traffic and the tattered-looking people flowing into the Detention Center. "You were right," May said. "You were right all along. We should have taken the phials back when we had the chance, because they're going to be expecting us now." He made a fist and slammed it into his thigh. "And I blew it, Vonn! I wanted to avoid the slinking and the explosions and the killing because I was so damned sick of it, but it's like these things are cursed. And I'm not going to be rid of it until they're—they're—"

"Destroyed?" Winters asked.

May calmly looked into the big man's eyes. "If it comes to that, yes."

"What about the *Angel's Luck*?"

May shook his head. "That's the least of my problems. What matters now is that we get Duke out of there. We owe him our lives. The least we can do for him is die trying."

"So be it," Vonn said. He held out the bandaged remains of his right hand. Winters placed his right hand on top of Vonn's, and after a moment, May followed suit. Winters placed his left hand on the stack, and after a nod, May did the same. Vonn capped it with his own left hand and gave the others a hard look. "May here is practically a brother, Winters. I think we can forgo the swearing ceremony."

"So be it," Winters said.

"For Duke," Vonn said.

"For Duke," Winters said.

"For Duke," May said.

With a shout, they broke the show of hands. Then they set off down the street, a determined look on their faces.

TWO

> "I'll bite," Burris said. "What do you know that we
> don't?"
> "You're going to waste all your time on Duke and me and
> you're going to lose the real prize. That's what we know."

Burris shuffled the simfiles across the top of his desk with a
satisfied smile. There was nothing in the universe quite like the
feeling he had at that moment—the feeling of having complete
and absolute control over one's life, the security of knowing that
the last unpleasant variable had been eliminated.

He rose from the desk and walked out of the office at a brisk
pace, heading for the lab quarter. It was time to see how their
guest was doing and begin the process of seeing how their product had fared after a decade of storage. There was much to do,
but he had the luxury of knowing that he had all the time in the
world to do it.

He paused on hearing his name called and waited as a young
corporate type hurried to catch up to him. Burris cocked his
head, trying to remember the man's name.

"It's Surber, isn't it?" he asked. "With legal logistics?"

"Yes," the corporate type answered, juggling a stack of simfiles and slates under his arm. "If you don't mind, I've got a
couple of questions about your memorandum from yesterday
morning."

"Yes," Burris said. Once Surber had caught up, he continued
on his way to the lab quarter. "But make them fast."

"To be honest, sir, I'm not expecting an answer now. There
are just some considerations I'd like you to be aware of. For
example, there is the question of whether the test subject—"
Surber looked at one of his slates for information. "Mr. Arbor.

I have some serious doubts as to the validity of his indenturement."

"Nonsense. The corporation paid to bail him out of jail, so we own him. No questions asked."

Surber cleared his throat and shuffled quickly to keep up with Burris's brisk pace. "Actually, sir, some very valid questions have come up as to our right to bail him out. I appreciate the fact that our claim is based on the fact that he allegedly has possession of one of the early Essence bioadd products—"

"Not one of the first," Burris corrected. "*The* first."

"But that has yet to be proven."

"Give us a week," Burris said.

"There are still problems," Surber continued. "The value of the product in question had a one-time maximum of one point five million credits, and you've paid more than six times that to get him here—"

"I know," Burris said. "The son of a bitch wrecked my car, too, okay?"

"I do wish you'd take this seriously, Mr. Burris."

Burris stopped and looked the legal tech in the eye. "This company is my life," he said. "I take it damned seriously. That's why we're ready to take off now." As if to add emphasis, he started down the hall again. "Over the last ten years the field of bioadds has opened wide. And those of us who started the whole idea sat on our hands and watched everyone else pass us."

"Those were your wishes, sir."

"You're damned right they were. We were still in bed with that gangster Hiro. There was always the chance that if we got too big, he was going to dangle the distillations over our heads and threaten to make our deal public unless we sweetened his cut. All of that is over with now. We have the phials in hand, we're going to find out how well they assimilated for our own curiosity, and that's going to be the end of the matter. Our perceived colossal blunder has made this company a legend, and we're going to enhance that by coming back with a vengeance. Is there anything else you're going to bother me with, Surber?"

Surber cleared his throat again. "Some members of legal logistics have expressed the belief—"

"Some members," Burris scoffed. "Legal logistics isn't paid to think. I tell you what to think. You're paid to tell me what I can or can't get away with."

"There seem to be some doubts as to whether you're going to get away with keeping Mr. Arbor."

"Who is expressing these doubts, Mr. Surber? Would you mind telling me their names?"

Surber looked around uncomfortably. "It was me, sir."

Burris nodded. "You've saved your own job, Mr. Surber, and I'm giving you a raise for being so brave. Now, if you'll excuse me . . ."

"There are some distinct liability problems encompassed in our keeping Mr. Arbor on the premises," Surber protested. "First of all, if it turns out that his claim of possession of bioadds is fraudulent—"

"Then he deserves everything that's going to happen to him in the testing stage."

"There's the possibility that he can sue us for false indenturement. His grounds are precarious, I admit, but our grounds for indenturement are just as precarious. It could make for a very ugly case. On the other hand, I've been reading the law-enforcement center reports of the incident at the Black Orchid that Mr. Arbor was involved in, and there's the distinct possibility that the Eric Dickson bioadd product could have been responsible for his actions."

"In which case we have every right to retain him. What the hell is your problem?"

"The problem," Surber replied, "is that with any bioadd product there is an implied warranty that says the product has been certified safe for human use. No such work was done on the distillations—"

"Of course not," Burris shouted. "We were up to our ass in lawsuits at the time, and the frigging court had slapped us with two hundred separate injunctions, one for each bottle—"

"Nonetheless, immediately prior to the lawsuits the company was preparing to market the Series One Distillations and was contracting out to various parties for Series Two. That alone implied perfected product, which may give Mr. Arbor a very good case for a lawsuit."

Burris stopped again and locked eyes with Surber. "Why are you telling me all of this?"

"You said it yourself, Mr. Burris. It's what you pay me to do. I'm merely warning you that you've engaged in an enterprise for which there may be a terrible retribution. With the right team of lawyers, Mr. Arbor—"

"Mr. Arbor can afford *nothing*."

"This is a case which many would take as *pro bono* for the publicity value. With the right disclosure of information, a settlement could be handed down which would result in the complete and utter liquidation of this company."

Burris took Surber by the shoulders. "I appreciate all you're doing for me, but I assure you that nothing is going to happen to this company. No matter what the outcome of our tests, Mr. Arbor will *not* be filing any kind of suit against us."

"The Targis-Hillary decision stated that a waiver signed within a standard week before or after indenturement—"

"Mr. Arbor did not sign a waiver," Burris said impatiently. "And I most certainly would not put faith in what's written on a slate to save this company. If you must know the truth, as soon as our research is done on our guest, I plan on selling his contract to the field procurement section of the Nimrev Company."

"That's no guarantee—"

"*After* having him brainwiped." Burris stared hard into the young man's eyes. "Are there any more questions?"

Surber shook his head.

"Good. Thank you for your concern." With a curt nod of dismissal, Burris sidestepped the legal tech and carded his way through a security door into the lab quarter. Halfway down a short hall, he carded another lock and stepped into a darkened room where Dr. Melrose sat before a host of video monitors. Several showed different angles of a small room where a tall, skinny man paced circles on the floor. Others showed different series of waving lines and three-dimensional constructs of biological patterns. Melrose himself was in a large, cushioned chair with controls on both armrests. He stared intently at the center monitor, which was three times the size of the others, and nodded at something he was hearing through a thin headset.

"How's our guest?" Burris asked.

Melrose pulled the headset out of his ears. "Normal," he said. "Almost too normal." He hit a key on the armrest, and the view on the central screen switched to a compilation of biosigns. "Mr. Arbor regained consciousness approximately fifteen minutes ago and spent about two minutes looking over the cell. Now he's into a solid routine of pacing, almost like he's doing some kind of exercise in order to keep in shape."

"What's so terrible about that?" Burris asked.

Melrose tapped the monitor. "His biosigns show no sign whatsoever of agitation. His blood pressure, breathing, heartwave, brainscan, all show normal. It's too normal for someone who has just wakened inside a strange jail cell."

Burris pulled a padded stool next to Melrose's command chair and eased down onto it. "Maybe our friend here is a chronic jailbird."

Melrose shook his head and handed Burris a slate. "Not according to this. It's a public data access record of common knowledge about Mr. Arbor."

Burris studied it. Arbor had just turned twenty-three in the last week and had the uneventful background of a commodities broker from Tetros 9, a slow-paced agrarian world that was out of the way of most of the well-traveled lanes. It was not until the last three months that a series of charges had rapidly piled up against him.

"There," Burris said, thumping the record with the nail of his middle finger. "Jail time on three different occasions. The port *Saint Vrain*, brig time on the passage ship *Hergest Ridge*, and right here on Council."

"But the record is limited," Melrose said. "That time has only accumulated over the last three months and is not significant enough to be a factor in his reaction."

Burris tossed the slate onto the worktable. "What about his juvenile record? We don't have that."

"Legal logistics be damned, my friend. A habitual juvenile delinquent does not spend six quiet years at a community college on a small agrarian world studying to certify as a commodities broker. It doesn't fit."

"So," Burris said, shifting on the stool. "Has he shown any manifestation of the presence of our lost distillee?"

Melrose thumped the main screen. "I think this is one of them."

"Don't get cute with me, Vinnie."

"I'm not," Melrose protested. "The fact that this quiet little boy from a farm world is not pulling his hair out upon finding himself in a strange detention cell is significant."

"You're saying that our distillee was a lowlife? You watch your mouth—"

"Think about it," Melrose interrupted. "Remember the allegation that Eric Dickson was the one put into Mr. Arbor, and consider that story your father used to tell about how he came to sign Dickson to the program? I remember the night he came in after signing him, he was worried to death that perhaps he'd made a mistake. But things worked out right, and he used to laugh like hell telling the story years later."

"That's what you think?"

Melrose nodded.

"As you're my father's friend, I can respect that opinion. However, I think we should take more of a direct approach."

"I think it's a mistake to start with drugs right now."

"You people," Burris grunted. "Always going off and thinking for yourselves. Did I say anything about drugs, Vinnie? No. The direct approach we should take now is for you and me to go in there and interview Mr. Arbor to see what we can find out about his situation."

"It's the same difference," Melrose said. "You're going to end up having me drug him." The doctor shook his head. "What makes you think he's going to give you the time of day after the way you treated him or his friend? You have this incredible capacity for forgetting the past."

"Vincent," Burris said sternly. "How long is it since my father died? Fifteen years? Twenty?"

Melrose nodded.

"Except for being exiled here by the board of directors, haven't I done an efficient job of taking his place? If you think I haven't, I'd be more than happy to review your contract."

"If you want to risk the interview, you may," Melrose replied. "Just remember that Eric Dickson was a violent personality, which may make Mr. Arbor unpredictable. Their two personality types are worlds apart."

"You're talking like Dickson's knowledge of piloting is going to be dangerous to me. Hell, even if we'd done a complete brain transplant, there's no way he could hurt me with that kid's body. That agrarian nit down there is strictly from the lower percentile."

Melrose ran his fingers across the armrest controllers and one by one, the screens went blank. "No sense in waiting around here, is there?" He rose from the chair, and Burris followed him through a door snuggled between rows of monitors, then down a short set of steps into a long hallway. Stopping at a metal box set into the wall, the doctor unlocked it with his ID badge and started to take out a Comealong, but Burris chided him.

"You won't need that, Vinnie."

"Standard procedure," Melrose said, pocketing the device. "For all unbalanced subjects."

"Unbalanced," Burris scoffed.

They continued down the hall until Melrose stopped at one of the doors. He carded a video monitor active and watched for a moment, checking the position of the subject on the other side of the accompanying door.

"What are you waiting for?" Burris asked.

Melrose swept his arm toward the door's card reader. "This is your project."

Burris removed his ID badge and laughed. "I like that about you, Vinnie. Always watching out for your own ass."

"Someone's got to do it."

"You just don't like having to answer to people." Burris laughed, carding the door. "Me, I answer to no one."

"What about the board of directors?" Melrose asked quietly.

Before Burris could reply the door to the cell lifted and the jab was forgotten. The two walked in to see the subject at the sink, drinking water from his cupped hands.

"We have utensils for you to use," Burris complained.

"Then why don't you get me some—" Duke turned to see who was addressing him, and as he did, his insult cut short. "You."

Burris shrugged. "You've got something of mine. I'd like to know how it works."

Duke shut off the faucet. He let the water drip from his face and hands.

"You want to tell me about it? You want to tell me about how you came to be in permanent possession of Eric Dickson?"

"No," Duke said bluntly. He sat down on the bed.

"I hope you'll consider being more reasonable about this, Mr. Arbor. This is very important to this company."

Duke slowly exhaled. "All right, I've given it three seconds' worth of thought, which is all that such a preposterous statement deserves. My answer is no."

"Have you had any manifestations of Eric Dickson's presence in—in your brain?"

"Why don't you ask him?" Duke asked bitterly.

Burris pulled up a short stool and sat, staring intently at Duke. The corners of his lips turned up. "You mean—he's *here*?"·

Duke said nothing.

"Mr. Dickson?" Burris said loudly. "Hello? Can you hear me?"

"I'm not deaf," Duke said.

"Eric Dickson?" Burris asked excitedly.

"No. William Arbor. *Mister* Arbor to you."

"I want to speak with Eric Dickson," Burris said, color rising in his face.

"If I had him," Duke said, "I sure as hell wouldn't let him talk to you."

"You can control his—his presence? His knowledge? The manifestations?"

Duke folded his arms around his upbent knees. "They have an expression back where I come from. It says, 'Go piss up a rope.' Does that mean anything to you?"

Burris bolted up from the stool, toppling it to the floor. "You had better cooperate with me, Mr. Arbor. I know you've got him. Your merchant friend told me all about it."

The commodities broker's face was inscrutable.

"It would be in your best interests to cooperate fully," Burris continued. "I can make your life very uncomfortable."

Duke laughed. "You already have, Mr. Burris. You have taken from us what is rightfully ours. You have ruined the life and career of the man who is quite possibly the best friend I've ever had. You've deprived me of my freedom and of the chance to return to my home and put my life back into order; you've ruined the chance for another man to repair his ruined hand." He shook his head slowly. "And I've got another friend, he's mentally retarded. I was actually idealistic enough to consider asking if your product could help him. What a joke *that* turned out to be."

"Perhaps if you realized the power I wield . . ."

Duke uncurled from the bed and stood. "I think I could guess what you wield, Mr. Burris, and it doesn't scare me. You forget that I've faced the *Yueh-sheng* and come out of it alive. Just what the hell are you going to threaten me with? Death? Go ahead and kill me, right now. You can always process my brain and give it to someone else. And if you're lucky, he'll remember enough to tell you that *he's* not afraid of death, so you can do it *again*—"

"All right," Burris said impatiently. "You've proven that you've got an above-average pair of testicles. How would you like to see them—"

"Mr. Arbor," Melrose interrupted. "In the interests of halting this rather annoying show of brinksmanship between yourself and my boss, allow me to ask one rather slight question. What would it take for you to reconsider your decision against cooperating?"

"Sheets for the bed," Duke said. "A pillow. Soap and toothpaste and a razor—"

"Liquid depilatory," Melrose said. "I can't allow you to take any sharp—"

"Dash and a towel and a cup to drink out of."

"Anything else?" Burris asked sourly.

"That's not unreasonable," Melrose said. "He's only asking to be treated like a human being."

"You forget," Burris countered, "that he's supposed to be at our mercy."

"For that," Melrose asked, "you'll reconsider?"

"For five seconds," Duke said. "I'll double that for a meal. A bottle of your best beer, a good selection of the local vegetables, and a prime rib steak, at least a kilo's worth. And don't try to palm off any crap on me. I was a commodities broker, and I worked beef."

"What will it take for your complete cooperation?" Burris asked, voice reeking of sarcasm.

Duke sat back down on the bed. "You deliver to James May, captain of the *Angel's Luck*, three hundred million credits *cash*."

"This interview is terminated." Burris carded the door open and waited for Melrose to leave before exiting himself. "I want you to go with drugs, Vinnie," he said as the door closed. "I want a complete regimen set by morning."

"At least let me work on him," Melrose said.

"You want me to pander to the son of a bitch? Is that it, Vincent?" He walked up the stairs and pushed through the door to the surveillance room. "I pay you—"

"You pay me to do after you think," Melrose said. "You've made it clear to me year in and year out. Well, I've got some thoughts of my own, and I'm not about to apologize for them. This is an important project for the company and I really would hate to see the research potential ruined because you let him get under your skin.

"You've got to show a little patience with this one. Remember that you've waited a decade to get out from under the threat of Hiro. How long had you resigned yourself to waiting as a third-rate bioadd company before Arbor and his mercenary friends walked in here? You told me yourself that you've got all the time in the world, so why don't you relax and let me try it my way?"

Burris stared as the doctor eased into the control chair. "Well?"

"Three hundred million credits," he snarled.

"Let's start with a cup and soap. See how much goodwill I can generate that way before we get too drastic."

"All right." Burris nodded. "I'll humor you, Vincent. I'll give you a week."

"That's not a lot of time—"

"You'll make do with it."

"I don't understand why you're in such a rush."

"Yours is not to understand," Burris threatened. "You should be happy in the knowledge that I'm acting in the best interests of the Essence Corporation. I've waited too long for something like this to happen, and I'm not about to see it ruined by some sub-par shitkicker from a green world."

"Can I petition you for more time?"

"We'll see what you come up with in the first three days." Burris turned and walked out of the surveillance room and down the hall. On the approach to his office, Sergeant Emerson appeared from down the hall and flagged his attention.

"Excuse me, Mr. Burris, but there's a rather unpleasant man in the lobby who wishes to speak with you about the location of the Series One Distillations."

"Give him the brush-off, Sergeant," Burris said. "I'm busy right now."

"I tried to," the sergeant said, tugging at his collar, "but he was rather adamant. He claimed that you had all of the surviving phials except for one."

Burris slowed. "He did?"

The guard nodded. "He said something about an insurance policy, and not wishing to cash it in because he knew you were a man who could listen to reason."

"He did, did he?" Burris came to a complete stop and blew a sigh. "Well, I suppose I could humor him, now, couldn't I?"

He started again, this time following Sergeant Emerson out to the lobby. James May was there, leaning against the reception desk and smiling malignantly.

"Captain," Burris said, "why is it that I'm not surprised to see you? Did you come to pay me for the damage done to my car?"

"You know why I'm here," May said quietly. "Aren't you going to invite me into your office?"

"No," Burris said bluntly. "Whatever you need to say can be spoken right here. And then you can leave."

May looked at the guard and the receptionist. "Ask them to leave."

"They stay." Burris folded his arms. "You're not only a crackpot, Captain, you're dangerous. Now speak your piece and be done with it."

"You have the phials," May said.

"I have the phials you brought us," Burris corrected. "They have yet to be verified as genuine. I wouldn't go holding my breath, though. There have been many clever fakes."

"You didn't get them all."

"Yes," Burris said. "I believe you did say something about an insurance policy. You want to explain that to me?"

"One of the phials you didn't get," May said, "was Eric Dickson."

Burris unfolded his arms and looked around the room mockingly. "Is it just me, or does everyone else get the feeling that I've heard this story before? Captain—"

"Eric Dickson was injected into my colleague Duke, the one who was with us on the day you took the phials from us. Currently, he's in jail—"

"How long do you intend to keep wasting my time with a repeat of this story?"

"Just long enough to remind you of what's at stake here. Duke is currently incarcerated for a particularly violent homicide which I contend was caused by your product—an Essence Series One Distillation. I have Duke's legal counsel working on that angle right now—"

"Captain," Burris said loudly, "first of all you've got to prove that you had the phials to begin with, and as I've said, I've got my people working on their verification."

"Don't give me that line about verification. You and I both know that what we turned in to you was the genuine article. Now I'm willing to credit you for taking them from us and leaving us without a leg to stand on. That was a really nice move on your part. But as long as I've got Duke, I don't think I need them."

Burris narrowed his eyes. "What are you getting at?"

May produced a WORM disc and held it up for Burris's inspection. "I've got a friend who is into instant database searches, and she's come up with a very interesting list of names for me. They're all former employees who worked on the distillation project, all of whom left within twenty-five months of your taking over the company after your father's death. There were varying reasons given for their departures, but I'm wondering if some of that wasn't because of your being in bed with the *Yueh-sheng*.

"I've already been in touch with some of them, and they've expressed a great interest in seeing Duke. If I can get enough expert testimony lined up, I won't need the remaining phials to prove my case."

"Why, Captain, are you trying to blackmail me?"

May pocketed the disc. "No. Of course not. It had just occurred to me that nobody had ever gone to court over the alleged validity of the phials they were returning. This would be a first for you as well, and since my case would be rather compelling, I thought you might be inclined to listen to reason."

Burris looked at the receptionist, then at the guard. After a moment, he returned his gaze to May. "Tell you what, Captain. If it makes you feel any better, you go right ahead with your court case. I'm sure that my corporate legal counsel would love to hear from the people working for your percentage. Be advised, though, that when you lose this case—and you most assuredly will—I will have every justification for filing a countersuit against you for slander, libel, harassment, and a dozen other charges. I daresay you won't fare as well as the defendant."

May gave a gracious nod. "I was hoping you'd be more receptive to reason, but your response doesn't surprise me. I'll see you in court, Mr. Burris." He turned and walked out the doors.

Shaking his head, Burris forced himself into a skeptical laugh for the benefit of the receptionist and the guard. "Can you believe it?" he asked. "Can you honestly believe it? Every year they get bolder and more desperate." Without another word, he turned and walked back to his office.

As he walked, he began to shake. He knew, dammit, that arrogant son of a bitch merchant captain had been playing with him. He had no more intent of filing suit against him than any of the ones who had brought in counterfeit phials. It was true that a court case such as the one the captain had mentioned would be disastrous for Essence—even if the company won—but that had not been the intent behind the visit.

The merchant had no plan to ever file suit against the company, He had *known* that Arbor was being held there, and the whole purpose of the visit had been to confirm that. And I, Burris thought, I, like a fool, had to taunt him and play right into his hands. I should have just given him the cell number while I was at it.

Still shaking, Burris let himself into his office and sat hard behind his desk. It never ceased to amaze him how fleeting the sensation of total security was. There was always something, some damned thing that served to upset the balance.

A smile began to surface as he stared at the wall.

Yes, there was always something. But this was a something over which he had some control.

What would the merchant be up to? The cosmos only knew. If he went the legal route, he had first to convince a legal counsel of the validity of the claim that the Essence Corporation was holding a man hostage for medical experiments. That meant that the counsel would have to be willing to work for a percentage of whatever money was rewarded to his client—a tidy sum if the court awarded the captain the full reward due for bringing back the phials.

Unfortunately, most of the counsels who would listen to the captain's story would be shysters. Alas, there were even shysters out there who knew too well what they were doing and how to manipulate corporate fear in their favor.

The other option Burris gathered from the captain's company—the two battered-looking men who could only be mercenaries.

Legal or military action? Which would the captain choose?

It did not matter. Not really.

The key to the case was William Arbor. And if he could open up the doors to the company to prove that Arbor was not there, then so much the better.

In either case, time was working against the merchant. He needed time to find counsel, or time to gather together a team for the assault to rescue his friend.

Burris looked at a small box that rested on his desktop.

"Phone," he said. "Ring Dr. Melrose, please."

"Obliging," it replied.

After a moment, there was a click, and another voice came through the box. "Melrose here."

"Vincent, we have a slight problem. I'm not going to be able to honor the week of research time you requested. I'm only going to be able to grant you three days, commencing immediately. If at the end of that time you have made no appreciable progress, we are going to be forced to go to the regimen of drugs."

"I see," Melrose replied. "And what happens after that?"

What indeed, Burris thought. It was a big universe. People disappeared all the time.

2

May walked through drizzle, across the concrete lot, and through the gates. Across the street from where he stood, a battered van sat at the side of the road, idling. When the traffic thinned, he cut across the boulevard and let himself in through the rear of the vehicle.

"Well?" Vonn asked as May seated himself on the floor.

"They've got him, all right," May said. "Burris practically begged me to try and pick him off in court. He wouldn't have done that unless he knew that the person who would be our star witness was in their custody."

"You were right, Mr. May," Winters said, drumming the steering wheel with his palms.

"That leaves the question of how to get him out of there," May said.

"I know how you feel about direct action," Vonn said, "but it's our only viable option."

"I think Mr. Vonn's right," Winters said. "We should go in there and blow the fuck out of them."

May stared at the big man. "I think you've been in the business too long."

"But we can do it, May," Vonn said. "I can get the men. There's two guys who were under Bachman's employ on the *Hergest Ridge* who owe me. I'm sure they're still around; maybe they've got stringers. We could have a dozen men inside of a week."

"We don't have a week," May said.

"Your legal way sure as hell isn't going to cut it," Vonn snapped.

"I know," May said, trying to shout the mercenary down. "I told you I was through with violence. And I don't think Duke would appreciate us blowing our way in. If it was him going in for one of us, he'd try to find another way."

"May's right," Winters said. "There's probably another way."

"Use the law," Vonn said. "Take months. Maybe years. And we get Duke back, and he's some frigging vegetable."

May shook his head. "I can't trust the law, either. Not on this one."

"Well then, what are you going to do? Hope that the good Mr. Burris has a change of heart and *gives* Duke to us?"

"Maybe he will," May said, smiling.

Vonn rolled down the window and spit in contempt. "There's only one thing in the whole wide universe that Burris cares about, and it *isn't* the Fifth Region."

"I know that," May replied. "And I also know that there's something else without which money is not complete."

"Of course there's something else," Vonn said. "Power."

"Absolutely," May replied, then dreamily looked out of the front windshield. "I wonder if Maggie's busy tomorrow afternoon?"

3

Duke felt as if he were dreaming, and in a sense he was. He was standing in a sleazy hotel looking across walls whose cheap wallpaper was covered with dark, drying splatters. Slowly, his gaze sank to the figure on the bed, two fist-sized wounds side by side in his chest, a cutlass with a dull metal finish clenched in one hand. A medtech stood to one side of the bed, hands pulling and tugging at the weapon, trying to avoid the sharpness of the blade while trying to wrest it from the corpse's grip. With a final tug the cutlass came free and was unceremoniously tossed to the floor.

Another medtech came in with a gravgurney, and he and his partner set about the task of moving Thomas Fortunado's body. Duke turned away, leaving them to their work. He expected to see Rhea there waiting for him, but she was gone. Dickson, he noticed, was gone, too, and the remaining people in the room were going about their work as if the young Tetran were not there.

It was odd, he thought. The scene was not an obvious construct, as the encounter with Leigh Brand had been, yet what he saw happening was not solidly ingrained in any of Dickson's memories. It was as if what he was seeing was a cross between the two, a solid memory of the room and the smell of death augmented by the memory of something else. Perhaps it was something overheard from a man on a bar stool, laughing over a few beers at how poor old Thomas Fortunado had been reluctant to let go of his cutlass, even in death.

Duke looked back at the scene. Something was very wrong. The medtechs' motions were slowing down, as if they were moving through thick fluid. The vivid colors were beginning to fade into bland tones of sepia. Finally, the scene froze and began to fade. The bloodstains, the medtechs, the tasteless pornoprint on the wall, all vanished into nothingness, leaving nothing behind but a body and a bed on a vast field of gray.

This was it, Duke realized. The end of the line. Like the once-ambitious Great Desert Highway back home on Tetros, never finished, and in the middle of the night on a beer drunk, he and a carload of friends had driven past the sign that warned ROAD ENDS 2 KM, right to the edge where the road quit and became sand. His gut was tightening in much the same way now, and the feeling he had to turn and run back the other way was much the same as it had been those five standard years before.

As he turned, he was looking across a vast gray plain, occupied by nothing but himself and Fortunado's deathbed. With great relief, he found that the door was still there, and when he opened it, it led into a hallway that was fast fading. He stepped out and hurried down the hall back to Dickson's room. Rhea was there waiting, seated on the bed, staring at the floor, hands folded in her lap.

"You're still here." He laughed nervously.

"Yes," she said. "I'll be here until the end."

Duke looked out the door. The hall to the stairs was just as Dickson remembered it, but back toward Fortunado's room there was nothing but a gray wall.

"He never went down that hall again," Rhea volunteered. "Even when he had to bathe or go to the bathroom, he'd go all the way up to the next floor."

Duke reached his hand out into the gray. His hand fell on nothing, yet there was resistance, as if something strange were pushing back against him. He looked back at Rhea. "Why are you telling me this?"

"I'm not," she said bluntly. "This is how you remember it."

Is that what it's coming to? Duke thought. The memory leaks in by fits and starts, and then I have to go digging to find out the rest. If only there was time. A dim memory of his own peeked out, one of a small cell and two men talking to him. One man leaving in disgust, the other following him out, and the sinking feeling that things were only going to get worse. A memory of going over the cell a centimeter at a time, knowing that they would be watching but damning them anyway, looking for something, anything that could be used to escape. The realization that, even though he was new at all of this, he held the knowledge to escape.

"I came here," Duke said. "On my own."

"Don't we all," Rhea answered.

"Where's Eric? I need to talk to him."

Rhea remained passive. "You'll know."

Yes, Duke thought. Of course.

He left the room and started down the section of hall that remained, making his way down the stairs, through the decaying lobby, and into the small lounge that was attached. Stopping at the doorway to look around, he soon spotted Dickson, sitting on a stool before the bar, a bottle of Aiaagan gin and a small shot glass in front of him. Duke sauntered over and climbed onto a stool between the pilot and a heavyset man who was laughing and drinking from a large mug of beer.

"So then," the fat man said, chuckling, "these techs are in there to take him away, right? And they're getting ready to load him into the bag, only, see, he's still got this weapon in his hands. So the one tech, he tries to pull it away, only his fingers is still wrapped around it, and he's getting kind of elastic by now, if you know what I mean, so his hand snaps back like he's trying to keep it for himself." He laughed uproariously, pausing to wipe a tear of mirth from his eye. "Can you imagine that, now? He wants to take it with him!"

Dickson suddenly turned as if to shout the fat man down and was quite startled to see Duke sitting next to him.

"I mean, this guy, he answers the door stark raving naked with nothing but a cutlass in his hand, and there's this big daddy on the other side with an autoshot. *Boom!*" The man continued to laugh.

"Just be glad it wasn't you," Duke said quietly.

"What?" the fat man asked.

Duke hooked his thumb toward Dickson. "My friend here is a friend of the family. He's taking this incident rather hard. I'd appreciate it if you could laugh about it somewhere else."

The fat man blinked at Duke and Dickson through rheumy eyes and raised his beer mug as if in apology. "Certainly, certainly. I'm very sorry about all of it, really. Unpleasant business. Gives the place a bad name." He tagged his cohort on the shoulder and moved away from the bar.

"Well," Dickson said, pouring himself a shot of gin. "You seem to have saved me from another night in jail."

Duke closed his eyes. "I remember," he said. "You broke his nose and both of his arms." He opened them. "There seemed to have been some kind of technicality, and you were never prosecuted for it. It's there, but I can't quite put my finger on it."

"That's because I never really understood it. Every world has it's own set of stupid, petty laws."

"I know," Duke said. "I've been there."

Dickson laughed, downed his drink, and poured himself another. "Yeah," he said. "You *think*, farm boy. You think." He downed the second drink, then poured himself a third.

Duke looked around the lounge. Dickson's memory of it was so vivid, right down to the smell of smoke and the barely audible computerized music. "Why don't you go easy on that stuff," Duke said as Eric put the third drink away.

"Why don't you make me," Dickson growled, pouring himself a fourth. He started to raise the drink to his lips, but Duke reached over and placed his palm across the open mouth of the glass.

"You know I can't do that," Duke said. "Not if this is a memory. I can't rewrite the past."

"But you have," Dickson countered, setting the drink down. "You kept me from going to jail for assault."

Duke shook his head. "I caused you to jump memories. This is a different time you're remembering now. It's winter, you've been outside and you're cold. You haven't been up to see Rhea yet, and when you go upstairs—" He lifted his hand away from the glass and Dickson stared down into it.

"She'll be gone," the pilot said.

Duke motioned with a finger. "Go on. Finish it. Three more drinks and the memory gets hazy. Then you need to finish the bottle in your room. At least, I think you finished the bottle. There's a certain point beyond which things get dark and there seems to be a gap of about two standard—"

"Why are you doing this to me?" Dickson snapped, standing suddenly and spilling Aiaagan gin across the cheap lacquer surface of the bar. "What are you pushing me for? Why can't you leave me alone to enjoy this in peace?"

Duke folded his arms and turned in his stool, looking out across the darkened room. "You expect me to believe you're enjoying this?"

"Don't you believe in letting a man suffer alone?"

"Certainly," Duke said. "But you're forgetting one thing. You're not alone, not anymore. You're with me now, and it's my life you're ruining with this behavior. Do you understand that?"

"I never asked for this to happen," Dickson said, and swallowed the fourth drink. He wiped his mouth with his sleeve and pointed at Duke with one finger. "And don't give me a line about how you never asked for it, either. I've seen the memory, you asking those mercenary friends of yours if they'd ever heard of me and then pocketing the bottle with me in it. Like the old saying goes, be careful what you wish for." He began to fill the glass a fifth time.

Duke unfolded his arms and grabbed the neck of the bottle. With less force than he thought necessary, he turned the bottle back up and set it down on the bar with Dickson's hand still clasped around it.

"You're getting weak," Duke said. "It's a wonder this stuff didn't kill you."

"What you want?" Dickson growled.

"An audience with you, preferably one of your sober versions. One with a little anger would be nice, like the version who was held in the Vicarage for the murder of Derrald Deakes."

"What for?"

"In case you hadn't noticed, friend, we have fallen into the hands of the enemy. We're being held by someone named Burris, a high-up in the Essence Corporation, and he's very interested in what is making us tick."

"You told him to go jump." Dickson smiled. "I was proud of you for that one."

"Then you're naive," Duke said, "or you've ceased caring. Do you really think that he's going to take no for an answer? I don't believe for a minute that he's going to sit here and wait for me to change my mind. This is a laboratory, Eric, and we're the experiment."

"You're the experiment, Duke." Dickson lifted the shot glass and sipped at it delicately, as if it were an exotic wine. "Me, I've already been the experiment once. It's not all it's cracked up to be."

"I don't care," Duke said. "I want to be out of here, and I want to be—" He stopped himself and looked away.

"Say it," Dickson challenged. "Go ahead and say it. You want to be rid of me."

"I want to lead a normal life again."

"Sure." Dickson laughed and poured himself a sixth. "You want to go home to those two little pixies you abandoned. They're not even pretty, Duke. But maybe that's how they grow them on Testes."

"Tetros," Duke snapped. "And it's not that bad compared to the places I've seen since leaving."

"You want out of jail?" Dickson asked. "Get out. Make your plan and do it."

"I need your help."

"What, you want rid of me but not before you've pillaged my life for whatever you could get out of it? What a shitty attitude."

Duke slumped down on his stool. "I thought I could get you to listen to reason."

Dickson's reply was a loud swallow as he sent the sixth drink home.

"After all," Duke continued, "you're the big war hero. You're the one who keeps telling me that death is not what it's cracked up to be."

"I'm not scared of nothing," Dickson said. "Not anymore. Not after what I've been through."

"After all you've been through," Duke said, "you don't even have the decency to try to make someone's life easier? You don't even have the feeling to try and make someone else's life a little easier because you know what it's like, because nothing is what it's cracked up to be?"

Dickson said nothing. He traced his index finger around the outer rim of the shot glass.

"You called me a coward," Duke said. "I remember that. But I'm going to remember *you* as the coward. I'm going to remember you as the person who was so busy being a real man that he didn't have time to show that he gave a damn about anything else. *You're* the coward, Eric." He grabbed the bottle and spilled liquid into and over the glass, puddling it on the bar. "Have another. And another." Duke pulled out a handful of bills and slapped them hard on the counter. "Have a couple more bottles on me. Don't forget to go upstairs. You've got a date with Rhea."

Duke hopped off the stool and stormed out of the lounge, hands thrust deep in his pockets. He felt that the encounter had gone all wrong. True, he had gotten some feelings off his chest, said some things to Dickson that he felt needed saying, but he had not succeeded in getting the pilot's help. Still, he felt strangely vindicated, as if he had scored a minor victory. Sighing, he wondered to himself, Is this what makes May the way he is? Is he addicted to that moment of truth?

His reverie was interrupted by a shout that reverberated across the inside of the sleazy lobby. He turned and saw Dickson standing by the clerk's desk, a gin bottle in each hand.

"I've decided you were right," the pilot said. "I've decided that there's no use in my being mad at the entire universe. I'm dead, after all."

Duke pulled his hands from his pockets and nodded. "Thank you."

Dickson gestured with his hands, the bottles winking in the dim light. "All of what I have—what I have that you've got now—is yours. I won't restrict you anymore. Take anything you need to escape from your situation."

Duke raised his fingers in the civilian salute of respect. Dickson flagged him back with a salute reserved only for dignitaries and started up the stairs. Hands knotting into fists with excitement, Duke watched the pilot vanish from sight.

Yes, this is it, he thought. That wonderful feeling of having Angel's Luck. There's nothing else like it in the universe. No wonder May runs himself crazy across the known galaxy. It's an opiate.

All he had to do was put the knowledge to use. There would be no more eerie feeling of someone standing over his shoulder, telling him what he was about to do wrong.

All he had to do was put the knowledge to use. It was simply a matter of finding it . . .

Duke broke out in a wave of cold sweat.

All he had to do was find the knowledge . . .

"You bastard!"

He spun on his heels and hit the stairs at a run, charging up them and screaming the pilot's name. At the first-floor landing he started down the hall, toward the gray wall, stopping at Dickson's room. The door was locked when he tried it, so he kicked at the knob. The cheap wood splintered, and the door flew open. Rhea was inside, still sitting on the bed. She was wearing a floor-length black dress, a broad-brimmed black hat, and a dark veil over her face.

"Where is he?" Duke demanded.

Rhea looked up. Through the veil he could see that she had aged badly. It was almost as if her face had mummified.

"It's too late," she said. "He's dead."

"No." Duke shook his head. "He's still around. I can feel him."

"He left a message," Rhea said.

"What?"

"He said . . ." Her voice was slowing and dropping in pitch as if it were a recording being played back on a dying piece of equipment. Duke looked around the room and saw that the colors were fading.

". . . that if you wanted the knowledge . . ."

She paused. Her black dress was fading, and the walls around her had bled into sepia. Duke waited for her to speak again. It took an agonizing number of seconds for her to blink her eyes.

"Yes," Duke said loudly.

"That—you—would—knowwww . . ."

"What, dammit?"

"Wherrrrrrrrre . . ."

"Come on!"

". . . toooo—finnnnnnnnnnd . . ."

"Rhea!"

"It." The last word sounded startlingly final, and Rhea's fade into two dimensions was complete. The image began to crack and peel, and an invisible wall of static electricity surrounded Duke and began to push him back toward the door.

"No," he shouted, fighting against the wave. "You can't do this to me, you *bastard*!"

There was a loud snap, and a bolt of electricity caught him squarely in the chest. His muscles jumped, and he hit the floor. A moment later he regained his senses, and the smell of ancient carpet filled his nose. Duke pulled to his hands and knees and looked inside what had been Dickson's room. Like the remainder of the hall, it had been consumed by a flat, gray wall.

From all around came laughter. Dickson's laughter.

"It's not over," Duke said. "Not at all. Not by a long shot."

The laughter continued, and Duke recognized it. It was the laughter of having pulled a grand prank on one of the green plebes at Narofeld Station. He picked himself off the floor, dusted himself off, and, with as much dignity as he could muster, went back to the stairs and down to the lobby.

4

Under May's grip, the *Reconnez Cherie* made a lazy circle around the platform. To the uninitiated eye, the orbiting station looked to be a scene of chaos, with the appearance of something that was assembled in great haste out of cheap material. An upended teardrop shape bristled with metallic spines that glowed with flashes of blue light. Tugs and small cargo hoists came and went at random intervals, and some turned back after appearing to go only a few kilometers away. Hovering all around the structure were tiny points of light that swarmed about the scene, thick and unorganized like a host of flies.

James May, however, was able to interpret the scene for what it was. The gigantic stretched pod shape was in fact a luxury ship, its spines the repair platform that had been carefully constructed around it. The tugs and hoists were carrying out routine acts of maintenance and repair, as much to the platform's structure as the ship's. And the small points of light were actually individual members of the repair crew in EVA suits, and their individual movements had a true rhythm and purpose.

"Running the blockade beat the hell out of it," Peter Chiba said from the copilot's seat.

"You should've seen it before," May said. "It's got a month's worth of repairs on it now."

"I'm glad I slept through it," the salvor said.

"I wish to hell I could have." May sighed. "That was one of those things that—how can I say it? They can fix up the damage on the ship and make it look good as new, but the damage to us was irreparable."

"No offense," Chiba said, "but I did all right."

"Then you're the exception," May replied. "I can only hope that Maggie came out of it as well."

"You know she did. She's probably the UTE Fleet's top commander now, a big heroine for bringing the Arcolians in safely."

"I can only hope you're right."

Chiba gave an understanding nod. "Let me put it this way, James. Outside of misterbob, you'll not have a more influential person on your side."

May sighed. "That's the big question, Peter. Is she going to be on my side?"

"Why shouldn't she be?"

"Why shouldn't she," May echoed with a cynical laugh. "I keep forgetting that you weren't there." He uncurled his fingers from the control yoke and replayed the frosty conversation he'd had with his ex-wife in a lift on the *Hergest Ridge*. She had been through with him once and had let him know in no uncertain terms that she was through with him again and had no intent whatsoever of letting the third time be the charm.

"You don't understand," she had said, almost uncomfortably. "Always you don't understand, Captain. This lift stops on my requested deck. I get off to meet the company reps. You stay in the car. The door closes, and we do not see each other again. Ever. *Now* do you understand?"

"You all right?" Chiba asked.

"Give me a minute," May said.

Chiba took over the yoke and made a long ellipse around the damaged luxury liner. May stared hard out the window, marveling at how much the *Hergest Ridge* had recovered since the last time he had seen it.

That's going to be the story of the *Angel's Luck* if I can pull this off, he thought. Just one more little favor, one more little act of goodwill, while you're at the peak of your career. Then I'll be gone, I really will be done with you . . .

"Look over there," Chiba said.

May followed the salvor's gesture to a sleek, aerodynamically shaped craft that was streaking toward the ad hoc repair platform. "A Surface Direct Transport."

"Doing Sub 10 if it's doing a meter," Chiba said. "That's no ordinary SDT, either. Looks like there's some important company arriving ahead of us."

What am I going to be interrupting now, Maggie? May thought. Is the Prime Minister of Council going to drape the Medal of Respect around your neck? Am I going to step in for a muddle this time, as well? Will the higher-ups look down their noses while I plead my case for some farm boy who slipped through the cracks of the system's penal code?

He could see the look on her face when she saw him. He could read the first words out of her lips just by looking in her eyes.

"Yes," May whispered. "I understand now." He looked over at his acting copilot. "Take us back to the *Angel's Luck*."

"What?" Chiba asked.

"I didn't understand before, but now I do. She's got a life—she's had one that's totally apart from me. When she pulled in the *Angel's Luck* it was back to the old days of my ideas and her giving and giving, and it nearly cost her. It damn near cost her, Peter."

"But this is an exception. She can really help you—"

"She's always been able to help me. And it's just occurred to me that I've never done anything to help her."

"Don't kid yourself, May. You've done plenty."

"Only when it served my own purposes. Now it's time I served one of hers." He looked down at the control yoke. "Are you going to take us back, or am I going to have to do it?"

"What about Duke?"

"You've got brains, I've got brains, Vonn's got brains. We've all got brains. Maybe it's time we started to use them."

Chiba shrugged. "You're the boss." He leaned in on the yoke and the *Hergest Ridge* swayed out of sight.

"Don't look so disgusted," May said. "You'd do the same for Roz."

"But I love Roz."

"And I still love Maggie. I swear it by the Fifth Region." Chiba nodded.

"Any more comments?"

"One," Chiba said. "What's the point of such a magnanimous gesture if she's not even aware that you've done it?"

May clapped the salvor on the back. "That's exactly the point, Peter, my friend. That's exactly the point."

5

Bleary-eyed, Burris pulled his car onto the plaza in front of the Essence building and cut the headlights. A guard was there to meet him with a word of rebuke, but when Burris flashed his card, the guard retreated and let him through the door. Dismissing the invitation of an escort, Burris went straight through the darkened halls to the laboratory, where he found a haggard-looking Melrose standing behind one of the young staff assistants.

"This had better be good," Burris growled. "Bringing me here at this hour."

"She got me out of bed, too," Melrose said. "I think you'll find this interesting." He extended his hand to the assistant in the control chair. "Dinah?"

The woman punched a view of Duke's cell onto the main screen. "This is a distinctly anomalous behavior," she explained, pointing to the screen. "Notice how the subject is sitting on the bed in a cross-legged position. There's a distinct hunch to the shoulders, and the eyes are darting about the room in concentration."

Burris looked at the scene for a moment and grunted. "You brought me all the way back here for this. What the hell's he trying to do, chew a hole in his wrist?"

"I suspect he's gnawing at the fabric on the sleeve of his suit," Melrose said. "If you'll watch, he's about to—"

The left arm came away from Duke's mouth, and with thumb and forefinger, he picked at a spot on the sleeve.

"I thought you were giving him enough to eat," Burris scoffed.

"I suspect that he's trying to gather thread to use in an escape attempt," Dinah said.

"Fine. Cut his food off. Make him eat his suit. Dammit, Vincent, can't you make that kind of executive decision without me?"

"That's not the reason you were brought here," Melrose said.

"We believe the behavior we're seeing is not inherent to the personality of William Wesley Arbor," Dinah said. "This is not the typical pattern of concentration that we have cataloged him as using."

Burris clucked his tongue. "And because we've had him here a few days already, we, of course, know *all* about him."

"Not all about him," Dinah said, unaffected by Burris's sarcasm. "But we do have a nice catalog of behaviors built up." She leaned forward and began to work the control panel. The main screen erupted into static and then changed to another view of Duke. He had unzipped the top half of his jumpsuit and had tied the sleeves at the waist, walking bare-chested around the cell.

"My time is money," Burris complained.

"Watch this," Melrose said. "This is significant."

While they watched, Duke lowered to his knees before the toilet and plunged his right hand into the water. Looking away, he reached down into the water evacuation port as if feeling for something.

Dinah froze the scene. "This is typical of Arbor's concentrating behavior. Not looking at the subject in question, eyes closed as if he's seeing another image, one that is coming from the tips of his fingers. We have this documented a number of times when he was checking out different parts of his room."

Burris yawned very deliberately, without covering his mouth. "You'll forgive me if I don't get as excited as you are about this."

"That was always your problem," Melrose said. "You never had your father's curiosity."

"Father didn't have my money, either. It was an even trade, I'd say."

"Dinah, show Mr. Burris the other loop."

"I don't know if I can stand the excitement, Vince."

"Quiet," Melrose said. "You want confirmation of the viability of the distillations? We'll lay it out for you."

The image on the screen was again Duke, now fully wearing the jumpsuit. He was pacing in slow circles around the cell.

"I don't suppose that this is typical of his boredom behavior," Burris said.

Dinah thumbed a switch and sound filled the room: Duke's footfalls, and then his voice.

"Eric?"

He continued the pacing, looking around into each corner of the cell.

"Eric, where are you?"

Then he stood for a moment, arms at his side, eyes closed in concentration. It looked almost deliberately posed for the camera.

"Dammit, Eric." He scowled.

Melrose reached down and stabbed a button. The scene froze. "There it is. Three times. He distinctly said 'Eric.' As in Eric *Dickson*."

Burris shook his head.

"It's about damn time you learned to think," Melrose said, punching buttons angrily. The scene lurched forward at high speed, and the image of Duke did a frantic gavotte around the inside of the cell. All at once Duke's arms came into play, giving the illusion that he was trying to flap his way to freedom. Melrose punched it down to normal speed. "Now watch," he ordered.

Duke turned slowly on his heels. "Then you're naive, or you've ceased caring. Do you really think that he's going to take no for an answer? I don't believe for a minute that he's going to sit here and wait for me to change my mind. This is a laboratory, Eric, and we're the experiment."

As Burris watched, Duke's features changed. In an instant his eyes lost their anger and glazed over with complacency.

"You're the experiment, Duke." The sound that came out was Duke's voice, but it was different somehow. It sounded lower, but not as if the subject was consciously trying to make a different voice. It sounded unnervingly natural. "Me, I've already been the experiment once. It's not all it's cracked up to be."

Fire sprang back into Duke's eyes, and he whirled in the empty cell. "I don't care. I want to be out of here, and I want to be—"

"Say it." The other voice was back, and it brought gooseflesh to Burris's arms. "Go ahead and say it. You want to be rid of me."

His mouth falling open in awe, Burris reached over and froze the scene. He blinked numbly at the screen, and slowly the stare of disbelief became a smile. "It's him. It's Eric Dickson. By the power of the Fifth Region . . ." He unfroze the scene.

"I want to lead a normal life again," Duke said.

"Sure." The Dickson voice laughed. "You want to go home to those two little pixies you abandoned. They're not even pretty, Duke. But maybe—"

Burris froze the scene again, his features becoming animated. "Tell me about this."

"It's really quite simple, if you think about it," Melrose said. "Each of us grows up in a unique culture and unique environment. We all learn to speak, but we all use our vocal cords in different ways. Some people are gifted mimics—"

"But that wasn't a funny voice that Arbor was doing, was it? That was—"

"Eric Dickson," Dinah said. "And he has that gravelly sound because he's using Duke's vocal cords—"

"In a way they've never been used before." Burris threw back his head and laughed. "Then that person in there with the unrecorded concentrating behavior isn't William Wesley Arbor. It's—" He paused for a moment and blinked, as if it was too unreal to believe. "Eric Dickson, back from the dead."

"As near as we can interpret," Dinah said.

"Perhaps not his soul," Melrose corrected. "But certainly his memories."

"Damned if it isn't his soul," Burris said. He found the small screen where the real-time image of the cell was. "Look, that's him, right damn there, and you're telling me that's just *memory*?"

"Memory and instinct," Dinah said. "It appears that contemporary estimation of their power has been somewhat underestimated. This type of manifestation—"

"That's one hell of a manifestation," Burris shouted.

"At this point, we're unsure of what Mr. Arbor's current mental state is. It could be that he's relying on Dickson's memories of how to accomplish the task of unraveling the sleeve, and is employing the same instincts."

"Then what about that conversation?" Burris demanded, pointing at the big screen. "There's something going on inside of that kid's head that we hadn't counted on."

"It's only speculation at this time," Melrose said, "but it is possible that under specific conditions, the host personality could be suppressed enough for the memory and instinct to make use of the host body."

"Then that could very well be Eric Dickson sitting in there."

"His memory. We have no real way of knowing at this point—"

"Like hell we don't." Burris started toward the small door.

"We need to gather more data," Dinah said.

"That's exactly what we're going to do. Come with me, Vince. We're going to go talk to him."

"*Talk* to him?" Melrose took a halting step toward the opening door. "But what—"

"You're the scientist," Burris challenged. "You'll think of something." He clapped Melrose on the back and ushered him to the door.

Melrose paused for a moment, then turned back toward Dinah, wagging a finger uncertainly. "Put the Pacification Jets on standby," he told her. "And if anything starts to go wrong, flood the room with Restcure."

"Nothing's going to happen," Burris urged as the door closed behind them. "If everything is going according to what you've told me, it'll be like going in and talking to the man."

"Talking to his memories," Melrose corrected. "There's going to be a distinct difference. Remember, he was one of the first ones processed, and even then it was a decade and a half before Series One was complete. What we're going to be conversing with are the memories of someone who has missed a quarter century of human history."

"Yeah," Burris said, anxious to get on with it. "I'll try not to let slip that the guy who wrote all of those Stalwart White adventure vids is dead."

"It's more serious than that," Melrose said, stopping outside of Duke's cell. "Eric Dickson was a pilot during the Arcolian War. We should be careful not to mention anything about the Accord."

"Oh, bullshit," Burris said. "He was alive at the time the Accord was signed. Don't give me that."

"Still," Melrose cautioned. "You shouldn't mention the recent arrival of the Arcolian delegation to this world. He came from a time when they were the Most Deadly Enemy—"

"Yeah. Right." Burris carded open the cell door. "Like it's going to come up during the course of a normal conversation."

Their prisoner was still sitting on the bed, gnawing on his sleeve. He paused on hearing the door open, then slowly turned to regard the two men with cold eyes.

"What's wrong?" Burris asked. "Isn't Vincent feeding you enough?"

Without looking at the worried sleeve, Duke lowered his arm and smiled. "This is really strange," he said in a coarse voice. "I *know* you two."

Before Burris could open his mouth again, Melrose took a step forward. "Why is that so strange?"

There came a toothy grin. "Because I could swear I've never met either one of you before."

Melrose and Burris exchanged glances.

"A party, perhaps?" Melrose continued. "Perhaps we saw each other but never met."

Duke closed his eyes. "Nope. I can safely say not that. The last party I was at—" He stopped cold and furrowed his brow.

Burris started to step forward, but Melrose stretched out his arm to hold him back.

"Tell us about it."

Duke opened his eyes. "It was a bust. I got drunk and hit some guy who thought he was a big shot and got thrown out on my ass. And then . . ."

He broke out in gooseflesh, and his head twitched in a motion that was half shiver and half shake. "There was some trouble. Anyway, I think I can safely say that we never met there. Like I said, a bust."

Burris nudged Melrose's arm aside and finished his step forward. "Perhaps if we introduced ourselves. Does the name Burris ring a bell with you?"

The answer was a sustained laugh.

Burris smiled. "Is that a yes?"

"Maxie Burris?"

"Maximillian. Yes."

"Boy, did I ever put one over on him. Hell, he put one over on himself. He came to me with some loony frigging story about how he wanted my brain after I was dead because he was going to make some kind of medicine out of it. Something about helping the mentally deficient."

Melrose nodded. "That was his original intent, yes."

More chuckling. "Yeah, he was a crazy old loon. He gave me—get this, now—twenty-five thousand credits for what he called 'the postmortem rights' to my brain. And I had to go in and have this little biochip implanted in the back of my neck, supposedly so they'd know when I was dying, so they'd know when to come and collect me. I don't know what ever happened to him. Gave up on me, I guess. Probably doesn't want me now. Hell, that money he gave me went to good use pickling my brain." Duke's eyes became distant, and the hard stare softened. "I had a lot of stuff I wanted to forget. But dammit, that's all I'm able to remember right now."

The scientist waited a moment, then extended his hand. "I am Vincent Melrose."

Duke reached up to shake, but the hand came into an accusing point. "*Doctor* Vincent Melrose? He's the guy who put that tracking chip in my head." He absentmindedly rubbed the back of his neck in search of it. "Where the hell is it?" He shrugged. "But you *can't* be Dr. Melrose. He was a young guy, and it wasn't that long ago."

"Times change," Melrose said.

Duke turned to Burris. "And sure as hell you aren't Maxie Burris. You could be his son, but the one I did meet was this ten-year-old monster with a *real* shitty attitude. Wanted to meet me so bad I thought he'd piss his pants, and then the little bastard bit me on the elbow." He rolled his sleeve back and pointed to his elbow in testimony. "I still have the—" He looked down and rubbed at the smooth skin. "Where the hell is that scar?"

"It doesn't matter," Burris said quickly. "What does is that the doctor and I would like you to join us in a little chat. You don't mind, do you?"

"Why should I? This is your soiree." He waved his hand about the cell in an amicable gesture. "Have a seat."

Burris and Melrose both looked at the single stool at the same time. Melrose did not budge, so Burris nodded, a signal for the older man to take the seat.

"And yourself?" Burris asked. When it brought a confused look from Duke, he elaborated. "Your name. We've introduced ourselves, after all."

"You already know who I am. I suspect that's why you're here." Duke began to nip at the sleeve of the jumpsuit once more.

"I really wish you wouldn't do that," Burris said. "Those do cost money."

Duke looked at Burris and, with a pop of lips and tongue, spat a small bit of string to the floor. "Then you've been screwed. These things don't unravel worth a damn."

Burris shrugged. "My mistake. We don't have much use for those here."

"Why are you being so polite to me?" Duke did not look up, busying himself with scratching at his suit with a thumbnail. "I thought threats and intimidation were more your style."

Melrose shifted forward on his seat. "Excuse me, Mr. Dickson, but if I may point out something here . . . you claim to have not met us before—"

Duke hooked his thumb at Burris. "Him. You and I have met."

Melrose nodded. "Yet you speak with authority on your perceptions of Mr. Burris's personality. Can you explain why this is?"

Duke blinked for a moment. "No. I can't explain it."

"Can you elaborate on why you have such a negative impression of Mr. Burris?"

Duke laughed. He caught a bit of string between the nails of his thumb and forefinger and started to pull. The outer rim of the sleeve began to fray. A good twenty centimeters came loose before it cut short. He swore. "I don't have a very good first impression of him."

"I merely pointed out that you're making a ruin of my company's property."

Duke shook his head. "The first impression I have is of your being an egotistical thief. Somebody worked very hard to bring you something, and you took it out of their hands without so much as a word of thanks." He put the length of string aside and rubbed the bridge of his nose. "Damn. This is giving me a headache."

"What else do you feel about Mr. Burris?"

"That he's being a big, fat toady. That he's standing here sucking up to me and talking nice because of who I am—who I was, rather, when I know for a fact that he's bullied others who have occupied this room."

"Which—" Burris started, but he saw Melrose hold up his hand. He nodded, and the scientist took over.

"Who you were, Mr. Dickson? What do you mean by that?"

Duke picked up the string, wrapping a bit around each index finger. He stretched it out taut and then snapped it repeatedly, testing its tensile strength. "I'm not even going to pretend to be humble. I was a pilot, and a damned good one at that. You've heard of the relief column that went into Bering's Gate? I *led* that sucker. I've got a whole chest full of medals stored up in a cigar box somewhere. The word is *hero* to you."

"I see." Melrose nodded to Burris.

"What about the others you mentioned?" Burris asked. "You said you have knowledge of others in this cell?"

"Indeed." Duke looked up, his expression one of distaste. "Why is it I don't care for that word all of a sudden?" He shrugged again. "What the hell. What I'm saying is that I know you've kept at least one person in this cell against his will, and you made this big show of trying to intimidate him. Something to do with—" His face became pale, and he swayed.

"Something wrong?" Melrose asked, rising.

"Hell of a note. It's like I get to certain memories and there's this hazy gray wall that I can't get through." He shook his head and his color returned. "Anyway, what you don't know is that this friend of mine has faced a hell of a lot worse than you in the last few months, and he's come out of it in damned fine shape, considering his background."

"What's this friend's name?" Burris asked.

Duke shook his head. "I'm not playing that game. We all know who we're talking about."

"Let's keep it neutral, then," Melrose said. "Tell us how you met."

Duke closed his eyes and rubbed his head. "Strange. The first I remember of him, I was trying to show him how to overload the engines of a ship so they'd produce a nice explosion."

"You were deliberately trying to destroy the ship?"

"No." Duke laughed. "It was a trick I came up with while we were getting our asses chased out of the Bering's Gate system after the relief column went in. This really hot Arcolian destroyer was chasing us, picking off members of the sortie one by one. They got a lock on three of us, and they thinned it down to me. The bastards wanted to catch me, that must have been what it was. I gave them a run for their money. I went shifting in and out of phase until my engine reactor was a nice little runaway hydrogen bomb, and then I ejected it right into their path. It let the others get away, and a couple of them doubled back after the explosion and pulled me in."

"You were trying to teach him this maneuver?"

Duke nodded, then busied himself with working another string out of the garment's sleeve.

"Mr. Dickson," Melrose said tentatively, "would you excuse Mr. Burris and me for a moment? I have something I'd like to discuss with him."

Five centimeters of string came out of the sleeve and then snapped. "If you have anything to say about me, you can say it in front of me."

Burris shrugged. "It doesn't bother me."

"I don't think," Melrose said, scowling at Burris, "that Mr. Dickson would appreciate the delicate medical condition that is involved in our discussion."

"It's my condition, isn't it?" Duke asked.

"He does have a point," Burris agreed.

"I don't think," Melrose said through clenched teeth, "that my esteemed colleague realizes the seriousness of this condition. Before I can make a final diagnosis, I need to confer with him."

"I don't like that idea," Duke said.

"Vincent," Burris said patronizingly. "You're making our guest unhappy."

"I'm not your guest, I'm your prisoner," Duke said. "And I was already unhappy and angry. What I'm getting is pissed off." He broke off another string at twenty centimeters, then patted around the surface of the bunk in search of the first one.

"This is very important what we're seeing here, and I don't want to spoil the effect." Melrose looked to the camera, hoping that through the link, Dinah could give some kind of support. "This needs to be studied in depth. It's an aspect to the distillations that we hadn't yet reckoned on."

"I'm not some damned lab animal," Duke complained.

"I'm seeing your point, Doctor," Burris said. "Mr. Dickson, if you would excuse us."

"No," Duke said, rising. "I most certainly will not."

Burris stood his ground. "You don't have a hell of a lot of choice."

Melrose stepped between the two of them. "If you will both listen to reason, I'm sure there's a way that this can be settled—"

"As far as I'm concerned," Duke said loudly, "this is a fucked proposition. You bring us in here and you think you can experiment on me and experiment on Duke as you please. Well, there are some things that you haven't taken into account."

"Duke's accomplices have been dealt with," Burris said calmly. "They're no concern of yours."

"That's what you think. I've got memories of them, although I'm damned if I can explain where they come from—"

"This is upsetting you both," Melrose said, pushing Burris toward the door. "I suggest we continue this at another time."

"No," Duke shouted. "This will *not* continue, not ever. I am not going to cooperate."

"See what you've started?" Burris snapped at Melrose. "Now we have to negotiate with *both* of them."

"No, you won't," Duke said. "You have to negotiate with one person. Me. I am the sole acting agent for both myself and William Wesley Arbor."

"We've already been talking to Duke—" Burris started.

Melrose grabbed Burris's arm. "We have to terminate this conversation immediately," he said in an urgent whisper.

Burris shook the scientist's hand loose.

"There's some kind of transition going on in the subject's mind," Melrose continued quietly. "When we came in he had no recollection of us and seemed ignorant of our intent. In the last few minutes he's come to know us very well—or so he believes—and he's become very streetwise. There seems to be some kind of inner turmoil. Perhaps Dickson is tapping information from Arbor's memories."

Burris looked down into Melrose's eyes. "I thought we were dealing with a manifestation of a memory here."

"So I thought. Either your father's procedure for mapping the brain and extracting memory was off the mark, or else we're seeing some kind of synergistic reaction that we hadn't anticipated."

"Memory learning from memory?"

"Exactly. And this has to be studied—"

"Do you mind?" Duke said loudly. "This is rude as hell. The whole reason you stayed is to keep me in the conversation."

Burris cleared his throat. "Dr. Melrose was merely afraid that I was agitating you."

"I was agitated the moment I realized I was cooped up in this shitty cell of yours. As far as negotiating with Duke, he's an all right kid, but he doesn't know what he's doing. He's hoping to buy enough time for his friends to figure out that he's here and come swooping in to save him. He thinks it's just a matter of time before they do something about it." He put the back of his hand against Melrose's chest and gently nudged him aside, then stepped up to Burris. "You and I both know differently, don't we?"

"What do you mean?" Burris said coldly.

"You and I both know that they've already figured you've got him. You and I both know that it's only a matter of hours until something happens. You and I both know that someone isn't going to live long enough to be found on these premises."

"Not exactly."

"Well, there are all sorts of ways to keep from getting caught with the meat in your mouth, aren't there? And you're a creative sort, aren't you, Burris? I'm sure you've got something planned."

"The operational question," Burris said, standing his ground, "is what are your plans?"

"I'm certain that my plans don't matter," Duke said. "You've got me bottled up in here, and even with this inadequate body I could leave the both of you dead, though I'd never make it out of the building alive. You've got me cold, and damn what I do, you're going to have what you want out of us." He started to laugh.

"I'm intrigued," Burris said. "You seem to find this situation quite amusing."

"Amusing, no." The cold look was back. Melrose was shocked by the way the face could change so quickly. Was that all Dickson's personality, or was it a vestige of Duke struggling to get out? "Funnier than hell. That's what it is." There came a wry grin.

"I'll bite," Burris said. "What do you know that we don't?"

"You're going to waste all of your time on Duke and me, and you're going to lose the real prize. That's what we know."

"This conversation has gone far enough," Melrose warned. "We'll come back."

"One more thing," Burris said, face burning.

"He's manipulating you," Melrose said, sotto voce.

Duke laughed, long and rich.

"*Damn you!*" Burris lurched forward, but Melrose caught him around the waist.

"Pseudoase," Duke said, very much amused. "Is that the best your old man could do?"

"That wasn't my father," Burris said defensively. He calmed, and Melrose dropped his grip. "That was Loevell."

"Doesn't matter. It was a ridiculous notion."

"Pseudoase was brilliant!" Burris shouted. "It kept the distilled knowledge from being destroyed by the body's immune system and facilitated its absorption into the brain—"

"Don't you see what he's doing to you?" Melrose demanded.

"Too late. I've already done it." Duke shook his head. "When you think about it, Pseudoase is such a poor substitute for the real thing."

"What real thing?"

"The genetic code."

The tension suddenly left Burris's body, and he shared the laugh with his antagonist. "Oh, that's a good one. That's really terrific. The big pilot who barely got through the final form of school is going to tell me all about it."

"I got it from Duke."

"A farm boy from a class C—"

"Duke has a rudimentary knowledge of genetics, although he couldn't compete with a college student specializing in the subject. He has made a very valid process of reasoning for the improvement of your distillations. Using genetic engineering, the protein chains could be restructured to retain their stored knowledge while overcoming the main stumbling block. I don't completely understand that part of it. Something about tissue cross-matching and blood types."

"A valid point," Melrose said.

"The only difficult thing is cracking the code." Burris's voice was rising. "Nice try, fly-boy, but the joke's over. Better men than Loevell have tried cracking that one for centuries and have nothing to show for it but blown blood vessels. Unless your friend has the genetic code tucked in his pocket, we can forget about continuing this conversation." With a disgusted shake of his head, he turned toward the door.

"The Arcolians have the genetic code," Duke said.

There was sudden silence.

"The different forms, the A's, B's, and C's—they're not different breeds of the same animal. They were specifically engineered for a specific task. The E-forms, for example, were arranged specifically to interact with us."

Burris slowly turned, his face pale. "You can't prove that."

"Duke's plans were to return to his home world, but he was thinking that he might try and get to Arcolia to see if they could use their knowledge to . . . *undo* me from his brain."

"You're dreamers, both of you. There's no way—"

"There's an Arcolian called misterbob who is part of the delegation that arrived here a few weeks ago. He split off from them to study us and our native interactions."

"You don't realize what you're saying. The protection—"

"But there is no protection, Mr. Burris. He's traveling with a merchant and his crew. The merchant happens to be Captain James May."

Burris looked at Melrose. Melrose shook his head, stepped back, and popped the seal on the door.

"Bring in the dogs if you don't believe me. Better yet, send a representative over to the Arcolian Embassy complex under a pretense and ask to speak with Ambassador misterbob. I'm sure you'll find him unavailable with no set time for his return."

Melrose held his hand out toward Duke. Duke regarded the doctor with the pilot's eyes, then reached out and shook.

"You're an amazing man, Mr. Dickson. I've never met anyone quite like you, past or present." Melrose turned and, putting his hand on Burris's back, began to usher him out the door. "We'll continue this discussion later."

Duke tipped his fingers to his brow in the salute of respect. "For you, Dr. Melrose."

"Fascinating," Melrose said as the door sealed behind them. "Absolutely fascinating. The interaction of the memories, the evolution of memory and personality right before our very eyes. This data will be worth a fortune to us."

Burris was silent. For once, the prospect of profit had not impressed him.

"And his manipulative talent is fascinating," Melrose said, trying to boost the spirits of his superior. "He read you and had you right where he wanted you. I don't know what kind of intuitive insight he had, but in the space of a few short minutes he thought he'd stripped you of any pride you had in this company."

Burris stopped at the door to the observation room. "That wasn't intuition," he said numbly. "He knew it. That son of a bitch destroyed me, Vincent, and I couldn't do a thing to stop him."

Melrose gave him a patronizing pat. "Let me pull up some of the old records we have on Dickson. He was that kind of a guy, used to having his own way, and he was skilled at getting it. You'll see."

"I was the one that bit him," Burris admitted. "He even knew that. I barely remember it, yet he had me pegged. All I remember is that Dad promised I would meet this hero and he introduced me to this—this human being." He reflected on that as he entered the observation room. "But human beings make mistakes, and Dickson's made a serious one. He's improved things for his captors while getting nothing in return."

"I wouldn't be so sure of that," Melrose warned.

"What's going on?" Dinah asked.

"I'll explain it later," Melrose said.

"If the Arcolians have the genetic code," Burris said, "then I'll get it. And you, Vincent, are going to go with me to the board of directors, and we'll see how they react when they see what their exiled son has brought them. This'll truly bring Essence back out into the forefront, and we're going to stay there. They won't be able to ignore me any longer. I'll have my father's legacy back."

"Aren't you forgetting something?" Melrose asked. "This entire dream of yours hinges on the fact that you have access to an Arcolian and that—"

"But I do have access to an Arcolian," Burris said. "Captain James May has one."

"You believed what Dickson was saying?"

"I have no reason not to. I'll have my people check the facts, and then I'll have my Arcolian."

"These are intelligent beings you're talking about. You can't go treating them like property."

"I'll do as I please," Burris informed him. "As it happens, I have someone who is very dear to James May. We'll see just how far their friendship will go."

"We still have to study the effects of the distillations—"

"Forget the distillations," Burris growled. "With the genetic code at our fingertips, nobody will care about them."

Melrose bravely pointed a finger as Burris left the observation room. "You'd better be certain that you're not hanging this dream of yours on nothing, and that Dickson wasn't handing you a line."

"I'm a step ahead of you, Vincent." Burris laughed and closed the door.

"Am I hearing things?" Dinah asked. "What's all this business about the genetic code and getting an Arcolian?"

Melrose hurried around the perimeter of the room, checking monitors and entering new information into the system. "You'd better put a full scan on that boy in the cell. The time we have to gather data is going to be extremely limited."

"What's going on? Is that really Eric Dickson in there?"

"It's either him, or someone who has absorbed more than the basic memory that Max and I were distilling. It's someone who has absorbed the wit and wiles of a very clever man. Either way, the distillations seem to work better than we had hoped."

"What's going on with Mr. Burris?"

"Our friend in there has learned to manipulate him. And in return, Burris is going to try and manipulate Captain May, who is very concerned over our friend."

"You think Arbor has engineered some kind of setup?"

"I don't know who is engineering what," Melrose said. "All I know is that this is going to be one hell of an interesting conflict. Here, let me swap out those data-blocks for you."

6

The words on the wall of the meeting room said MARGARET O'HEARN. May gave them a wistful look, picked up a fat static pen that was lying on the table, and drew a large X through them.

"You still didn't tell me what she said," Vonn grumbled.

"It's not important," Peter Chiba said, coming to May's defense. "Suffice it to say that she's busy with problems of her own."

May gave the salvor a look of gratitude, then marked out another pair of words: LEGAL ACTION. "I think we can rule this out as too slow."

"I think you can strike the idea of going to the media," Roz said.

"But it's a beautiful idea," Vonn said. "It's fast, and it'll bring down a ton of shit on Burris's head. After what he's done to us, he deserves that."

"Nobody would believe what we done," Winters said.

"There are plenty of media people who would," Vonn countered.

"I don't doubt that," Roz answered, "but I also know that the ensuing publicity would make us targets of the Yueh-sheng again. That defeats the whole purpose of freeing Duke. What good is it to get out of jail and be hunted by someone else?"

May scribbled out GO TO MEDIA.

"Indeed," misterbob said, clicking its fingers together with a steady beat. "Our list of options has quickly narrowed. I understood that it would come down to this, jamesohjames."

May got the distinct impression that the ambassador was pleased. He turned and looked at the remaining three options:

POLITICAL INFLUENCE, PHEROMONAL INFLUENCE, and MILI-TARY STRIKE, which had been added at Vonn's insistence.

"I think we can rule this out," May said, putting a line through the political option.

"It is the easiest option," misterbob said. "By going through our embassy we can have misterduke declared a political pris-oner, and this company would be compelled to release him on what you call humanitarian grounds." The creature's head made its characteristic nod. "A most fascinating concept."

"It's too risky," May said. "For one, it'll bring publicity, just as certainly as going to the media."

"But we would not explain why misterduke was to be freed."

"We wouldn't have to," Vonn said. "That bastard Burris would do it himself. It might ruin his ideal of having the phial legend live on, but it would certainly insure that we'd be found by the *Yueh-sheng*."

"Not so much that," Roz said, "but there are political as-pects that we haven't even considered. For one, misterbob is supposed to be traveling with us incognito. There are people around who would make targets of us—or worse yet of mister-bob—because of that."

"You flatter me too much," misterbob purred, "putting such a value on The Life in me."

"The Life in anyone is of great value," May said.

"If word got out—and it certainly would," Roz continued, "that an Arcolian was intervening against the Essence Corpo-ration, every anti-Accord kook in the known galaxy would come out in their support."

"Burris would love that," Winters said.

"Similarly," May said, striking out PHEROMONAL INFLU-ENCE, "this poses an equal risk to misterbob. Besides, we'd never get near the Essence Company to pull it off. And politics is involved. For misterbob to do that would violate the trust our people have put in the Accord. We've got a generation coming up that thinks the Arcolians are wonderful creatures and that the days of pheromonal attack are over. If word got out, the damage would be irreparable."

"The Sapient A-forms have such fragile minds," misterbob observed. "I have accumulated such a great list of things which damage them."

"You've only scratched the surface, Ambassador," Roz said.

"The key here it to step lightly, to be low-key and subtle," May said. He turned to the wall and saw the last remaining option: MILITARY STRIKE. He shook his head in dismay. "Did I somehow manage to undo everything I've just said?"

"It makes sense, May," Vonn said, rising. "It's the only option that works fast with the minimum amount of danger."

"Have you listened to yourself?" May asked. "You're not making a lot of sense."

"Sure, there's the initial risk of violence," Vonn said, "but that's all there's going to be. That's what's so beautiful about the situation. That bastard Burris might want our necks, but is he going to go to the press and admit to having an illegal prisoner? Never mind the fact that this prisoner was taken because he had knowledge from their fabled lost Series One Distillations. Their hands would be tied."

"He could still go to the *Yueh-sheng*," Peter Chiba said.

Vonn shook his head. "I don't think he'd do that, and I don't think the *Yueh-sheng* would be interested in keeping the phials again."

"I don't want that to happen," Winters said, concerned.

"Aren't we forgetting something?" May asked. "I seem to have made the point that a military strike was not what Duke would want."

"Hell," Vonn said, waving his hands in the air. "Right now, Duke probably doesn't know *what* he wants. If he's capable of wanting anything, it would be to get the hell out of there."

"I have no argument with that."

"That's why military action makes sense."

"We don't have time to recruit your friends," May said. "And we'd never get near the place if we did. I'm sure that Burris has advance guards all over the place."

"So what?" Vonn protested. "We don't need more people. Those of us in this room could do it. I've been thinking about this, May. There should be room enough in the *Reconnez Cherie*'s cargo space for that rented van. You and Chiba can set down right on the plaza in front of the Essence building. Roz can stay on the ship to guard it—"

"I *beg* your pardon," Roz said.

"If you want," Vonn said, holding his hands up defensively. "The rest of us pile in the van with weapons and drive it through those pretty glass doors."

"Count me out already," Chiba said.

"So we'll rearrange things to make everybody happy," Vonn snapped. "I thought we were doing this for a friend."

"Go on," May said.

"You can't be serious," Roz said.

"He deserves to be heard."

Vonn gave the merchant a courteous nod. "We pull the van right into that big lobby and go in shooting. Most of those guards are rentals anyway, and they're carrying nothing but popguns. We could go in for Duke, and kick their ass while we're at it."

"Nice idea," Chiba said, "but how do you find your way around the building once you're inside?"

"If I may interject," misterbob said. "I believe that look-cheech could track the kickass participants with remaining computer systems of the *angelsluck*. With proper access codes she could produce floor layouts of the building complex."

May raised his eyebrows. "Indeed, Ambassador?"

The Arcolian's arms rose in an approximation of a shrug. "I realize that this poses inherent dangers to the personal possession of The Life, but I understand that such a sacrifice is considered to be noble among the Sapient A-forms."

"You're not going to sacrifice—"

"Indeed, jamesohjames. I believe that mistervonn has thought this out well. I am inclined to agree that military strike is a viable option. This action of kickass is something I desire to see firsthand."

"Yeah," Winters chimed. "I promised him that."

"Supposing we did this," Peter Chiba said. "What would you need in the line of weapons?"

"We'd need to make sure that we have the rented guards outgunned," Vonn said. "To be safe, I'd want an even split between machine pistols and assault rifles, or better yet a couple of autoshots."

May nodded. "That's not unreasonable."

"I think Winters should take a grenade launcher or an anti-tank rifle in case we have any heavy doors to deal with. And we'll need Danteum Gel, twenty-five meters of det cord, and at least one person should be lugging a VX-1200."

"Yeah!" Winters said, shaking a fist in the air.

"No!" May shouted, then waited until everyone was looking at him. "In case you hadn't noticed, you're making this into a full-scale assault, the likes of which this planet has never seen."

"There's no such thing as a low-key military strike," Vonn pouted.

"Then how about keeping it down to a covert action?" May gave a sarcastic smile, then turned and scribbled until he had obliterated the last option.

"You're writing off Duke, you know that, don't you?" Vonn said.

"That's a matter of opinion, Vonn. There's a way to do it, I'm sure. We just haven't thought of it yet."

"They're probably dissecting him right now," Vonn said.

"Will you stop it!" May shouted. He looked at the faces of the others. All save misterbob were showing signs of tiring. "Okay," he said. "Let's give it a break. Everyone's got things to do for themselves—let's take an hour."

"Another hour that—"

"Enough," May threatened.

The group in the conference room began to dissolve. Vonn was the first out, muttering under his breath about being hamstrung by indecisiveness. Winters stopped on the way out, patted May on the back, and offered his obedience to whatever the merchant decided. Roz and Peter Chiba hurried out together, anxious to see if anyone was trying to contact them for tug service. May quietly pushed a button on the table in front of him, and the scribbling on the wall slid off and formed a pile of dust on the floor. Looking up, he saw the Arcolian watching him, patiently perched in a corner. May pulled out one of the chairs and wearily flopped into it.

"Et tu, misterbob?"

The Arcolian cocked its head at the merchant. "Indeed, jamesohjames?"

May shook his head. "Sorry about that. It's a literary allusion."

"Indeed. So many fascinating behaviors. This tendency to relate one's life to that which has been recorded in past as fiction—"

"But this wasn't fiction." May raised his finger as if to try to explain it but ended up shaking his head. "Yeah. I see what you mean."

On each hand, misterbob interlocked his fingers. "jamesohjames, there is something I have been meaning to discuss with you. Your insistence in not involving me with your attempt to free misterduke is most distressing. If I understand this correctly, you value The Life in him above even that of yourself, which I scent in your consideration of doing all in your power to free him."

"True," May said. "Although I don't seem to have a hell of a lot of power right now."

"This is not true," misterbob said. "You do have power,

jamesohjames, in great amounts of hell. Perhaps you cannot yet scent this.''

"Perhaps."

"I do not wish to make you tedious with accounts of explaining your behaviors to me, but there are some I find I cannot ignore. There is this scent I have that you made no contact with margarethearn. Is this accurate?''

May nodded. "I chickened out. Uh . . ." He waved his hands in the air. "I made a last-minute decision that consulting with her would not be in her best interests.''

"Indeed, you do not think that she would show concern over the state that misterduke is in?''

"I'm sure she would, misterbob," the merchant said. "And I'm sure that even though she said that she never wanted to see me again, that she would help if I asked her to. But I can't do that to her. She endangered her career for us on the blockade run, and it's something I can never repay. I can't ask her to do something else which I cannot repay.''

"Do I scent a longing in you?''

"Of course you do. And it's not because of something that Maggie could do for me. It's a longing for what Maggie and I would do when we were together.''

"You must be truthful with me, jamesohjames. Was I wrong to submit you to pheromonal restoration of the bond which once existed between the two of you?''

May shook his head. "No. And I'm sure that Maggie would agree. That moment where you had us holding each other on the floor of the brig? I'll treasure that forever.''

"Yet," misterbob said, "you elect to avoid further contact with margarethearn.''

"Because I love her.''

"You must explain this process to me," misterbob observed. "This ritual breaking of bonds for the alleged mutual good in spite of existing emotional ties . . .''

"It's not always like Maggie and me," May said. "Most divorces are ugly or out of convenience. I'm sure you can scent it, misterbob. I still love her.''

"As you might say, you love her as all of hell.''

"Close enough.''

"I do not scent the logic of this.''

"We don't always scent of logic with bonding, misterbob.'' With a sigh, May looked around the room. "Tell you what. How are you at metabolizing human food? Are there any foods that you have problems with—like those with alcohol in them, for example?''

The Arcolian thought for a moment, then shook its head. ''We seem to have an extreme compatibility with your food-stuffs, which is inherent to our design.''

May nodded and rose from his seat. ''Then I want to introduce you to the joys of beer.''

''Indeed.'' The Arcolian clicked its fingers together. ''A suspension of liquefied vegetable matter contaminated with the waste product of *Saccharomyces cerevisiae*. I have heard much of this.''

''No,'' May said. ''Beer. A golden elixir which is generally partaken of by those of my species and sex during a process called male bonding. I'm going to introduce you to both.'' He started for the door.

''I should explain,'' misterbob said, ''that while I am interested in observing and participating in Sapient A-form rituals, I do not think our respective reproductive systems would be compatible.''

''Not *that* kind of bonding,'' May said. ''This is where we become friends by getting drunk together. There's no reproduction involved.''

''Indeed,'' the Arcolian said.

Before May could leave, Cheech appeared in the doorway, a stern look on her face. ''Captain,'' she said politely, ''I hope I'm not interrupting anything.''

''jamesohjames was going to allow me to get drunk,'' misterbob volunteered.

''I was trying to explain, uh, male bonding,'' the merchant explained sheepishly. ''What's wrong?''

''Nothing,'' Cheech said nervously. ''I have a long-wave transmission coming in, and the source is requesting a conversation with you.''

''Me?'' May asked guiltily. ''Who is wanting to get in touch with me?''

''Burris,'' she said.

''That's not funny,'' May snapped.

''It's true.'' Cheech pointed at the wall where the writing had been. ''You want me to put it up there for you? I just finished rewiring it.''

''You were supposed to be working on the CHARLES.''

''I'm waiting for a part. Do you want the call or not?'' Cheech looked straight into May's eyes.

May said nothing. He blinked and considered the options, studying the blank expression on her face.

The Arcolian's chest fluttered with the information it was receiving.

"Of course," Cheech said, face flushing. "I'll put it right through." She turned smartly and hurried out the door.

misterbob's head nodded excitedly and its fingers rattled. "Indeed, indeed. That was a most gratifying exchange."

May's arm raised into a point and aimed at a corner. "You'd better sit over there, Ambassador, so you'll be out of sight—" He cocked his head and frowned. "What do you mean 'gratifying exchange'?"

misterbob raised up and began to shuffle in the direction May had indicated. "I scented a distinct conversation between yourself and lookcheech. She came to this room scenting of apprehension, which began to dissipate as you spoke. Your words sounded harsh, but your angerscent seemed to calm her, which allowed me to scent the underlying message of her seeking approval, which she received."

"But I didn't say—"

The Arcolian backed into a corner and eased into its sitting position. "As your expression goes, not in so many words, jamesohjames. Human conversations are full of wonderfully rich subtext."

"That's called semantics, misterbob," May said gruffly. "It's part of our language."

"Indeed," the Arcolian mused. "But I have noted a distinct . . . I believe the expression is 'chemistry' between yourself and lookcheech."

May snorted. "Indeed yourself." He thought back on the glance that he had exchanged with Cheech and shivered. "If there's anything between us, it's *paternal*, misterbob. I'm certainly old enough to be her father." He dusted off his sleeves as if that was the final word on the subject. Alas, it was not to be, for misterbob started to say something about differences he had noticed in carescents. May looked to the wall for relief and smiled when he saw it erupt into a wall of scrambled color. Cheech's voice came over the audio and announced that she was patching the signal through. May looked to the Arcolian and put his finger to his lips. The Arcolian nodded.

There was a loud pop from the audio and a picture snapped and rolled, filling the wall with the image of Burris. He stared blankly at May for a moment, then, as if prompted, put a smile on his face.

"Captain May, you're a difficult one to get hold of!"

"Not if you know where to look for me," May answered sourly.

"This is rather important, Captain. I wanted to discuss with you the situation of William Wesley Arbor."

"You mean you're going to admit that you've illegally taken him prisoner? Awfully big of you, Mr. Burris."

Burris's image nodded as if admitting a fault. "Yes, Captain, we do have him here at the Essence labs, but as to the illegality of our holding him—"

"I don't want to hear it," May said. "I want to know why you're calling. Are you wanting to charge for Duke's room and board?"

"As a matter of fact, I did want to discuss something with you, so I hope you'll hold your tongue long enough for me to explain."

"Go on." May crossed his arms and gave a sidelong glance at misterbob. The Arcolian was studying the screen intently.

"Suffice it to say that we've learned what we wanted to from Mr. Arbor about the effects of our distillations on him—"

"That didn't take long," May said. "Some product, huh?"

An exasperated look crossed Burris's features and he glanced away, as if looking somewhere else for moral support. "Please bear with me, Captain. This is very difficult for me to say. I realize that I've been unfair, and it's my wish to make it up to you." He paused. "I've done some research into your situation, and I understand that you're in the process of having your merchant ship repaired. Is that correct?"

"I was," May said, trying to keep his voice under control. "For some reason I can't afford it now."

Burris nodded. His image faded momentarily, covered over by a wave of interference.

". . . turn this around and use it to our advantage," Burris was saying as he returned. "That's why I've decided to return Mr. Arbor—Duke—to you, along with a substantial portion of the promised reward money."

"How much?" May demanded.

"One hundred million," Burris said.

"Congratulations," May said in a sarcastic tone. "That should about cover the repairs to my ship, excluding the engines. I might add that this damage was done while bringing your phials out of the Cosen system where you conveniently had them taken."

"How much do you need to repair your ship?" Burris was looking away again, as if the idea were paining him.

May thought about it for a moment. "One hundred fifty million."

"One hundred ten."

"One forty."

"One twenty-five."

"Done," May said. "What about my other debts?"

"Other debts?"

"I still owe thirty-five million on my ship. I had planned on paying it off."

"All right," Burris said, choking.

"There are other debts."

"Be reasonable, Captain."

"Legitimate business expenses that I had planned on paying off. I owe a friend for a load of fuel; I owe some finance companies for some hardware I had planned on reselling; and there's a matter of Duke's back pay and shares to the mercenaries for their part in bringing the phials out. Then there's the money I was planning on using to get my trading started up again."

"How much?" Burris sighed.

"Hundred million."

"Fifty million."

"Ninety."

"Fifty-two."

"You bastard. A hundred million."

"Sixty," Burris said quickly.

"A hundred twenty-five."

"Seventy-five."

"One fifty."

"Eighty-five," Burris gagged. "And not a credit more. If you can't deal with that, I'm sorry."

"You're talking the safe return of Duke plus two hundred forty-five million credits? I can live with that."

Burris made a weary smile. "I'm so glad, Captain."

"Now what's the catch?"

"Catch?" Burris raised his eyebrows.

"C'mon, you sleaze. People like you always have a catch, and the terms are usually a bitch."

Burris sighed. "We are a company dealing in biological commodities, and we are always looking for new and different products."

"Which means you've thought of something I've got which would more than return your initial investment of two hundred forty-five million credits. Now tell me what it is."

Burris set his jaw. "It has come to my attention, Captain, that you are in the possession of an E-form Arcolian. What we ask is that we be allowed to study his physiology and biological processes—with his permission, of course."

"That's the most ridiculous thing I've ever heard," May said, laughing. "Whatever gave you—"

"I have it on good authority," Burris advised. "Firsthand authority, you might say."

"You bastard," May said. "You living bastard."

"I'm sure that in our study of their form, we could find something of value from which we could get a return."

"I can tell you the answer already. It's no."

"Be reasonable, Captain. I expect a return on the initial investment merely from the initial sale of data on Arcolian physiology to other companies. Since the Accord nobody has been able to make a truly in-depth study, and it would be in keeping with our reputation as innovators to get the jump on the other companies."

"And it would be in keeping with your reputation to turn the ambassador into a permanent guest of your lab. One experiment would beget another, and there would never be enough answers. Well, I'm not giving in to that, Burris. The Arcolians are sentient, just like you and me. They're not house pets and they're certainly not lab animals. What you're asking is a crime, and it would be criminal for me to go along."

Burris lowered his head. "A shame, Captain. I tried to be reasonable."

"Not by a long shot."

"You know, you were right to a point. We have incurred expenses while keeping Mr. Arbor here. And unfortunately, it behooves me as head of this branch to recover as much of them as possible. If that means selling Mr. Arbor's indenturement to another company, then so be it."

"You bastard," May said again.

"What makes it difficult is Mr. Arbor's limited range of experience. Not much use around here for someone with an agrarian background. Of course, the Nimrev Company has a standing request for contracts. It seems they're always short of hunters—''

"You wouldn't dare," May challenged.

Burris shrugged. "I must keep our books in the black, Captain May. I'll do it one way or the other. Fortunately for you I'm a reasonable man. I'll give you ten hours to think about it."

"Burris—" May said.

"Must go," Burris said. "This conversation is running up Mr. Arbor's expenses."

"Burris!" May shouted as the screen went blank. He stalked across to the now-blank wall and pounded it with his fist. "I only wanted things to go right," he said to the wall. "All I wanted to do was pay off my frigging ship."

"If I might question you, jamesohjames," misterbob asked. "What is this company Nimrev that was referred to in conversation?"

May turned away from the wall. "Clothing," he said. "Namely, exotic furs. Expensive as hell. Their most famous line is a series of cloaks and wraps of an extremely rare nature. Each one of them comes with this official paper certifying that at least one human life was lost in the procurement of that particular fur."

misterbob's head shook. "It is not good that misterduke goes into their employ."

May rubbed his face, hard. "That's an understatement."

"Then you must allow me to go to the Essence Corporation."

"Out of the question," May said. "They'll make an experiment out of you. I won't allow that to happen."

"And they are not doing the same to misterduke?"

May walked a tight circle across the inside of the room, giving his face a chance to cool. "You don't understand, misterbob. This is a case where keeping you alive is more important than what happens to Duke."

"But I thought The Life was important to you Sapient A-forms."

"It is, but in this case, you're looking at Duke's life weighed against the lives of others. This includes your life, misterbob, because like it or not, your life is more important than Duke's."

"But this means nothing to our race."

"I realize that, but try and look at it like a Sapient A-form would. You have finally made peace with a race you have regarded as the enemy for a long period of time and the first delegation has come to live on a world set up exclusively for reasons of diplomacy. Then you find out that an ambassador who has gone to live with the native forms was sold by your own people for money."

"You are speaking of slavery," misterbob said. "Indeed, I understand. This is a crack in the chitin for you."

"There's more. Because of what has happened, perhaps others would make it difficult for the diplomatic party to live on this world. Perhaps another misunderstanding would arise between the two races and there would be war again."

"The lives of many hang in the balance," misterbob said. "A most interesting dilemma."

"And there's greed involved, too. I'm worried about what would happen to me if such a thing happened, and I'd worry about what would happen to Vonn and Winters and Peter Chiba and Roz. You remember what I told you about Bachman and his plot to steal you and the others from the *Hergest Ridge*? By allowing you to go with Burris and his cohorts, I would be no better than he was."

The Arcolian's head nodded. "So what you call reputation is valued above The Life?"

"Never," May said. "At least it shouldn't be. But sometimes it is."

"Yes," the Arcolian rattled. "This is most gratifying. I can comprehend your position and appreciate it. I find these dilemmas that confront you most delicious."

May shook his head in dismay. "Then I'd like your recipe." The Arcolian cocked its head in question, but the merchant quickly protested. "That was a joke. You said delicious and I said—never mind. It's Sapient A-form humor."

"I do not wish to add to your dilemma, jamesohjames, but I think that there is something about my race that I should explain. Perhaps it is something which you have not yet considered in making your decision. As an ambassador, I request that you give this a full hearing before making your final decision."

"I respect that, Ambassador. Go ahead."

misterbob rose from its sitting position and shuffled across the floor in an attempt to mimic May's pattern of pacing. "If your scentsense was properly developed, I could better explain to you the history of my race and perhaps cause you to speculate on why The Life means so little for us. Let me, then, merely perform cardiological vivisection—"

"Uh," May said politely, "I believe the expression is 'cut straight to the heart of the matter.' "

"Such quaint idioms," the Arcolian mused. "My race thrives when it is challenged, when it is confronted by newness, by when it is forced to learn and adapt."

"So is ours."

"But we differ as well. I scent that your race is not satisfied until it conquers. Ours is not satisfied until it assimilates." misterbob made a sweeping gesture with its arms that made May look at it from head to toe. "What you see in me is from our efforts to more effectively communicate with you. Please do not request that I explain more about that. It may crack your chitin."

"Go on," May said.

"As you can rightfully assume, one of the traits we find so fascinating is the manner in which you deal with The Life. It is beyond value, yet you buy and sell—"

"It makes us a species of hypocrites, I know."

"—yet you have this unprecedented capacity for caring, which transcends all of our understanding. This idea of sacrifice, of the individual forfeiting The Life for that of another. Unthinkable to our culture. We have a high rate of volunteering for medical research, yet these things are to advance the species. Such sacrifices are not even thought about, for the shedding of one's form is an investment in the future."

"That's the same thing—"

"No," misterbob said. "It is not, jamesohjames. An individual Arcolian at a critical transition point will either live or die by its own means. It passes on to the Z-form without protest or grief. There is none of what you would call leaping into the fire."

"I scent this now, I think. All for the good of society or nothing at all."

"Quite," misterbob said. "Now my ambassadorial duties include to learn all I can about your natures. If that requires that I make this sacrifice, then so be it. It is no damage to our chitin."

"But our chitin—"

"Indeed, jamesohjames. By not allowing me to do this you are frustrating my very reason for being."

"I am terribly sorry, Ambassador, but I am responsible for your welfare. If anything happened to you . . ."

"It would be of no political significance to relations between our two races."

"Perhaps not, from what you've told me," May said. "But

let me be selfish for a moment. If anything were to happen to you, I would have lost a friend.''

misterbob bowed its head. "You flatter me.''

"And I think Duke would feel the same way about it. I don't want to do that to either of us.''

"Such a charming sentiment,'' the Arcolian purred. "You do me a great honor by talking in this way.''

May cleared his throat and looked away. "I mean it.''

"Allow me to express one thought, jamesohjames. If you would close your eyes—''

"No influence,'' May said sternly.

"I wish to express an idea.''

"All right.'' The merchant closed his eyes. "What now?''

"Relax. Just for a moment.''

May drew breath and took his time in exhaling. With the next breath the scent came, rich and yeasty.

"What does this make you see?'' misterbob asked.

"Beer,'' May replied.

"Allow me to adjust. This is a new expression to me.''

The scent shifted, gathering warmth and spice.

"Oh,'' May said, almost startled.

"Yes?'' the Arcolian encouraged.

"Somebody cooking things. Bread, and beef roast with onion, and something with cinnamon . . .''

"Indeed. What you would call—''

"The smell of home.'' May opened his eyes. The Arcolian's head was bobbing excitedly, and it was making a pleased murmur.

"A most successful interpretation. And what is it you feel when you scent this, jamesohjames?'' misterbob rapped itself in the chest with chitinous fingers. "What do you feel internally?''

"Hunger from—no, that's not quite right.'' May closed his eyes for an instant. "I feel—safe.''

"Yes, yes. And what does this say to you?''

There's a message to this? May thought. He studied the ambassador for a moment, wondering what the creature was thinking. Then, in a flash, it dawned on him. To understand it, he had to try and think like an Arcolian, and if an Arcolian was scenting of somewhere safe . . .

"You feel no danger to your own life,'' May said. "No matter where you go, you are safe. If things start to get bad, you are perfectly capable of manipulating your captors.''

"Yes," misterbob said with a gleeful tone. "That is it. Oh, this is a delightful thing, to have successfully communicated this concept to you through a means to which you are unaccustomed."

May nodded. "Perhaps we're not as unaccustomed as we think."

"The Sapient A-forms catch on quickly," the ambassador said.

"Indeed," May said. "And we also catch on to each other quite quickly."

The Arcolian's head cocked.

"We play games with each other, misterbob," May explained. "And the person who is the best at manipulating the others is the one who comes out ahead." He stepped over to a small comm panel set into the far wall and thumbed a button. "Right now that bastard Burris thinks he is ahead."

"Am I to understand that thinking one is ahead is not the same as being ahead?" misterbob asked.

"That's exactly it. Burris thinks he's up on me because he's got something I need, and that he's put me into a bad situation. But knowing your abilities and his weaknesses puts me ahead. And his weakness is terrible indeed."

"Indeed?" the Arcolian parroted.

"Indeed." There was a burst of static from the comm box, and Cheech's voice flowed into the room.

"You rang?"

"Cheech, do you have the coordinates for returning a transmission to the Essence Company?"

"Aye aye," she said.

"Prepare a message to Mr. Burris. Tell him that we have agreed to his proposed exchange on the following terms. First, Duke is not to undergo any further study from this point on. Any research involving his assimilation of the Eric Dickson product and any research done in counteracting the same is to be turned over to us at the time of the exchange, which will be determined after his acceptance of these terms."

"That it, Captain?"

"There's one more thing," May said, smiling at misterbob. "The price he offered isn't enough, not when we're going to have to buy into medical research. I want five hundred million in secured credits or the deal is off, Duke or no. Tell him that."

There was a long pause. "Will do. Anything else?"

"That's it." He punched the button to cut the connection.

"That, sir, is how you stay ahead in the game. Burris plans on making money off of you, and I want him to know that I know. Of course, we won't allow anything to actually happen to you."

"I thought you understood I would be safe, jamesohjames."

"I know you will be," May said, walking to the open door. "And if you'll come with me, I'll see that the odds stay stacked in our favor.

7

The room where the hearing was being held was unpretentious. It reminded Duke of the *Angel's Luck* cargo hold because of its size, although it was nothing more than a glorified hangar for the Vacc Fighters that were parked out in the midday heat. A raised platform had been built in one corner so the presiding triumvirate could look down on the proceedings. A shorter platform provided a stage for the lead players in the game: the uniformed officers who took the roles of prosecution and defense and bailiff. On the hangar's concrete floor was a sea of folding chairs, fanning out in a semicircle from the occupied corner of the hangar. It was a place that had seen many large gatherings where the martial law of the Narofeld Station was determined or upheld, and many was the time when the room had been packed. On this day, however, the audience was hard-pressed to outnumber the triumvirate and the other major players. A handful of pilots and ground-support crew took their places in a scattering of seats, most of them using the hearing as an excuse to get off the sweltering tarmac.

It was under those circumstances that Duke had wandered in. As the upstairs of the rooming house had slowly dissolved into nothingness, he sat in the lobby, frustrated that Dickson had managed to lure him away and leave him. That damned cryptic remark that Rhea had left him with—"if you want the knowledge, you know where to find it"—gave him no idea of where to look.

Only after uncounted hours of sitting in the lobby, waiting for Eric to return and realizing that he wouldn't, did Duke decide that something had to be done. He tried to explore the upstairs again, but to no avail. All that remained of Dickson's floor was the hall, which ended in gray. Likewise, the two rooms he had been familiar with revealed a similar cloudy wall when opened. Those rooms that Dickson had no knowledge of were merely impenetrable black. Duke had managed to go up to the second floor, just to find that the hall went only as far as the bathroom, and that all of the residential rooms were the same shade of black. It made sense to him after a while; Rhea had said something about Dickson's unwillingness to pass the room where Fortunado had died, and the only way around it was to use the plumbing on the second floor. It still existed there, in a part of the memory that Dickson had not managed to blot out. Unfortunately, it was doing no good.

The first floor of the hotel had been equally unenlightening. Attempts to enter the kitchen, the manager's office, or the custodian's workshop resulted in the same walls of black that had greeted him above. While Duke had discovered that he had an unlimited tab at the bar and that it carried any obscure drink he asked for, including the Tetran-brewed Dooley's Beer, whatever quantities he drank had no effect on him. Likewise, the small café had obligingly brought him a two-kilo brick of Cesslian Cheese Power, and the worn-looking waitress had not even flinched when he ordered thick steaks of imported Tetran beef. Similarly, the hotel management had no problem with his sleeping on the battered Naugahyde couch in the lobby, and the vidscreen always had something that Duke wanted to watch on it, although it seemed to be limited to things he had already seen.

It was no time at all before Duke grew weary of this hospitality and decided to make an earnest effort to track down Eric Dickson. He awoke one morning after a dozen bottles of Dooley's with no hangover at all and realized that in his endeavors to explore the inside of the hotel, he had never once thought to set foot outside. Shrugging off the feeling that he needed a shower and a meal—which he determined was largely imaginary—he walked to the hotel doors, pushed both of them open, and stepped outside.

He was not disappointed. He found himself squinting in the brightest sunlight he had ever known. Searching his memory, he realized that the light came from the twin suns of the Narofeld system, and that he must be at Narofeld Station. The sensation made him laugh. He had read of Narofeld in the accounts of Dickson's life, and he had heard Dickson himself talking about different things that had happened while on the station, but to step into whole memory, complete with heat and suns and sticky asphalt tarmac, was something else again.

Duke took a few steps, then turned to look back. He was standing on acres and acres of pavement, painted and marked into lanes and rectangles and grids, landing and storage zones for the assortment of military craft based there. Incongruously, the hotel, which he remembered from a later time as being on a seedy side street, stood squarely in the middle of the landing field.

He shrugged and, glad to be out of the hotel at last, started across the landing field toward where the borrowed memory told him there would be others to talk to, fliers and military people who would know something about Eric or possess the same knowledge he did.

As he crossed, a strange whining came into the air, almost making him shiver until the new part of his memory reminded him that it was the sound of Vacc Fighters making a landing approach. Duke hurried across, trying to get off of the landing field before they started to slot in, but to his surprise, there was only a small handful, not more than a score of them. They came down all around him in a less than coordinated ballet, something he knew to be wrong from the memories he had taken from Eric Dickson. Not only were their slot-ins sloppy, but the ships looked battered and worn, and the pilots were jumping out of the cockpits, screaming and cursing in frustration. Many tore pieces of life-support equipment from their uniforms and kicked it across the asphalt. Others beat their fists on the foils of their ships. One woman took her sidearm and, tears streaming from her eyes, emptied the clip through the window of the cockpit. The words from everyone's lips all echoed the same sentiment. Bering's Gate was a disaster.

An eerie sensation had crept into Duke's spine, making him break into a dead run for the line of buildings. Before long he arrived, drenched with sweat, and he wove in and out of the complex of hangars until he found the one where the hearing was being held. He almost passed it by until he heard the mention of specific names and places that bore him a glimmer of recognition, so he slipped in and occupied one of the folding chairs near the back, trying hard to listen to what the principals in the drama were saying but never quite being able to hear. The feeling it gave him was like the most frustrating parts of a vague memory.

Nonetheless, Duke stayed in his seat. While there was no true air-conditioning, the hangar did afford shelter from the direct light of the suns, and even though he had a nagging doubt that it should have been even hotter in the corrugated metal building, it felt no less comfortable than the hotel had been.

At last there came some action. Both the prosecution and the defense made imperceptible closing remarks, after which the triumvirate rose and vanished out a side door. Duke glanced at his watch, wondering if perhaps he should run back to the hotel for something to eat. No matter. The triumvirate was returning already. Thinking it had not taken long, Duke checked the time again to see how long it had been and was quite astonished to find that seven and a half hours had elapsed. He stared at his watch in horror, trying to figure out what kind of a mistake had been made, when the middle member of the triumvirate rose and cleared his throat.

"In the matter of Narofeld Station Security, acting security agents for the United Terran Transplanetary Navy, versus Cadet Eric Leland Dickson in reference to the death of Cadet Commander Derrald Deakes. Having heard much compelling testimony from both sides and having considered the facts as presented surrounding both sides of this incident, we have reached the following conclusion."

An unheard murmur went through the crowd. Backs straightened and necks stiffened. All eyes were riveted on the front dais.

"Wait a minute," Duke said, under his breath. "I know how this is going to turn out."

"Colonel Gratiot, General Biej, and myself have unanimously concluded that Cadet Dickson cannot be blamed for the death of Cadet Commander Deakes."

The few people watching began to talk all at once, and were silenced when the center figure raised his hands.

"The injuries given to Deakes by Dickson would most certainly not have resulted in the death of the cadet commander. Until more compelling evidence can be given to show the guilt of Cadet Dickson or another party, the matter is hereby closed. The death of Cadet Commander Deakes is ruled as misadventure until which time a proper investigation of infirmary personnel can be mounted."

The voices started up again, but the triumvirate head continued, "In the matter of the assault of Cadet Commander Deakes by Cadet Eric Leland Dickson, we hereby issue a verbal reprimand to Cadet Dickson and entreat him to not repeat such behavior. This is wartime, and it is in our best interests to not waste time in prosecuting our own talent, especially that of Cadet Dickson's caliber.

"In the matter of Cadet Dickson's volunteering to make the cargo run to observation post P-3-A, thereby restoring the Narofeld monitor system, we hereby acknowledge the cadet's willingness and bravery and cite the same as an example to this most recent class of cadets. However, we decline the recommendation by Major Feliz that Dickson be decorated for such meritorious service. Cadet Dickson will instead by given a verbal acknowledgment of appreciation for his trip to P-3-A, as well as a verbal reprimand and a stern reminder that there is no excuse for letting one's success go to one's head and that it is certainly no excuse for striking one's fellow or superior officer.'' The man in the middle cast a stone glance down at one of those sitting in chairs on the concrete floor. "Is that understood, Cadet?"

A young Eric Dickson nodded. "Yes, sir. It is understood."

"Very well," the man replied with a nod. "If there are no further comments or remarks, this hearing is dismissed."

The members of the triumvirate rose and vanished out the side door. Duke bolted up and made straight for Dickson, who was standing and shaking the hands of his defense team. But the closer he got, the thicker the crowd became, until Duke was convinced that it had grown to the size of the entire population of Narofeld Station. He reached out, trying to close the distance between Dickson and himself through the crowd, but it was to no avail. Dickson was encircled, trying to shake the hands of the well-wishers who surrounded him. The cadet was far from being flushed with victory, Duke noticed. He was still pale, and his sunken eyes gave the impression that he had been given a last-minute reprieve from the gallows.

Duke pushed forward, but as he did, Dickson fell into a crowd of cadets and was drawn away, and then up, and then out of the hangar, riding on the shoulders of his peers. Stunned, the broker watched the crowd dissipate, shaking his head and searching his mind for the memories that would corroborate what he had seen. To his chagrin, all he had witnessed was still fresh enough in his own mind to make the task impossible. With a sigh, he slumped down in one of the chairs, shaking his head. If Dickson had been intent on getting out of there without having to confront his physical host, he had done a smashing job of it.

Duke was about to head in the direction the crowd had taken Dickson when he glanced out one of the open hangar doors and noticed that dark clouds were gathering on the far horizon, and that the sky between him and the hotel was already a darkening mix of grays. A cool breeze struck him full as he rose, and he decided it would be a good idea to get back to the hotel before things got too bad.

The breeze went from cool to bracing in the time it took him to walk out of the hangar. As he darted across the asphalt, he noticed a strange circulation of air, as if it were rising hot from the flat of the landing field on one step and falling down cold on the next.

Less than a dozen meters from the hangar, the first fat drops of rain began to fall from the sky. The water was cold, and the shock as they hit Duke was electric. After a score or so of the drops had hit him, he became used to the cold and welcomed it as a relief from the incessant Narofeldian heat. He continued on his way, hurrying across the landing zones, marveling at the way the mist was rising up off of the cooling asphalt.

Another few steps, and suddenly Duke was in the middle of a downpour. The rain was coming down in sheets, instantly drenching him and blanketing the field in fog. He halfheartedly turned, looking back toward the hangar and considering its value as a shelter, but the rain was falling so hard and fast that it was invisible to him. Turning, Duke hunched up his shoulders and carried on, heading in the direction that he had last seen the hotel, marveling at the rain.

Just like the rainy season on Tetros, he thought. A warm rain, hard and fast, and it would do this for days . . .

His steps began to slow. He squinted against the rain and blew air from his lips, forming a wet spout.

Narofeld rains aren't like this, not the way Dickson remembered them, he told himself. They were those big, fat, cold drops, and it would rain hard and fast for maybe half an hour, and there were usually tornadoes with the rain and everyone was scrambling like hell to get their ships to safety—

Duke broke into a dead run, arms and legs flying, pushing against the wetness that pounded from all sides. Something was terribly, terribly wrong. Either their memories were mixing and blurring, or else someone was interfering, trying to manipulate the situation.

Is it Dickson, is it Dickson? Duke puffed under his breath. You'd think by now he'd learn that two can play at this game, that I'm catching on to—

Out of the rain a large silver shape appeared so suddenly that Duke cried out, his shout of surprise lost in the sounds of the downpour. His hand went to his chest and he staggered back, sinking to his knees and then sitting on the asphalt. He could feel his heart pounding under his ribs, and it was only when he calmed that he could see the shape for what it was, the hulking frame of a Vacc Fighter, water running in rivers from its stream-lined shape.

A way out of the rain, he thought. You know the drill by now. Up and away.

He suddenly broke out in gooseflesh, and for the first time since the rain started he felt cold. That wasn't my idea. I didn't put that thought there. That was Eric Dickson, *you bastard*!

Slowly he rose and stepped toward the craft. Across the nose was a black streak of paint, but beneath it he could still see the raised impression of the lettering it covered.

LOVELY LEIGH

Below that, in the same hand, a legend had been painted in haste and anger.

COLDBRINGER

"So that's it," Duke said against the rain. He shook his head. "Not this time. I know what you're trying to drag me into, and it's not going to work." He placed his palms against his temples and pressed. "I'm not going. I'm not going to take it." Squeezing his eyes shut, he scanned the artificial darkness for a sign of the pilot. "If I come to you it's going to be on my own terms. Do you hear me? *On my own terms!*"

With a deep breath, he opened his eyes and quickly skirted around the fighter, shielding his eyes against the deluge. He placed one foot after the other, following each step with another until a shape began to rise out of the flooding grounds. Duke pushed forward and through, until bright blue letters began to cut through the haze, flashing HOTEL in their language of cheap neon. In another moment he was up the steps and in the door, watching water drip from his clothes to puddle on the tiled floor.

"I know where the knowledge is hidden," he said. "I'm going to take it now."

The hotel clerk looked up from his broom and regarded the sopping figure. "What did you say?"

"Not meant for you," Duke said with a shiver. "But I have something I want to say to you. Remember when I came in the door just a minute ago? Didn't you wonder how I did it?"

"Wonder how you did what?" the clerk asked.

"How I came in from that torrent out there and managed to be bone dry. Don't you remember that?"

The clerk shook his head.

"Funny," Duke said. "That's how I remember it."

Instantly the dampness was gone. The clothes were no longer clinging to Duke's body; his hair was no longer plastered to his head. The puddles on the floor were gone.

"I'd like to go see Eric Dickson," he said, heading for the stairs.

"A little late," the clerk said. "He's checked out."

"No, he hasn't," Duke said. "He's hiding."

"Whatever you say." The clerk shrugged. "Will you be staying the night?"

Duke grabbed the handrail and started up. "I don't expect to be long. Not long at all." He ascended the steps quickly, stopping on the first-floor landing to look down the hall at the gray wall. He gave a resolute nod, more to comfort himself than for show to any possible onlookers, and started toward the wall.

At five meters he could feel a low thrum. At two meters he could feel its tension raise the hair on his body like static electricity. At half a meter his body began to fill with a tingling sensation.

"This wall is not going to hurt me," Duke said, fighting hard to keep his voice calm. "It can't. It's my body. It's my mind. He's the parasite."

He dropped his hands from their defensive posture and, with a giant step, walked into and was engulfed by the gray.

8

At two A.M. local, the road winding through the small forest was deserted. Even someone passing through on the way home from a late meeting or a liaison would have missed the pleasure craft that sat darked out in a nearby meadow, and they most certainly would have avoided the van at the side of the road, which sat with its hood up while two hard-looking men studied the engine compartment.

Vonn stuffed his hands in his jacket pockets and stared up at the stars, listening to the insects.

"Reminds me of the beginning," he said. "A ship parked illegally in the woods, a van full of desperate men, an approaching convoy carrying a precious cargo—"

"Vonn," May grunted, trying to act as if he were fixing the engine. "Shut up."

The mercenary laughed. "Yeah, I get the prehit jitters, too."

"Yeah," May snapped. "And I'll bet the big question every time you get them is whether or not you're doing the right thing, isn't it?" He paused for a moment, and his teeth chattered.

"Give it a chance, May. The mercenary business is different."

"Sure it is. You get in the middle of a firefight, and you probably sit there and count the number of bullets left until you get paid. You don't have to worry about any of the moral consequences because there's always somebody there to take the heat for that part of it."

Vonn shrugged. "It does give me a chance to be the best at what I do."

"Be glad," May said quietly. "Be glad you don't have to think. Be glad that all you have to do is kill."

"I don't just kill," Vonn said, offended.

"You know what I mean."

"Yeah," Vonn agreed. "You're worried about this whole thing hanging on Winters. But he's competent, May, he really is."

"All he has to do is get into the truck carrying Duke and drive like hell for the *Reconnez Cherie*. I think we can handle the rest."

"Yup." Vonn sauntered around the front of the van and opened his coat to reveal a snub-nosed autoshot dangling by a cord from his left shoulder.

"You're not going to have time to use that," May warned, slamming the hood of the van shut. "And I don't want you to use it, not with all of the drugs you've been taking."

"I never go anywhere without a covered ass, pal."

"Then why didn't you wear any body armor?"

Vonn closed his jacket and patted it. "Not enough room."

"You've got a really screwed set of priorities. Anyone ever tell you that? Just make sure you don't lose it and turn that thing on misterbob."

"Why do you think I filled up on drugs?"

Shaking his head, May walked to the driver's side of the van and climbed in.

"jamesohjames," came a voice from the back. "Is it time yet to engage in kickass?"

"Nearly," May said.

"Now there's someone with his priorities straight," Vonn said, easing into the passenger seat.

"This is a most curious situation," misterbob said. "I am

getting a strange amalgam of scent. Yours seems to be sharp with apprehension, while mistervonn's seems to be quite smooth with anticipation.''

"Depends on how close you are to screwing things up," May said. "Do you understand what you're supposed to do, Ambassador?''

"Indeed." May could hear the creature's rattle in the darkness. "You are to lure those who have taken misterduke out of their transport vehicle by giving falsescents to them about my condition. This will enable bigguy to take control of the vehicle."

"Right," May said.

"As mistervonn opens the doors to reveal my presence, I am to douse him with scentkill. When he steps out of the way, I am to scent strongly to the others with tigerscat. This will cause them to—how did you explain it, mistervonn? 'Lose control of their bowels'?''

"Not exactly," Vonn said. "But it should scare them into a state of disorientation. While they're trying to rally, I'll jump in with you, and May and Winters will drive to the *Reconnez Cherie*. We'll leave their truck behind and drive this one right into the cargo hold, and Peter Chiba will get us the hell out of here."

"I understand this."

"Do you also understand that you do not have to do this?" May asked. "In spite of what you've told me, I want to give you every opportunity to bail out. No one will think the lesser of you for it."

misterbob's reply was a scent, one dry like chalk dust but with a latent sharpness to it. "mistervonn, can you scent what I am trying to convey?''

"I'm sorry, misterbob, but I don—" Vonn turned to look at the Arcolian, and his voice pitched upward as if his throat were suddenly being squeezed shut. He followed with a loud gulp, managed to squeak "Excuse me," then hopped out of the van. May saw him reach into his pocket and pull out a small bottle of pills.

"Apologies," May said. "These Neurodowns don't last long in highly stressful situations. At the very least your presence is going to make his skin crawl."

"Indeed. What I was trying to convey, jamesohjames, is this strange sensation that this situation has produced. It is one of dread, but most certainly I find myself looking forward to the experience. Is this common to your species?''

May nodded. "Why do you think Vonn stays in the business?''

Vonn returned to the van, wiping his lips with the back of his hand. "Sorry," he said, shaking the pill bottle. "These things don't work worth a damn.''

"I could scentcalm you, mistervonn.''

"Save it," May said. "You're going to need all of your strength to Tigerscat the others.''

The rattling approximation of a laugh came from the back of the van. "That is like a Sapient A-form saying save your energy to speak. This is a very natural thing for us to do, as natural as your speaking.''

"I know," May answered. "But speaking persuasively sometimes takes a great deal of mental energy. Besides, I want Vonn scared. He's supposed to paint a picture of you as this big, fearsome animal, and it'll help if he looks the part.''

"Thanks a lot, pal," Vonn groused. "Well, Anders always did say you should stand up to your fears, and I never have been scared of much.'' He drummed his foot nervously on the floor of the van. "Damn it to hell, what's taking those folks?''

May checked his watch. "It should be any—''

He was interrupted by a loud crackle from the portacomm that rested between the front seats.

"Big Guy to Lucky One, Big Guy to Lucky One," came Winters's voice. "Come in please. Come in, Lucky One. This is Big Guy calling. Where are you, Lucky One? Come in, come in . . .''

May swore and grabbed the device. "If he'd let me get a word in—''

Vonn's hand fell onto the merchant's shoulder. "We're all scared, May.''

The merchant nodded. "Thanks. I forget." He waited for Winters to finish babbling, then keyed the switch and asked for a status report.

"I can see really good," Winters said. "I'm up in this tree on the big hill going up by the road, and I can see all the way into town even without the optoculars. And there must be a *zillion* stars up in the sky.''

"Big Guy," May said. "That's all very good, but why are you calling us?''

"Oh, yeah. There's this big truck coming down the road. It's got letters on the sides, the ones I think you wanted me to look for, the E-N-S-E-N-E-S. It'll be up to us in a minute or so.''

"Very good," May said. "When I'm done talking you turn off the radio and come down out of the tree. Climb in the truck when everyone gets out and then drive it to the clearing after misterbob scares them. All right?''

"All right." The static went dead, then returned after a moment. "This is Big Guy signing off from Lucky One. See you at mission rendezvous point." Before May could think of formulating an appropriate response, the line went dead again.

"If he hadn't done so well for us on Cosen, I wouldn't believe that he could survive in the business," Vonn said.

"Let's hope he survives this business. Are you ready, misterbob?''

There was a clatter from the back of the van. "Indeed. I will await the opening of the door.''

With a nod, the merchant climbed out of the van and walked around to the vehicle's rear. Vonn met him there, giving a sign of relief. "It's weird. Just knowing there are steel doors between me and it—''

"Stow it," May said sharply.

"Don't panic," Vonn said. "This is going to be simple. We're going to be going up against a bunch of out-of-shape corporate big shots and security guards who have gotten fat from eating too many Leth'rian spice rolls.''

"Don't underanticipate and keep our ass covered, all right?''

"But I thought you didn't want me to use—'' Vonn patted the bulge under the left side of his coat as a set of headlights swept across the road and then blinded them. The crackle of slowing tires on pavement filled their ears, and a large, rounded shape stopped not a dozen meters from where they stood.

May stared at the vehicle and spoke to Vonn. "Remember, misterbob is the scariest thing you've ever seen in your life.''

"I won't have any trouble with that.''

"Step out of the light.''

Vonn moved to the side of the road as a passenger door opened on the new vehicle and Burris stepped out, wiping his nose on a kerchief. He pocketed the cloth and stepped around to the front of the truck, where he was joined by the driver, a broad-shouldered sort who was at least a full head taller than Burris. Leth'rian spice rolls, May thought cynically.

"Car trouble?" Burris asked innocuously.

"Money trouble," May said. "But I think you know all about that."

"I can probably help you with that," Burris said, "although I think your price is still a little steep."

"It's a drop in the bucket compared to what you stand to make on this. What are you going to do, market an exclusive line of products? Coffee mugs and bath towels and sponsorship of Zeeball matches?"

"We're a biotechnological company," Burris said. "I'm sure we'll find some useful applications. Did you bring your friend?"

"Did you bring yours?" May retorted. "Five hundred million of them, plus one friend of mine."

A door opened on the rear of the Essence truck, and another figure stepped out, lugging a large suitcase.

"The board of directors is going to be very upset with me for complying with your demands. I had to liquidate a great deal of our holdings in order to comply."

"You'll have it back in six months."

"Our research will take considerably longer than that." The guard with the suitcase came to stand by Burris's side. "Give it to the merchant captain."

The guard approached May with the case.

"Stop," May ordered. The guard complied. "Set it down right there. Lay it flat and open it." After looking to Burris for a nod, the guard keyed the latches. There was a tone, and he opened the case.

"Lay it open flat and start taking out the contents."

With a shrug, the guard laid the case flat on the road and began to remove bound bundles of what looked like credit chips. "They're all the same," he complained.

"I want to make sure there are no surprises," May said.

The Essence driver sneezed.

"Bless you." May nodded.

The guard continued to stack money on the road.

"Vonn, check it."

Vonn stepped over to the guard and looked down at the stacks of money. "Give me one of those."

The guard reached into the case and offered Vonn a packet.

"Not that one." He gestured to one of the packets lying on the road. "That one." The guard handed it up, and Vonn broke the seal on it, quickly riffling through to check the amount. "There's a million here," he said. "It's secured." He stuffed the money into his pocket.

"Five hundred packets?" May asked.

Burris nodded.

"I've seen enough." The merchant nodded at Vonn, who backed out of the pool of light. "Pack it back up."

"Yeah," the guard snuffled.

May turned his attention to Burris. "Duke," he said.

"The Arcolian," Burris replied.

"I want to see him," May demanded.

"Likewise, I for the Arcolian."

May shrugged. "All right."

"I don't think that's such a good idea," Vonn said from the darkness. The last few Neurodowns were already starting to wear off and gave the mercenary's voice just the right note of panic.

"Why not?" Burris asked. He gave the merchant a disappointed look. "Captain, you're not trying to pull something on us, are you?"

"I think what my friend is trying to tell you is that you probably don't want to open the van until you're ready to take the Arcolian out. If you go playing peekaboo with it, there's going to be more of a struggle than you want to deal with at this point."

"I thought the E-forms were docile."

"So are a lot of animals," Vonn said from the darkness. "Until you start screwing with them."

"I don't think you have the Arcolian in there," Burris shouted. "You don't have any protection against its pheromonal attacks."

"You're the one who said it was docile," May said sourly. "Give me some credit for my intelligence. You get a couple of guys in gas masks, a couple sheets of myoplast seal, and a roll of bulkhead sealing tape, and you can work miracles."

Burris took a hesitant step forward. "You didn't hurt the scent organ, did you?"

May shook his head. "Just covered it up."

"I don't think you've got the Arcolian in there."

"All right." May tossed his hands in the air. "I give up. Vonn, open the door."

"I'd rather not, May."

"Then I'll do it." May stabbed a finger at the guard who was repacking the money in the suitcase. "Just leave it there when you're done. I'll have—" He froze, then smiled wryly. "People who live in glass houses, Mr. Burris."

Burris licked his lips. "Whatever do you mean, Captain?"

May stepped into the center of the lighted area. "How do I know you have Duke?"

"That seemed to be a foregone conclusion."

"In the back of your truck."

"Like the Arcolian, Captain. You don't know for certain."

The guard snapped the latch on the suitcase and stood, dusting off his knees.

"Pick up your suitcase," May said, "and give it back to your boss."

"What?" Burris said, outraged.

"I can't deal with this," May said. "We can't trust each other enough to make a simple transaction." He started out of the light, toward the driver's side of the van. "Let's go, Vonn."

"You can't just walk away from this, you bastard!" Burris shouted.

May spun on his heels. "Watch me," he snapped. "It's my ass hanging on this one, Burris. If there's another war, I'm the one who'll take the blame. Yeah, I've got a friend and his life is at stake, but what's one life compared to millions? For all I know, you've already killed him by digging into his brain, trying to see what the distillation did to him."

The guard standing by the money looked back at Burris, astonished. He had not been told.

"All right, Captain. You win." He waved his hand at the driver. "Escort Captain May to the back of the vehicle and allow him to speak with Mr. Arbor." The driver retreated and slapped the back of the truck. "Fair enough?"

May nodded. He stepped back into the light and took the suitcase from the guard. "Just the three of you going to take the Arcolian?"

"Now you underestimate me, Captain." The rear of the Essence truck opened and another tall guard stepped out. May walked toward the truck, suitcase banging against his leg.

"Duke?" he called.

"May?" came a thin voice. "Is that you?"

"Is that him?" Vonn shouted.

"Are you all right?" May asked.

"I'm okay," came the reply. "But listen, May, you shouldn't be doing this. It's not worth it, trading the Arcolian for—"

"That's enough," Burris snapped. "The Arcolian."

May stopped by the side of the truck, staring up at the Essence logo on its side, wondering how close Winters was. "All right, Vonn."

"You're sure about this?" The mercenary's voice cracked as he stepped into the light. He shifted nervously from foot to foot as the driver and the first guard walked out to meet him. The second guard passed May, wiping the end of his nose with two fingers as he went by.

Funny, May thought. Must be something going around.

The second guard joined the others, with Burris taking up the rear. Vonn was slowly stepping back toward the double doors of the van, hands up with palms out, trying to slow them.

"I've got the big guy in there with the critter," he was saying. "Do you have something to put it in?"

The second guard produced what looked like a fine mesh net.

"Okay. Great. You're in business."

There was a rustling from the back of the truck. May reached up and thumped the wall with his fist.

"It's all right, Duke. We'll have you out in a minute."

Vonn raised his hand to the latch. "Don't crowd," he was saying. He looked pale in the quartz light, and his skin glistened from sweat. "This thing's a mean fucker."

There was a sneeze from May's right. He turned to see another guard climbing out of the truck.

"May," a voice said. "Is that you?"

The merchant shot a glance back at the van. The four were advancing on Vonn, not heeding his instructions.

"It's okay, Duke, I—"

"I'm okay. But listen, May, you shouldn't be doing this. It's not worth it, trading the Arcolian for—"

The guard paused, looking up into the truck, glaring and shaking his head. He sneezed.

"C'mon, guys," Vonn urged, backing away. "This thing is—"

"I'm okay," Duke said. "But listen, May, you shouldn't be doing this. It's not worth it—"

The third guard suddenly brought up the butt of a rifle and slammed it against the side of the truck. The voice cut short and the rifle started a downward arc.

"*Abort!*" May screamed. "*Abort! Vonn, Winters, we've been screwed!*"

The rifle butt came flying at May's head. The merchant brought up the suitcase and deflected the blow. The rifle discharged, and the guard staggered back, trying to regain his footing. The truck's engine fired and filled the air with a low bass rumble.

"Winters! No!"

May turned for an instant, and the guard brought the weapon to bear. The merchant raised the suitcase up to shield his face and charged. From behind, Vonn shouted for help and was cut off. There was another explosion and the suitcase burst, throwing shards of nylon and plastic into May's face. He fell back, arms crossing over his face, and did a clumsy catfall down to the pavement. The truck roared and moved toward the van. May rolled out of the way and came up to find himself staring down the barrel of the rifle.

"No," he said.

The guard smiled. He raised the rifle to his shoulder, and the smile shattered into a grimace. A bright flash of silver burst out from his lower abdomen and began to rip its way up, catching on his rib cage and physically lifting him into the air. The weapon slipped from his hands and fired as it hit the ground.

"The truck!" Winters shouted, pulling the blade out and letting the body fall to the ground.

May scrambled to his feet and pumped his legs, almost catching the truck before it put on a final burst of speed. From over the roar of the engine came a quick series of concussions from an autoshot, and someone began shouting obscenities. May threw himself down to the concrete and heard Winters dive into the brush. Tires screeched, and there was a sickening crunch, followed by the hiss of glass spraying on pavement.

"Son of a bitch!"

"Get the xeno! *Get the xeno!*"

The autoshot sounded again, followed by the sound of pellets hitting metal.

"Other side! Other side!"

May looked up from his cower to see one of the guards circling around on the driver's side of the truck. He stopped at the back, looking May's way, then pushed open the rear door.

There was a rustle from behind.

"Hey!" Winters shouted. "You get away from that!"

The guard spun and sprayed the area with gunfire. May yelped and rolled off the road into the ditch. A large figure hit the ground next to him, breathing hard.

"Winters!" the merchant whispered.

"I'm okay," the big man gulped. "We're pinned. Shoulda got that piece of shit rifle. Better'n nothing."

There was a shout of "Hurry!" May inched forward and peered down the road. The driver appeared, his arms full of a woven silver wrap that squirmed and wriggled, slowing his progress. He stumbled to the back of the truck and hefted the bundle up, where it was caught up by a waiting pair of hands.

"You *bastards*!" May rose up, shouting, but a massive hand fell between his shoulder blades and dragged him back down as another volley of shots scarred and tore leaves from the surrounding trees. "They've got misterbob!" he growled at Winters, who calmly put his finger to his lips.

"Don't get excited," Winters said. "Look at the other side of the van. Don't say nothing."

May crept up again and squinted into the night. After a moment he could see it—a shadow flattened against the passenger side of the truck. Its left hand held something long and slender, the other end of which was cradled in the crook of the shadow's right arm.

"Get him," May whispered. "Get him, Vonn, *get him*!"

"Go for them when he fires," Winters said, "but keep your ass down."

May nodded and growled, *"Get him, Vonn . . ."*

Burris appeared around front of the van. "The xeno?" he asked.

"Stowed," said the guard with the weapon.

"Get him—"

"Shh," Winters urged.

"The others?"

"Pinned," the guard said.

"No survivors," Burris said. "We'll take all the bodies and leave the van. Meantime, close that door. We don't want that thing to get away."

The driver and guard nodded. Burris produced a cloth, blew his nose, and started to walk away. The door of the truck started to lower, and the guard raised his weapon and started toward May's position.

"Oh, boys," he called. "I'd like you to meet my friend Rosalita."

Winters giggled. "It's bad luck to call your gun that."

The humor was lost on May, who had locked his gaze on the shadow against the side of the truck. "Dammit, Vonn! *Vonn . . .*"

The driver reached up to grab the handle of the door, and as he did, Vonn whirled away from the side of the truck and fired two shots. The driver suddenly spun up on his toes in a skewed pirouette, then went strangely limp and hit the ground. The guard turned and sprayed the back of the truck with fire, but Vonn was gone. With a scream, Winters was up and running, with May half a heartbeat behind him, shouting for the big man to stop. Winters took two more steps, there was a flash and a thunderclap, and the big man was airborne. He hit the guard, and they both went down as bright red light flooded the scene.

May stopped for an instant to assess the situation and heard the cry of bending metal.

"The truck!" he shouted.

Vonn stepped onto the road as the truck lurched back; the rear bumper clipped his side and pitched him back into the brush. May took two steps and grabbed the fallen guard's weapon as the truck ground to a stop, then, in a squeal of tires, lurched forward.

"The tires!" someone shouted, but it was lost. A primal cry ripped from May's throat, followed by every obscene word he could think of. He brought the weapon up, and it hammered and bucked in his hands, bullets tearing and sparking off of the back of the vehicle. There was a sudden rush of air across the front of May's face, and something jolted the gun from his hands and tossed it to the ground with a fresh bend in the barrel. He watched the truck vanish into the night, his ears ringing from pounding blood and the sounds of violence.

Gradually, words found their way into his brain. "Bastard! You stupid bastard! The tires, I said! You aim for the frigging tires!"

May shook his head. It was like waking from a dream. Vonn was pacing around him, shouting at the top of his lungs.

"That's no armored truck like we took the phials from! Those bullets could have gone right through! What if you iced mister-bob, Captain Frigging Hero? You think of that?" He paused for a moment, salting the air with a few well-chosen epithets about May's lineage. "From now on you fly the damn ship and leave the fighting to professionals, okay?"

"*Professionals?*" May shrieked. "You 'professionals' let us get taken by a bunch of coffee-swigging spice roll addicts! Think about that."

"Where the hell was our ground support, May? misterbob was supposed to spray those bastards with that nuclear-powered scent of his. Where was that? He sat on his fat clam-shell ass while ours got kicked!"

May took a deep breath. "It was there," he said. "It had to be. They didn't smell it. They all had colds or something, didn't you notice? They probably all shot up with allergens before coming because they expected something like this."

"Hey, guys," Winters said, limping over. "Are you done fighting? I got—"

"Are you okay?" Vonn asked quickly.

Winters nodded. "I was kinda close when you took that last guy and got some pellets in my leg. I'll be okay."

"What do you want?" May asked, trying to control his trembling.

Winters pointed. "This one's still alive. He wanted to say something to you."

With a nod, the merchant shuffled to the guard Winters had tackled. He squatted down beside him, reached down, and loosened the collar of his uniform.

"Let's put this unpleasantness behind us," May said. "We'll get you some help."

The guard raised a quivering finger and aimed it at Vonn. He fought for a moment to get his breathing under control, then said, "Nice shot."

Vonn turned away.

May tore a strip of cloth from the guard's uniform and began to fold it into a compress. "You wanted to say something to me?"

The guard nodded. He drew a deep breath, and his face twisted in concentration.

"Easy. There's time."

The guard's cheeks puffed out and popped, and a warm, sticky blob struck May in the face.

"*You*—" May cried, and his hands darted for the guard's throat, but Winters held him back.

"It's too late," the big man said. "He's gone."

Slowly May brought the makeshift compress up and wiped his face. The guard was limp, his eyes staring blankly up into the night.

"What now?" asked Vonn, who had not turned back to look at his handiwork.

"Every turn—" May said. "Every move I've made, that son of a bitch has seen it coming. I guess the time has come to try and do something he doesn't expect."

"What's that?"

"First, we don't panic. I think he's counting on us to flee the scene and leave our mess behind. How many dead?"

"Two guards," Vonn said. "The driver."

"We pick them up. We put them in the van. We bundle them up, and on the way back to the *Angel's Luck* we have Peter Chiba drop them into a high-decay orbit. They should burn up on reentry, and we'll be rid of that much evidence."

"Do we dump the van?" Vonn asked.

May shook his head. "We might need it yet. I haven't explained the damage from hitting Burris's car, and the rental company's not going to be happy about it—"

"They're going to be pissed," Vonn said. "That truck really creamed it."

"As long as it runs." May pulled to a standing position. "You're sure you're okay, Winters?"

The big man nodded.

"All right. We need to hurry. Vonn, open the back doors, and Winters and I will bring the bodies over."

Vonn walked down the road without comment.

"It's not his fault," May said. "It's not yours, either."

Winters shrugged. "You're not supposed to feel nothing because you get paid, win or lose. But you still feel bad when your boss don't win."

May managed a smile. "Bet it makes the boss feel like hell, too." He tapped the guard's body with his toe. "Let's start with this one."

They had no sooner bent to the task when there was a shrill scream from the van. They dropped their load and ran over. They found Vonn two meters from the caved-in rear of the van, sitting in the middle of the road with his right hand over his chest.

"I'm not getting in there," he said, shaking and pale. "I'm not getting in that van."

"What the hell's your problem?" May asked.

"misterbob," Winters said. "He's scared of misterbob."

May shook his head. "Burris *got* misterbob."

"Not all of it," Vonn said, trembling.

Grumbling, May slipped up to the van and pulled at the door. It opened with a metallic grunt, and the air that drifted out from inside choked May and caused his eyes to water.

Ammonia, he thought. The halls of the *Hergest Ridge*. Not that, not that . . .

He swallowed and peered in. A light flickered on, and May's breath stopped.

It was lying on the middle of the deck. It was long and brick-

red, and yellow fluid still seeped from one end. On the other
end, stilled and peaceful, were two sets of opposable, chitinous
fingers.

9

Duke fought hard to keep his wits about him. He felt as if he
had been walking for years, and all he could see in any direction
he looked was the same shade of gray. In spite of the tingling
numbness that filled his body, he kept moving forward, one step
at a time, pausing occasionally to lift his hands up before his
face in order to assure himself that he could see something besides the blankness that surrounded him.

As he plodded away from the hotel, he found himself wishing
that Dickson would show up to torment him with some an-
guished moment from his past. Even that would be better than
this current state of nonexistence. As he thought about that prospect more, he found himself shaking his head. He knew exactly
where he was going, and he knew that Dickson would be waiting
for him.

He continued on—for two or three centuries, it seemed—until
at last the nothing that he was walking on seemed to become
solid and then began to clang under his feet like plates of rein-
forced metal. Duke's gait began to slow. He had the sensation
that the bottoms of his feet were sticky. When he checked his
feet, he saw what was happening. He was wearing the bottom
half of an EVA suit, and the feet had magnets in the soles so he
could walk without drifting.

A good thing, he thought. Since I'm so terrible at catfalls—
although I could probably borrow Eric's.

His breathing began to resonate in his ears, and he started to
grow warm. Now he was wearing a complete suit, including the
helmet. Instinctively, he stopped and grabbed a high-intensity
beam from off of his utility belt and shone it in front of him.
The gray was beginning to clear, and he was standing in a corridor of corrugated metal. In front of him was an airlock door,
which had been left standing partly open. With a resolute nod,
he pulled the door open and stepped into the lock.

The inner door was open as well. Duke understood then that
he was on a derelict ship. He turned to the control panel next to
him and let Eric's knowledge punch in the orders to seal the
hatch behind him. Having done that, it was simply a matter of

going inside to the support bay and seeing if enough atmosphere had been saved to repressurize the inside.

No, that's not what Eric is wanting you to do, he told himself. He just wants you on this ship. Duke looked warily at the inner door. The sounds of his own breath rasped in his ears. You're not even going to greet me at the door with your smile and say "Welcome aboard the *Cloud of Magellan*," he thought. You're going to let me find out all of this stuff for myself.

Duke fought to control his breathing. It was hot in the EVA suit. Shining the light with one trembling hand, he reached out with the other for the inner door.

"Beef," he told himself as he touched the door. "Sides of beef. Home. The abattoir."

The door opened noiselessly, and he stepped into the hall. At first glance, he almost laughed in relief, for it looked as if the walls were lined with his uncle's product, all cleaned and hanging in one of the Arbor Company freezer bays, waiting for a drunk nephew to sell them to an equally drunk merchant captain. But as he took his first halting steps down the hall, he could see what really filled the halls of the *Cloud of Magellan*. Duke's breath roared in his ears as he fought to keep it in check.

The hulks lining the walls were people, or rather, what remained of them. The skin from the bottom of the rib cage to the top of the pelvis was gone, as were all of the internal organs. On each and every one, the eyes and mouth were open in shock or surprise, and a finely crafted silver nail was driven through each forehead, securing the body to the bulkhead.

They had been disemboweled and nailed to the walls of the ship with large metal spikes.

Duke continued on, trying to keep from losing his breath. He aimed his light straight down the hall, but it was no use. They lined both sides of the wall, corpse after corpse after corpse, until the passageway ended half a hundred meters away.

"Meat," he said, trying to set his jaw. "Abattoir. Home. The busy season. Hot and hanging—take the clients to the nice, cool freezer."

It did not help. The suit was too hot, the remains too human. It might not have been so bad had the memories not come flooding in from what he had gotten from Eric Dickson. Some faces were familiar—there was Denis Weir, Miriam Hastings, Jack O'Donnell, D'rinda MacKenna.

"Something's wrong." Duke whispered. "This isn't the same. This isn't the same ship he showed me when we were being chased by the *Yueh-sheng*." He continued down the hall, losing his initial revulsion, stopping occasionally to examine vacant faces with the light he carried.

The *Cloud of Magellan*, he remembered, was smaller. According to the book, and what he could remember from Dickson, the *Cloud* was the first ship ever found in that condition.

Duke swallowed against the heat in the suit. The light was shining in the faces of some cadets he had seen at the hearing in the Narofeld hangar.

But this was not the *Cloud*. It was worse. The light was trembling now, and he could not keep the beam still. Sweat poured from his face inside the helmet, and the view plate was starting to fog.

This was from later. Much later. This is—

The light fell on one last face. Hair cut short into a pilot trim, soft but strong features, and a vacant look in glazed eyes. Well-muscled and dead, a spike in the forehead—

Leigh Brand.

"It's the sortie from Bering's Gate."

Duke screamed and turned, the bulk of the suit pulling him to the floor. He threw his light at the figure that had spoken, but it bounced harmlessly down the hall. The figure, also in an EVA suit, made an exaggerated nodding motion. The radio plug in Duke's left ear hissed.

"It's about time you got here. You should've taken the fighter."

"You *bastard*," Duke said. "This isn't the *Cloud of Magellan*."

"That would have been worthless," Eric Dickson said. He absently played the light off the various corpses hanging in the corridor. "I'd already showed that to you once. Its effectiveness is gone."

"Effectiveness for what?" Duke reached around, trying to get back on his feet. After a moment, he gave up and sat, arms crossed.

"An object lesson. I thought you'd want to see what you were perpetuating by sucking up to those Arcolian bastards."

Duke fought to slow his breathing. "Those Arcolians are not the same as the ones who did . . . this."

"What's the real difference, Duke? You know, I've been looking through what you remember and what you've experienced, and it seems to me that you've let yourself get so awed by the Arcolians that you've forgotten what savages they really are."

Duke shook his head. "No more than us, Eric. We make war among ourselves, we sell out our friends for money, our uninhibited sexuality gets us into trouble . . ."

"You've seen what the Arcolians have done."

"This was a long time ago," Duke said. "And we were at war then. And I'm sure we did things to them that they were outraged about. That our two species could meet at a table and work out our differences is a tribute to our maturity as a race."

Dickson stared up at Leigh Brand. "That won't bring her back."

"Of course not. You've got to leave her, Eric. She wouldn't want you to do this."

Dickson whirled on him, aiming a gloved finger like a weapon. "Don't say that. Don't you give me that line. I'm not buying it. That's what my evaluator said—it was a joke then, and it's worse now."

Duke uncurled and managed to rise to his feet. "Leigh was another casualty of war—"

"No!" Dickson shouted. "She was tortured and mutilated by a bunch of xeno—"

"What would you have said," Duke interrupted, "if Leigh had died in her fighter? What if her ship had been one of those blown out at Bering's Gate, if she had been killed by the initial ambush?"

"It's still the same thing."

"Humor me," Duke urged. "What if it hadn't been the Arcolians? What if it had been a *Yueh-sheng* ship? What if it had been pirates? What if she had been working a blockade against some planet and had died in an attack?"

"But she didn't."

"If she had?"

Dickson shook his head. The gesture was almost invisible because of the bulk of his suit. "There's nothing wrong with dying in the line of duty."

"And what was her duty?"

"To fight."

"For what?"

"For us."

"So dying like that is a brave thing to do."

"Brave, hell. Gallant. With honor. Better you should die in the line of duty than like poor old Thomas Fortunado. Better to die like that than like some diseased old wreck—"

"All right," Duke said. "Now, what if it turned out that the

Arcolian War hadn't sprung up because of sudden xenophobia on both sides, and if it hadn't been perpetuated by the differences in our cultures? What if we had fought it for some noble cause—does that make it any less wrong if we were convinced we were doing right?''

''What are you getting at?''

Duke slowly paced the hall. Because of the suit and the magnetic grips, his movements looked slow and meaningful. ''The Arcolians wanted to end the war as badly as we did. It came down to a matter of not being able to accurately communicate with us. They understood the situation—we did, too, Eric, but we weren't as clever as they. Thus, we took what they were doing to be an atrocity, but they were convinced that what they were doing was right. You have to understand the Arcolian mentality.''

''You're an expert, I suppose.''

''Arcolians have no reverence for their own lives like we do. If a demand is made of them by their society, they give without thinking. They merely assumed that we felt the same way. Hence, they took it upon themselves to design an Arcolian that could communicate with us. And to do that, they had to study us—''

''Which means they had to look at our DNA. Yeah, I remember that you heard that line from one of the ambassadors. Swallowed it pretty good, too.''

''They had to know.''

''They had to do the spikings, too, I suppose.''

''Maybe it was a cultural thing,'' Duke said. ''I don't know. All I know is that the deaths of these people was a very important point in the war—''

''Because we learned what bloodthirsty—''

''Because the Arcolians were able to create a form of their own kind that could interact and learn with us. And all of these people died for that cause, and while they didn't die in combat, their sacrifice meant more to the war effort than the deaths of any other combat forces combined. Their sacrifice was one worthy of an Arcolian. They died for the good of society as a whole.''

''That's the whole idea of a war,'' Dickson scoffed.

''You know what your problem is?'' Duke asked. ''You have the belief that if you don't die in glorious combat, you haven't the right to go into soldier's heaven. Well, I submit to you, Eric, that you'll find Leigh and all of the others nailed to the walls of this ship there. They died with honor. They died in the line of duty, each and every one of them.''

"Then why the spikes?" Dickson demanded.

"I can only speculate. Perhaps they have a tradition of returning the bodies of their enemies. They're chitinous creatures, remember. Maybe they shed and think nothing of nailing up their old, discarded skins. Maybe they thought that we did the same thing, too. They didn't know our culture, and we didn't know theirs.''

Dickson remained silent. Duke continued his slow, stately pace, moving around the pilot.

"It doesn't matter now. It's all beside the point. Leigh made a noble sacrifice, and the war is long since over. It's time to get on with other things.''

"For you, maybe," Dickson pouted.

"For me, especially," Duke said. "I'll learn to deal with you in time, Eric, but right now more pressing matters are at hand.''

"You won't have to worry about me," the pilot answered. "At least, not for much longer.''

"Of course not," Duke said. "We're going to get along fine. We'll work this thing out. But this isn't the time for that. You have to keep up your end of our agreement, Eric.''

"What agreement?"

" 'If I wanted the knowledge, I'd know where to find it.' This is the place, isn't it? You wanted me to come in here and see Leigh Brand, didn't you? Well . . .'' In the heavy suit, he pulled himself to his full height. "I did it.''

Dickson nodded sullenly. "Nothing, I suppose, is going to keep you out of being in bed with the Arcolians.''

"I need to get out of here," Duke said. "*We* need to get out of here.''

"Well." Dickson leaned against the wall and stared blankly in Duke's direction. "I wish you could appreciate what a difficult situation that puts me in. My whole reason for being was to kill Arcolians.''

"Not your whole reason," Duke said.

"Perhaps not. But I was trained as a machine to destroy the enemy, and the Arcolians were the enemy for so damned many years.'' He laughed and looked sullenly in the direction of Leigh Brand's corpse. "You know what she always said to me? She said I'd come out of the war with no problems, that I was a survivor. She said that peace would kill me.''

"We have another enemy now," Duke said. "Burris. We've

got to break out of here before May does something stupid trying to do it for us."

There came a satisfied smile. "I wouldn't worry about that if I were you." Dickson raised a finger and tapped the top of his helmet. "I've already done something that will deliver Burris into the hands of your friends. All he has to do is not drop the ball when it's handed to him."

Duke shivered. "What?"

"Of course," Dickson mused, pleased with himself, "I had to be true to my own nature. I had to do something about my feelings, as well. You have to remember that what you consider a threat, I might consider—"

"What did you do?" Duke said, voice rising.

"And it played so well. One side played against the other. You should've been there to see the look on Burris's face. He's one of those types, Duke, I can work him, and it's not even hard—"

"What did you do?" Duke shouted.

Dickson looked down and studied the palm of one of his gloved hands, rubbing the fingers together as if to dislodge some invisible piece of dirt. "I told him about the Arcolians and how they had the secret of the genetic code."

"You did *what*?"

"It was really great." Dickson laughed. "You should have seen the look on Burris's face. He wanted it so damned bad, worse than he wanted to hang on to us. He got suckered right into it. I'm sure he's going to get in touch with May."

"What makes you so sure?" Duke's hands knotted into fists.

"Simple," Dickson said, pushing off from the wall and hunching forward. "I made a recording for him. Just some simple things, in your voice. A little practice, and I sounded more like you than you do. Nothing fancy, a couple of standard lines like 'May, I'm okay,' and 'May, don't listen to these bastards.' He told me if I did it that he'd let us go once he had the Arcolian."

Duke took three running steps and grabbed the pilot by the straps on the front of his suit. "You trusted him?"

"Hell, no. I set him up to get killed or captured, whatever your friend has in mind. And I kept our asses clear out of it. Don't you see? If Burris is killed, the news hits the wires and we walk out of here. If May captures him, then a big exchange is set up and we still walk out of here. Simple enough."

"No." Duke shoved Dickson back and turned away. His voice

crackled angrily through the headsets. "It's never that simple. What about the betrayal?"

"According to you, Burris deserves it."

"Burris doesn't enter into it! You've betrayed me, you've betrayed the Arcolians—"

"More's the pity," Dickson mumbled.

"And you've betrayed the Accord—"

"The Accord killed me," Dickson said. "This was a damned unique opportunity to get even. Revenge is a dish best eaten cold and all of that shit."

"And you've betrayed everyone who worked for the Accord and fought for the Accord and died so the Accord could be signed. You've cut your own throat, you stupid bastard, because you've betrayed Leigh Brand!"

The helmet muffled Dickson's reaction. He was shaking his head. "No. You're wrong."

Duke started a slow pace back Dickson's way. "I'm right. Because Leigh Brand became a pilot to beat the Arcolians or force them into peace. And she died trying because the Arcolians captured her, and she was eviscerated and disemboweled and had her blood and bone marrow drained. And others had their brains sucked out or their spines removed, or their eyes or their inner ears. And the Arcolians took that stuff, Eric, and they studied it, and they studied the DNA in all of the cells and figured out how we ticked. Then, because they could, they started doing the same thing to their own people, rewriting the genetic code and experimenting until they had the E-forms which they sent out to be captured by us. And heaven only knows how many of those we blasted and chopped up in anger before a handful of them were brought back to study and one of them happened to recognize Admiral Studebaker and said—"

"I know what was said," Dickson said quickly.

"The Arcolian talent for genetic manipulation was sacred," Duke said. "And you gave it to Burris." He shook the pilot. "That makes you a pimp, Eric, a frigging pimp. And since Leigh Brand died to make that possible—"

"Don't," Dickson said.

"—you know what that makes her?"

Dickson tried to back away, but Duke held him fast. "Don't you *dare* profane her memory."

"I don't have to!" Duke shouted. "You've already done it! You've made a mockery of it! You've made Leigh Brand—"

A cry began to well up in Dickson's throat, threatening to overload the speaker in Duke's ear.

"—a whore!" Duke cocked his arms and pushed with all his might, hoping to smash Dickson back into the wall. But when his arms flexed out, they snapped at vacuum as if nothing had been there to begin with. The sensation caught Duke off guard, and he stumbled forward, windmilling his arms in a catfall to reset his balance. After he had steadied, he looked around the halls of the ship and the abattoir it had become.

"She's a whore, Eric," he said contemptuously, hoping the pilot would hear it in whatever recesses he had retreated to. "And it's your fault."

He took a moment to collect his thoughts, and as he calmed, he realized that he was quite alone on the derelict vessel. The hairs on the back of his neck bristled, and he tried to brush them down but was thwarted by the suit's bulk.

Duke kicked at the bulkhead and swore. "How in the hell did he find out about the Arcolians knowing—" He suddenly checked himself. "Never mind," he said, trying to stay calm.

Slowly, he walked back to the airlock and stepped through into the gray wall.

10

Burris took the last tissue from the box and blew his nose violently. "That was foul stuff," he complained to Melrose. "And what's worse, we didn't need it. We grabbed the Arcolian with no problem."

"That foul stuff is the reason there was no problem," Melrose told him, giving a handful of pills to Sergeant Emerson, the one surviving guard. "With your sinuses blocked from the allergic reaction, you weren't able to smell when he emitted his defensive scent."

Burris finished wiping his nose and tossed the soaked tissue into the waste disposal. "What made you think they even had a defensive scent?"

"All that crash research you laughed at me for doing. Several face-to-face accounts from the war years stated that troops which landed in Arcolian-held territories were seized with an unreasonable fear of any aliens that were found. They were convinced that even the C-forms, which resembled nothing so much as protoplasmic jelly, were going to suddenly transmute into some terrifying fanged and clawed creature. It was like the scent was releasing some hidden race memory of a creature like Sol's Bengal tiger.''

"What did they smell?" the guard asked mockingly. "Its breath?"

"Its feces," Melrose said bluntly.

"Oh, yeah," Emerson said bitterly. "Well, you should have given us something to protect us from those mercenaries."

"But we got the Arcolian," Burris said triumphantly.

"At what price?" the guard demanded. "We had a sixty-percent casualty rate. That's obscene, considering you told us that we'd be taking that thing from some overweight, low-gee-weak spacers. They acted quite professionally, for being such losers."

Burris clapped his hand on the guard's shoulder. "That's all behind us now. The Arcolians are going to make the company rich, starting with you. By virtue of your performance, you have also earned the bonus money that would have gone to the others, as well as your own."

"By virtue of survivorship, you mean," Emerson snapped. He threw a used tissue on the floor. "Keep it, sir," he said contemptuously. "Or better yet, send it to the families of the dead. They'll need it a hell of a lot more than I will." He stomped out of the medical lab.

"You certainly didn't inherit your father's sense of tact," Melrose commented.

"It doesn't matter," Burris said. "When I get the charts run on the Arcolian and its systems, and get it to give us the secrets of the genetic code, I'm going to get my father's chairmanship back. And I'm going to have the head of every member of the board of directors who voted to stick me out here. They're going to pay for what they did."

Melrose cleared his throat. "I've been meaning to talk to you about this business of the Arcolian divulging the information you want. I think a little common sense is in order."

"That's why I held on to Mr. Arbor," Burris said with a grin. "If the xeno holds out, we threaten to vivisect its friend in front of it."

"I don't think it'll react to that," Melrose said. "But that's not what I was talking about."

"It doesn't matter," Burris replied. "It has what I want, and I'll be damned if I don't get it. Everything's got its button, Vinnie, *everything*. If the xeno's button isn't William Arbor, then I want your people to find out what it is, and then I'm going to push it.''

Melrose was silent, giving a slight shrug.

"Are you ready to go see it?" Burris asked.

"Whenever you are," Melrose said noncommittally.

With a nod, Burris walked out the door of the treatment room, Melrose at his heels. They walked down the corridor, past the surveillance room, and to the end of the hall, where they stepped through an airlock into a small anteroom where Dinah sat behind a row of controls, half in and half out of a clear plastic cleansuit. She was looking through a double set of windows into a large, white room, in the center of which was a table canted at an angle. Strapped to the table was the Arcolian, minus its usual purple robe. Its head was pivoting on its shoulders, arm waving in the air, giving the appearance that it was having an animated conversation with the cleansuited figures that staffed the inner room.

"What's the outer airlock doing open, Dinah?" Burris asked.

She turned suddenly, startled to see him there. "There's an airlock and a negative pressure seal between us and—"

"Seal it, please," Burris said. "We can't afford any mistakes.''

Behind him, Melrose nodded.

Dinah keyed an order, and the doors behind them closed with a hiss.

"And put the rest of your cleansuit on."

Dinah gestured at a row of readouts before her. "The Arcolian is only putting out minute traces of particle scent. It could be likened to what normally comes off of a human, only in a little greater concentration. We get some occasional low rises, and my assumption is that he's talking to himself.''

"It," Burris said sternly. "This is not a human, and therefore it is certainly not a he or a she. It is an Arcolian, and therefore an it. You will address it as such from now on."

"But his—its—personality is so distinctive, it's so intelligent, we just assumed—"

"Never assume anything," Burris advised. He pulled two wrapped cleansuits from a shelf and tossed one to Melrose. "Especially not over anything this important."

"That thing is driving them crazy with questions," Dinah said. "It's asking them about everything."

Melrose tore the wrapping off the cleansuit, glancing up at

the rows of video monitors that lined the upper part of the room and studying the different angles they showed of the Arcolian. "How about the injury?" he asked. "Does it seem to be in any pain?"

"It hasn't complained," Dinah replied, zipping up the torso of her suit. "In fact, it's been almost too casual about losing the arm. It let our people look at where it was attached, and they said that there isn't any damage to the chitin. The wound seems to have closed itself off rather neatly, which is a lucky thing. Ultrasound shows that this thing has an open circulatory system."

"So?" Burris said, stepping into his cleansuit.

"An open circulatory system has no veins or arteries to carry the blood," Melrose said. "The internal organs are literally bathed in the blood matter and directly absorb what they need. With the right kind of injury, there would be no self-sealing veins or arteries, and the creature could bleed to death."

"Leak to death, you mean," Burris said smugly.

"It's really a remarkable piece of adaptation," Dinah said admiringly.

"How does the creature's brain get enough blood?" Melrose asked, working his arms into the stressed plastic sleeves. "Most open-circulatory animals are notoriously slow-witted."

"They've found a shunting system," Dinah said. "Like three open-ended hearts attached end to end with tendrils running to three body cavities where the blood tends to pool. It squeezes blood upward to the top of the cranial cavity and keeps the brain well soaked—more so, they speculate, than any of the other major organs with the possible exception of the main heart."

Burris pulled the hood up over his head, adjusting the elastic so that only his face was visible through the plastic. "I don't see why we have to go through all of this," he complained. "Why don't you just give us another round of allergens?"

"The allergens were a quick fix," Melrose said, handing Burris a large mask. "We don't know what their scents are based on. They may be something that can be absorbed through our skin with the same effect as inhalation, which gives it the potential of being even more subtle and insidious."

Grumbling, Burris fitted the mask over his face and tried to adjust the straps in the back.

"But mostly," Dinah said, "we've got very sensitive instruments measuring the air in the clean room, and we don't want your body's scents fouling up our readings."

"Yeah. Right." Burris's voice was muffled, but there was no mistaking the contemptuous tone.

"You haven't got a good seal," Melrose said. He stepped over to his taller colleague and adjusted the straps in the back. "How's that?"

Burris waved his hands and spoke. His words were indistinguishable.

Melrose smiled and winked at Dinah. "That's about a perfect fit, isn't it?"

Burris stamped his foot and spoke again. The front of his mask began to fog, and its seal began to flap from the increased air pressure, then to rattle against the plastic hood, making a low fricative sound.

"No, no," Melrose said. "You can't breathe hard or shout. You'll ruin the seal and contaminate the clean room with elements of your breath."

Burris's arms crossed, and he said something else.

"I'll be right there." The doctor pulled the hood over his head. "Wait for me at the inner airlock."

Burris shuffled off, trailing a string of garbled epithets.

"That's a definite improvement," Dinah said quietly. "Is that the one that's defective?"

Melrose nodded.

Dinah suppressed a giggle. "What are the odds that we can keep him in that mask all the time?"

Melrose's answer was a sad shrug. "What are the odds that we can save the life of that poor creature in there? If the boss doesn't get what he wants out of it, I'm afraid it's going to end up on the vivisection table."

"He's such a bastard," Dinah whispered, casting a careful glance at the inner airlock.

"The research on this one is going to be slow, if you know what I mean," Melrose said in low tones. "Take your time in seeing that the data is compiled into the central memory. Sit on some of it if you have to."

"I already have been," Dinah admitted.

"Good girl. Maybe I can arrange for an information leak to the press, if I can think of a way to have the boss come out of it looking good."

"You could always say that the Arcolian volunteered to let itself be examined."

"The problem is getting the ambassador to corroborate that story." Melrose grabbed a mask and began to fit it over his face.

"By the way, what are we dealing with, Dinah? Is it a 'he' or a 'she'?"

She shrugged. "We haven't been able to determine a sex as of yet. There's no visible genitalia, and we haven't been able to determine the purpose of all the internal organs we've found. Since there are different types of Arcolians, our guest may not have any."

Melrose looked up at one of the monitors. That strange double-pupiled eye was blinking and looking around at the humans in the clean room. "So 'it' it is. Poor guy."

"Good luck," Dinah said as Melrose secured his mask and walked to the inner airlock. He gave her a thumbs-up and closed the hatch behind him.

"This is a pain in the ass," Burris said as air cycled through the locks.

"I'm sorry," Melrose lied. "I can't understand you."

"Understand this, then." He made a vulgar gesture that had been imported from the Elregg system.

The two approached the table. One of the workers was taking readings from a rack of instruments that had been wheeled in, gloved fingers fumbling with the writing instrument.

Melrose laid a hand on the technician's shoulder. "Tell us what you know about our guest, Reg."

"Not a lot yet." Reg shrugged. "That pulpy mass you see in the center of the chest is the communicative apparatus. It makes the scents and both smells and tastes the air for others. The mottled pink and blue you see is because it also uses it as we would lungs, exchanging gases in its blood."

"That's not bad," Melrose said. "You've been making progress."

"That's it, though," Reg said with a disappointed tone. "All the rest is the boring basics. One hundred seven centimeters in height, weight fifty-three kilos. Most of that, we think, is the outer shell, which means that our friend here must have some extraordinary musculature inside."

Burris said something loudly. It came out as a random spill of consonants, punctuated by the loud *brakkk* of the mask's seal.

Melrose waved his hand. "No," he said. "You can't do that."

Burris stamped his foot and mouthed the words, "I'll damn well do what I want. It's my damn lab," but the exertion started to fog the face plate again, and the seal of the mask went *blurt, blurt, blurtttt* against the side of his head. Melrose looked at Reg, who had turned away to conceal his laughter. Through the window, Dinah had cupped one hand over her face and was visibly shaking. Burris's face grew redder, he shouted louder, and the mask continued to vent air. The situation would have degenerated further had there not been another sound, a low and resonant croak carefully formed into syllables, coming from the table.

"I understand," it said.

Every human in the room froze.

"There is no reason to show embarrassment," the Arcolian said, concerned. "I understand that the Sapient A-forms play host to a number of colonial bacteria and are forced to expel the gaseous secretions of these bacteria in a manner they consider distasteful. It is a common condition, and I have learned to disregard the involuntary message carried by the scents involved."

The room filled with muffled laughter.

"I scent that I have amused you A-forms?"

Melrose turned to the tech. "It's reading us through these suits?"

Reg nodded. "We think it's picking up on our breath."

"But the expirations are vented through charcoal and—"

"As he would tell you," the Arcolian said, "my sensory apparatus is most sensitive."

Melrose smiled under the mask. "You'll have to forgive me. I've never had to think of something that looks like an animal as being—"

"Sapient? Indeed, I have had to make the same adjustment."

There was more laughter, which ended suddenly when the air was split with a string of bitter oaths. All eyes fell on Burris, who had torn off his mask and tossed it to the floor.

"Dammit!" he shouted. "I can't believe the way you people are sucking up to this—this *thing*." His finger rose and singled out Reg. "*You*. Calling that thing a friend . . ."

There was a chitinous clatter as the Arcolian clicked its fingers together. "Ah," it said. "I believe I know you. You must be bastardburris."

Burris froze, momentarily nonplussed by the fact that the Arcolian had addressed him directly.

"Indeed. I fear that I must rely on falsescents since I have no direct scent, but your voice I recollect from your transmission to *angelsluck*, and your face is similar to that which was in the broadcast. Yes, you are the one which jamesohjames refers to as bastardburris."

"Am I now?" Burris said, having gathered his wits enough to try a threatening tone of voice. "And what should I call you?"

The organ on misterbob's chest pulsated and fluttered. Reg and Melrose took a cautious step back. "The malevolence I scent in your attitude tells me that you would probably be happiest in addressing me as bugface or xenomenace. I believe those are the popular vulgarslangs for my race. However, you must always address me as—" The Arcolian raised its arm and tapped below its mouth in thought. Seeing it raised gooseflesh on Melrose's arms and back.

"As what?" Burris said impatiently.

"Ambassador," misterbob said. "Indeed, you must always call me 'ambassador.' " Its chest continued to pulsate.

"I suppose you think you're clever," Burris said. "I suppose you think that I'll call you that because you have me intimidated and that doing so will keep me from harming you."

"Indeed not," misterbob said. "You are of the type who would not stop at harming any of the individuals in this room. I have no experience at influence of the subtlety of which you speak. I ask this because of what you would call social convention. The other Sapient A-forms in this room all scent that you should call me some term of high respect such as 'lord' or 'avatar' or 'madame.' I believe that 'ambassador' would be sufficient."

"You sons of bitches," Burris said, looking around at the others. He checked himself and focused on misterbob. "You mean to tell me that the people in this room are all on your side? What did you do, Ambassador, dose them all with some kind of Super Ferocious Tiger Scent?"

"No," misterbob said quietly. "That is the belief I scent, and as you are their leader, I shall not interfere with the manner in which you exert control over them. But that is what they believe, and if you do not believe that I have not influenced them in any manner, then I humbly suggest that you should bring in the dogs."

The others present gasped.

"Indeed, bastardburris, were it in my plans to pheromonally influence the others, I could well have done it by now. If I were to use what you call 'tigerscat,' I would certainly have directed it at you when you removed your mask. That I have not done so should show my sincerity."

Reg reached up and pulled off his mask. Melrose quickly did the same, and the others followed suit.

"Why are you so concerned about appearing sincere to us," Burris asked, "when all you have to do to manipulate us is—"

"Indeed not," misterbob interrupted. "I shall not manipulate you. Not in this situation. It would not be in keeping with my status as ambassador to your race. You are of the type, bastardburris, that you will do what you will to me, and no amount of my influence will stop that. Contrary to the popular belief among the Sapient A-forms, my powers are finite. Perhaps you should consider that I am here to use my abilities in another manner."

Burris folded his arms and took a step toward the Arcolian. "You mean that you didn't try to defend yourself last night? What did you do, allow yourself to be captured?"

"If that is your interpretation, bastardburris, I will not argue with it."

"We took you," Burris said, voice raising. "My doctor injected us with allergens so you couldn't frighten us, and my people got themselves shot to pieces by your mercenary friends, and now you're telling us that you let yourself get caught?"

The Arcolian nodded, and the sight made Melrose shiver. "I was aware that you had allergens and were incapable of scenting my messages. That caused me some distress, but not as much distress as I received from another message. Indeed, bastardburris, I scented from the start that you did not have misterduke with you, and that you had no intention of turning him over to jamesohjames."

"Mr. Duke? Who the hell is—"

"William Arbor," Melrose whispered.

"Quite correct," misterbob said. "Your intent of leaving my hosts dead and taking me was quite clear, but the disastrous outcome of our meeting shows that you underestimated their strengths as they underestimated yours. It would not have taken much on my part to turn the encounter against you. Had I indulged in what you would call passive resistance, that would have bought time enough for mistervonn and bigguy to rally and kill you."

"So you surrendered."

"Indeed not. I merely decided to submit to you so I could insure the safety and release of misterduke."

"How noble," Burris sneered. "And how do you plan on doing that?"

The Arcolian cocked its head at Burris. "From what I understand, many Sapient·A-forms believe that there is much money to be made from the Arcolian physiology. A group on the *hergestridge* believed that and attempted to steal me. From what jamesohjames has told me and from what I scent of you, you will cooperate if—as your race is wont to put it—the price is correct."

Burris looked at the others in the room and laughed. "You make it sound like I'm the one who is the prisoner."

"That is your own supposition," misterbob said.

"What makes you think I'm going to cooperate with you, Ambassador? After all, I'm the one who has your misterduke, I'm the one who has you—"

"When the time comes," the Arcolian interrupted with a tone that had altered just enough to sound menacing. "When the time comes, bastardburris, you will not stop misterduke from walking out of here on his own power. He will do it with your blessing or without."

"He will only do it *with* my blessing, I can assure—"

"bastardburris," misterbob said coldly. "The determination of greed is no equal to the determination of loyalty. I need do nothing, and misterduke will still walk out of here because of who his friends are. It is best that you cooperate and gain your profit. Certainly you do not wish to see your fine employees want for employment."

The room filled with murmurs and chuckles.

"Out," Burris barked. "Out. All of you."

The others in their cleansuits stared.

"Now, dammit! You don't need to listen to the rest of this conversation." He raised an arm and flagged it at the two closest departing figures. "Vinnie. Reg. I want you to stay here." He turned back to the crowd forming at the airlock. "One of you, tell Dinah to ready the digital recorder. We're going to see just how sincere Ambassador Bugface is."

A dim rattle came from the examination table.

"What the hell is that?" Burris demanded.

"I believe," Reg said, "that the ambassador is laughing."

Burris swore violently and paced until the last of the technicians had left the room. When the airlock door sealed shut for the last time, he turned to the window and demanded to know if the recorder was ready. Dinah nodded. "All right," he said, addressing the ambassador. "We're going to continue this without your putting undue pheromonal influence on my people. I don't know what you were using, but fortunately I seem to be immune to it.''

"You will forgive me for failing to sound humble," the Arcolian replied, "but my influence on them was not pheromonal. The word for what you claim immunity to is *charisma*."

"Let's just say that I'm on to you," Burris said. "But I'm going to see how sincere you really are. If you want your friend to stay safe, I'm assuming that you came prepared to divulge some secrets of the Arcolian physiology."

"We have no secrets," misterbob said. "We are all taught of our nature since roehood."

"But you have one thing that you've kept from us, haven't you, Ambassador? You've failed to tell your new allies that you know how to perform genetic engineering."

"Genetic engineering," misterbob said. "Ah, yes. misterduke used the term once. We were discussing manipulation of the spiral code."

"Yes," Burris said. "The genetic code. Don't deny it."

"I would not deny such a thing," misterbob said, sounding indignant. "We do not openly discuss such a thing around Sapient A-forms because we understand that this is a break in the chitin to them."

"Well," Burris said with a smug grin. "You're going to tell me all about it." He looked out at the observation room. "Dinah, start the recorder."

The woman nodded.

"Ambassador."

misterbob shifted on the table. "Where would you like me to begin?"

"With an overview," Burris said. "The good Dr. Melrose will be asking you questions to fill in the gaps."

"Very well." misterbob shifted as if it was about to relate a long tale. "My ancient ancestors would get falsescents of stars in the sky and dream about what they were. Since we had no scent of them it was many generations before we were able to understand that these were other worlds for us to occupy."

"Get to the point," Burris growled.

misterbob annoyedly rattled its fingers. "This is a part of the story," it said. "My ancestors realized what they were seeing and then came to realize that in their present form—the horizontal axis—they were condemned to remain on motherworld, which you call Arcolia. If only, they lamented, there was a way to change their forms, to adapt, to become the creatures which could build the vehicles to take us there. We were a sapient race, bastardburris, but our primary forms limited our technology. Most ancestral Arcolians lived and died within a fifty-kilometer radius of the place of their hatching.

"But these stars of which we had no scent were beguiling. Some of them were worlds that circled our own motherstar. We had to find a way to alter our forms. Fortunately, our medical technology was not one which suffered. And we had one other trait which did not slow our research, even as you have been slowed in your research, bastardburris. Our people were willing to undergo tests of the new technology for the common good of the race. It was a mere thirteen generations between the time we realized the potential of manipulating the spiral code to the time at which the process was perfected and put into common practice."

"That's a long time," Melrose said. "How did you manage to keep such a persistent vision for so long?"

"Primarily, we are much shorter-lived creatures than yourselves. Indeed, with your hundred twenty years, you will outlive five of my generations. The other reason is that early on we discovered how knowledge was stored in our brains, and we discovered how to pass it from one generation to the next so the original genius of the visionaries would not be lost. It is very similar in principle to the crude manner in which your company does it."

"Crude?" Burris shouted. "Crude—"

Melrose stepped between Burris and the Arcolian. "Easy," he said.

"Within a few generations we had sufficient forms with the proper tactile skills to build the devices we needed for research, to prove the mathematics we had until then deemed theoretical. We colonized our motherstar system, bastardburris, and each time we set down we found worlds inhospitable to us. This did not daunt us. We merely rewrote the code so we had sufficient forms which could inhabit these new places."

"You have more than the six known forms?" Melrose said. "Incredible."

"Many more," misterbob said. "And we were able to accomplish this through a mutual racial cooperation. I have found one destructive flaw in the nature of the Sapient A-form. As a race, you creatures are seriously shortsighted. If something cannot be done in your lifetime, or in a proscribed amount of your lifetime, you lose interest in it. It does not matter. Perhaps you should think as we do, bastardburris. We merely have a lifetime in which to perform, but it is not twenty-five years. It is twenty-five million years. It is the lifetime of our race.''

"Yes." Melrose nodded. "I understand." He looked at Burris. "He's saying it's ours, he's saying we can have it, but only if we stop thinking of the individual and start thinking of the race.''

"That's really nice," Burris snapped. "I didn't want a damned history lesson.''

"The recorder is running," Reg said.

"Fuck all that. It doesn't matter. None of what he said does. I'm not going to wait for my great-great-grandchildren to claim my rightful place as the head of this company." He wagged his finger at misterbob. "That thing has the secret of the genetic code, and it's going to give it to me now or misterduke Arbor is going to wind up on the Expendable List of the Nimrev Company.''

"With proper respects intended," misterbob said. "I will not be divulging what you refer to as the secret of genetic engineering.''

Burris's hands knotted and shook with rage. "Why not? Because it's a crack in our chitin? You little bastard!" He bolted for a table and grabbed a laser scalpel. "I'll show you a crack in the chitin, you miserable insect. I'll give you such a frigging crack—''

He lunged for the Arcolian, but Reg and Melrose grabbed him and wrestled him to the cold stone floor, shouting his name and slamming his hand down until the device rolled harmlessly under the examination table.

"Stop it!" Melrose shouted. "Stop it! It's given us the secret already, can't you see it? You can take what you've learned and become an innovator—you can make this company the greatest in the entire galaxy!" He stared down into Burris's face, trying to get through the hardness he was seeing. Melrose continued quietly, "All you have to do is ask for volunteers.''

"I want it now." It came out as a half whine, half growl. "It's got it, and I've got to have it!''

"No," misterbob croaked from the table. "Even if I had it, I would not divulge such information to a person such as yourself.''

Burris struggled against Melrose and Reg. "You lying bastard! I'll make you talk! I'll bring Arbor into this room and eviscerate him in front of you until—''

"At the risk of bringing misterduke's life to premature end," misterbob interrupted, "were I even willing to give such information, I would not be able to."

"Why the hell not?" Burris grunted through clenched teeth.

"I tried to tell you this," Melrose said.

"I could no more tell you how to manipulate the spiral code any more than you could describe to me the nuances of interfactional rivalry between members of your race and its effect on provisions of the Accord. I am simply not trained in that field. For the information you want, you would have to travel to one of our frontier worlds and procure a roechanger."

Melrose nodded. "A genetic engineer." He felt the fight leave Burris's body and relaxed his grip. Reg followed suit.

"You're an ambassador," Burris said, sitting up and spitting on the floor.

"Indeed. And what I can tell you of roechanging is equal in content to what you might tell me of the signing of the Accord between our two races."

Wiping his mouth with the back of his hand, Burris stood. "I see. I see that now. Yes, I've made a mistake. A very serious tactical error." He nodded sadly at Reg. "Do you have quarters prepared for the Arcolian?"

Reg nodded.

"Take him there. I've got a lot to think about. Vincent, I'd like you to come with me."

Reg stood and crossed to a table to retrieve the Arcolian's purple robe. "If you'll allow me to change the angle of the table, Ambassador . . ."

"Indeed," the Arcolian said. "You must call me misterbob."

Shoulders sagging, Burris stepped through the open airlock door. "It is time to cut our losses," he said as Melrose joined him.

The doctor nodded. "I'm sure you're doing the right thing."

Burris palmed a switch and waited for the hiss of the door before speaking again. "Give the ambassador and Arbor the rest of the day and a night's rest. Starting tomorrow morning, I want you to run every test you can think of. I want crews on them every minute for the next three days, and I want everything you can out of them before that time is up."

"The Geretz Method?" Melrose asked. "You can't be serious. That's—"

"It's what I want."

"Doesn't leave that much room for error."

"It doesn't matter. Do what you have to. Proper disposal of the bodies is the least of my worries." The outer airlock door hissed open and he stalked out, not bothering to remove his cleansuit as he left the observation room.

"Why do I have the feeling that things could have gone better?" Dinah asked as Melrose entered, unzipping his suit.

"He's fine as long as he's in control," Melrose said. "But he's lost control and he can't stand it. He gets desperate and does foolish things in order to right the situation."

Dinah shrugged. "He's never been in control. Not really. He's just thought it."

"Well, he doesn't think it now, and he's going to get us all hung for it. He wants us to use the Geretz Method to see what we can learn from Arbor and the Arcolian."

Dinah paled. "That's awfully hard on the subjects."

"It's hard on everyone involved, but he's beyond caring. I'll tell you something, Dinah. If you've ever entertained any ideas about accidentally letting the doors to this place stand open so our guests can walk out of here, you'd better act on it soon. As of tomorrow morning, they won't have a prayer."

11

The chime from the door of the cabin wakened May. The return to lucidness made him dizzy, and he lifted his head to look around. He had gone to sleep in front of his private computer terminal. He had been writing a letter to the Council branch of Port Authority, but without the CHARLES unit working to transcribe it for him, May had been forced to type each word painstakingly in by hand. Reading over the words he had put in the night before, he decided that this approach would get him nowhere, and with a few key strokes, he cleared the screen.

The chime sounded again. Yes, that was what had wakened him, wasn't it? He leaned over and thumbed a switch. "Yes?"

"Cheech here. May I talk to you, Captain?"

"One moment." He stood and brushed at his jumpsuit, then wondered why he was bothering. Cheech was probably coming up to discuss parts for repair work that he could not afford to pay her for. There seemed to be no end to the situation.

Although, he noted to himself, she had never come to his cabin before to discuss business. She had never come to his cabin before, period. She had always talked to him when he was in the bridge checking on her progress.

Well, he thought as he walked to the door. There's a first time for everything. But the instant before he opened the door, he decided to step out into the hall to speak with her.

"I hope I didn't wake you," Cheech said as the door rose. "I didn't think of that until it was too late."

May shrugged and rubbed the side of his face. "No," he mumbled. "Well, yes, you did wake me, but it wasn't what you'd call a quality sleep." Watching her expression fill with dismay, he tried to change the subject. "What did you need, Cheech?"

"Well," she said hesitantly, "I heard that you lost the Arcolian. I just wanted to say that I'm really sorry about that, Captain. I know what you've been going through."

"Don't worry about it," May said. "It's not your battle. Besides, even if it was, there was nothing you could have done."

"But maybe there was something I could have done," she said quickly, as if she had been waiting for May to say what he had just said. "I feel like maybe I could have made a difference."

May shook his head. "If you'd been there," he told her, "you might've gotten your ass shot off. Don't worry about it."

"But I do."

"What could you have possibly done to change things for me, Cheech?"

Cheech's expression was blank. "I don't know. It was just a feeling, Captain."

"Call me James."

"Shouldn't we step inside your cabin?" she asked. "I mean, what if someone comes along?"

May looked up and down the hall, momentarily confused. "Did I miss something?"

"What do you mean?"

"What's this sudden interest in privacy?"

"I don't know," Cheech admitted. "I thought that maybe if someone came wandering down the hall, you wouldn't want them to hear the conversation."

"Anyone that would come wandering down the hall of this ship," May said, "is authorized to be here and subsequently knows about what is currently going on."

Cheech flushed. "You're not making this any easier for me, Captain—James."

At least she doesn't call me "jamesohjames," May thought. With a final shake of his head, he turned to the door of his cabin and gestured for her to step in. He followed, sealing the door.

"This is nice," she said, looking around. "I've always heard that merchants had the nicest cabins."

"That's because the ship is our home."

Cheech fingered the top of the terminal. "This could use an upgrade, though."

"Add it to the list of things to be done," May said, losing patience. "Why did you want to talk to me, Cheech?"

The techette avoided his glance for a moment and then looked him straight in the eye. "I don't want you to take this wrong, that's all."

"I can't take it wrong," the merchant said calmly, "if you don't tell me what's going on."

Cheech folded her arms and kicked at an imaginary spot on the floor. "I know that it would never work between us."

May's jaw tightened, and he broke out in gooseflesh. He almost asked "*What* would never work between us?" but immediately thought better of it.

"I mean," Cheech continued, "you're old enough to be my father, and yeah, I know that doesn't mean anything because with rejuv you could be my physical equal—" She waved her arms to punctuate herself.

Have I missed something important? May thought, trying to keep a neutral expression.

"But I want you to know that I really care about you, and I worry about what your future will be like and what's going to happen to you."

"Look, Cheech," May said, "that's very nice, but—"

"Please let me finish," she insisted. "I know you've got a lot on your mind with what's happened to Duke and—and the Arcolian. And I don't want to make the same mistake twice, so I'm going to come right out and say it. Captain—James—if there's anything I can do to help you correct this situation or get Duke and—and the Arcolian out of there, I'll do it. You just ask."

May's chest felt tight. He cleared his throat. "We had considered something, but due to its violent nature, I don't think—"

"I don't care."

"I mean, you're perfectly capable of assisting, but because of the tenuous legality of what we'd be doing—"

"I said I don't care."

"And I don't know what kind of pay—"

"I wouldn't be doing it for the pay, Captain. If that's all there was to it, I sure wouldn't have hung around here for as long as I have."

"Actually, I had been meaning to talk to you about that."

"It doesn't matter. I'm doing this for you, Captain, not the money. Because I know that probably after this job is done, I'll never see you again. But maybe you won't forget me, and maybe we'll cross paths again when the difference in our ages has caught up."

Like when I'm a hundred and you're seventy, May thought. He managed a smile. "Thank you," he said. "I appreciate that."

Cheech stared him down. "Promise," she said.

"Promise?"

"Promise that you'll ask me to help when you do something to help your friends out of their situation. I know you're going to do something, and I want you to promise that you'll ask me to help."

"If there's something—"

"No," she insisted. "I can do a lot of other things besides work on computers. You promise me."

"All right," May said, nodding. "I promise."

Cheech beamed. "Thank you." As she turned to leave she paused and kissed the merchant on the cheek. The next moment, she was gone.

May looked at the door in astonishment. Then he slowly lifted his hand to his face where the moistness of her kiss still burned.

I guess misterbob was right, he thought. Why is it I'm always the last person to know about things like this?

12

Duke was on his knees, hands folded and propped against the metal chair in front of him. The voice that filled the hangar was that of the chaplain of Narofeld Station, a man whose face had grown increasingly gray and haggard in the days since the discovery of the ship bearing the remains of the captured sortie of Bering's Gate. The initial reaction had been to have a mass memorial service for the dead, but a group of surviving pilots— which included Dickson, if Duke's borrowed memory served him correctly—had insisted on services for each individual. As a result, the chaplain was now in the third day of a marathon, staring hour after hour into empty and hurt faces as he eulogized each missing person as best as he could.

". . . and thus," the chaplain droned, "we commit to our memories the soul of Leigh Sucarita Brand, friend and comrade-in-arms, fighter for the freedom and integrity of the race . . ."

Duke broke his reverent stance and looked around the hall. Dickson was there, he had to be, yet Duke could find no trace of him. He stood and wandered among the scattered crowd, able to identify by sight most of those who were present. As the invocation ended, the crowd slowly rose, maintaining an eerie silence.

"There will be a five-minute recess," the chaplain said hoarsely, "after which we will remember Major Denis Weir."

The crowd maintained its silence. Some of those present sat down to wait for the next service, and others quietly walked out, to be replaced by those coming in for Weir's memorial. Duke paced around the outside of the block of metal chairs, rubbing his face with his hands and massaging his temples.

"Dammit, Eric," he said under his breath. "Where the hell are you? How many times do I have to replay this thing before you show up?"

One more time, he thought with a sigh. He sat on the nearest chair and, elbows on his knees, placed the palms of his hands over his eyes.

All right, remember it. Remember it. You came in about half-way through the memorial for Olivialii Stamms, and you felt bad because you'd always liked her, and you were still a little drunk and you took too much Leuten's and it started to make you sick, but somehow when they started to talk about Leigh—

Suddenly Duke flinched. Something inside his head had popped, like his sinuses suddenly opening after a long bout with his allergies, only he was not sure it was a physical sensation so much as psychological. He looked around the hangar again.

". . . Olivialii Carvella Stamms, rank of major in the war-time forces of the . . ."

Something pricked the inside of Duke's nose. It was heavy and oily at first, very similar to transgear fluid. Even though it was distinctly industrial, there was an odd purity to it and the strong metallic taste it brought to his mouth.

Duke looked up. The light in the hangar was getting brighter, and the figures around him were mere outlines, thin line draw-ings of the flesh they once carried. He reeled back, closing his eyes, and the smell assaulted him, stinging his eyes, coating his throat, burning his nose. After a strangled gasp he tried to cry out, but the corrosive sensation stopped the sound short before it reached his lips. Knotting his hands, Duke flailed his arms, swinging wildly. He fought the urge to exhale but finally relented, and when he drew breath again, it was like inhaling grains of broken glass, which slashed and weighed upon his lungs and caused them to fill with blood.

He convulsed, and a wild grunt slipped from his throat. He pitched forward and snapped to a stop.

He was in the Essence Corporation cell.

Panting heavily, he looked down at his hands and marveled at being able to see and control them and at the regained sense of touch, something he had missed in his recent shadowy state. The scent, whatever it was, had done something that Duke himself had not been able to accomplish. It had forcibly dragged him out of Dickson's memories.

But what?

He remembered something that the CHARLES had given him once on the *Angel's Luck*, some kind of liquid to counteract the effects of Restcure gas. The lucidness he felt had the same quality as before, but something was wrong. The nasal cannulas were not there, nor were Burris and Melrose, who most certainly would be on hand to observe the drug's effect on him.

If not them, then who?

Suddenly there came a quick barrage of scents: roses, manure, cordite, ammonia, hot transgear fluid, and the nauseating fishiness of Aiaagan gin.

All at once, Duke understood.

"misterbob," he said.

13

"You know what the worst part of all of this is?" James May asked.

Cheech looked up from her work. She was wearing the pair of magnalenses, and a solderlase crackled in her hand.

"It's not the prospect of getting killed. It's not even the prospect of losing Duke or misterbob, although the Fifth Region knows what a nightmare that really is. It's having to admit to Vonn that he was right." He gave a sad shrug. "That's the reward I get for trying to play straight."

"You can't play straight," Cheech said, "when everyone else is working with jimmywired randomizers."

"Indeed," May said, and then shook his head as if a bad taste had risen in his mouth. "Dammit, listen to me. I'm even starting to *sound* like misterbob."

Cheech looked back into the small component she had been working on and began poking at circuits and junctions with the tool. Green flashes reflected off of her face.

"You know what's ironic about this?" May continued. "A long time ago, back around the time we stole the phials from the *Yueh-sheng*, I made this promise to myself that when it was all over, I'd go back to being a harmless little merchant. All I wanted was to take a back seat to galactic affairs and turn a nice profit. The only problem was that it never ended. I have the feeling that those damned phials are going to haunt me for the rest of my life."

"It'll end," Cheech said through tight lips. "Everything ends."

"The question," May said, "is when."

Cheech clicked off the solderlase and laid it aside, then pulled off the lenses. She dusted off her hands, then picked up a small metal plate and secured it over the components she had been working on. "There," she said. "It's ready to go." Rummaging through a pile of junk, she produced a strap and clicked it to the sides of the component. "Who are you going to place at the computer terminal?"

"Roz."

"All right. She'll assist me in gaining access to the layout of the building." She handed the component to May, who gently turned it over in his hands. "This gizmo will tell me where you are, and I can corroborate that with the floor plan. With the building's floor plan uploaded, I can guide you around like you owned the place."

"Terrific," May said. "You realize that you—"

"Don't even start with that," Cheech said. "I'm looking forward to this. It's been a long time since I've done any intrusion on corporate datafields. I've been keeping clean since working for Dirk, but I always hoped that I'd go out with a bang. I'm looking forward to making a little noise."

"All right." May slung the device around his neck. "I don't know how to thank you for this . . ."

Cheech gave him a thumbs-up. "Bring 'em back alive," she said.

He returned the gesture. "Okay. Thanks, Cheech." He paused suddenly and cocked his head.

"Something wrong, Captain?"

"I was just wondering what the hell kind of name Cheech is for someone like you."

"It's my—"

"I know how the techettes work. Isn't there something else I can call you?"

Cheech flushed and shrugged.

"How about your real name? Most people like you come from a home where they gave you a sensible one."

Cheech reached out and fidgeted with the solderlase. "Kimberly," she said.

"Kimberly," May said. "Kimberly what?"

"Kimberly that's-all-you'll-get-out-of-me."

May smiled. "Good enough. It was nice working with you, Kimberly." He turned to leave but she shouted him down.

"I'll have none of that kind of talk, James May. You're coming back, right? Then dispense with this 'nice working with you' and give me a 'see you later.' If you're going to inflict that name on me, the least you could do is come back to apologize."

"Okay then." May tipped his fingers to his brow in a civilian salute of respect. "See you later, Cheech."

He turned and walked out of the door as Cheech nervously tapped her foot on the floor. His behavior was probably frustrating to her, he knew, but he preferred to keep it that way, in spite of what misterbob had said. Things were just too precarious, and there was such an obvious difference in their ages. Cheech could very well have been the daughter that he and Maggie never had.

I'm just collecting a whole damn family here, he thought, pacing down the halls of the *Angel's Luck* to the cargo hold. Son Duke and daughter Cheech and misterbob, the family pet . . .

The idea amused him until he walked across the hold to the *Reconnez Cherie*. Roz was walking up the ramp with a large box of ruined components that Cheech had discarded, so he gently took it from her, holding out Cheech's tracking device for her to carry.

"What's with all the junk?" he asked her.

"It's an idea of Peter's," she said. "Since you can't very well land undetected, and you can't divert the planetary radar nets like Vonn said you did last time, we're going to confuse them." She directed May to a back corner of the pleasure craft, where she had him place the box in front of a large chute. "We've filled the disposal hold with all sorts of metal junk, and while we're reentering, Peter's going to jettison it. Instead of one unidentified to track, they're going to have hundreds."

"Most of this stuff will burn up on the way down," May said.

"It won't matter by then." Peter met them in the hallway and gestured for Roz to empty the box into the hold. "We're leaving as soon as the captain and I are strapped in."

She nodded and opened the door. Chiba started down the hall to the pilot's compartment, and May fell in step behind him.

"I've been running through some of the figures for stress boost going and coming," the salvor said, "and I was wondering how attached you were to that van."

May shrugged. "It's a rental. What's the problem?"

"There's the consideration of time in getting it back into the cargo hold. Plus there's the fuel consumption for getting it off. If we're to be leaving quickly, I want to have a comfortable margin. We could take the van out with us, but that would be cutting it closer than I'd like, especially if we have to break it off and meet at the rendezvous point." He stepped through the door and eased down into the pilot's seat.

"I've put so much damage on it that I'll probably end up paying for it anyway," May said with a laugh, making his way to the copilot's position. "I almost hate to leave it behind. It's been through a lot."

"It's your decision, May." Chiba reached up and buckled himself into the seat.

"We'll worry about it when the time comes."

"Just don't take too long to decide about it." He put on a headset and gestured at May. "Seal us up, would you?"

"Everyone on board?"

Chiba nodded. "Roz in the back. Vonn and Winters in the passenger lounge. You and I."

With a nod, May began to flip switches and check status lights.

"Just don't spend too long on the decision, okay?"

"What?" May looked up from his task.

"Don't take forever deciding about the van."

"Right." The merchant turned back to his work.

"Roz," Chiba said into his headset, "give me a green light when you're buckled in. All other hands show secured status. We'll be leaving momentarily."

From down the hall came a loud whoop, a war cry from Vonn.

"Dammit," May said, keying the last of the switches.

"Something wrong? I just checked the status—"

"Not that," May said, securing the seat's webbing around him. "It's Vonn. He's going to be insufferable, I'm afraid. Dammit, I hate to have to resort to this."

"It's not like you didn't try other channels. You exhausted the possibilities."

"Like maybe I should have gotten in touch with Maggie."

"You did the right thing, May. Believe me."

"That's the problem, Peter. You have no idea what this does to me. I guess that deep down inside, I really believed that there were places where you could still get ahead by doing the right thing." He shook his head in surprise. "Oh, damn, now I'm starting to sound like Duke."

Chiba leaned over his console and flitted his fingers over a keypad. The pleasure craft began to vibrate, and a low whine filled their ears as the drives kicked in. "There are still places like that, May. The problem is, this isn't one of them." He tapped a pressure pad on the side of his headset. "I've got a green light from Roz. Cargo stowed, all hands ready. You can open the doors, Cheech."

They heard nothing else over the whine of the *Reconnez Cherie*'s power plant, but before them the doors of the *Angel's Luck*'s cargo hold began to part, revealing below them a huge disc matted with shades of green.

"Energize cargo hold on my signal," Chiba continued. "Negative to negative, and I'll ease us out." He looked at May. "Give us a point two negative hull charge."

May held his palm against a small black pad until the readout gave him the appropriate reading. "Done," he said.

"All right, Cheech," Chiba said, grabbing the control yoke. "Tweak the grid."

"Wait a minute," May said as the ship rose and began to slide out of the *Angel's Luck*. "Cheech doesn't know how to operate the magnetic grid system."

Chiba shrugged. "She does now."

The *Reconnez Cherie* eased into space, and the dirty swirl of green that was Council 5 began to fill the window.

"Get ready to goose it," Chiba said. "I want full negative hull energization on my mark." Aside, to May, he said, "I'm hoping for enough of a push so we can make capture range without having to fire the engines. It'll give us that much more fuel to play with.''

"I hope Cheech knows what she's doing.'' May wiped his palms on the leg of his trousers.

"Relax. She's got the magnetics grid up, she has some different system components operating and has restored the inner logic board of the CHARLES unit. She'll do fine.''

"Then I hope you know what you're doing.''

Chiba nodded. "Get ready to energize this critter's hull. I want maximum negative in minimal time.''

May hovered his palm above the black pad and nodded.

"Ready, Cheech?'' The salvor paused, then nodded. "We're ready here. Both of you, on my mark.''

Chiba began to count down, guiding the *Cherie* out at an angle down and away from the *Angel's Luck* and the platform on which it was docked. Then he gave the order in a loud bark and May slapped his hand down, watching the reading go from point two to ninety-nine point three in the twinkling of an eye. The lights in the cabin dimmed, and the ship swung about hard, causing the merchant's stomach to plunge.

Out the window, the green skies of Council rushed toward them.

From his seat in the lounge, Vonn gave another war cry, this one long and drawn out. Then another one came, and Winters joined him, sounding more scared than anything else.

Can't say that I blame him, May thought, tightening the muscles in his abdomen so the plunge would not make him ill.

THREE

Indeed, misterbob, you mean to explain that the entire success of your helping the A-forms is contingent upon a spontaneous and therefore untried and unproven course of action?

Yes, redbutler, but you must understand the psychology of such behavior as it is most fascinating. It is called "long-shot."

Duke sat with his back against the cell door. His arms circled his knees, and his feet were pivoting on their balls and slapping a nervous tattoo on the floor. What to do, he thought. Whatever to do? Ever since misterbob had successfully communicated its presence to Duke, a steady barrage of scents had made their way into the cell. While the Tetran was able to identify a majority of them, he was at a loss when it came to interpreting their meaning. Was misterbob trying to talk to him, or was this some kind of pheromonal smoke screen? Should Duke try to communicate back? If so, how? He briefly thought that this could be another of Melrose's tests, but how could he possibly have gotten the right combination of scents to conjure up the image of the Arcolian on the first try?

Most importantly, if it was truly misterbob and not some experiment that he was the subject of, what was it doing here? Duke had no idea of the effective range of an Arcolian's scent, but the strength of the odors he was receiving seemed proof enough that the ambassador had to be somewhere in the building.

Dickson had said something about telling Burris and Melrose about the Arcolian gene-engineering technology. Had Burris somehow captured misterbob? Had May attempted some kind of trade that went wrong, and now the Arcolian was crying for help?

Or perhaps they were coming to get him out. Perhaps things had been settled peacefully. The ambassador could be giving the Essence scientists a demonstration, and what Duke was scenting was the spillover.

He hated not knowing. Lolling his head back, he let it bump against the metallic side of the door, closing his eyes.

If that message is for me, how can I possibly answer?

He could shout, or bang on the walls. But even if the racket did find its way to misterbob, the Arcolian might not put any credence in a message from one of the false senses.

How can I possibly communicate all that I've been through in a way that misterbob will trust?

Duke's stomach rumbled. He folded his hands over his belly, fearing that he had become institutionalized. Here it was, time for dinner, and his stomach was telling him that his meal was late in arriving.

The corners of Duke's lips turned up. Maybe he could bribe the orderly who brought the food to take a message to the Arcolian.

He shook his head. It would never work. He had nothing to bribe the orderly with, and an Essence employee certainly would not be interested in doing any favors for an indentured medical experiment.

Still, it was the best idea so far. It was the one chance to get something outside the cell—something that could be carried up and down through the halls. Something that the Essence people would interpret one way without realizing that a message was being transmitted. It required deception, but it had to be deceptively simple. Something with the indelible stamp of William Wesley Arbor.

Duke rolled his head forward, then opened his eyes as his stomach protested. There was a bed built into the wall, a stainless steel toilet, a matching sink, and the cup he had fought so hard to get.

Oh, yes. That was it.

The plan was so simple that it made him smile.

2

The *Reconnez Cherie* was buffeting wildly as it plowed through the thin beginnings of Council 5's atmosphere. Peter

Chiba threw a hand signal at May, who reversed a series of switches and watched their accompanying lights all flicker into the green.

On a screen above their heads, a single image blossomed suddenly into hundreds of tiny, shimmering objects, all trailing with the same downward trajectory.

"It's working," May said.

"If nothing else," Chiba answered, "they're going to think we broke up during reentry."

"Shouldn't we have saved some of that for our escape?"

The salvor shook his head. "Wouldn't do us any good."

"What are we going to do about escaping any unwanted attention?"

"Let's worry about getting Duke and misterbob out first. Maybe the ambassador can use some of his political influence to divert any curiosity if we get caught."

May's look soured. "In other words, you don't have the slightest idea of what we're going to do, and probably won't have until the situation hits."

Chiba gave a guilty shrug.

"Change your ways, Peter," May said in disgust. "You're too much like me."

3

misterbob sat on the floor of its cell, lids locked over its sight organ, and neurons to the hearing organ voluntarily disconnected. The center of its chest organ pulsated as it produced scent, and the outer rings fluttered as they checked the air. There was an interesting array available, even over the chemical disinfectants that were used to keep the cells clean. The sheets on the bed gave a history of the last few tenants of the cell, and the currents wafting in from the other side of the door let the Arcolian catalog the numbers of Sapient A-forms and their varying states of mind.

One of them came and went lethargically, scenting strongly of ennui and increasing contempt. After a while the contempt gradually began to fade, accompanied by a dramatic rise in the presence of a distinct chemical pattern. The personality then began to alter until misterbob could describe it in no other way but the Sapient word "numb."

Two others were together, one smelling of glandular agitation and the other of obligation. They disappeared for a time, and when they passed again, their scents had blended. The agitated one had calmed to a great degree, and the other had become frustrated.

Still another kept passing back and forth, scenting of high emotional agitation and indecision. When the scent was on the verge of tipping into panic, another Sapient appeared on the scene, smelling of duty and then annoyance, a change that happened as the two communicated. They began to fade away, and when their traces were almost gone, the agitated one had tipped into full-fledged panic and the annoyed one had become quite angry. Their scents began to close in, and as they did, misterbob realized there was a third one there, one with a familiar composition.

william. wesley. arbor.

At first it almost eluded the Arcolian, so intent was it on trying to figure out which interaction had caused the change between the other two A-forms. Yet there it was, distinct, although not quite right.

WILLIAM. WESLEY. ARBOR.

The scent was tainted with compounds and low blood sugar and confusion and escalating blood pressure, yet it was very distinct and became almost overpowering as the other two sapients passed by.

WILLIAM!!!WESLEY!!!ARBOR!!!

misterbob drummed its feet on the concrete floor in excitement. It was such a pleasure to deal with these creatures, and exciting when they were able to communicate—albeit crudely—in the truesense of scent.

It slowly rocked back and forth on its natural pedestal, pleased with itself and trying to figure out the next step. Trying to make contact had been exhausting, and some time would be required to rest in the event that a major pheromonal assault was required. Then there was the problem of which message to send back to misterduke. And how would misterduke respond, given the limited capacity of the Sapient A-form to communicate pheromonally? Things were becoming more complex than the ambassador had imagined.

Indeed, it thought. It seems I have located misterduke, yet I have no plan for getting us both out of here. How typically Sapient of me. What would jamesohjames do in such a situation? misterbob stopped its motion.

After thought, the Arcolian realized that the question was not what jamesohjames would do were he in the same situation. It was what jamesohjames would do knowing that his friend and an Arcolian ambassador were held by the same company that the merchant scented as the epitome of why things were going wrong in his life.

Yes, yes. That was it. That was the message to send to misterduke.

The Arcolian began to rock again, chest fluttering and filling the room with scent. As if to make the meaning clearer, misterbob forced air through his specially designed chitinous passageway and formed the words against tongue and lips, putting them out in the Arcolian approximation of a whisper. It had observed such conversation with self among the A-forms, and doing so seemed to comfort them as if what they referred to as "angelsluck" was capable of hearing them and acting accordingly in their lives.

misterbob had no real evidence as to whether or not it really worked, let alone whether there really was anything behind "angelsluck" or "regionfifth," but it reasoned that if such a thing was out there, it might as well be petitioned.

"Patience, misterduke," it sang. "Have patience, have patience. Be a patient Sapient, misterduke, and our time will soon come."

4

Dinah stood below the air duct, eyes closed, the current of air stirring her hair.

"What does it remind you of?" Melrose asked.

"Cooking," she said. "Some kind of meat."

"Pork hybrids," Melrose said.

"Close," she replied. "Bacon."

"Yes." Melrose sat up and spoke to the computer. "Next cataloged scent. Frying bacon."

"It seems to like this one," Dinah said. "It hasn't changed yet. It's been this way for a minute or so."

Melrose looked at the data on the screen. "That makes one hundred nine distinct scents in the last hour," he said, "that you and I could notice. I wonder what the Arcolian is up to."

Dinah walked away from the air duct, shrugging. "Maybe it's talking to itself."

Melrose chuckled. "You know, I could think of sounder explanations that would seem more ludicrous."

Dinah idly paced the room, examining the monitors that

showed the Arcolian in its cell. At the present time, it was letting the water run full stream into the sink and had settled down into its sitting position, eyes closed as if in sleep. "This is really a missed opportunity," she said. "I know that the terms of the Accord restrict medical experimentation on either side, but there's so damned much we could learn through simple observation." She reached up and clicked off the screen to allow the ambassador its privacy. "This plan of Burris's has me worried, Vincent."

"Save data, compile," Melrose said to the screen. The machine obediently went to work, and he rose from his chair. "I keep wondering if an anonymous phone call to Port Authority would do it."

"They'd take forever to act," Dinah said. "I got as far as keying in the number. I've got this friend in Transgalactic Affairs . . ."

"But you couldn't do it." Melrose sighed.

Dinah shrugged.

"We're damned. We're in too deep. We blow the whistle to stop the madness, but we end it for both of us. So we let the monster do his evil."

The air was suddenly split with profanity. Reg bolted into the observation room, arms held away from his body and a large stain that occupied the better part of his tunic.

"What's wrong?" Melrose asked.

"That son of a bitch Arbor. Or Dickson. Or whoever the hell it was . . ."

"What did he do?" Dinah asked.

Reg stopped inside the door and winced. "One of the orderlies came to me and said that Arbor hadn't returned his dinner tray. It'd been over an hour since they were collected, and the count came up short. He knew that Arbor hadn't turned his back in, but he'd waited so long to report the discrepancy that he came to me for help. He was afraid you'd have to write him up, which means that Burris would fire him."

Dinah took a step his way. "So?"

"So I went to Arbor's cell to try and talk him into giving the tray back. By now it's been nearly two hours since they were gathered, and the orderly is about to have a stroke. I go in and Arbor is sitting on his bed, and the tray's in the middle of the cell. 'By the way,' he says to me while I'm picking it up, 'it occurs to me that you forgot to get my urine sample this morning.' I told him it was no big deal, we'd take care of it tomorrow, and he says, 'No, I'd like to take care of it now.' And he heaves it on me. He had that damned cup of his full of—''

Dinah put her hand over her mouth and nose and backed away. "Oh. I can tell."

Holding his breath, Melrose inched around Reg and opened the main door for him. "You'll probably have to change into a set of guest standards," he said. "I can have those washed for you."

Reg scurried out the door. "I want to file a report against him. I don't care *what* Burris said about being nice."

"You'll have it," Melrose said. "Take your time in the shower. It'll calm you."

Reg's final comment was cut off as Melrose sealed the door. He turned to see that Dinah had moved back under the air vent.

"Arbor or Dickson?" he asked.

"Just a minute," she whispered. She put one hand over her mouth and the other around her throat.

Melrose crossed the room and keyed cool air to flood the room. "Pungent, isn't it? That sweetness must be coming from feeding him all of those—" He froze.

Dinah gratefully inhaled the fresh air. "Something wrong?"

"How long to get from Arbor's cell to here? A minute, maybe? Another thirty seconds to stand there and shout 'Why did you do that, you little bastard?' Plus a minute or two to stand dripping warm piss onto the floor while giving one of our famous orderlies instructions on mopping and cleaning the cell? And when you come up, you pass the Arcolian's cell?"

"What are you getting at?"

"How long since we've been getting that bacon smell from the Arcolian?"

Dinah checked a timer on the console. "Coming up on four—" She became visibly pale as the words caught in her throat. "Oh," she said. "misterbob was not talking to himself. He was talking to William Arbor."

Melrose nodded. "Exactly. And William Arbor just replied. That urine sample wasn't meant for Reg."

"Then that means that the Arcolian now knows what Arbor has been through." Her mouth dropped open, and she puffed air. "I think I'd better sit down."

"Why don't you go home?" Melrose suggested. "Call it a night."

"I'll be okay, I just—"

"Go home, Dinah," he ordered. "Because I don't think either of us wants to be around here for much longer."

"What about you?" She took a deep breath, trying to compose herself.

"I've got to go talk to Burris. We're supposed to report any anomalous behavior to him."

"You're going to warn him?" she asked.

"I'm going to tell him that Eric Dickson manifested himself in the form of an escape attempt, which involved drenching one of our people in urine. I'm also going to tell him that I've sent the staff home because we've got a busy day tomorrow."

Dinah nodded as Melrose started out the door.

"Vincent," she said quickly. "It's been nice working with you."

He smiled. "And I shall miss you too, Dinah. Would you be a dear and shut off the lights when you leave? I'd hate for them to be left on."

"Of course," she said, and a lump formed in her throat as she watched him leave.

5

Duke was doing a long series of push-ups, trying through exercise to burn off the agitation he felt. His attempt to communicate with misterbob had been a success, he was sure of it. There was no longer a quick series of odors, but instead one constant one of cooking meat.

Something, he knew, was about to happen.

The problem was that he did not know *what* was about to happen. Was the scent from misterbob a direct message, or a general indication? In either case, what did it mean, providing that it was meant for Duke to begin with? For all that was going on, the message could be something that Burris and Melrose had induced during the course of an experiment.

A grunt escaped his lips as he pushed up from the floor. He lowered himself back down, and a memory peeked out: doing push-ups fast, pushing off so hard that he could clap his hands before going back down. It caused a laugh to spill from his lips. That was something, the memory of doing something he knew he could not do.

Your reflexes need work, Duke . . .

Another grunt and he pushed up. For some reason he was finding the going tough. Maybe it was the gravity. Was it heavier here than on Tetros? It felt no different. Perhaps all that time in space had weakened him. He held himself up until his arms started to quiver.

You didn't have enough upper body strength.

He collapsed to the floor with a grunt. Panting, he shook his head and told himself that he would never get in shape fast enough. There had to be another way.

You're such a loser, Duke.

Duke froze to the floor.

"No," he said.

There was laughter in his head, and the room began to spin. A feeling welled up behind his eyes and threatened to shut them. Duke fought against it, looking frantically around the cell.

"Not now," Duke said. "Dammit, this isn't the time."

There was more laughter. Duke tried to sit up, but his body would not respond. He tried to push with his arms to inch along the floor, but to no avail.

"Get out!" he shouted. "Get the hell out of here!"

And then came something that confused him. In his thrashing on the floor, he forced his eyes open and caught a skewed view of the cell door. There was a black military boot partially covered by a cuff of gray—the battered-looking leg of a flight suit. The figure wearing the suit had one fist resting on a hip and the other gripping a bottle of cheap liquor. The face was stretched and pale and looked old—older than it had appeared in any previous memories. It took a long pull from the bottle, and as the hand came down, Duke could see a name screened onto one side of the chest.

DICKSON.

The figure swallowed the liquor, wiped its lips with the back of a hand, and started to laugh.

6

Roz's voice came over the speaker, distorted by interference. "That's it, Peter. The last of it's been dumped."

"Absolute," he said, and eased the control yoke forward. The *Reconnez Cherie* pitched forward, and there was a dropping sensation in the pit of his stomach. "You know," he said, "I've always wanted to do this, set down somewhere in the dead of night when the stars are out, and nobody knows what's going on."

"I hate to burst your bubble," May said, "but we're going

to make a hell of a lot of noise coming down and even more when we take off. We're hardly running stealth options here."

Chiba shrugged. "I know that. It's the romance of it, May. Salvors don't see a lot of touch-and-go work."

"Romance." May laughed. "I can tell you haven't been through much. It might look good from the outside, but when it's happening to you, it's never worth it. Remember that, Peter. Don't make some of the same mistakes I've made. It might look like a game, but it costs."

The salvor sighed. "We're, uh, looking at touchdown in fifteen minutes."

May nodded. "Everyone should assemble. I want the ramp open the minute we're down. We're going to take the van right through the front doors."

"How long should I give you?"

"Roz will tell you that. And if something comes up, break off and get out. We'll meet back at the rendezvous point, that meadow from the other night. That should let up on some of the pressure." He unbuckled and started out of the control cabin.

"How close do you want me to get to the Essence building?" Chiba asked.

"Don't sweat that part. Just put us down in the parking lot. We'll do the rest."

Chiba saluted as the merchant stepped out of the cabin and made his way back to where Winters and Vonn were strapped in.

"Time to saddle up?" Vonn asked.

May glared at him. "What the hell does that mean?"

The mercenary shrugged. "Something I've always heard. Never really thought about it."

"Well, don't lose any sleep over it. We've got a job to do."

The three of them made their way to the front of the pleasure craft, where Roz sat waiting by the van. She was running her hand across the long gash put in by the encounter with Burris's car and looking nervously at the damage done by the Essence truck.

"Is this thing going to make it?" she asked.

One of the rear doors gave a metallic cry as Vonn muscled it open. "All it has to do," he said, "is get us in the front door." With his left hand he opened a chest and pulled out a small hand weapon. He chambered a round by pressing down with the palm of his mangled hand, then held the gun out to Roz.

"Take this," he said.

She stared at it, hesitant. "I'll only be in the computer room."

"Everyone has to pack," Winters said apologetically. "That's one of the rules."

She took the weapon and snapped the safety on. "That's the one thing I learned from you."

Vonn handed her a shoulder holster and a belt of extra clips. "It'll take more than that if you get into trouble."

Taking the equipment, Roz holstered the weapon and slung it over her shoulder. "The trouble we're looking at, this won't help us," she said. "But I'll respect your rules."

"You've got to take care of yourself," May said. "Cheech couldn't get the multichannel relay working, so you're our lifeline to Peter and the ship. If anything goes wrong, you tell Cheech, and she'll tell us."

Roz walked across the small hold and knelt beside a small case of electronic gear. "Have you ever had Angel's Luck, Captain? I mean really, truly had it?"

May smiled wryly as Vonn handed him an autoshot and two belts of ammunition. "Not pure Angel's Luck. For everything that ever went right there was something else that went wrong." He pumped the action of the weapon to chamber the first round. "And yourself?"

She shook her head.

"We'll all need it tonight. Every one of us."

Vonn swore a blue streak as he tried to bring his weapon to bear. It was a machine gun with a central, cylindrical magazine, and he was trying to grip the trigger with his left hand and aim the barrel through the crook of his right arm. "You want to trade weapons?" he said to May.

May looked down at his weapon, then at Winters, who was carefully taking grenades from three different crates and clipping them to his combat vest. "After what happened when Bear was killed, are you sure you want Winters to carry those?"

"He's going to have one of these, too," Vonn said, shifting the weapon in his arms. "Besides, the grenades, those are *his* weapons."

"He could have destroyed the ship, tossing them off like that."

"I want that quality," Vonn said. "If I catch the one with my name on it, I know that Winters is going to waste the son of a bitch that fired it."

"If he remembers to pull the pins," May said bitterly. He looked at Roz, who was checking the communications gear.

"Do you want to trade weapons or not?" Vonn asked.

May shouldered the autoshot. "No," he said. "This is *my* weapon." He walked away, leaving the mercenaries to their business.

"What did I ever see in that man," Roz whispered as May approached.

"You can bow out," May said. "Nobody would blame you—"

"Would you cut it out," she snapped. "I owe Duke my life. We all do. There's no question, May. Really."

The merchant stood staring at the battered van as Vonn related to Winters some tale of being overrun on Solina B. "If only there was another way," May whispered to Roz. "I wish to the Fifth Region that there was."

7

Burris drummed the writing stylus against the desktop and wrinkled his nose. The list of scents that Dinah had been cataloging had ceased to be interesting. For the last half-hour, the same entry, BACON (FRYING???), had appeared at the rate of once every twenty seconds, filling the screen to the point where the other listings had been bumped off to make room. Burris wondered why she continued with the reports. Perhaps she was expecting change soon, or perhaps she was trying to get a list of normal reactions before they commenced with the Geretz Method. Certainly there would be no normal reactions once they were through. The intensive regimen of biological and psychological testing was usually fatal—and the rare few that survived it spent the rest of their days institutionalized. The Geretz Method was trying on those performing it as well, but for all of its drawbacks, there was no faster way to gather hard data on a subject.

Tiring of the readout, Burris asked for the KELLY unit, and after a moment it responded to him with a polite "Yes, Mr. Burris?"

"Tell Dinah that she can lighten up on her observations. I think the Bugface is sleeping, and this is its way of snoring."

"Would you like that verbatim, Mr. Burris?"

"Yes, yes," he hissed. "And come back in half an hour and talk dirty to me."

"Very well."

The screen before him flickered, and the scent listings returned. Well, he thought, we'll know all about this soon enough.

There was a knock from the doorway, and he looked up to see Melrose staring back in at him. He put the pen down and switched off the monitor. "Yes. Vincent. Come in."

"Too busy," Melrose said. "I wanted you to know that the Arcolian's scent seems to have stabilized and is showing no signs of change."

"I noticed," Burris said. "I think it's asleep. I just sent a message to Dinah to tell her to quit being so damned obsessive about record keeping."

"She's just being thorough—but that's not the point." Melrose paused for a moment and shoved his hands in his pockets. "If you didn't mind, I thought I'd go home for the night. The next few days are going to be hectic, and I'll need to be in top form."

"I have no problem with that."

"Might I suggest that you do the same? It's going to be trying—"

"Point well taken. I'll consider it, but there's a lot I have to do yet this evening."

Melrose nodded. "In the morning," he said, and disappeared.

"In the morning," Burris murmured. He turned the monitor back on and watched the listing of Dinah's entries. The rate had slowed to once every 300 seconds, and the report was still showing that the Arcolian was putting out a smell like BACON (FRYING???).

"KELLY," he said. "Is there a response from Dinah?"

"Yes, sir," the KELLY replied. "She advised that she is going to run a spectrographic analysis on this particular scent to see if there are any subtle variations."

"That's fine."

"Which scenario did you prefer for our conversation?" the KELLY asked. "You seem fond of the lesbian transgear puller."

"Let's cancel, shall we?" Burris said, stretching. "I need to rest for tomorrow."

"We could do a quick scenario," the KELLY offered.

"Thank you, no. But hold the thought." He reached forward and snapped the down switch. The monitor and the interface system winked out, cutting off the KELLY's voice in mid-suggestion. Someday, he promised himself, this company will offer a real woman with one of those built in.

Burris rose from the chair, grabbed his topcoat, and started down the hall. He turned and walked through the lobby, noticing as he put on his coat that strange shadows were playing across the vacant parking lot. His pace slowed as he approached the glass doors, and he studied the circular patterns of light that inched toward the small concrete plaza. The patterns were steadily getting smaller and growing brighter, making Burris look up to find their source.

Through the glare of the inside lighting, he could barely make out the object, but once he spotted it, there was no mistaking what it was: a small stellar craft whose approach lights were making the patterns he had been seeing. As the vehicle grew closer, Burris could tell that it had every intention of landing near the main doors.

He knew too well who would be inside.

"So, Captain May, you resort to desperate measures." Burris laughed and started back through the lobby. As he turned toward his office, he saw a lone figure walking the empty hall, eyes wandering from door to door.

"That you, Mr. Burris?" the figure asked.

"Sergeant Emerson." Burris smiled. "How fortunate that you should be on duty this evening. It'll give you a chance to avenge your colleagues."

"Vengeance?"

"The merchant responsible for their deaths is landing in our parking lot right now. I suspect he's come for the Arcolian." Burris motioned at the Comealong that Emerson carried on his hip. "I suggest you get rid of that toy and check out something a bit more intimidating. Are you trained to use a machine pistol?"

Emerson nodded.

"Get one. They're going to be coming into the lobby in a matter of minutes." Burris pointed down the hall. Pure white light flickered from the direction of the lobby. "See that? He's touching down now. If you hurry, you can draw first blood."

Emerson nodded and started down the hall at a quick trot. Burris stood and watched him go, then continued down the hall and palmed into his office.

Of course, he told himself as he rifled through the drawers of his desk, the merchant and his mercenary friends were entirely capable of drawing second blood. But then Emerson had not exactly been happy with the way the snatching of the Arcolian had turned out.

It would work out for the best. Surely James May was not the type to lead a charge, so only a few of his complement would fall to Emerson's ambush. That would leave the good merchant's guard down.

Burris found what he was looking for. It was made of molded hardpoint plastic, and the clip jammed into its side carried a half-dozen cartridges that were specifically designed for shipboard combat. They would not pierce a bulkhead, but any hit to the main body cavity usually made a mess that was ultimately fatal.

Mutiny pills, they were called.

Just what was needed to put the damper on that merchant's reactor.

8

A klaxon sounded, once, through the halls of the *Reconnez Cherie*. It made everyone jump, even though they had been listening for it from the instant that a lurch told them the pleasure craft had touched down.

"That's it," May said, turning to Winters. "We're down."

In front of them, the jagged hallway began to drop down. As it did, they could see the face of the Essence building not more than a dozen meters away.

Winters beamed. "Mr. Chiba did a great job of setting us down."

"Let's do it, then," Vonn said.

Winters leaned forward in his seat and started the engine. The van swayed with power.

"Wait for it," May said. He looked out the windshield at a line of flickering red lights. The flickering stopped for an instant, and then they all changed to green. "All right," he said. "The ramp is locked in place. Let's go and get our friends."

Winters's hand hesitated over the gear selector.

"What's wrong?" May asked.

Winters pointed out the window. "Steps, Mr. May. We're gonna be driving down *steps*."

"Yes," Vonn urged. "And if you don't drive down them *now*, we're going to lose the initiative."

Winters ground the vehicle into gear, and it pitched forward.

9

Emerson turned the corner and was struck blind. The light was bright and searing and felt as if it were burning into his brain. He shielded his eyes and took a few hesitant steps forward. As he did, he heard a metallic scraping from outside, and the lights cut off.

He hurried into the lobby, and sure enough, sitting on the outer edge of the plaza was a struts-down pleasure craft, hull blackened and steaming with the heat of reentry in the cool evening air. As he approached the reception desk, the front of the ship started to open. Emerson pulled the Comealong from his belt, tossed it down, and punched a security code on a pad. A control panel lit up and he stared at it, wondering if he should ring for law enforcement, bring up the early warning alarms, or wait to see if Burris was right about the ship's occupants.

There was a scrape from outside, and Emerson looked up. At the top of the stairs sat a pair of lights, not as bright as the landing lights, but shining like a pair of malevolent eyes.

What in the name of the Fifth Region . . .

The eyes lurched and then started forward, rapidly bobbing up and down, convulsing in an almost comic manner, getting bigger, closer . . .

And then Emerson realized: It's a vehicle, a truck or a van, and if they're not careful, it's going to hit—

The lights connected with the first of the glass doors, which began to crack and shatter a split second before the rending sound made by the impact. Emerson watched in awe as the vehicle plowed through, lights glinting off the jagged bits of glass exploding against the marble floor. There was a nervous instant of quiet, and then it hit the second set of doors, spraying more glass and rending the metal door frames from their housing. The vehicle skidded to a stop in the middle of the lobby, and Emerson went numb with recognition.

It was the same battered van that the Arcolian had been taken from. There was a clamor from inside, and the front passenger door fell off. A short man hopped out and brought an autoshot to bear in his direction.

"Don't do it," the man demanded in a very familiar voice.

"I wasn't going to," Emerson said nervously. He hoped it sounded like the truth, because at that point it was.

"You do me a favor," the man said, "and I'll let you live."

Emerson stared hard at the man with the autoshot. He looked tired and haggard, and his expression showed that, while he was trying to sound tough, he wanted to be anywhere else in the galaxy at that particular moment. *This* was the merchant that

Burris had feared, the one intent on bringing the Essence Corporation down? He looked more like a tired old man.

"Living," Emerson said, stalling for time to think. "Hey, that's for me."

Other doors on the van opened, and more people emerged. There was a tall man with a too-big head and a very trusting face, a woman who was scared and uncomfortable, and another man who was trying to juggle some medium-tech assault weapon against a blood-streaked bandage on his right hand.

In looking at them all, Emerson thought, *these* people are a threat? None of them except the one with the bandages looked as if they really wanted to be there, and he was coming across as being too clumsy to be taken seriously.

"Tell me," the man with the autoshot said, "where the on-line computer maintenance room is. The one that controls temperature, airflow—"

"I know which one you want," Emerson said. He was supposed to exact revenge against these people? What could Burris have been thinking?

"Well, where is it?"

Revenge. Ah. Of course. That's what he was thinking.

Emerson smiled. He gave them exact directions to the computer room.

"Thanks," the big-headed man said, trying to sound mean. "Now you should get out of here."

"Wait a minute," Emerson said quickly. With one hand, he gingerly unclipped the ID card from his breast pocket and flipped it toward the leader. "That's got my code on it. It'll make it easier for you to get inside the computer room."

The man with the bandages trained his weapon on Emerson while the woman picked up the card.

"It looks legit," she said.

The man with the autoshot gave a polite nod. "Thank you," he said. "Now if you don't mind leaving . . ."

"Leaving," Emerson said. "Hey, that's for me." He turned his back to them and walked out the hole the van had made, not looking back, pausing only for a moment to look at the oddity of a pleasure craft parked on the plaza. He tipped an informal salute to the unseen pilot, then started across the parking lot.

Revenge, he thought. Yes. That's the name of the game, isn't it, Mr. Burris?

The night was warm and clear, and the stars were out. Emerson walked home.

10

"Angel's Luck," Roz said. "I don't believe it. I've finally had—"

"Hush," May whispered. "Don't you dare say it. Don't even think it."

"But—"

"It's bad luck to mention Angel's Luck on a hit," May insisted. "An old mercenary superstition."

"I never heard that one," Winters said.

"I just made it up," May said. "Keep moving."

They shuffled down the hall, following the directions the guard had given them. After several meters they took a right and continued until that corridor dead-ended with a large gray door, the word NETWORK stenciled across it.

"He told us the truth so far," Vonn said.

"Let's hope he carried it all the way," May said. "Winters, go back down the hall and make sure that we don't have any surprises behind us."

Winters nodded and walked away.

Roz held the card out to May with a trembling hand.

"Go ahead," he said, nodding at the access slot.

"Don't worry," Vonn said, cradling his weapon. "I'll protect you."

Tentatively, she eased the card into the slot. There was a brief tone, and the door slid open. Vonn pushed ahead of the others and stepped into the room.

A man with a long tangle of hair started to rise from a terminal.

"Emerson," he said. "It's about time. I thought I heard glass—" He looked up at Vonn, yelped, and started to throw himself sideways.

"No!" Vonn shouted, and he jerked the trigger of the weapon, fighting to guide the spray of fire with his right arm. The shots scarred the walls and decimated a bulletin board cluttered with notes, then found their target, picking him up, spinning him around, and pitching him over a bank of humming mainframes.

With a shout, May jumped and slammed his shoulder into Vonn, knocking him to the floor. "You had no right to do that!"

"He was going for a weapon, May!"

"Like hell he was! Now you've alerted everyone in the galaxy to our presence!"

"Like driving through the window is discreet?"

"Is everything all right?" Winters was standing in the doorway, brandishing his weapon.

"Fine," May growled. "Vonn just smoked the person who was supposed to help us, but other than that—"

"If you gentlemen wouldn't mind, I could use your help."

They looked over at Roz. She had dropped down on one knee and was taking a handful of components out of her satchel. "Cheech gave me something—an uplink interface, I think—she said it was supposed to home the data dish onto the *Angel's Luck* so she can access the Essence System Frequencies."

"The map," May said. "Of course." He knelt beside Roz and pulled a tangle of black boxes and wires out of the satchel. "Here," he said, handing the mess to Vonn. "Sort these out. Roz gets the two direct links. You and I'll take the quietlink."

"Why can't we take a direct link?"

"Roz is going to need to talk directly with Cheech, and we won't have time to keep track of Peter Chiba. Roz will."

Vonn pulled at the twist of wires until he had the quietlink in his hand. He flicked it on.

> ReaD eRRoR No iNPuT DeTeCT <

"Oh, yeah," he said sourly. "This works really well, May."

"Can I help it if it's old?" May found a case filled with small tools and took it to one of the terminals.

"Old? Ancient. Why couldn't you have gotten a multilink? Then we wouldn't have to mess around with all of this pass-the-secret type stuff."

"Can I help it if I used to be a cheap bastard? We'll get a multilink before the next job, I promise."

"Messing with this shit," Vonn hissed, "is going to get us cut off."

From down the hall, a buzzer sounded, alternating between two tones, one near and one distant.

Roz jumped. "What's that?"

"An alarm," May said. "We're already cut off."

11

"What are you doing here?" Duke asked.

Eric Dickson sauntered across the cell and sat on the stool. For some strange reason there was no sound to his movement, and when the pilot spoke, Duke heard him on some private channel inside his head. Yet there he was . . .

"A more appropriate question," Dickson said, "is what are you doing here?" He shook his head. "You xenophiles make me sick."

Duke shook his head. "No. I'm not going to listen to any more of that, Eric."

"You wouldn't," the pilot sneered, "because you've managed to put yourself in bed with the Arcolians."

"It doesn't matter who I'm in bed with," Duke snapped. "I could be in bed with Leigh Brand—"

"You leave her out of this!"

"—and I still wouldn't measure up to your exacting standards. You know I don't understand what she saw in you, but with enough time, I'll figure it out."

"No, you won't," Dickson said. "The end is near."

Duke grunted. "You know, it must be boring to be right about everything. I've met some people with huge egos in my time, but you win the prize."

The image of Dickson circled around the inside of the cell. "What are you talking about?"

Duke crossed over to the mirror that was set into the wall and studied his face. He looked tired. His eyes were bloodshot, and he needed a shave and a haircut. "There's a difference between thinking you're something and being something. Between being the best and thinking you're the best. Do you see what I'm saying?"

"I had to be the best," Dickson snapped. "I survived the entire Arcolian war. That didn't just happen—"

"Thomas Fortunado survived the war," Duke said quietly. "With considerably less effort than you expended."

"Misfortunado's dead."

"So are you!" Duke spun to confront the figure. "And I certainly wouldn't call the way you lived after the war as surviving. Not drinking yourself into oblivion like you did. It was almost as if you had planned it."

Dickson looked vaguely troubled. His image flickered.

Duke advanced a step. "What was that?" he demanded.

"Nothing," the pilot said quickly. He looked around the cell and resolutely set his jaw. "We did what was needed to win the war."

"We didn't win the war," Duke said. "It was called off. We had to relearn something we'd taught ourselves a long time ago— that war is not profitable for the health of a sentient species."

"Peace isn't healthy, either," Dickson said. "We lose something of ourselves."

"Of course," Duke said. "We lose part of our aggressive nature. And during times of peace, those raised to be warriors suffer the most."

Dickson flickered again.

"They've got nowhere to go, nothing to do. What happens to those people, Eric? What happens to the perfect warrior once peace comes? What did it do to Thomas Fortunado?"

"No!" Dickson cried.

Duke closed his eyes.

Before Madeline there had been Veruca, and before Veruca there had been Celeste, and before Celeste there had been Lareae, and before Lareae it had been rumored that he had actually nailed General Biej, not long after the Accord had been signed . . .

"He became an inveterate womanizer," Duke said. "And after the Accord, all of his women had one thing in common, didn't they? With the exception of General Biej, who could have arranged to have him shot, they were all married women."

The expression on Dickson's face changed, and the image took a step backward.

"That was it, wasn't it, Eric? That was how Misfortunado Farmbuyer bought his ticket out. During the war he was the clown prince, but what good was someone with a talent for cratering out Vacc Fighters in peacetime?"

"That wasn't it at all,"

"Of course you're right," Duke said, watching the image as it started to fade and then suddenly sharpened again. "Only in this case you *have* to be right, because if you're not, then you have to face the truth. And the truth is that you knew what Fortunado was doing, didn't you? You even discussed it with Rhea. You knew that Fortunado was checking out, and you let that poor, trusting fool do it, didn't you?"

Dickson completely disappeared. Duke nodded, then sat on the bed.

The pilot reappeared. "You don't understand what it was like to be groomed and trained for a purpose and then have it all taken away."

"Wrong. I understand because I have your memories."

"The only thing we were good for was war. This business with the Arcolians coming to Council hurt me. It was betrayal—"

"The Arcolians coming here," Duke said, troubled. "What about that?"

Dickson began to fade.

"No, you don't!" Duke shouted, and the image became clearer than it had ever been. "All of what I went through on the *Hergest Ridge* with assaulting the Arcolians and going to the transgear bay. That was you, wasn't it?"

"It had to be," Dickson said. "You got my memories, so you reacted as I would have."

"No. You would have reacted differently. I can feel that, Eric. I was acting like I would have, only . . ." He rose and paced around the cell. He rubbed his forehead. "I don't know how I was acting. I was so sure I was helping you, but what was I helping you to do? I was so convinced that you were in trouble."

"I was in trouble."

"But your attitude. You weren't worried about the outcome of the Narofeld trial because you'd already lived through it. You'd come out of it clean. I'd have known that if I could have finished your biography, but I never could bring myself to read it. Yet, by sheer logic, I should have been able to reason that you were going to be okay, because you had to survive the war and sign up for the Essence program. For some reason I couldn't access those memories."

Dickson flickered.

"Stay," Duke ordered. "Why is it that I can only pull you up under stress?"

"You're not under stress now."

"Why can't I access all of your memories, only selected bits?"

Dickson shrugged. "The lot must take time to assimilate into your brain. You're getting my life as I lived it, a day at a time."

Duke shouted again as the image began to fade. He studied the uniform the pilot wore, then nodded. "You kept me from accessing those memories, didn't you?"

"No. That was a side effect. Think about what you've been through. Think about what it takes on your part to assimilate someone's whole life—"

"A hell of a lot you know about it!" Duke shouted. "That was you, wasn't it, making me do all of that stuff on the *Hergest Ridge*? You wanted to see war break out so you could live again, *in my body, you son of a bitch!*"

"I'm dead—"

"I know," Duke snapped. "And death isn't all it's cracked up to be, is it? What was I supposed to be? Your second chance?"

"No," Dickson replied. "I'm *your* second chance."

"What did you do in your life to make you manipulate me like you have been?"

"What I did is important only if you learn from it."

"*What was it?*" Duke shouted.

Dickson rubbed his eyes in concentration and began to fade.

"No!" Duke ordered. The image obeyed. "I'm in control now, Eric. And now you're going to tell me all about what happened to you."

Dickson dusted off the sleeves of his uniform. "You tell me."

Duke closed his eyes again.

Rhea. Rhea had talked of trying to save him. She had talked of trying to save him from—

"Yourself," Duke said. "Just like Fortunado."

"No. Not just like Fortunado."

"With Maximillian Burris's money."

"Terminal anesthesia."

"Why couldn't you have let Rhea save you?"

Couldn't you see that, Duke? Because she would have succeeded. Because I would have lived a long time, and I would have been miserable; I would have been a son of a bitch to live with if I couldn't do what made me happy, which was slaughtering Arcolians. Hell, I was a son of a bitch anyway.

"She loved you, Eric."

And I loved her, Duke, more maybe even than Leigh Brand. I couldn't do that to her. I made her cut her hair and dress like Leigh so I wouldn't forget. It made it easier to drink.

"Easier for you to kill yourself."

Understand, Duke, that it was important for me. All my life I'd been this self-centered hot-shot pilot-hero. I put Rhea's life ahead of my own. I'd never even done that for Leigh. That took more from me than leading the relief column to Bering's Gate. It was a hell of a brave thing that I did.

"It's braver to face life."

That doesn't matter. What does matter is that you've gotten stronger. You're getting control over me. All that remains is one more thing. You have to kill me, Duke.

Duke found himself laughing. "You'd like that, wouldn't you—having me pull the trigger for you? Talk about cowardice. You can't face life, so you make it as unbearable as you can so it's easier to drink yourself under. And when you find you've been given a new lease on things, what do you do? You tell me I've got to kill you." He shook his head. "If you're going to take the coward's way out, the least you could do is be brave enough to do your own dirty work.''

But you don't understand, Duke. I'm reaching the end.

''It ought to be easy enough for you to face, then, since death isn't all it's cracked up to be.''

There was silence. The image of Dickson appeared to be frozen in time.

''What's wrong?'' Duke asked. ''Can't you answer your own justification?''

The figure seemed to rise to its full height and then began to stretch, face puffing, shoulders broadening, chest swelling. All at once there was a metallic click, and the image winked out.

''Eric?''

The door hissed open. A guard stared into the cell, a weapon in his hand. Duke noticed that it was not a Comealong but a pistol.

''Arbor,'' the guard said. ''Come with me.''

Duke looked around the cell. He couldn't see or feel Dickson.

''Drag it out here,'' the guard growled.

With a shrug Duke stepped into the hall. The guard waved the barrel of the weapon, and Duke started walking. Behind him, the door slammed shut with a chilling finality.

''What's going on?''

''Mr. Burris wants to see you.''

Duke sighed. ''It's late for a social visit, don't you think?''

The guard said nothing.

''Really,'' Duke said. ''What's going on?''

''You're a hostage,'' the guard said.

Duke stopped and turned to the guard. ''And I wasn't already?''

''Keep moving.''

With a shrug, Duke continued.

''Burris wants you in his office for insurance,'' the guard said. ''Your merchant friend is coming for you and the Arcolian.''

At the word ''Arcolian,'' Duke froze.

''Move it,'' the guard snapped.

Duke tried, but it was impossible. Something was blocking his legs from moving and had locked the air in his lungs so he could not explain.

''I said *move*!''

Duke could do nothing as the barrel of the weapon poked between his shoulder blades. His chest was about to explode from holding air in when the halls darkened and a siren sounded.

"What the hell—"

Duke jerked forward helplessly, one step, two steps—

"No," he cried.

He rose up on the ball of his left foot and started to spin. His right leg came up and aimed for the pistol in the guard's hand. It connected and sent the weapon into the wall. The foot went down and an elbow came up, raking across the side of the guard's head. With another fluid motion, he stepped over to the gun and grabbed it off the floor with his left hand. Left tossed to right, fingers snapped the safety catch, and with a wrist flick, the pistol spun twice and came to bear on the guard.

"All right. Where's the Arcolian?"

The voice in Duke's ears sounded foreign but clearly came from his own larynx. The guard looked up from his sprawl and shook his head, surprised to see that the gun had suddenly changed hands.

"I'm on a short fuse, dammit! Where the hell is the Arcolian?"

Don't tell him, Duke thought. Don't tell him oh don't tell him in the name of the Fifth Region . . .

The guard opened his mouth and gave explicit directions on how to get to the cell.

All right, Eric, you got what you wanted now lock him in my cell and let's work this out.

"No, Duke," the strange voice said. "I'm not talking to you now."

The guard looked confused. "You talking to me?"

"No," the voice said.

'No!' Duke cried.

He calmly squeezed the gun in his hand and put two bullets into the guard's head. After rifling the body to get the master access card, he turned and ran deeper into the cell complex.

12

So this is what it was like for him, Eric Dickson thought. To be in complete control, yet have the feeling that someone was watching you over your shoulder. In this case the feeling was saying *damn you, why did you have to do that when there was a perfectly good alternative, you were right, I should have killed you . . .*

And the problem was that the feeling could not be reasoned with and would not be consoled. The overall sensation was eerie—that of total dominance while still being helpless to stop the feeling's tirades.

Still, the feeling did not matter. He was in control. A feeling could be ignored.

He thought obsessively about the guard's directions. It felt wonderful to have a memory that worked well, unfettered by the fog of alcohol. "You don't know how good you have it," he said to Duke. "Even though your body is lacking, your mind is so clear. By the time I was your age, I'd already screwed mine up."

The feeling chose to ignore him, instead continuing its condemnation of his actions. He ignored it again, and as he followed the guard's directions, the protests became a distant buzz. He was in a short hallway that terminated in a single door. A sign told him MAX SECURE.

This was it.

Flesh crawling, Dickson stepped up to the door and made sure there was a round in the chamber of the weapon. He slipped the master access card into the slot and keyed up the COMMUNICATE mode.

A hissing noise came over the speaker. "Yesssss?"

Dickson's stomach turned at the shock of hearing a xeno talk. Yet there were some memories that confirmed it—the one that had talked to Studebaker, and Duke knew that they talked. It was enough to settle him. He cleared his throat and tried to speak in his most Duke-like voice. "Do you know who this is?"

"Indeed I do."

Dickson bounced with excitement.

"I scent that you are the one who assaulted redbutler on the ship *hergestridge*."

He cursed and slammed his hand into the wall. The bastard knew! And yet—it should have been expected. There was a tease of information, not "bring in the dogs," from the Accord negotiations, but something from Duke about the actual level of sophistication—

So this is what Duke went through as he learned about me. The helplessness, the frustration of it all . . .

"Yes," Dickson said.

"You are the Sapient B-form I was told of," the Arcolian said. "And you currently inhabit misterduke's A-form."

"That's right. Do you know why I'm here?"

"Indeed. It is most obvious."

"Tell me, then."

There was no reply.

"Tell me, dammit!"

"I refuse to give you the pleasure."

"Well, then," Dickson said, licking his lips, "I'll give it to myself. I owe you something from a long time ago. You cut up a bunch of my friends on Bering's Gate—"

"This was during wartime?"

"Yes. And I had a friend—"

"You may spare me the details. Your confession does nothing to alleviate your malevolence. I humbly suggest you participate in what is called 'getting the event over with.'"

"Smartass," Dickson said. He punched in the order to open the door, and it started to rise.

"Of course," the Arcolian said matter-of-factly, "you are forcing me to engage in self-defense."

No, no, no—shit! Duke, you made me forget!

Dickson's hand struck the controller, and the door began to ease down. As it did, something rolled up at him. It was a scent so strong that he was sent reeling backward, blind and dizzy. The breath locked tight in his chest, and his saliva stopped flowing, the inside of his mouth puckering from the odor's bitter sharpness. His sinuses instantly plugged up to keep it out, but it was too late. It had already sent burning spikes of fear into his brain, driving in so hard that he could feel the impact as surely as if someone had struck him full in the face. His arm pivoted wildly, hand squeezing the gun, trying to get off a lucky shot, but nothing happened. Fingers touched an empty palm. He was trembling, and it was not until the smell in the hall subsided that he realized that he was lying flat on his back, his weapon on the floor a few meters away.

For a split second, Dickson reasoned out a complete and effective plan of action, but before he could implement it, it was lost forever in the scent's tangle of fear and confusion.

It was horrible, awful. Worse than anything he had ever felt before.

Dickson put his hands over his eyes, and in the final seconds before darkness closed in, he began to cry.

13

Duke was lost in gray. The last thing he remembered was looking down the barrel of a cocked revolver, finger biting down on the trigger, and the look of horror on the face of the man who was the target. He had tried to turn away from the scene but could not. There had been an explosion that had sent him reeling, and when he recovered he was lying on the rain-drenched tarmac of Narofeld Station.

He got up and made straight for the hotel, straight up the stairs, straight for the gray that waited. When he came face-to-face with it he stopped, staring hard, trying to see through it.

No, he thought. Dickson would not be there. He had already made a lesson of the scene on the ship, and going back would be a waste of time. Duke had to find something that could put it all together and bring Dickson under control.

He stepped back.

No. Not something. Someone.

"Rhea," he said.

He turned and walked to the blank that had been Dickson's room. Rhea had been there before she had faded into oblivion. Perhaps she was still there.

Duke held his breath and extended his finger toward the blank. There was no sensation as he touched it, no feeling, no resistance. It did not seem to be an actual barrier, other than the eerie illusion that the tip of his finger had simply ceased to exist.

He drew his finger out. It was still whole, seemingly none the worse for wear.

Duke stuck it back in, and the digit vanished all the way to the knuckle. He could wiggle it but could not see it.

Biting his lip, he pushed his hand in all the way to the wrist and snapped his fingers. He could feel his hand making the motions, but there was an absence of sight and sound.

What is this? Duke asked himself. Was Rhea on the other side? There was only one way to find out, and it was damned important that it work.

His resolve set, he took a step. A rumble passed down through the hall, and the floor beneath him warped and buckled, knocking him into the opposite wall. He tried to stagger back toward the blank, but the entire hotel was shuddering, plaster falling from the walls and ceiling. Duke fell to the floor, and something began to drag him back toward the stairs.

He tried to grab onto something so he could resist the pull. There was nothing but cheap carpet and wooden floor beneath. His palms raked across it until they burned, and he snapped his hands back in pain as the wood buckled and fired jagged splinters into the air.

Duke looked at his hands in awe. They had blistered.

What's going on? he thought. I've never felt pain in this place . . .

The force pulled him to the edge of the stairs and unceremoniously nudged him over. He rolled down the first flight, arms and legs flailing in a perfect catfall that had been taught to a young Eric Dickson decades before. A strange feeling tingled the back of his neck—for the first time in ages, he was actually mindful of protecting his twice-broken right arm.

At the turn of the stairs he was able to stop his descent. He pulled to his feet and started back up the stairs, shouting Tetran epithets about Dickson's lineage. He went three steps, and his feet plunged through the wood as if they were feeble sticks. Duke threw himself forward, trying to pull himself up, but the impact smashed him through what remained of the staircase, and he went spinning down amid a hail of rotting wood chips. He tried another catfall, but he had broken through to a universe where it did no good—he fell at light speed toward an infinite plain of flat black glass.

Duke screamed and his eyes flew open. He was sitting in the hallway of the Essence Corporation's detention unit, drenched in sweat and panting hard through a wide-open mouth.

He blinked. His eyes felt gritty.

Slowly the trembling stopped, and he was able to look around. He was sitting with his back against a wall. Not more than a meter from his limp right hand was a revolver, and a cell door was in front of him.

Duke rested until he was sure that the hall was not moving, then tried to swallow. He was somehow out of his cell. What did he do now? What did he need to accomplish?

Before he could decide, a thin rattle reached his ears. The rattle was bent and shaped into a pattern he had recently learned to recognize.

"misterduke, are you there?" it said.

Duke reached up and wiped his mouth with the back of his hand. He felt weak, and he realized that he was only conscious through a great effort.

"mister . . . bob?" he panted. "I'm . . . dying . . . I'm afraid . . ."

"Nonsense, misterduke. I scent that your physiology is merely recovering from the effects of a direct hit with tigerscat. It will pass."

"Tigerscat?" He tilted his head back; the motion seemed

to make it easier to breathe. "What did . . . I do . . . to deserve . . ."

"Oh, my dear Sapient," misterbob chortled. "You did nothing to deserve. I was most unfortunate to have to use it as a defense against the Sapient B-form that shares your physiology. It seemed intent on my destruction."

"Eric . . . Dickson?"

"After my defensive assault, a most remarkable thing happened. The Sapient B-form began to scent of new death, and then I began to detect the scent of you, misterduke. Is this possible?"

The question made Duke's head spin. Was it? Dickson would be using the body as only he could. Would that account for the pheromonal change that misterbob had noted?

"I scent I have confused you," misterbob continued. "Disregard my query. Suffice it to say that I am glad you are alive and in health."

"I . . . feel . . . rotten."

"As I have said, this will pass. Now you must endeavor to open my cell door, misterduke. It would be of most urgent profit that you do this quickly."

"Urgent . . . profit?" Duke tried to shake his head, but the movement came out as a shiver. "Never mind. Be there . . . in a minute." He tried to push himself into a standing position, but his legs flopped uselessly against the floor.

"I might add that—what is your idiom? I believe it is that 'time is hellishly inadequate.' "

Duke leaned forward and flopped onto his belly. He reached out with shaking hands and tried to grip the tile floor, fingers trying to find some purchase so he could pull forward. They did nothing but slide back toward him across the cold slickness.

"Damn," he said disappointedly. "Can't move."

"But you must do it, misterduke!" the alien said excitedly. "This situation is most urgent!"

"I *know*!" Duke said angrily. He put his palms flat against the floor and pushed up. His body shifted, and he tried to pull his knees up. All he managed to do was roll onto his side.

"Indeed," misterbob said. "I know you will be able to do this. The Sapient A-forms have many homilies which stress the importance of triumph against the condition of adversity. 'The tragic musical entertainment has not ended until the diva has lost weight.' 'If you do not obtain the desired results, then you must obtain them again.' 'Surgical procedures at present render further surgical procedures unnecessary—' "

"misterbob," Duke said weakly.

"—when you have lost everything, then it is time to lose nothing.' 'That which is deemed relatively important under current wisdom soon reaches a juncture at which—' "

Duke kicked with his legs and managed to inch forward. It caused his head to spin madly, and he closed his eyes and tilted his head back, breathing through his open mouth. *"misterbob!"* he shouted.

"Yes?" the creature asked softly.

"Shut up," Duke said. And then the feeling he had been fighting overtook him, and he crumpled to the floor.

14

Burris stopped. He had been pacing around his desk, waiting for the guard he had dispatched to get Duke. Was it his imagination, or was the guard taking forever to go to the cell complex and escort the prisoner back?

He looked at his watch. It was not his imagination. Something had happened. Either the guard had deserted his post, or Dickson had surfaced and overpowered him. Or perhaps something else had delayed them. Maybe Arbor had told him of the riches that were due from the distillations and had offered the guard a cut for switching sides. That seemed the most plausible; Arbor was obviously skilled at negotiating with low-life mercenary types.

Burris picked up the pistol and opened the breech to make sure that a round was in the chamber. Then he pulled on a jacket, slipped the weapon into his pocket, and walked out the office door.

One shot at May, that's all he asked. One, right between the eyes.

15

Cheech's voice crackled in Roz's ear. "Do you have a green light on the transducer?"

Roz glanced over the maze of winking lights on the small box in front of her. "Uh, which one is the transducer?"

May reached down and tapped one of the lights for her. She nodded.

"Green light," she told Cheech.

"Steady?" the programmer asked.

Roz looked at May. "Steady?"

"The light is burning steady, yes."

Roz flushed. She looked out at May from a tangle of wires surrounding her head. The hear/speak unit to Cheech was attached to her right ear, and the unit to Chiba in the *Reconnez Cherie* was attached to her left. "You're sure you want me to do this?"

"Unless you want out."

"It's a little late for that." She sighed. "Cheech? Steady green light."

"One moment." The transmission hissed. "All right. Winking now?"

"Winking," Roz said.

"You're on-line," Cheech said. "Let me see if I can cut that alarm for you."

Roz turned to give May the message as the alarm went silent. She laughed. "You're a miracle worker, Cheech."

"This is the simple stuff. I'm going to send a message to the boys."

"Is the quietlink on?" Roz asked.

May checked the screen.

ReaDy To Go GeT DuKe? <

"Son of a bitch," Vonn said.

TeLL RoZ To BRiNG uP aTTaCHeD TeRMiNaL <

"Power up the secondary terminal," May said. "She's going to go into the floor plan."

Roz obediently leaned across the desk and activated the slave unit.

"Can you hear Chiba?" Vonn asked.

"Peter," Roz said into the left mike. "You there?"

"Ready and waiting," the salvor answered in her left ear.

"He's there," Roz said.

May looked at Vonn and Winters. "You guys ready?"

Winters snapped back the bolt of his weapon. "Let's kickass for Mr. Duke and misterbob."

"Let's just get them out of here alive, all right?" May turned to Roz. "You want one of us to stay?"

"Get out of here," she said uncertainly, "before I change my mind."

May gave her a salute of respect and walked out the door, followed by Winters. Vonn paused for a moment.

"Close the door behind us," he told her.

"I will," she replied, and smiled at him for an instant.

He turned and joined the others in the hall, and the door sealed shut. "All right, where do we go?"

May held up a hand as he looked at the quietlink. "Just a minute. Cheech is accessing the floor layout."

> RoZ SayS HoPe you HaVe a. L. SayS you'D KNoW WHaT THaT MeaNT <

"We have *what*?" Vonn asked.

"Don't ask," May said.

> aM iN THe SySTeM. FRoM CoMPuTeR RooM TuRN RiGHT Go @) MeTeRS. <

May swore bitterly and fumbled a message onto the quietlink's keypad.

> CHeeCH WRiTe NuMBeRS ouT <

> TWeNTy MeTeRS < came the reply.

May punched in > TKS < and nodded his head to the right.

"I don't like this," Vonn said. "If we get in trouble, we're not going to have a chance to type out an eloquent request for help."

"That's why," May, said, "you've got to quit bitching and be on your toes. Give me some cover."

Vonn muttered and made a sweeping motion with the barrel of his weapon.

> you CoME To iNTeRSeCTioN TuRN LeFT Go FiFTeeN M. <

May pointed left. Vonn flattened himself against the wall. May waited for Winters to glance toward them from his position behind them and gestured in explanation. The big man nodded. The merchant slung the quietlink around his neck, took his pistol in a two-handed grip, and slid around the corner. He covered the hall until Vonn and Winters appeared and occupied positions farther down the hall. May scrambled between them.

"What's the link say?" Vonn asked.

May checked the screen. "Through the door, down the hall to a T intersection. Cells to the right."

"Ready on the door," Vonn called to Winters.

Winters crouched and brought his weapon to bear at the door. May brought his pistol back up, and Vonn slapped the switch with his left hand.

The door raised. There was nothing except more hallway, which terminated in the described intersection. May put a finger to his lips, and they slipped through, Vonn in the lead and Winters moving backward, covering the rear. Once Vonn was satisfied that their path was clear, he gave a hand signal, and they moved toward the intersection.

>FiFTeeN M. To CeLL DooRS. May HaVe To BReVKK 7oKK<

"Dammit, Cheech," May said, squinting at the readout.

Vonn hissed and put a finger to his lips. May typed into the quietlink.

>CHeeCH SiGNaL GoiNG BaD<

>DuKe iN Ce77 # \\ — aRKo7iaN N Ke77 . ..!*¦¦¦<

"Vonn," May whispered.

Waving for May to be quiet, Vonn flattened against the left wall and inched his way to the intersection in a semicrouch, peering down the right hallway. Stopping short of the intersection, he hand-signalled for Winters to come and take the point. May pointed at the quietlink, and Vonn made another emphatic gesture that expressed his opinion of the equipment in question. May checked the screen one last time.

>¦¦¦¦¦¦¦¦¦¦¦¦¦¦¦¦¦¦¦¦¦¦¦¦¦¦¦¦¦¦¦¦¦<

The merchant unslung the device from his shoulder and laid it on the floor, which earned a gesture of approval from Vonn. Readying his pistol, May crouched next to the mercenary.

"On three," Vonn mouthed. "You left, Winters right."

May nodded.

Vonn started to take his hand from the trigger of his weapon, but May stopped him.

"I'll count," May whispered. Both mercenaries nodded.

The merchant inched around Vonn until he was next to the left corner. He held up one finger, and then two, and then Winters cried out and swung his gun toward May's position. May jumped at the sound. He tried to roll into a catfall and keep his pistol trained but became tangled in something soft that grunted and fell to the floor as part of a tangled heap. There were shouts from the two mercenaries, the sounds of Vonn trying to keep Winters from firing on a target that now included May.

May turned his head to examine the tangle he was in and looked directly into Burris's eyes. Burris's face lit with recognition, and he scrambled to his feet and ran. May was up an instant later, following and shouting for Winters to fire at the fleeing man's legs. Winters tried to aim; Vonn swore loudly and ended up tossing the big man to the floor.

Hearing the clatter behind him, May pumped his legs. With a deft leap, the merchant caught Burris by one foot and both went to the floor. May bounced in an aggressive catfall and landed hard on Burris's back, threw his arm around the man's neck, and cranked it up at a painful angle.

"Don't try it!" May shouted. "Let me see those arms, out front!"

Burris splayed his fingers apart and stretched out his arms.

"Give me one reason why I shouldn't blow your brains out right this very second. *One reason*."

"You don't have your weapon." The voice came from behind. It was Vonn. "You left it on the floor, May."

"Forget it." He tightened his grip, and his prisoner grunted.

"That was stupid, May," Vonn hissed. "Really stupid."

"Whose side are you on?"

"Winters would have blown your legs off. You hired me for a reason—"

"It turned out all right, didn't it?"

"He's the enemy," Vonn said, shouting and pointing. "It's *him*, May, not us! It's not my job to baby-sit Winters!"

"It's all right," Winters said, joining them and tagging Burris with the toe of his boot. "Maybe I'd have figured I was gonna hit May." The quietlink was in the big man's hand, and he hung it from his shoulder by the strap. "Your little box is broken, Mr. May."

"But we've got Burris, and he'll take us anywhere we want to go. Isn't that right?" There was no answer. May increased the pressure. With a grunt, Burris spit at May.

"That's it!" May dropped his grip and kicked Burris away. "I'm not playing that game with you. Kill him, Vonn."

Vonn shrugged. With the assault weapon in his left hand and May's pistol in the remnants of his right, he would not be able to do it.

"All right," May said, standing. "Winters, you do it."

"Be happy to." The big man swung the weapon up, and Burris cried out. May held his hand out to stop the execution.

"You wouldn't," Burris said, trying to sound calm. "Not really. You're a reasonable man—"

May shook his head and pointed at Winters. The weapon came up again.

"The money!" Burris cried. "The reward money, every penny of it, the three hundred—"

May stayed Winters.

"It was five," Vonn said.

Burris nodded rapidly. "Yours."

"That's not what we came for," May said icily.

"Of course. Your friends—"

May shook his head. "Just like you to put money ahead of them, isn't it? You're in no position to bargain for them, Burris. They're ours."

Burris paled. "Dammit, man, you've got to have a price."

"Oh, yes," May said quietly. "I've got a price."

Vonn studied the merchant with a cocked head.

"We're going to go and get my friends out of your lab, and they'd better still be in good health—"

"They are," Burris said, voice breaking. "In the name of the Fifth Region, they are!"

"But first, you're going to take us to where the phials are, and you're going to give them back to us."

"*What?*"

"You heard me. Even if they're never used, there's too much power in them to stay in your hands."

Vonn stepped forward. "May, this is one hell of a time to get idealistic."

"Shut up!" the merchant shouted.

"What about repairs to your ship?"

"We can finance it by selling the phials to someone else, someone reputable, but that's not what matters right now. What does is that he shouldn't be in charge of so much corporate power. I want him taken down. Getting the phials back will do that.''

"May, nobody's going to buy those phials, not when—"

"Then it doesn't matter. We'll have the satisfaction of knowing the truth, won't we?''

"I don't like this," Vonn said.

"You don't have to like it. I'm your boss and those are my orders.''

Vonn held the pistol out for May to take. "Let it be known that I wish to file an official protest against these orders.''

"Noted," May said. He stepped up to Burris and pulled him from the floor, then pushed the barrel of the pistol into the back of the businessman's neck. "Lead on.''

Stiffly turning, Burris began to lead them away from the cells.

16

"Any word yet?"

Cheech drummed her fingers on the worktable, trying to figure out how to answer Roz's question. The lines across the screen of the quietlink were disquieting. Drawing breath, she fumbled the mouthpiece closer to her lips. "They're in the hallway before the main cell block. I suspect they're trying to breach the lock.''

"You said the same thing five minutes ago," Roz said urgently. "What's keeping them?''

Cheech shrugged. Realizing that Roz could not see the gesture, she tried to formulate an answer.

"Ask them," Roz demanded. "Please get on that thing and ask them what the delay is.''

"Okay," Cheech said, not wanting to complicate things any more. She flexed her fingers and ran off the first few words of a message.

>!!!!!!!!!!!!!!!<

It was useless. The linguistics circuit had failed, and she had no time to troubleshoot it. If only there was something she could substitute . . .

She leaned back in her chair, looking around at the makeshift repair shop she had made of the *Angel's Luck* bridge. Her eyes fell on a familiar molding of plastic and synhair which made her smile.

No, nothing to substitute. But there was a linguistics board that was *almost* working.

"Come here, CHARLES," she said, and grabbed the component head of the ship's android.

17

Peter Chiba sat in the cockpit of the *Reconnez Cherie*, squeezing the armrests of his seat and tapping his feet on the floor. The novelty of working with mercenaries had long since worn off, mostly because he had been designated to stay behind with the escape vehicle. He had tried to chat with Roz about their next job, but she had resolutely ordered him off of the frequency. She needed to keep her head clear in case Cheech called, she had said, so he should only call her if there was an emergency.

Stretching until the bones in his neck cracked, Chiba looked down at the event clock. The others had been gone a little under fifteen minutes. Further proof, he mused, of relativity. For those in the building, time must be whizzing by as quickly as the bullets past their heads, if any shooting was going on. But for the salvor left to wait, it seemed as if a century had dragged by.

Chiba leaned back in the chair and stared out the viewport. The Essence building blocked most of the view, but out of the corners he could see part of the city's skyline. He lazily gazed out one side and then the other until a series of blue and red flickering lights caught his eye. On instinct, he reached for the external camera controller, brought the image up on the screen, then magnified it.

It was a police car, and the sight of it made Chiba laugh. He had been in space for so long, spending time on tankers, way stations, and luxury ships, that he had forgotten that planetary law enforcement had to utilize vehicles in getting from one place to another instead of using lifts and gravity wells.

His fingers played across the controls and brought the magnified image up closer. The vehicle was sleek and aerodynamic looking—another rare sight in space. The front had a series of lights that aimed out in an arc across its front, and the strobes of red and blue were set along the sides of the front windscreen.

The vehicle was stopped, so Chiba nudged the camera to give him a closer look, boosting up the infrared gain to compensate for the darkness outside.

What he saw made him gasp.

The driver of the vehicle was looking straight at him through a pair of optoculars. Then the man waved as another law-enforcement vehicle pulled up. He walked back and began talking with the driver of the second vehicle. As he spoke his arm came up and pointed straight at the *Reconnez Cherie*.

It stood to reason. The sight of a pleasure craft settled in the parking lot of a major corporation on a world where landings were restricted was bound to raise eyebrows. In fact, it was bound to raise a lot more than eyebrows.

Fixing his eyes on the screen, Chiba called up Roz's frequency and keyed in an alert tone.

"What do you want?" Roz snapped.

Chiba paused for a moment. She was probably alone and scared. He could forgive her.

"I told you not to call unless there's an emergency, Peter."

Under different circumstances, Chiba would have smiled. It was almost as if she wanted an emergency so she would have an excuse to leave.

"I thought you'd better know we're attracting a lot of attention," he told her. "Better tell the boys to get moving."

"All right," Roz said nervously. "I'll have Cheech call them."

18

You're right, Eric. I should have done something about you.

Duke awoke to find his face flat against the cold tile floor. There was a sharp throbbing behind both eyes, and his stomach was in knots. He pulled his hands in, and they squeaked on the floor. He pushed up and tucked his legs under until he was in a kneeling position, then blinked at the cell door in front of him.

"misterbob?" he asked hoarsely.

There was no reply.

Duke rubbed his eyes. His strength felt as if it was returning, but he was still weak. "misterbob?"

Still nothing. Duke moaned and leaned forward, inching into a standing position by bracing against the wall.

"They didn't get you while I was passed out, did they?"

A thin croak came from inside the cell. "Indeed, you wished to speak to me, misterduke?"

Duke laughed in relief. "You're still here."

"Are you expecting me to answer you?"

The Tetran rubbed his head. "That's right. I didn't offend you, did I, misterbob?"

"Certainly not," the ambassador said. "But you did request that I maintain aural silence. Is it safe to speak?"

"As safe as it's going to get." Duke spotted the card that Dickson had left sticking out of the lock and leaned on the release button. The cell opened to reveal the Arcolian, patiently waiting.

"Nice to see—" Duke's jaw dropped. "Your arm," he said. "What happened? What did they do to you?"

misterbob rose and calmly shuffled out of the cell. "Indeed, nothing was done to harm me. I sustained the injury during an accident—"

"You've got to be helped—"

"I am intact," misterbob insisted. "Our most urgent need at this time is to find the hell of this building and remove it."

"No matter how you say it, it's a great idea." Duke shook his head to clear the last of the disorientation and stared at the place where the arm should have been. "Are you sure you can travel? I mean, haven't you lost blood or whatever it is that you call it?"

"Yes," misterbob said. "Fortunately, Arcolian forms have capacity to quickly remanufacture lost bodily fluid. Such a trait is necessary to the survival of our race."

"What about your arm?"

"It will grow back, misterduke. You must not concern yourself with my welfare. Yours is by far the most important right now, and we must hasten before jamesohjames does something foolish such as come after us. Pleasantries can be exchanged later."

"Of course." Duke looked around and spotted the discarded pistol. "We'll need this," he said, and bent to pick it up.

"Sadly, you may be correct. All the communication I have done over the last few hours is beginning to tire me."

Duke held the gun in his hand and stared at it. It felt strangely cold and heavy in his hand. "I'll bet you never thought life in the Ambassadorial Corps would be like this."

"Indeed not." The Arcolian's head pivoted to take in the hallway. "In which direction must we go, misterduke?"

Duke did not answer. He continued to study the gun.

"misterduke?" The Arcolian's chest fluttered and it concentrated. "Indeed, this is most remarkable."

Duke still had not moved.

"Hello?" misterbob said. "Sapient B-form?"

Duke slowly looked up from his stare. "What did you call me?"

"You are the Sapient B-form who inhabits misterduke. You have returned."

Duke nodded.

"I scent that you have a growing feeling about me. A most curious mixture of fear and hatred. I realize that you cannot scent me, otherwise you would know of the compassion and pity I feel for you."

Duke lifted his gaze from the gun.

"I should warn you, however, that I will not allow you to harm me. I have defended myself once, and I do not think that you wish for me to subject you to tigerscat again. If you do not attempt to assault me, you will also have my word that I will not attempt any undue pheromonal influence of your feelings. Do you understand me, B-form?"

Duke nodded again.

"Any conclusion which is reached must be done on your own volition. We must reach an equitable solution to the problem of your inhabiting the A-form of my friend misterduke. Do you understand, B-form?"

"You called him your friend."

"That is correct."

"Are there more of . . . your kind . . . coming?"

The Arcolian nodded. "Just as your race will be coming to share frontiers with us. Acceptance is not yet universal, and it will never be complete. But once the generation which remembers us as a feared and hated enemy has passed, there will be much more blending of our scents."

"And Duke . . ." Duke looked down at the floor. "He's part of that."

"He and his *angelsluck* friends are the first of your common citizens which have been allowed to interact with my race. It has been a most gratifying experiment."

Duke sighed. "It's strange—no, I take that back. When I think of all that's happened since I've been gone, it's not strange at all."

"Of what were you about to speak?"

"Duke. He has these memories of you, and . . ." He stared into space, looking for the right words. "You're a hell of a nice guy, misterbob. And that goes beyond your being—what you are. You would've made a great human being."

"Indeed." misterbob nodded its head, pleased. "I was designed with that intent. The roechangers will be pleased to be scented of this development.''

''There's no denying change, is there?''

''It is foolish to,'' misterbob said. ''I do not know how much you know of my race's history—''

''I have what Duke remembers.''

''Then you are aware of the manner in which we embrace change.''

''Yes. And I remember something else. I remember a derelict ship full of mutilated people. I was there, misterbob, I was on that ship.''

''War has regrettable consequences.''

''But I also remember something you told Duke. It had to do with the way you view change and the way we view it. You—your race—did that to help bring the war to an end.''

''History has shown that you attempted the same type of experiments.''

Duke shook his head. ''There was a universe of difference between them. There's something else I seem to remember, correct me if I'm wrong, Ambassador.''

''Indeed.''

''I must call you misterbob. I remember that, too. But I remember another member of your delegation.'' He stopped for a moment and took a deep breath. ''I remember one called . . . I remember one called Leigh—''

''leighbrand,'' misterbob said.

Duke nodded. ''I don't want to, but I understand you. You know, it was so comfortable being right back then. It was so easy to make a career of hatred.''

The Arcolian said nothing, but cocked its head in study.

Duke laughed wryly. ''You know, I kept telling Duke that death wasn't all it was cracked up to be. Looking at what's happened, it really wasn't. You know what the bad part was, misterbob? The bad part was coming back to life.''

''What are you telling me, B-form?''

''I'm giving you the solution to the problem with your friend. I was attempting to take control and have a second chance. It was a great prospect, especially since I screwed up so badly the first time. But I can't push for it anymore. I'm surrendering.'' He laughed bitterly. ''I can't imagine anyone wanting to live past a hundred and fifty. Beyond that, there's so much change.''

misterbob rose and began to shuffle toward Duke, but Duke backed away.

"No, that's all right, Ambassador. I'll be all right."

"I scent no fear from you, B-form."

He took a cautious step back. "It's coming. I've been using Duke's positive memories to keep it suppressed."

"Indeed. You have learned something from Duke even as he has learned from you."

"I've learned more." He started to turn. "Thank you, Ambassador. It's been an education."

"B-form," misterbob said. "Where are you going?"

"I've got some unfinished business to take care of." He shifted the pistol to his left hand and gave the Arcolian the highest salute of respect. The Arcolian mimicked the gesture, and Duke turned and started down the hall.

misterbob stood in the hall, trying to scent what was happening to Duke. It was getting difficult to figure out—it had been a long day and rest was required.

After a moment, however, the Arcolian realized that while it had found Duke's scent, the Tetran had gone his own way. On top of that, while the cell was no longer confining, the building still was.

misterbob rattled its throat in disgust and started to wander down the hall, chest pulsating and tasting the air. After a time, it started to pick up impressions of scent, faint but distinct.

There was no mistaking what was happening inside the building. If that was the case, then there was another way to help misterduke. True, it was untried, but one thing that misterbob had learned from the Sapient A-forms was their pragmatic approach to problem-solving, even when the potential solutions defied what they called common sense. Or as they were so apt to put it, the tragic musical entertainment was not ended until the diva lost weight.

The creature's Arcolian heritage bristled at the prospect. It could almost hear the words of rebuke that redbutler might use: *Indeed, misterbob, you mean to explain that the entire success of your helping the A-forms is contingent upon a spontaneous and therefore untried and unproven course of action?*

Yes, redbutler, but you must understand the psychology of such behavior as it is most fascinating. It is called "longshot."

misterbob's head shook with the excitement of the prospect. *Longshot.* It was so simple, so obvious.

So human.

Indeed, it might even work.

19

The van sat inside the lobby, idling.

One of the rear tires, impacted in two separate accidents and now resting on shards of glass, finally had its seal breached and slowly began to go flat.

Inside the engine compartment, a piece of metal was crushed against the synthplast hose line that fed transgear fluid to the inner engine compartment. As the engine ran, the vibrations caused the metal to rub against the line, scraping the surface until a small patch began to wear thin. When enough had been sheared away, the hose burst, and the slippery fluid began to spray out in a fine mist, coating the inside of the engine housing.

Some drops stayed where they landed, and the fluid continued to do its job of remaining perfectly inert. Others, shaken by the increasing vibrations, succumbed to gravity and began to puddle on the lobby floor.

The engine continued to idle.

20

Cheech answered the line with a brisk "Yo!" which annoyed Roz Cain to no end. With everything that was happening, the technician's humor was more than Roz was able to bear.

"When," Roz asked, "will the guys have that door open?"

There was a long silence.

"Well?" Roz banged her fist on the console. "You've been messing around long enough, Cheech. What's going on?"

The mike on the *Angel's Luck* opened, but there was a stifling pause before Cheech spoke.

"I don't know yet."

"*What?* I thought you were a genius at this sort of stuff!"

"It's not my fault. The linguistic circuit in the quietlink went dead."

A cry broke from Roz's throat and turned into a sob.

"It's not as bad as it sounds. I've got another that will work as well if not better. But I need to modify it first."

Roz took a deep breath. "All right," she said, trying to sound calm. "How long will this take?"

"I'm almost done."

"I need a *time*. Minutes. Hours. Days."

"Ten minutes, tops. All I have to do is tap into the primary cerebrosynthetic processor and—"

"Don't explain it, do it. And any time you could shave off that would be appreciated."

"Aye aye."

Roz poised her finger to cut the connection. It hovered for a moment, then folded into her fist. "Look, Cheech, do you still need me here with all of this stuff?"

"Negative. I'm in the system. I could be assisted through any terminal in the building." Cheech paused, leaving the circuit open. "Roz, is there something you're not telling me?"

Roz swallowed. "Absolute. Peter tells me that the *Cherie* has caught the attention of local law enforcement. You've got to get that thing up and running and tell the guys to get out of there."

"Two minutes," Cheech said. "I should have enough to go on by then. Meantime you get out of there, girl."

"All right," Roz answered. "Color me gone. Tell the boys not to wait for me." She pulled the line to the *Angel's Luck* from her ear and tapped into the one to the *Cherie*.

"Peter?"

"You rang?"

"Cheech is going to call the others off in two minutes."

"Good. This meeting is turning into a party. I count four vehicles now, but so far it looks like they're still at the discussion stage."

"Cheech doesn't need me anymore, so I'm coming out. Be there in a minute."

"I'm not going anywhere."

She disconnected the line and checked the equipment that had been slaved into the Essence computer network. After a quick survey to make sure everything was in order, she opened the door, and when she was certain that the hall was clear she stepped out, sealing the room behind her.

It took a moment for her to get her bearings, and then she made for the lobby. The whole situation struck her as strange; the trip to the computer room had seemed to take no time at all. Perhaps it had something to do with being in the company of three armed men.

Roz hurried through the darkened halls until the lobby was in sight and she could hear the dull thrum of the van's engine. She paused for a moment, looking back toward the computer room.

There was a flash of color from one of the halls. Roz turned to see a figure standing in the hall, staring back at her, a pistol in his hand. After a moment of study, he looked away in a lack of recognition and disappeared from the intersection.

"Duke?" Roz asked. Then she shouted, "Duke!"

She looked out at the lobby, and at the *Reconnez Cherie* resting beyond the broken windows.

If Duke is here, she thought, then May doesn't have him yet. And if Duke ran from me, then he's not in his right mind again. It must be Eric Dickson.

Without looking back, Roz hurried down the hall after Duke, calling him by his name and the name of the long-dead pilot.

21

Burris stopped in front of a door marked BIOSCIENCES STORAGE. May brought the pistol up and aimed it between the businessman's eyes.

"This is where they're kept," Burris said. "The distillations are stable at room temperature, but we like to keep them in cold storage."

May nodded to Vonn, who flattened against one side of the door. Winters did the same on the other.

"Open it up."

"I've got to get my access card. It's in my front breast pocket."

May pulled back the hammer of the pistol. "Slowly. Two fingers."

Burris opened his jacket and reached in with fore- and middle fingers to draw out a thin plastic chit. May stood motionless. Burris turned and inserted the card in the lock, sweating as he heard the merchant move to a position directly behind him.

The lock gave a green light, and May grabbed Burris around the neck and pushed the gun into his temple.

"There's nobody here this time of night," Burris grunted.

"There had better not be."

May eased toward the door and stepped through. Vonn came next, and Winters inched in last. May barked an order to close the door, and Winters slapped the switch. As the door sealed, a sharp beeping filled the air. May tightened his grip around Burris's neck and spun around.

"What the hell is that?"

"I don't know," Burris choked. "I swear to the Fifth Region—"

"Mr. May," Winters said, brandishing the quietlink. "It's your little box."

"It can't be. The oscillator on that thing hasn't worked in—"

Winters held the box out. It was the source of the noise. "There's letters on it, too."

May pushed Burris away, gave an order for Winters to cover him, then took the quietlink.

The screen said, >HeLLo HeLLo HeLLo HeLLo HeLLo< and then cleared to read >aTTeMPT To ReaCH May aND CoMPaNy<. The letters were not perfect and their image was wavy and flickering, but damn, May thought, at least it's working. Heart pounding, he keyed the ACKNOWLEDGE switch.

>May! So GooD To HeaR FRoM you! THe LaST THiNG i HaVe iN MeMoRy iS BeiNG PuRSueD By yueH SHeNG GaNGSTeRS<

Vonn looked at May's puzzled expression. "Who is it?"
May shrugged. "Myron Li's ghost?"
Winters whined and took a step backward.
"It's okay," May said, and keyed in a request for identification.

>Boy aM i DiSaPPoiNTeD! aFTeR aLL We'Ve BeeN THRouGH ToGeTHeR, you DoN'T eVeN ReCoGNiZe Me! DiD you HaVe My PeRSoNaLiTy ReCaLiBRaTeD? DoeS iT SHoW THaT MuCH? WiLL i eVeR Be THe SaMe? oH, WHaT'S HaPPeNeD To Me???<

"It's the CHARLES unit!" May cried. "Cheech must have it working!"

Vonn rolled his eyes. "Great. Let's get choked up about it later, okay? We're kind of in a tight situation, May."

The merchant looked up at Burris. "Where are the phials being kept?"

Vonn pointed at a large vault door labeled COLD STORAGE/ MAIN BAY. "Right in there."

"No," Burris said.
They looked at him.
"I could say that, and I could easily lock you in there and freeze you to death, but I won't. It's my hope that you'll listen to reason."

"Like you listened to us earlier," May said. "Where are the phials?"

"That," Burris said, gesturing at the main storage bay, "is long-term storage. We're still running checks on the distillations to see how they've held up over the last decade, so they're in short-term storage." He swung his arm to a double set of glossy white doors. "They're in that chest right over there."

May turned his pistol butt out and handed it to Vonn. "Make him open it."

"Move," Vonn said, wagging the gun in his left hand.

May typed again.

>CHaRLeS, DoeS CHeeCH HaVe uS BaCK oN THe TraCKiNG LiNe? iF So HaVe HeR PLoT THe FaSTeST RouTe To WHeRe DuKe aND MiSTeRBoB aRe BeiNG HeLD<

"This is going to take a little bit," Burris said, stopping at a terminal to power it up. "The system needs to verify that it's me."

"Just so you know," Vonn warned, "we've got someone tapped into your computer line. If you try anything funny, your brains are going to be all over that screen."

Burris shook his head. "I'll open it for you, but you've got to hear me out."

"Just open the vault," Vonn said.

>WHaT??? WHaT iS THiS??? WHaT HaS HaPPeNeD To LiTTLe DuKe??? WHo iS CHeeCH??? WHo iS THiS Mi-STeRBoB??? aNy ReLaTioN To THe Guy oN THe HoLo-SeRieS???<

May swore under his breath.

>No TiMe CHaRLeS CHeeCH iS THe WoMaN FiXiNG you aSK HeR THe QueSTioN<

Burris's fingers rattled on the keyboard.

"Why don't you use voice?" Vonn asked.

"Because this takes longer," was the answer. "It was designed to slow down this kind of situation."

>oH yeS HoW FooLiSH oF Me. oF CouRSe i KNoW CHeeCH. THaT ReMiNDS Me oF SoMeTHiNG<

"I swear, CHARLES," May grumbled, "I'm going to have your personality done over."

>i aM To GiVe you THiS MeSSaGe. SoMeoNe NaMeD PeTeR CHiBa aDViSeS THaT THe LaW iS CLoSiNG iN oN youR LoCaTioN aND you aRe BeST aDViSeD To eVaCuaTe iMMeDiaTeLy. oH CaPTaiN you HaVeN'T GoNe aND GoTTeN youRSeLF iNTo a JaM aGaiN, HaVe you??? <

May keyed in >MeSSaGe aCKNoWLeDGeD STaNDBy <. "Let's show a little motivation here, folks," May said.

"There," Burris said, jumping up from the console. Vonn swore and held the barrel of the gun inches from his face. "Uh, sorry," Burris said quickly. "The system is ready for my card."

"Be my guest," Vonn said.

Burris reached out to slot the card and stopped short.

"What's the problem?" Vonn asked.

"Before I do this—"

"Before nothing," Vonn spat.

"Mr. Burris," May said. "It occurs to me that one luxury you don't have right now is that of negotiation. Open the vault."

Burris slotted the card, and there was a pop as the doors disengaged. He grabbed the handle of each and swung them back, and cold smoke rolled to the floor. "There they are," he said, stepping away. "Second and third shelf—"

"I can tell," May said, wandering toward the storage unit.

"The rest are other bioproducts that you probably wouldn't be interested in, mostly experimental models of implants like the cat eyes."

"Box up the phials," May ordered. "Vonn, you count them. Make sure he doesn't hold anything back."

"No," Burris said loudly. "I refuse."

Winters aimed the assault weapon directly at Burris. "Didn't you hear what Mr. May said about no negotiations?"

"I want to be heard," Burris shouted. "These phials were my father's entire life!"

"Then you should have paid us the reward to begin with."

"You don't understand. My father worked with the colleagues of Dalton Loevell to perfect the distillation process and made it the commercially viable product that it was. Loevell was a scientist with a good idea that was grossly impractical. Father took that idea and created the Essence company."

There was another tone from the quietlink. May looked down at the screen.

> CHeeCH aDViSeD THaT PeTeR CHiBa HaS MaDe DiReCT CoNTaCT WiTH THe aNGeL'S LuCK. CHiBa RePoRTS LaW eNFoRCeMeNT uNiTS SuRRouNDiNG eSSeNCe BuiLDiNG. CHiBa RePoRTS He HaS LoST CoNTaCT WiTH RoZ. i KNoW you aRe My oWNeR JaMeS BuT iF SoMeTHiNG HaS HaPPeNeD To HeR i WiLL HoLD you PeRSoNaLLy ReSPoNSiBLe <

"Load the phials," May said, again hitting the ACKNOWL-EDGE switch. "We've got to get moving."

"I could have gassed you," Burris said. "One wrong keystroke and I could have filled this room with Restcure, but I didn't. Even with your person on the computer line, whom I very much doubt exists, it wouldn't have made a difference. My people would have had you, and I could have made an experiment out of you."

"Like you did with Duke," May said.

"Let him talk," Vonn said. "I smell money."

Burris nodded. "By rights, Captain May, this company was mine, but the board of directors ousted me and took control—"

"I can't say that I blame them."

"With those phials, I can get it back. I can claim what is mine."

"You'll never get it back," May said. "Not as long as—"

"You haven't heard my offer," Burris said.

"The reward isn't enough," May said. "Not even five hundred million. Not if it's your money."

"Let him talk, May!"

"Stay out of this!" May ordered.

"Through this terminal I can access all of the assets that this branch of Essence holds. I can give you cash, I can give you stocks, I can give you land, I can give you whatever you want, and your mysterious person on the other end of the computer can confirm that before you walk out of this room. Think of it, Captain. I won't give you three, not five, not even eight hundred million credits. I can give you a *billion*."

"That'll cripple the rest of the company."

"Exactly!" Burris laughed. "They'll be teetering on the brink of ruin! And that's when I step in with the distillations, which have been rescued from the jaws of the *Yueh-sheng* by a handful of brave men who understandably wish to remain anonymous. It'll make the Essence Corporation a legend twice over! I'll have my father's chair at the head of the company table, and you'll have your money, Captain, more fucking money than you've ever been able to imagine."

"I like the way this guy thinks," Vonn said.

"I don't," May said. "You notice that he hasn't said a word about Duke or misterbob. He's trying to buy us off."

"No," Burris said quickly, sliding into the seat at the terminal and keying in orders. "Not that. Not that at all. I'll free the Arcolian, although once I've got the Chair back, I'd appreciate it if you could convince it to volunteer for physical examinations by my people. What we would learn about the Arcolians would help the company get back on its feet."

"And what about Duke?"

"Duke. Yes, yes, I can set him free as well, Captain, although you must understand that he'd be better off staying with us. He appears to be quite sick from the product."

"And you have to ascertain whether or not your product has damaged him, right?" May asked. "You need him to determine whether you can really sell the product to the people willing to give anything for a product that had achieved such legendary status. You've thought this all out, haven't you? You're going to make that billion back by making the phials the latest chic—sell them to the fabulously rich and let them destroy themselves or their servants." He shook his head. "You can take your billion credits and go straight to hell."

Burris looked up from the screen. "Please listen to sweet reason, Captain. You'll even have the added pleasure of humiliating me, because I'll have to face the board after paying you off. Think of it, Captain, you'll be the recipient of the biggest reward purse in history!"

"I don't like it."

"No," Vonn said. "You wouldn't, but you're not thinking of the options. Duke could volunteer for examinations, and maybe they could even help him suppress Dickson. Think of what a cut of that money would do for me. I could go in for rejuv, and that would take care of my neural hardcasing, and I could get my hand—"

"So you could run out and get yourself killed, Vonn—"

The quietlink gave an urgent bleat.

> VeRBaTiM MeSSaGe FRoM PeTeR CHiBa Via CHeeCH. GeT youR aSS ouT oF THeRe. aLL HeLL aBouT To BReaK LooSe <

"Vonn, we've got to—"

"There," Burris said, gesturing at the terminal. "I've opened up access to the entire assets of this branch. You want office furniture, Captain? You want lab equipment?"

May said nothing.

"You want money?" Burris shouted, tears coming to his eyes. "Doesn't money mean anything to you? What about sex? There's my secretary . . . and listen, Captain, I've got this great lab assistant named Dinah who wouldn't give me the time of day. Maybe you'd have better luck than I."

The merchant remained stoic.

"Dammit, what do you want? You want me to beg, Captain? Is that what you want?" Burris fell to his knees.

"No," May said. "I don't want any of it. Get the phials, Vonn."

"What?" the mercenary shouted. "Are you out of your mind? You can't walk away from that kind of money!"

"Watch me."

Vonn threw down his weapon and grabbed May by the collar. "No!" he shouted. "I won't let you! Dammit, I lost my best friend and I'm not going to wear those things around my neck like some damned curse—"

"Winters!" May shouted, trying to push Vonn away. "Take this son of a bitch out of here!" He sank a punch into Vonn's solar plexus. The mercenary dropped his grip and staggered back.

Winters opened the main door, grabbed Vonn around the waist with one arm, and muscled him into the hallway. May puffed a sigh of relief. The quietlink caught his eye.

> May????? aRe you CoMiNG????? May????? aRe you THeRe????? <

"Captain."

Startled, May looked up. Burris had a small pistol in his hand.

"I always get what I want."

The first shot struck May squarely in the chest and knocked him back into the wall. Two more shots patterned on either side of the first before there was a feral cry from the corridor.

"Winters, *no*!" Vonn shouted.

The muzzle of Winters's assault weapon began to flash, and bullets tore Burris to pieces before he could change targets. He went down hard, dead before he hit the floor. Winters eased up on the trigger and studied the scene.

"Winters, I'm sorry, I—"

"You were right, Mister Vonn," the big man said. "It's those phials. They're a curse!"

"Winters—"

The weapon fired again, and the contents of the cold chest exploded, spraying glass and liquid and metal across the laboratory. He stopped firing for an instant and aimed right into Vonn's chest.

"All right, Mr. Vonn," he said, tears streaming down his cheeks. "Give me one reason why I shouldn't blow your brains out right this very second. *One reason.*"

"Because it's going to take both of you to carry me."

The two mercenaries looked at the body slumped against the wall. "May?"

"Mutiny pills," the captain gasped, pulling at the shreds of his shirt to reveal stained white fabric underneath. "Flak vest stopped them, but I got broken ribs."

Winters and Vonn scrambled to his side, looped his arms around their shoulders, and lifted him to his feet. He screamed.

"Sorry," Winters said.

"Forget it," May said. "Get me out."

"What about Duke and misterbob?" Vonn asked as they helped him out the laboratory door.

"Burris dead . . . this place . . . bust wide open. They'll . . . walk . . . out of here."

"But shouldn't we get them while we're here?" Vonn asked. "Dammit, May, we came all this way."

"And now . . . we go . . . back," May said, and then he lost consciousness.

22

There was no closing his eyes against the motion. Duke plunged helplessly through the building, up and down corridors, backtracking, doubling back. No matter how hard he tried to assert himself, Dickson was in complete control, and all that he could do was drift in the background, hoping to catch a stray thought that would explain what the pilot had on his mind. All he had to go on was a single, obsessive determination.

I'm going to do it right this time. Do it right.

At one point he saw Roz in the hall and was startled enough

that he momentarily gained control. Before he could react, Dickson had moved back in and started to run again, weaving through the building until he was certain that Roz was no longer in pursuit. Even when convinced, Dickson continued to run through the halls until Duke was sure that his body was close to exhaustion.

Panic was beginning to creep in, and Duke projected a single thought at Dickson: Stop and we'll talk. Stop and we'll talk. Stop and we'll talk.

Duke felt his body slow and then stop. Feeling crept in, and he was wracked with pain. The muscles in his legs burned, and he could not catch his breath. He bent over, but it did not help. He put his back to the wall and slid down, slipping sideways until he was lying on the floor.

Eric, you bastard. You do all the work and leave so I can deal with your overload of my body . . .

Don't get so pissed off, pal. You're going to be back in charge soon enough.

Duke was startled. He tried to sit up, but it hurt to move. From his limited vantage point, he could not see if Dickson had appeared, but he could hear the pilot's voice ringing inside his head.

"What do you mean, I'm back in charge?" Duke panted.

You're not back in charge yet. But you will be. I'm leaving.

Duke tried to swallow. "What?"

Don't worry about it, though. You're going to keep all of my knowledge, all the good shit.

"What are you talking about?"

This is where I get off, Duke. I thought maybe I'd take over, run things for you, improve your life, and once it got straightened out—

"Liar."

All right. I reacted badly, I'm afraid. You know, you get a new lease on life like that, you want to get out and kick up your heels, look up old girlfriends . . .

Duke felt a small amount of strength returning. If he kept Dickson busy with conversation, perhaps the pilot would not notice the improvement. "Unless they're dead."

Rhea's still alive, I'd wager.

"Seventy years old, if she's a day."

Maybe she's had rejuv.

"Only if you left her a fortune in insurance money."

Maybe she has a daughter. Maybe a granddaughter. Maybe

twins. *Poor old Thomas Fortunado was always talking about twins—*

"Spare me the details."

Anyway, things have changed too much for me. You're actually friends with that Arcolian thing. It might be a hell of a nice guy, Duke, but I can't deal with the way things have changed. I can't live in this universe, not anymore.

"So you're checking out."

Exactly.

"You're a coward."

The feeling was a distinct laugh. *I won't tell if you won't. Besides, sometimes it takes courage to know when you can't do any more good. It takes courage to know when to quit.*

Duke slowly sat up. "Well. It was nice knowing you. I suppose I owe you, as the mercenaries say. You got me out of a couple of pretty tight jams. On the other hand, you got me into some even bigger ones." His lips turned up in a smile. "Don't forget to write—"

Oh, but WAIT, Dickson said loudly. *There's one other tiny detail . . .* Duke's hand jerked up. It had a tight grip on the pistol. *There's the matter of my checking out.*

Duke pushed against Dickson but could not get his hand to ease the grip on the weapon.

Come, now. I've got to do it somehow.

"Not like that," Duke said. The pistol was close enough that he could smell its metallic oiliness. The hand twirled it, caught the butt in the palm, and thumbed back the trigger. "You do it that way, and you'll take me with you."

A minor detail, old buddy. Besides, you shouldn't be frightened. After all—

"I know," Duke growled. "Death isn't all it's cracked up to be." The Tetran's thoughts were whirling. There had to be a way to get control, to talk Dickson out of doing this. "Why does it have to be *this* way?"

Because I don't want to be brought back again. In another fifty years Arcolians and people are going to be living together as man and wife.

"But why the gun, Eric?"

Nothing personal, Duke, but it's your brains. If I blow them all over the wall, there's no way in hell that Burris and his cronies are going to be able to scrape them together and put them in another bottle.

The hand with the gun started to wave for emphasis but faltered. The hand trembled.

That was it, Duke thought. Stress. If he can take over when I'm stressed, then if he gets stressed enough . . .

Enough of this, Duke, it's time to—

"Wait," Duke said. "What was it like the first time?"

What?

"When you died. The first time." The hand faltered again, the grip loosening. All right, Duke thought. Keep him busy and steal his knowledge of how to unload the gun. Keep him thinking about something else.

You'll find out soon enough.

"No," Duke said. "I won't. This is going to be violent, Eric, and I'm scared. You drank yourself under, isn't that what happened? Was it alcohol toxemia, or did you do something stupid like choke to death on your own vomit?"

You arrogant little—

"Humor me, Eric."

The grip on the gun tightened again. *It was like—it was like— oh, hell . . .*

Duke was able to close his eyes. He tried to relax, reach out— what was it called? Automag pistol? Yes. They showed him how to strip and clean during Basic: "This little jewel is your second right hand if you're ever downed on a habitable world . . ."

*I'm sorry, Duke. I can't tell you much. It was like—*Another quiver, but the gun held fast. *I started to drink and I blacked out and the next thing I knew I was looking over your shoulder overloading the engines on that tin pot merchant ship of yours.* The arm moved and started to bring the barrel down.

"You know what I've always wondered?" Duke said quickly. He kept his eyes closed, could see the memory of turning a weapon over in his hands, quickly, quickly, the stopwatch was running . . .

What? It was a resigned sigh.

"I wondered . . ." It was close now. The safety catch—no! Better yet, eject the clip. That'll leave one bullet in the chamber to deal with—"Have you ever killed an animal, Eric, a clean shot, took the head right off? You know the way it convulses, like the body's electricity is firing in the muscles all at once?"

The hand with the gun began to tremble. There was a memory there, something dark and hidden. *I know, Duke, we're going to do that and we're going to be too dead to worry about it.*

"But what I wonder, does your brain fire off like that too,

once it's been breached? Does each little piece on the wall and the floor sit there and think whatever it had stored, mathematical equations and brokerage quotations and memories of Tetros and Narofeld Station, until the cells are all dead, and *will we be aware of it, Eric? Will we have one glorious moment of being aware that our mind has never been so alive before it's all over?''*

Trembling, the hand came down and pressed the barrel of the gun against his temple.

"And who'll be around to remember, Eric?" There it was! Clip eject, then slide back the housing, and the live round in the chamber will flip right out. "Who'll be around to remember two little pregnant girls on Tetros? The last memory of Leigh Brand and Rhea drying on the wall!"

NO!

Duke's left hand darted out and caught his right by the wrist, knocking it clear. The right hand fisted around the barrel of the gun, and a shot resonated through the corridor. Duke's left thumb found the raised knob on the handle and mashed it. The clip sprang out and clattered to the floor, and as if by involuntary reflex, Duke's left leg snapped out and kicked it down the hall.

NO! You bastard you bastard you BASTARD!

Duke convulsed and threw himself down on the floor, grappling with the gun. His left hand pushed, popping the bones in his right wrist.

There's still one left in the chamber and one, my friend, is all it's going to take . . .

Duke pushed his hand up to the top slide of the weapon and gripped it hard, trying desperately to push it back. The effort was all that was keeping Dickson from getting a good aim. When it looked as if there was going to be a stalemate, Duke's left arm suddenly went numb.

It's your body, pal, but I was always the physically stronger. If you'd had a little training, you could've done something with this pathetic body of yours.

"I'm smarter than you, Eric!" Duke shouted. "I've always been smarter, I've had the common sense and—" He was cut off when the barrel of the gun bore down and rammed into his mouth, bloodying his lip and banging against his teeth.

Good-night, Duke.

No, Eric. I won't let you do it.

The Tetran relaxed himself completely and concentrated on his trigger finger.

Damn you! Let go! Let me do it!

The barrel of the gun quivered in Duke's mouth. It was cold and metallic against his tongue, and the sensation of cordite was drying out his throat. He thought of nothing else, just that finger, frozen in time—

"Duke!"

His eyes opened and rolled toward the source of the sound. Roz was running down the hall toward him.

"Don't do it!"

A scream broke from Duke's throat, but it was too late. Eric Dickson surged through his nervous system, a burning sensation of overload, coursing down his spine and out the right arm, the right hand, and then the right finger caught fire—

Say good-bye.

The finger pulled and the hammer dropped, jarring as it impacted.

There was an explosion in Duke's brain, light and dark, fire, and ice . . .

23

"Anything from May yet?"

"No," the CHARLES said. "It's rather alarming. Do you think I offended him with that verbatim message from Peter Chiba? I know, it was when I said he was responsible for Roz's welfare. He always said my personality was overbearing. Maybe I should make the ultimate sacrifice and have myself recalibrated."

"Not now," Cheech said. The screen before her flickered, prompting her to lean forward and examine it. "How strange," she said then, keying in a confirmation. "There's been a status change on my intrusion program."

"Are they on to us?" the CHARLES asked.

Cheech shook her head. "We've actually been put deeper into the system. We've been given unlimited access to the Essence Company's financial holdings. What was May's last calculated position again?"

The CHARLES collated for a moment. "One of the cold storage labs, although they appear to be moving."

"Try and reach him again. Ask him what's going on."

"One moment," the CHARLES said.

24

Grunting and puffing, Winters and Vonn dragged the inert body of James May through the halls of the Essence Corporation.

From Winters's side came an insistent beep.

"What's that?" Vonn grunted.

"May's little box," Winters said. "It's tryin' to tell us something." He looked down at the screen.

> HeLLo HeLLo. CHeeCH aDViSeS THaT We HaVe BeeN GiVeN uNLiMiTeD aCCeSS To eSSeNCe CoMPaNy HoLDiNGS. Do We iGNoRe oR Do We PLuNDeR? <

"What does it say?" Vonn asked.

"I don't know," Winters said sheepishly. "I can't read. Do you want to read it?"

"Not now. No time. If it's important they'll try back. Can you get that thing to quit beeping?"

Winters fumbled with the buttons until he hit ACKNOWLEDGE. The noise quit, and the pair continued with their struggle.

"Not far to go," Vonn said.

The box beeped again.

> FoR CoNFiRMaTioN—ouR oRDeRS aRe To PLuNDeR eSSeNCe HoLDiNGS <

"Dammit, Winters, I told you to shut that thing off."

Without looking at the letters, Winters hit ACKNOWLEDGE again. That time the box stayed quiet.

25

"Plunder," the CHARLES said.

Cheech stared at the screen. "There's a small fortune here, a couple of billion at least. Are you sure?"

"I received an acknowledgement."

"This is going to ruin the company," Cheech said.

"Maybe they worked something out in trade," the CHARLES said. "You had said that the company refused to pay Captain May."

Cheech crossed her arms tightly and stared at the screen.

"Something wrong?"

"I wish I could talk to May directly. Something about this strikes me as being wrong. On the other hand, my boss is always telling me not to sweat every minor little detail. He's always complaining that I don't show enough initiative."

"What's your problem?"

"If this company liquidates, a lot of people down there are going to be out of work."

"Perhaps May is taking over ownership."

"I don't think so," Cheech said. "Otherwise I would have been given access to a different program. He must want me to collect his money out of this, but I hate to see all those people cut loose."

"C'est la guerre," the CHARLES said.

"Wait a minute," Cheech said jubilantly. "I've got it. This is more money than May can possibly use, right?"

"Well . . ."

"I know how I can get the best of both worlds. CHARLES, go into the Essence Files and bring up a list of all current Essence Employees and a list of the people Essence now owes money to. Add May's name to it and list the amount owed him as three hundred million." She got up and started across the bridge.

"Where are you going?" the CHARLES asked.

"I'm going to another terminal. I need to get on-line with the Auctionnet."

26

The hall was filled with bright light and wind. Vonn slowed as they approached the intersection. "What's going on?" he asked.

Winters tightened his grip around May's waist. "I don't know."

Vonn untangled himself from under May's arm. Winters wrapped his arms around the unconscious merchant to hold him up.

"Wait here. I'm going to take a look." Taking May's pistol, Vonn inched down the hall and peered around the corner. The light and the wind were pouring in through the broken windows of the lobby, wrapping around and whipping past the slowly idling van. A figure stood next to the vehicle, silhouetted by the lights.

"Vonn!" it shouted. "Is that you?" It started toward the mercenary.

"It's Chiba," Vonn told Winters, grabbing one of May's arms. "C'mon, let's get out of here."

The two dragged the merchant around the corner toward the salvor.

"What's with the light show?" Vonn shouted over the roar.

"Where are the others?" Chiba asked in return.

Vonn shook his head. "We got orders to scrub and break off. You said the law was closing in."

"They are," Chiba said. "They're starting to surround the place. I powered up the engines and hit all the lights to see if that would make them nervous. It didn't. We need to get out before they get someone airborne."

"All right," Vonn said. "Let's get May loaded and get out of here." He started to move toward the breached lobby doors, but Chiba put his hand against his shoulder and stopped him.

"What about the others?"

Vonn shook his head. "They'll be okay."

"No!" Chiba shouted. "We came for them, we can't leave them with Burris—"

"Burris is dead," Vonn explained. "The phials have been destroyed. Once the law sees what's happened here, they're going to be crawling all over the place, and when they find Duke and misterbob, the story's going to be out. It's all over, Peter."

Chiba tightened his grip on Vonn's shoulder. "What about Roz?"

"Roz? I thought she was with you!"

They both looked back toward the corridor.

"Damn it to hell," Peter Chiba said.

"We've got to leave," Vonn said urgently.

"I love her," Chiba said.

"Yeah," Vonn shouted. "Right. Like I got nothing at all invested in her, right? Well, you owe me, pal. If it hadn't been for me—"

"Hey, guys!" Winters yelled. "Can we go now? Huh?"

"He's right," Vonn urged. "Roz'll walk out with Duke and misterbob. Come on, Chiba. We can fight over her later, winner take all."

"You go," Chiba said.

"You have to fly—"

"You can fly."

"I got half a hand in case you hadn't noticed!" Vonn brought the pistol up to aim at Chiba's head. "Right now, Chiba."

"You don't understand—"

"Like hell I don't." Vonn pulled back the hammer of the weapon. "You have a legitimate excuse now. I held a loaded gun to your head, and you know I'm crazy enough to use it. Now move!"

Chiba turned and started through the lobby. Vonn and Winters followed, their boots crunching on broken glass.

"We did it," Vonn said to Winters. "We did it, big guy. We kicked this company's ass. They have to free Duke and mister-bob after this or else—"

Winters suddenly stopped short and stepped away from May.

"Fagin 3!" he exclaimed, sniffing the air.

Vonn's knees started to buckle under the weight that Winters was no longer bearing. "What?"

"That smell!"

"Fluid," Chiba said, moving in under May and helping Vonn to lift. "From the van."

"No!" Winters said. "Rekkfich! Fagin 3! I can find mister-bob! I can bring him and Mr. Duke right out!" He began to run back through the lobby.

"Winters!" Vonn shouted. "Come back!"

The big man stopped. "If I ain't back in an hour," he yelled, gesturing wildly at the van, "meet me at the place we're s'posed to meet at!" Then he vanished down the corridor.

"An hour?" Chiba asked.

"Five minutes," Vonn translated. "Let's go."

They carried May through the ruined door and out into the humid night air.

27

It took Winters two minutes to find the door to the cells. In another thirty seconds he realized that the door was locked and that it would take a card for him to get in. He spent thirty more seconds on the verge of tears, then remembered where there was a card.

He found his way to the cold storage room where Burris's corpse lay crumpled by the doors of the short-term storage vault. Winters deftly kicked the body aside and looked at each blood-spattered door.

There it was, still in the lock. Winters yanked it out, gave Burris's body a good, swift kick, and then ran out of the room.

Forty-five seconds later he plugged the card into the cell-block door and it opened. The overwhelming odor of Rekkfich poured out.

On the other side of the door was misterbob, chest organ pulsating. It opened its eyes and said, "bigguy!"

"misterbob!" Winters shouted jubilantly. "I knew it was you! I knew it!" He fell to his knees in front of the Arcolian and caught it up in a bear hug. "I'm so glad you're okay!"

"Indeed," misterbob grunted. "Your show of concern is most . . . disconcerting."

"Thank you," Winters babbled. "And guess what? I saved your arm! Mister May thought I was nuts, but I had a big fit until he put it in a freezer. Maybe we can take you somewhere and have it sewn back on!"

"That will not be necessary," misterbob said. "I will explain it later. If you would put me down, bigguy . . ."

"Right!" Winters relinquished his grip, and the Arcolian hit the floor with a thud. "Now we gotta find Mr. Duke and Roz. That's going to be harder because they don't smell like Rekkfich."

misterbob's chest fluttered. "I anticipate no problem in locating them."

"Great! Where are they?"

"Turn around bigguy."

Winters put a protective arm around the Arcolian and gazed out the cell-block door. "Are you all right?" he asked. "Did Burris do something to your brain and make you like me?"

"Be patient," misterbob said. "These things take time."

"But misterbob, we gotta hurry! Mr. Vonn is gonna leave us behind unless we get back—"

misterbob's chitinous arm rose. "Observe."

From the intersection not fifteen meters from where Winters and the Arcolian sat, Roz emerged from around the corner, leading Duke by the hand. Winters leapt up and ran to them but stopped before he got there. Duke had dark circles under his eyes; his face looked drawn and, except for a series of scratches on his cheeks and a bloodied lip, was devoid of color.

"What happened?" Winters asked. "You look like you came back from the dead."

"I did," Duke said hoarsely. He stopped to lean against the wall. "What's this about everyone leaving?"

"We've got to go right now," Winters said. "Mr. Vonn and Mr. Chiba are going to fly the little ship away."

"Can we get past Burris?" Roz asked.

"He's dead," Winters said proudly. "And I'm the one that did it. You shoulda been there, misterbob! I kicked his ass good!"

"Indeed," misterbob said. "Under the circumstances, I have decided that perhaps direct participation in kickass is not such a good idea."

"Anyway," Winters continued, "all we got to do is walk out of here. Except we got to hurry because the law is coming."

"You heard the man," Duke said, pulling to his feet. "Let's go."

Winters threw his arm around Duke, and they started off. Roz went to join them, but a strange scent filled her nostrils, and she found that her legs would not move.

"misterbob?" She looked back to see that the Arcolian was holding one finger over its lips to silence her.

"Forgive me for using influence on you," it said in a coarse whisper, "but you must tell me what is wrong with misterduke. I scent that he is not well. His condition is fragile at best."

The scent changed, and Roz regained control of her legs. "What about—" she said, pointing at Winters and Duke as they walked away.

"They have momentarily forgotten us. I wish to discuss this out of hearscent of bigguy, who does not scent well if there is bad news. I also do not wish to bring misterduke into this."

"All right," she said. "I was getting ready to leave the building when I spotted Duke in the hall—he didn't look like he recognized me. I tried following him, but he lost me. His trouble was, he'd go through such elaborate steps to keep out of my way that I'd find him again."

"He did not recognize you?"

"He looked at me like I was someone he wanted to avoid. That was all the recognition I got."

misterbob scratched its chin. "Yesss," it hissed. "It appears that you spotted misterduke during a manifestation of the B-form." Before Roz could question the Arcolian on the meaning of 'B-form,' it asked her to continue.

"When I finally caught up, he was lying on the floor with a gun in his mouth." Roz shivered. "I yelled at him to stop, and he looked up, like he was scared. He pulled the trigger."

"And he incurred a physical wound from this?"

"No," she said, shaking her head. "The clip was out of the gun. He'd unloaded it, but still . . ."

"The weapon did not harm him, then?"

Roz hesitated. "I don't know. He pulled the trigger and went into these convulsions. There was no shot, but I thought he'd actually fired the gun. I ran to him and grabbed him . . . there was no blood. Physically, he looked fine, but he was thrashing like he was dying.

"I started slapping him, and eventually he came out of it. He was disoriented at first, and he kept talking about a raid and scrambling to the ships. I thought he was talking about going back out to the *Reconnez Cherie*, but as I talked to him, I realized it was like talking to someone coming out of a very deep dream-state sleep. Before long he seemed fine."

"Except for his physical functions."

"I just saw him as pale and scared, misterbob. If you scented something . . ."

"Indeed. I must think on this. We must hurry to be with the others. I will summon them."

misterbob waddled down the hall with Roz at his side until Duke and Winters returned, embarrassed that they had gone off without the Arcolian. After a moment to regroup—Winters took the lead with his assault rifle, followed by misterbob, with Duke and Roz taking up the rear—they worked their way out to the lobby of the Essence building.

"Where is everybody?" Duke asked as they passed through corridor after corridor without seeing anyone.

"I can only speculate," misterbob said. "However, it is of low priority. I have other matters to consider."

"You're not putting out scent?" Duke asked.

"No," the Arcolian replied. "My ability is diminishing for want of rest and proper nourishment. The workers here were well intentioned but unfamiliar with the Arcolian diet."

"*Most* were well intentioned," Duke said. "Not all of them."

"Indeed," misterbob observed. "Remember my first few days with you on the *angelsluck*?"

"Point," Duke said. "But at least we didn't lock you in—"

"We're almost there," Winters said excitedly. "Look! There's the lights from the little ship!"

He ran ahead of the group in spite of shouts of protest from the others. Ultimately, they could not fault him for doing it; they had adopted a slower-than-normal pace in order for the Arcolian to keep up, and it had clearly tried the big man's patience.

Duke stumbled and fell against the wall. Roz rushed to his side and tried to feel his forehead, but he brushed her hand aside as he stood. "I'm okay," he insisted. "The food didn't do anything for me, either."

As Winters stood at the intersection the lights began to fade and the wind died down. "Oh, *no!*" he cried, and disappeared from view.

Duke lunged for Winters's last position, but Roz held him back.

"What if it's a trap?" Roz said.

"Then we'd have heard gunfire by now. Something else is wrong."

They rounded the corner and found Winters in the lobby, standing by the idling van.

"Son of a bitch!" he said. "They just left! Didn't see me, neither!"

"Who?" Duke asked weakly.

"Mr. Vonn and Mr. Chiba in the little ship. I only told them to wait for a hour or so."

"They couldn't wait," Roz said, stepping to where one of the windows had been. "But they were right to leave." She watched as the law-enforcement vehicles scattered, some circling the compound, others leaving the scene completely. "We've got to leave right now, before the law decides to come in and poke around. This is the time, while they're still disorganized."

Duke stared at the van. The front windshield was spider-webbed with cracks, and the front grill was caved in. There was a long gash smeared with red paint along the length of the driver's side, and the rear end had been caved in by an immense collision. A puddle of dark fluid was oozing out from under the vehicle, and the frame was sagging to one side as tires lost air.

"In this?" he asked, feeling suddenly weak. He leaned against the vehicle for support.

"Why not?"

"It looks like I feel."

"That's what we're s'posed to do," Winters said quickly. "Everybody get in the van, and I'll drive."

Duke's stomach burned and pushed against his throat. "Winters, I know what you're trying to do, but where in the hell are we going to go? Even if this crate could carry us, once word gets out, this planet won't be big enough to hide us."

"It doesn't matter," Winters said. He smiled as he came up to Duke, clapped him on the back, and led him to the passenger side of the van. "We don't have to get that far. We just have to get to the meeting place. There's a place where Mr. Chiba can hide the ship."

Roz came to Duke's side and helped ease him through the passenger door and into the back of the van. "He knows what he's doing," she whispered.

Duke waited until Winters went for misterbob. "You trust him to pull this off?"

Roz nodded. "Implicitly. He's got good instincts."

Duke grinned. "Too bad Vonn can't hear you talking like this. You sound like a brother."

"I'm glad he can't."

Winters came around the side of the van, the Arcolian in his arms. misterbob's throat rattled, and its arm waved wildly in the air.

"Be steady," Winters said, trying to sound soothing. "You're a heavy booger." He plopped the Arcolian on the passenger seat, and Duke helped it into the back. Roz climbed in and slammed the door.

"Confidence is high," she said. "Remember that."

"Confidence," Duke said. He looked at misterbob and wondered if the Arcolians had a scent that could stimulate that feeling in Sapient A-forms. He decided not to ask.

Winters plopped behind the wheel and ground the gears; the van lurched backward, tossing Duke and misterbob down and bringing protests from them both.

"Don't worry about it," Roz said. "This is an escape, not a pleasure cruise."

Duke crouched between the front seats and looked out the front windshield. Winters expertly backed out of the lobby and across the plaza, then spun the wheel and took the van through a J turn.

"Here we go," the big man said, steering straight for the gate. The failing tires made the van wobble from side to side.

"Does this thing go any faster?" Duke asked thinly.

"Wait!" The word was a loud croak, and it came from misterbob.

Winters smashed his foot down on the brake, pitching his passengers forward. "What?" he asked.

"What's wrong?" Roz asked.

"I must know something," misterbob said. "Things were so confusing that I forgot to ask. Is there any more left to this kickass?"

"One more thing," Winters said. "We're going to do it right now." His foot sank the accelerator as far as it would go, and they started to move, gently swaying at first and then violently pitching back and forth as the van shook over the compromised tires.

The van smashed through the front gate, and the windshield burst, filling the cabin with tiny chips of safety glass. Winters swung out onto the main highway as Roz leaned forward and peered out the window. Bits of glass fell from her hair as the wind streamed in.

Outside, the horizon beyond the line of trees was beginning to turn purple with flecks of gold. "You're going to have to hurry," she shouted. "The sun's coming up. If we want to get the ship off the ground without being seen . . ."

Winters fought the wheel as it rattled on the highway. He took one hand off long enough to hand Roz the quietlink. "Call May." Both hands took control of the wheel in time to swerve and miss a small animal that was crossing the road.

Roz thumbed the box on and started to enter a message.

>CHeeCH you THeRe??????<

>aND WHo iS THiS?<

"Oh, for pity's sake," Roz said with disgust.

"misterduke," misterbob said. "Would you come back here for a moment? I would like you to explain something to me."

"Just a second," Duke said.

>RoZ DuKe WiNTeRS MR. BoB aLL oKay aLL ouT oF eSSeNCe BLDG<

>RoZ!!! HoW GooD To HeaR FRoM you!!! i'M So GLaD you'Re oKay!!! THiS iS CHaRLeS!!!''

>CHaRLeS< Roz started to type. >i THouGHT THaT—

"There's no time for that!" Duke shouted. "Get through to May and tell him we're headed for the rendezvous point—wherever the hell it is."

"misterduke, I must speak to you about this," the Arcolian said.

Duke turned and made his way to the back of the van while Roz entered the information.

>CHaRLeS TeLL CHeeCH TeLL May WeRe ouT oF BLDG eNRouTe To ReNDeZVouS<

> RoZ i'M aFRaiD youR MeSSaGe DiDN'T MaKe SeNSe
To Me. iF you CouLD MaKE iT MoRe GRaMMaTiCaLLy
CoRReCT, PLeaSe. you KNoW HoW We aNDRoiDS aRe <

Duke crouched beside misterbob. The Arcolian was by the
back doors, peering at the road behind them through a tear in
the metal.

"I realize this is not the time, but I am getting eyescent of
something that I do not understand." It scraped at the hole with
its hand. "This pattern of lights, is it some form of portable
industrial complex? It seems to be traveling in the same direction as we."

> CHaRLeS GiVe CHeeCH MeSSaGe VeRBaTiM aLSo
GiVe THiS MeSSaGe VeRBaTjM—uNPLuG CHaRLeS
PeRSoNaLiTy iF iT CoNTiNueS To Be uNCooPeRaTiVe <

Duke peered out of the hole and watched the blue and red
flickering. "We've got a problem," he announced.

"I know," Roz said. She was staring at the screen of the
quietlink, which had just gone blank.

"Yeah," Winters said, squinting at the road. "The damn
sun's coming up too fast. It's in my eyes."

misterbob looked at Duke. "Can you explain what all of this
means, misterduke? I scent that individual levels of stress have
taken a sharp upturn."

"It means," Duke said, "that you're about to learn more than
you ever wanted to know about the way Sapient A-forms behave."
He turned and shouted. "Winters! We're being followed!"

"Lotsa cars on the road this morning," Winters said, squinting. The rays of Council were streaming in through the front of
the vehicle, helping the wind to blind him.

Duke was about to make a bitter comment about using the
mirrors, but he remembered that the one on the driver's side was
missing altogether. "This is the law," he said. "At least two
cars. They're gaining."

"I got the speed all the way up," Winters said.

Duke told misterbob to keep watch on the vehicles and
climbed up between the seats of the driver's compartment. Roz
looked at him. The light of dawn made her face look pale and
drawn. She held up the quietlink. The screen was still blank.

Duke was about to take the device when a smell tickled his

nose. It was hot and sticky—the transgear bay, he thought. The systems distributor. That big biomechanical heart. The heat—

"Dammit, Winters!" he shouted. "The engine—"

There was a loud concussion from under the hood, and the van began to slow. The engine rattled mercilessly.

"Dammit!" Duke shouted, stabbing his finger at the status panel. "Red lights, Winters! Engine temperature, fluid pressure, mechanical integrity! You're supposed to pay attention!"

Winters gritted his teeth, eyes filling with tears. "You know I can't read!" he shouted.

"I'm sorry," Duke said quickly. "Really. I know how it is when—"

"When what?" Winters yelled, rocking back and forth in his seat as if the action would make the vehicle speed up.

"Someone always tells you what's wrong. Looking over your shoulder." He turned to Roz. "He's not there."

"Cheech must have taken the CHARLES off-line," she answered.

"No" Duke said. "Dickson."

"You were expecting him?" Roz said cynically.

"Yes," Duke said. "It's hot. There's the smell, the lights, the stress . . ." He closed his eyes. "I can tell you how to fix the engine," he laughed. "All we have to do is check the level of—"

"That's great!" Roz screamed. "We'll stop at the nearest garage, and you can fix it right up!"

"I *remember*," Duke said. "It's me, not him leaning over my shoulder."

There was another report from the hood, and the vehicle slowed again. Winters cranked the wheel, and the van careened onto a gravel road.

"No!" Duke said. "What do you think you're doing?"

"This is the turnoff," Winters said. "They're gonna land this ship over here!"

"Great," Duke said. "And you're going to lead the law right to—"

Winters hit the brake, and Duke flopped forward and hit the dash. He shook off the stun and gave Winters an angry look. The big man was smiling and looking out the window. They were at a fork in the road. He pulled a grenade off his jacket.

"Here's what we're gonna do, Mr. Duke. You and Roz and misterbob are gonna go down that road there." He punctuated his statement with a wide swing of his arm. "That's the short

way to the meadow. I'm gonna take this long way and lead
everyone away."

"You can't—" Roz said.

"Sure!" Winters said. "And then I jump out of the van and
let it blow up! And then I sneak back and blow up their cars
when they get out to look, and then I run and meet you at the
ship!"

Roz opened the door and jumped out. "Get misterbob," she
ordered.

"What?" Duke said, outraged. "You can't!"

"Do you have any better ideas? They'll be here any minute."

There was a chitinous scrabbling sound behind him. "Indeed, misterduke, bigguy's plan scents of soundness to me. I
understand that its success will be made better by the concept
of longshot."

"Indeed," Duke said. He turned and grabbed misterbob to
lift—the Arcolian was much heavier than he had imagined—and
placed him on the seat. Roz helped the ambassador out of the
vehicle, and then Duke clamored out, pausing to give Winters
a salute of high respect. "You've really earned your pay this
tour, Winters."

Winters started to smile, and then his face twisted. "Oh, I
almost forgot!" He reached deep inside his body armor and
pulled out a long, slim cylinder. "I didn't tell nobody about it."

Duke's mouth dropped open as he reached out to take the
cylinder. It was the Acker distillation. He raised his head to
thank the mercenary, but the van was already listing and chug-
ging down the dusty road as fast as its dying engine could move
it.

28

As the first rays of morning struck the tops of the trees, the
birds began to make a racket, tweeting and twittering, making
their presence known to others and reestablishing their territory.
Vonn stood in the meadow near the edge of the woods, scowling
as he listened.

"Shut up!" he shouted, throwing a rock into the trees and
dislodging a large flock. "Happy little bastards," he muttered
under his breath.

"Shut up yourself," Peter Chiba whispered loudly. "You're
going to give our position away."

Vonn gave the salvor a sour look. Chiba was squatting by a

patch of fuzzy green, marvelling at the fog that blanketed the meadow and the dew as it formed. The look on the man's face was almost disgusting, but Vonn said nothing. He kept reminding himself that the space-bound Chiba had never before seen anything like this.

"Water," Chiba said, rubbing a film of it between his fingers. "Do the plants give it off?"

"Condenses from the air," Vonn said. "Like sweat on a cold beer. Is it time yet?"

Chiba shook his head. "We just got here. We agreed to give them an hour."

"A mistake." Vonn started to say it loudly but caught himself. "Winters doesn't know what he was talking about. He's—"

"I know," Chiba said. "But he deserves the chance, right?"

Vonn said nothing.

"I don't know a lot about your business," Chiba said, "and I don't want to. But I know enough to be able to tell when someone should change careers, and buddy, you've reached that point."

The mercenary looked down at his bandaged hand. "They had the place surrounded. Maybe they've found misterbob and he's explaining what's been happening." He laughed. "I wonder if they'll bring in dogs."

"The cars scattered when we started to take off," Chiba said. "Maybe they got away."

A voice rolled to them through the mist. "They got away."

Chiba and Vonn looked back toward the *Reconnez Cherie*. A hunched figure was staggering toward them.

"May?"

The merchant waved his hands to keep them still. "Don't look so surprised. Somebody had to answer the radio."

"What are you doing—"

"I woke up long enough to raid the medicine cabinet." Noting that Vonn paled at his words, he added, "Not as extensively as you had. Pain killer and oxygen supplement."

"We can handle this."

"Like you thought to leave someone behind to man the radio, I suppose." Vonn and Chiba exchanged sheepish glances. "You two would've been at each other's throats in another sixty seconds—" May stopped short, head turning. "What was that?"

Vonn crouched and picked up his weapon. Chiba straightened and glanced across the meadow.

The sound came again, the steady crunch of gravel.

"It's them!" Chiba called. He bolted across the clearing and into the woods nearest the road.

"No!" May called in a loud whisper. He waved his arms at Vonn. "Stop him! Stop him!"

Vonn dashed into the woods, following Chiba's thrashings. With a curse, he threw down his weapon and pumped his legs, arms crossed in front of his face to protect it from the spidery tree branches and hanging vines. He stopped for a moment. There was no more noise from the salvor, but he could hear the vehicle approaching on the gravel road, and he could hear an engine, one that was missing badly. He picked his way through the trees until he saw Chiba standing in the middle of the road, waving his arms at an oncoming vehicle.

"Stupid—"

The mercenary flew out from the woods and caught Chiba by the waist, folding him in half and taking them both down on the opposite side of the road as the van careened by.

"What are you trying to—"

Vonn stopped short when the van skidded, turned sideways, then flopped over on its side.

"Roz!" Chiba cried. He started to rise, but Vonn held him down and clapped his hand over the salvor's mouth.

The van exploded. Sheets of flame began to roll out of the windows and the holes in the body, and the undercarriage smoked with heat.

Chiba started to squirm violently, but Vonn put a containment grip on him and held him fast. He could hear another vehicle approaching. Looking through the dust that the van had raised, he could see flickering lights.

"Quiet," he whispered to Chiba.

In a moment, a law-enforcement pursuit vehicle sped by. It was followed half a minute later by a slower, bulkier vehicle with the same logo branded on the side. Both skidded to a halt meters short of the accident.

Vonn waited until his heart stopped racing to let Chiba go. "Now," he mouthed.

They slowly rose and slipped across the road. May was waiting for them, watching the burning van and the stopped vehicles in disbelief.

"I've got to go over there," Peter Chiba babbled. "I have to know, and damn you if you don't care enough—"

May raised his hands. "All right," he whispered. "Quietly."

The trio inched their way toward the accident scene, watching the officers as they backed their vehicles away and then stepped out of them to confer.

"Helluva mess," one said.

May stopped short and watched the van burn. A lump formed in his throat.

"How many in there?" the other officer asked.

"Fifth Region only knows."

Chiba's mouth dropped, and he started to wander toward the road. Vonn reached out to grab him, but May shook his head.

One of the officers swore. "I'll never get used to that smell." He walked down the road and vomited.

The other officer laughed. "Maybe it's justice. Our system would've just coddled them." He turned to his ill partner. "Now they're frigging barbecue."

May's heart leapt, and he snagged Chiba's arm before the salvor could step onto the road.

"No," Chiba said softly. "I don't care anymore."

"You must!" May whispered, trembling and sweating. "Just for another couple of minutes. Trust me, Peter. You've got to trust me."

Vonn shrugged. "Let him go, May."

May looked the mercenary in the eye. "It's misterbob."

"Yeah," Chiba said. "misterbob, Duke, Winters . . . Roz—"

"misterbob!" Vonn said, understanding. "Of course!"

May took Chiba by the shoulders, turned him around, and gave a mighty shove. "Quickly, Peter! *To the ship!*"

29

On the *Angel's Luck*, the auction was going well. Cheech had sold off the building, the ground it sat on, and the furnishings, and was loading a list of laboratory hardware to be sold next. She hummed softly as she watched the action on the screen. Things had gone slowly at first, but as the data was relayed to the major nets around the galaxy, a feeding frenzy had ensued. They would clean up when the time came to sell the on-site intellectual property.

"Excuse me, ma'am," the CHARLES said, "But I've been monitoring the list of people that money is going out to. I thought you'd want to know that Captain May has officially received his three hundred million credits."

"What?" Cheech said. "You mean the list is up to 'M' already? Is everyone getting their fair share?"

"All outstanding debts are being paid in full. All employees are receiving one year's severance pay."

Cheech whistled. "We've got a lot more stuff to sell."

"Is that a problem?" the CHARLES asked.

"Tell you what," Cheech said. "Let's get a list of the two hundred people who got processed for those phials. We'll set up a nice little trust fund for any descendants so their grandkids will get a windfall."

"Excuse me, ma'am, but it'll take someone to oversee that," the CHARLES said. "It'll also take money to find all of the descendants and determine who gets what."

"Then set up a fund to do that and hire detectives—whatever it takes. If somebody's family hits a dead end, find out what the donor's favorite charity was and sink the money into that. If there's anything left after that, divide it up evenly between the remaining Essence branches in the galaxy." She tagged a key and entered the listings for the Essence Corporation's intellectual properties. "I'll have those donor names for you in a minute."

"Very well. There was one more thing, ma'am—"

"CHARLES, I hate 'ma'am.' Call me Cheech."

"Very well. I was wondering if you were aware of the legal consequences of what you're doing."

Exasperated, Cheech looked up from her screen. "There are none. This was fully authorized by the head of the Council branch of Essence. He obviously reached an agreement with May."

"I can't help calculating that this agreement may have been made under some sort of duress. If that is the case, then there will be legal and moral consequences."

"What moral consequences? We're paying off all of their employees, aren't we? If they can't live off what we give them while they're finding another job, they're beyond help."

"I was talking about what will happen to the balance of the Essence Corporation after they lose this branch."

"CHARLES, you need to learn one thing. Nothing is ever black and white."

The android did not answer. Cheech accessed the file on the distillations and routed it to the CHARLES'S systems and told him to get the names of the distillees out of it, then continued to search through other programs.

"Ma'am?" CHARLES said after a lengthy search of the files.

"Cheech," she corrected.

"I've made a search of the files you gave me on the distillation volunteers, and I've found something interesting. It seems that Mr. Burris kept extensive records of his dealings with the *Yueh-sheng*. The information is very specific about names, places, and dates, and how it was arranged for the *Yueh-sheng* to take possession of the Series One Distillations."

"Why are you telling me this, CHARLES?"

"I want to know what you want to do with this information."

"What would you do with it?" Cheech asked, calling the records up on her terminal.

"Obviously," the CHARLES said, "the right thing to do would be to return these records to the Essence Corporation, since we had no right to access them to begin with. Then we would cease this auction and arrange for all of the buyers to have their money refunded—"

"Shut up," Cheech said. "That's not what you're going to do."

"I don't mean to be fatalistic, but I didn't calculate such behavior as your response."

"Then why did you ask?" Cheech growled. "Never mind. What you're going to do is make copies of the data and send it to all the other Essence branches. Then you're going to forward the main file to the Council branch of Port Authority. Got that?"

"I can't calculate Port Authority's reaction to illegally obtained evidence—"

"A starving man wouldn't turn down a hand-out, would he? Don't answer that. Just carry out the orders, CHARLES."

"But ma'am—"

"Shut up!" Cheech rose from her chair and crossed to the terminal where the android's head was mounted. She picked it up and grabbed up an electronic probe.

"Ma'am," the CHARLES said, "what are you doing?"

"Restoring your old personality," Cheech answered. "I don't care what May says—I liked you better the other way."

30

They came out of the woods and into the mist. As they crossed the meadow, a shadow grew in front of them in the shape of the *Reconnez Cherie*. There were shapes moving around in front of the boarding ramp.

Peter Chiba broke into a run. He went straight to Roz and grabbed her, picked her up, and held her close.

Duke, who was sitting on the steps leading into the ship, rose and walked out to meet the staggering May. As the distance closed, he could see the merchant beaming from ear to ear.

"Yes!" May whispered, and they fell into an embrace.

"You're wounded," Duke said.

"I'm okay for now," May said, "but I'll need medical help before the drugs wear off."

A short figure hobbled their way. "Indeed, this is a most joyous moment," it said. "I shall treasure it."

May sank to his knees, took the ambassador's hand in his two, and shook it. "I'm so glad to see you," he said. "And I've got to thank you for helping us out! We couldn't have done it without you!"

"I should thank you," misterbob purred. "You are the ones who risked The Life to make this possible."

"But you're the one who turned it around!" May said. "You made the scent of burning flesh that stopped the officers on the road! That was brilliant, misterbob!"

The Arcolian's head cocked and it studied the merchant at an angle. "Indeed, jamesohjames, what are you talking about?"

"misterbob's been with us," Duke said.

Vonn stepped into the conversation, visibly trembling at the sight of the Arcolian. "Where's Winters?" he asked.

"He's not with you?" Roz asked.

May shook his head.

"Last we saw him," Duke said, "he was in the—" His gaze drifted off to the column of smoke rising from behind the trees.

"No!" Vonn shouted. *"No!"* He turned and ran toward the line of trees, oblivious to the shouts of the others trying to stop him. A high-pitched rattle reached his ears, and he began to slow, thinking he recognized it.

It was Roz, screaming.

Vonn spun on his heels.

The Arcolian was shivering and hopping in tight circles, thrashing its arm wildly at things that were not there. "bigguy," it bleated. "bigguy, bigguy, bigguy . . ."

The mercenary looked down at his own trembling hand. It was covered with gooseflesh. In the name of the Fifth Region, he thought, that damned thing is human!

Duke tried to close on the Arcolian but was kept back by the swings of the arm.

"misterbob," he said. "We've got to go! Winters would want us to get out of here! If we don't—"

The Arcolian slowly stopped thrashing. "I understand," it said. "It would be a waste of The Life."

"Yes," Duke said, eyes filling with tears. misterbob reached out and touched one as it trickled down the Tetran's face.

"It must be nice," it said, "to have a physical manifestation of grief." It stepped back and turned to the others, speaking in a faltering voice. "I don't have tears. I must express what I feel. I apologize for my violence."

"No need," Roz said.

"We do the same thing, sometimes," Peter Chiba said.

"I understand it now, the importance of The Life in the individual Sapient A-forms. How foolish of us to see only the importance of the race! Oh, this grief you feel! It is sweet, is it not? The sense of loss burning, yet it makes you feel so—"

"Alive?" May choked.

"I am standing here by virtue of bigguy in the van, yet I would give that up, all of that, to have him standing here with us!" misterbob raised its head to the sky and wailed. "Sweet grief! Sweet, burning grief!"

Vonn got as close to the Arcolian as he dared. "Ambassador," he said. "misterbob. Duke is right. We must—" He looked out at the woods. "We must go."

"Of course," misterbob sighed. "We must. I shall never forget."

"None of us will," May said. "None of us will."

They stood for a moment in silence, and then misterbob began to waddle toward the boarding ramp. Once he was out of sight, Vonn followed, and then Chiba and Roz.

"It's time," May said. He put his arm around Duke's shoulder for support, and they started walking.

"I've got something for you," Duke said. He pulled the last Essence Phial out of his pocket.

May stared in disbelief. "What did you do, palm it the day we were in Burris's office?"

Duke nodded. "I thought we might need some evidence if there was more trouble."

May took the phial and turned it over in his hand. "If the law comes looking for me again, I'm surrendering. I'm tired of running."

He dropped the bottle in the grass. It made a most satisfying crunch under the heel of his boot.

EPILOGUE

Six months later, May and Duke were on an industrial salvage ship in high orbit over Council 5. Duke was looking out the window of the operations room and laughing.

"You know," he said, "I can't believe Vonn. He really is crazy, May. You know that."

"I admire him," May said. "He's facing his fears."

"He'll be tranquilized most of the time," Duke said. "He'll have to be."

"Maybe."

"You think the Arcolian roechangers will get his hand to regenerate?"

"If they do," May said, "then he's going to be riding high on the crest of a whole new industry."

Duke shivered. "I hope it works out for him. I've seen what happens to people when things don't go their way."

"The phials?" May asked.

"Eric Dickson," Duke said. "Let the biographers write what they will. He had a miserable life."

"Do you miss him?"

Duke turned and looked at May. "Not at all. misterbob is the one I'm going to miss. I wish he could go to Tetros with me. I'd show him how normal people live."

"He was on the holo the other night," May said. "Some political discussion program. He came across very well. The host praised him for his understanding of our ways." The merchant shifted in his seat. "Listen, there's something I need to discuss with you—"

"I'm going back to Tetros," Duke insisted. "I've got things I need to take care of. Now that I've got money, I can finally make some things right. I've got two kids that need a father, family to apologize to—"

"Impending nuptials," May said.

"Of course."

"You're going to be the envy of everyone on Tetros, you realize that. The kid who went into space for a year and came back a multimillionaire."

"If they whine about it," Duke said, "I'll tell them about the ones who didn't make it."

May sighed. "Duke, I know you're bound and determined to go back and set things right. But I think that with all that new knowledge, you might get restless. You may not settle back into an agrarian lifestyle. If that's the case—"

"You'll be the first one I call," Duke said.

The door from the hall slid open, and Roz peered in at them. "We're on approach, May. You wanted to know."

May thanked her and saluted. He waited for the door to shut before he continued. "Let me tell you, the thought of anyone going into debt for a ship makes my skin crawl."

"Peter and Roz will do fine," Duke said. "They're not merchants, right?"

"No." May laughed.

Duke rose from his seat and walked to where he had laid his baggage. "I suppose I ought to get things in order," he said.

"Not yet, Duke."

"But Roz said we're on approach."

"Not the platform," May said. He rose and went to a window on the opposite side of the cabin. "I arranged to have us swing by the refitters. I thought you'd want one last look at the ship."

"Absolutely." Duke stepped over to the large window. In the distance, he could see the merchant ship clamped to a long boom that reached out from the refitting yard. There were flashes of light from the engine compartment. "They're installing the engines?"

"Next week," May said. "They're rehabilitating the bay. The first on-line testing should be in six weeks, if you want to stay."

"I really can't." Duke continued to stare. As they rounded the merchant ship's port side, Duke could see a bluish sheen from the fresh coat of paint. "They did a great job with the hull," he said. "It looks brand new."

"It is," May said, "for all intents and purposes."

"A clean start." Duke nodded. "If anyone deserves one—"

"Before you go any further," May interrupted, "there's something else I need to tell you. It has to do with something Cheech told me about salvage law. When I bought the ship back from my ex-wife for a hundred credits, it was considered salvaged material and its past was erased. I was free to do whatever I wanted—strip it, sell it . . ."

"What are you getting at?" Duke looked back out the window. The registration number came into view, painted in flat black on the refinished surface.

89631.

"May! You reregistered the ship!"

The merchant shrugged. "In my name. Free and clear."

"This is great!" Duke grabbed May's hand and shook it. "You didn't happen to rename it, did you?"

May drew a deep breath, and his eyes began to mist. "As a matter of fact, I did."

Duke leaned against the window and watched as the letters came into view.

Winters Tale.

Nothing came out as Duke opened his mouth to speak. He drew breath and bit his lip. It was all too much right then, the realization that the ordeal was really over and that at last he was getting to go home. Or maybe it was the temperature in the cabin, which suddenly seemed too hot, or the farewell toasts, too many of them, that they had given to Vonn the night before. He had nothing to say, and no way to say it even if he did.

He wished for an instant that he could freeze this moment and keep it, stored in a small bottle like the Essence Distillations. Then, after a moment of thought, he changed his mind. Some memories were best left to the ravages of time.

About the Author

Joe Clifford Faust is the author of five science-fiction novels and a very strange play called *Old Loves Die Hard*. He also scripts stories for *Open Space*, a science-fiction title from Marvel Comics.

Besides writing, his interests include his wife, his two children, and obscure British pop bands. His weakness for the medium of radio led him to a top-rated FM station in northeast Ohio, where he daylights as a copywriter.

Mr. Faust is currently at work on a new novel.